## "I should be angry with you, you know."

"I know," Sara Beth said, averting her gaze. "But you're not, are you? Not really."

There was no way Taylor could overlook the sweetness of her smile or the blush on her fair cheeks. Her hair had become mussed during her ordeal and the loose curls made her look like an endearing moppet. "No," he said. "I'm not."

Her grin spread and her greenish eyes twinkled mischievously. "Good. I'd be terribly sad if you were."

"Sad enough to behave and stay safely away from the city center for a while?"

"Well..." Her soft drawl and the way she was gazing into his eyes made him melt inside like butter on a summer's day. "Don't look so worried. I promise I shall behave as well as is sensible."

"That's what worries me," he quipped. When she reached up and gently caressed his cheek, his knees nearly buckled...

*USA TODAY* Bestselling Author

# Valerie Hansen

and

# Allie Pleiter

# The Doctor's Newfound Family

&

# Mission of Hope

⬥ **HARLEQUIN**® LOVE INSPIRED®CLASSICS

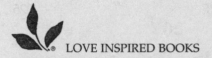 LOVE INSPIRED BOOKS

ISBN-13: 978-1-335-45466-9

The Doctor's Newfound Family & Mission of Hope

Copyright © 2019 by Harlequin Books S.A.

The Doctor's Newfound Family
First published in 2010. This edition published in 2019.
Copyright © 2010 by Valerie Whisenand

Mission of Hope
First published in 2010. This edition published in 2019.
Copyright © 2010 by Alyse Stanko Pleiter

www.Harlequin.com

Printed in U.S.A.

# CONTENTS

THE DOCTOR'S NEWFOUND FAMILY     7
Valerie Hansen

MISSION OF HOPE     225
Allie Pleiter

**Valerie Hansen** was thirty when she awoke to the presence of the Lord in her life and turned to Jesus. She now lives in a renovated farmhouse on the breathtakingly beautiful Ozark Plateau of Arkansas and is privileged to share her personal faith by telling the stories of her heart for Love Inspired. Life doesn't get much better than that!

### Books by Valerie Hansen

### Love Inspired Suspense

#### *Military K-9 Unit*

*Bound by Duty*
*Military K-9 Unit Christmas*
"Christmas Escape"

#### *Classified K-9 Unit*

*Special Agent*

#### *Rookie K-9 Unit*

*Search and Rescue*
*Rookie K-9 Unit Christmas*
"Surviving Christmas"

#### *The Defenders*

*Nightwatch*
*Threat of Darkness*
*Standing Guard*
*A Trace of Memory*
*Small Town Justice*
*Dangerous Legacy*

Visit the Author Profile page
at Harlequin.com for more titles.

# THE DOCTOR'S NEWFOUND FAMILY

## Valerie Hansen

Many are the afflictions of the righteous:
but the Lord delivereth him out of them all.
—*Psalms* 34:19

To my editor, Melissa Endlich,
who believed in me enough to let me branch out
and live a vicarious life in the old West, as well as
get into plenty of "trouble" in the present.

# Prologue

"A righteous man may have many troubles, but the Lord delivers him from them all."

—*Psalms* 34:19

*San Francisco, 1856*

Chilling, midnight fog from the bay swirled around the two men standing together in the narrow alley bordering Meigg's wharf. The taller one was clad in the tailored suit, coat and top hat typical of a wealthy merchant or banker while the other, shivering and nervously rubbing his own arms, wore the canvas pants, homespun shirt and cap of a dock worker.

The man in the tall beaver hat scratched a lucifer and lit his cigar with it, then slowly blew out a stream of smoke that was quickly lost in the mist. When he finally spoke, his tone was smooth and assured. "You understand what has to be done?"

"Yes, sir, Mr...."

"Shut up. No names. And if anyone asks, you and I have never met. Is that clear?"

"Yes, sir." The workman chafed his calloused hands together to warm them. "When do you want me to do it?"

"In a few more days. I'll get word to you when my plans are firm. Spend your evenings right here in old Abe Warner's so you're ready and waiting when the time comes. Just see that you stay sober enough to hit what you're aiming at. There'll be no further payment if you miss him and shoot me instead."

"I won't miss, mister. I know when to keep away from John Barleycorn."

"Glad to hear it."

"How will I know for sure which fella to shoot? I mean, won't he be dressed just like you?"

"Probably. I'll lure him down here to meet with me after dark, then light my cigar the way I did tonight. When I step back out of the way, kill him."

"How'll I see so's I don't make a mistake? What if there's more fog, like now? The new gaslights ain't workin' hardly anywhere in the city."

The elegant gentleman laughed quietly, menacingly. "I know that, you cretin. Who do you think arranged for the Board of Supervisors to stop paying those exorbitant gas bills? I want it dark, especially around here."

"You've got this all figured out, haven't you?"

"Yes. As long as you do as you've been told, all my troubles will soon be over."

# Chapter One

Something was terribly wrong.

Sara Beth awoke with a start. The darkness seemed filled with unnamed dread. She sat up in bed and strained to discern what had disturbed her usually peaceful slumber. At first she thought that perhaps there had been another minor earthquake, which were common in the city by the bay, but she felt no tremors. She did, however, hear plenty.

Downstairs, Mama's voice was raised, pleading, and although Sara Beth couldn't quite make out her stepfather's words, she could hear the rumble of his gruffsounding reply. That was very unsettling. Mama had married Robert Reese when Sara Beth was but five years old, and in nearly thirteen years she had almost never heard her parents argue.

Rising, she wrapped a shawl around her shoulders over her long nightdress, tossed her head to free her heavy, reddish braid, and tiptoed to the adjoining room to check on her younger half-brothers.

Peeking in at the small beds, she noted that all three boys appeared to be sound asleep. Josiah was the youngest and the most restless. As long as he wasn't stirring, there was a good chance none of the boys had been disturbed.

She gently eased the door to their room closed, went to the head of the stairs and paused at the banister to listen carefully. What she overheard made the fine hairs on the back of her neck prickle.

"Don't go, Robert," her mother pleaded. "Please. For the sake of the children, if not for me."

"You don't understand, Isabelle. I work with the man. I owe it to him to give him a chance to explain before I take my findings to the authorities."

"He's evil. I can see that even if you can't. How do you think he got so wealthy while we scrape by and live so meagerly?"

"Do you wish you'd married him instead? Is that it?"

"No. Of course not."

"Then stop acting as though you want to protect him."

"It's *you* I want to protect, not him. Can't you see that?"

Sara Beth crept silently down the stairway until she reached a vantage point where she could see both her parents. Mama was still dressed, as was Papa. It looked as if they had never gone to bed.

Jerking his arm from his wife's grasp, Robert Reese grabbed his top hat and greatcoat and stormed through the front door, not even glancing in Sara Beth's direction as he passed.

As soon as he had slammed his way out, she hurried the rest of the way down the stairway to comfort her mother. "What's happened, Mama? What's wrong?"

Isabelle covered her face with her hands and began

to lament. "I've buried one husband. Now I fear I shall have to bury another."

"Oh, Mama! Papa Robert will be fine. I know he will. We'll pray for him."

Sniffling and wiping furiously at her eyes, Isabelle shook her head. "No, he will not be fine. Not unless I can talk some sense into him before he goes too far." She cast around the cozy room, her eyes alight in the glow from the kerosene lamps, then moved quickly to her sewing table and took her reticule from the drawer. "You mind the boys."

Sara Beth's sense of foreboding deepened. She reached to restrain her mother, but was shaken off like a pesky insect. The older woman grabbed a hooded cape, threw it over her shoulders and strode purposefully toward the door.

"Mama. Wait. Where are you going?"

"Meigg's wharf. If I don't return by morning, go next door to Turner's store as soon as they open and ask them to send someone to fetch Sheriff Scannell."

"Why do you have to leave us?" Sara Beth asked, the quiver in her voice mirroring the trembling of her body.

"Because there's evil in this old world," her mother said. "And your father is determined to stand alone against it in spite of everything. I have to be by his side whether he wants me there or not." She paused at the open door, her expression somber. "If anything should happen to me, go to Ella McNeil at the Ladies' Protection and Relief Society. She'll take care of you just as she took care of both of us when you were a little girl."

The last thing Isabelle said before she closed the door behind her was, "I love you, dear heart. Always remember that."

\* \* \*

Sara Beth didn't even consider returning to her room or trying to sleep. She paced. She prayed. She fretted. Then she pulled herself together with a final, "Please God, help us," and decided she must act.

She had no doubt that it would be foolish to venture out on foot at night, especially down toward the wharf, although her mother had done exactly that. She also knew that the fate of her entire family might rest on her being there to render aid. That was why Mama had gone after Papa Robert, wasn't it? How could she do less?

It wasn't as though Sara Beth had never been to Meigg's wharf before. She knew the old man who ran the menagerie off the alley down by Francisco Street. Abe Warner had been friendly to her and the boys every time Mama had taken them there to see all his amazing animals. And he'd always let them feed peanuts to the monkeys that roamed free in his watering hole dubbed the Cobweb Palace.

That establishment was run-down and dirty even without all the resident spiders that he refused to kill, but the old man was jolly and Mama had deemed him harmless. If Sara Beth could reach that section of the wharf safely she knew she'd find sanctuary.

The trouble was, she couldn't run off and leave her little brothers alone. Therefore, the first thing she had to do was rouse them and see that they were warmly dressed.

Lucas, the eleven-year-old, would help if she could manage to awaken him sufficiently. And Mathias was pretty self-reliant for being only seven. If they couldn't manage to dress two-year-old Josiah properly, she'd tend to his needs herself.

Rushing up the stairs, she barged into the boys' bedroom, raised her coal-oil lamp high and shouted, "Everyone up. We're going on an adventure and we have to leave right away."

The shot echoed through the rickety frame buildings and resounded along the docks.

An elderly, balding man in his nightshirt stuck his head out the window of his bedroom on the second floor of his establishment and squinted down through the fog, seeking the source of the noise.

Directly below, a woman screamed. Another shot was fired. Then another.

The old man ducked back inside, fumbled into his trousers, tucked in his nightshirt and stuck his bare feet into run-down boots as he pulled his braces over his shoulders. He didn't know what had happened but he'd bet his bottom dollar that somebody was in need of a doctor. And he knew just where to find a good one. He only hoped that whoever had been injured could hold on long enough for proper help to arrive.

By the time Sara Beth got her brothers ready to go and led them out onto the street, the fog was lifting and there was a pale pink glow beginning to warm the springtime sky just over the hills to the east.

She had hoped to be able to tuck Mama's little single-shot pistol into her pocket for protection, but when she'd gone to fetch it, it was missing, which was comforting because it was probably with her mother.

Sara Beth would be armed only with her wits, her courage and the "full armor of God" that the Bible spoke of. That would be sufficient. It had to be.

At the last minute she'd taken one of Mama's bone knitting needles and had stuffed it up the narrow sleeve of her coat. It wasn't much defense, considering the riffraff they might encounter, but it gave her courage a slight boost.

"Luke and Mathias, you tend to Josiah," she said as she led them down the front porch steps and onto the street. "Take turns carrying him if you must. Just keep up with me, stay very close and don't say a word, you hear?"

Luke obeyed as expected. Mathias was his usual ornery self. "Why?" he asked in a shrill whine. "Where's Mama? And why do we have to go out in the dark? Papa will be mad."

"If you must know, we're going to meet Mama and Papa." Sara Beth used her most commanding tone to add, "Do as I say or I'll tell them you misbehaved and you'll get a whipping."

Mathias made a sour face and scrunched up his freckled nose, but he fell into step as instructed. Sara Beth turned away so he wouldn't see her start to smile. There was a lot of her own orneriness in her little brother, and his antics often reminded her of herself. Luke was the serious one. Josiah was the inquisitive imp. But Mathias and she were kindred souls, never satisfied to bide their time and always questioning authority.

"I hope and pray I'm doing the right thing this time," Sara Beth whispered to herself as she led the way along the plank walkway toward the Pacific shore. "I truly do."

In the misty light of approaching dawn, she could see a few figures moving silently in and out of the deep shadows. Their presence gave her a start until she realized that none seemed the least interested in her or her little band of children. That was just as well, she reasoned, marching ahead boldly to allay her own fears, because until she reached the safety of the Cobweb Palace she was more vulnerable than she'd ever been.

The shortest distance to Meigg's wharf was via Francisco Street, so that was the route she chose. Feral cats, busy raiding the rotting garbage dumped at the edges of the raised walkway, hissed and spat as she and the boys passed.

Time and again, Sara Beth glanced over her shoulder to make certain her little brothers were staying close as instructed.

The moist, damp air blowing ashore from the bay seemed to press in on her, its cloying smells almost overpowering. Never before had she noticed how filthy this neighborhood was. Nor had she anticipated how desolate it would seem at this time of the morning.

Always before when she had been there, the area had been bustling with all sorts of people, men and women, rich and poor, intent on their own business or simply out seeing the more colorful sights of the city. To find the neighborhood so apparently abandoned was unsettling.

Suppressing a shiver, she boldly marched on. They were almost there. Her breathing became shallow with anticipation, her heart pounding even more rapidly.

There were lights shining from the windows of the Cobweb Palace when she rounded the final corner. Moreover, many of the local inhabitants who had been out of sight during her approach had apparently been congregating in front of Mr. Warner's menagerie building. The crowd there was considerable, and it was growing.

Sara Beth paused a moment to assess the situation, then gathered her brothers to her, relieving the older ones of baby Josiah.

"Keep close to me," she ordered. "Grab a handful of my skirt and don't you dare let go until I say so, understand? This crowd is very big and I can't hold all your hands at the same time. We mustn't get separated."

"Yes, ma'am," Luke said, his brown eyes wide.

Mathias, too, nodded, although Sara Beth could tell he'd be off in a jiffy if one of Abe Warner's tame monkeys scampered up and wanted to play tag. Reinforcing her command she glared at him. "You, too, Mathias. Promise?"

He made a silly face. "Okay."

"Good. Now come with me. I think I see Mr. Warner in the doorway of his store and I want him to watch you while I find out what's happened."

She didn't voice all that she was thinking, partly because she didn't want to frighten the boys, and partly because she wasn't ready to accept that her parents might be at the center of the knot of men gathered on the rough, weathered walkway.

The moment Abe spotted her, he hurried over. "You children shouldn't be here."

"I had to come," Sara Beth said, handing the still-sleepy Josiah to the trusted old man. "Is it…?"

"Come inside," he said. "There's no need for you young'uns to see all that. No need at all. No sirree."

Sara Beth grasped his coat sleeve and stopped him. "Tell me. Please?"

She saw him look to the boys, then shake his head. The sadness and empathy in his expression told her more than any words could have. Much more than she wanted to know.

Biting her lip and fighting dizziness, she passed all her brothers into Abe's care, then whirled and ran back into the street, pushing her way through the gaggle of onlookers.

A young, dark-haired man in a black frock coat was crouched down next to three bodies that lay on the walkway. Two had already been covered and he was laying the muddy folds of a wool cape over the face and upper torso of the third to mask it.

Sara Beth immediately recognized the fabric of her mother's skirt and gave a little shriek.

The hatless man quickly stood, focused his dark, somber gaze on her and grasped her arms to stop her from proceeding.

She tried to lunge past him toward the bodies as she fought to free herself. "No. Let me go!"

"I'm sorry," he said, holding her fast. "I did all I could. By the time I got here they were gone to Glory."

"No. That can't be true."

"Unfortunately, I'm quite certain it is," he answered. "I'm a doctor."

"But you're wrong! You have to be wrong."

"I am sorry, miss."

Truth and sympathy were evident in the man's darkly serious gaze.

Bright lights sparkled in Sara Beth's field of vision. Her head spun and she felt wobbly the way she sometimes did during an earthquake.

Her mouth was dry, prickly. She took several shuddering breaths and blinked rapidly, trying to clear her thoughts, to accept what her heart insisted was impossible. It was no use.

Darkness akin to a starless night began to close in on her. She sensed herself descending into a bottomless pit of hopelessness and despair.

No longer wanting to see or hear anything that was transpiring around her, she closed her eyes and let go of a reality too painful to acknowledge.

She was only vaguely aware of someone's strong arms catching her as she sank blissfully into the welcome void of unconsciousness.

# Chapter Two

Dr. Taylor Hayward's boots clumped up the creaky wooden steps as he carried the unconscious young woman into Warner's Cobweb Palace.

He laid her atop the bar rather than lower her onto the dusty floor. Hopefully, she wouldn't be offended when she awoke to find herself the center of interest in the old saloon. In his opinion the bar was the cleanest area in the entire building and therefore the best choice as a makeshift fainting couch.

He didn't think the girl was ill or would be in need of his services once she regained consciousness. She had simply received a shock when she had stumbled upon the grisly scene and would surely come around soon without medical intervention. Still, he planned to stay close to her until she was in possession of her full faculties and to offer smelling salts if need be.

Suddenly, there was a high-pitched shout and a sharp pain in his ankle. He looked down to see a reddish-haired boy of about eight drawing back to give his shin another whack. Before the child had a chance to kick him again, Taylor lifted him by the back of his coat collar and held him at arm's length.

"Whoa, son. Take it easy."

The wiry boy wriggled and swung his fists in the man's direction even though his arms were far too short to reach his intended victim. "What'd you do to my sister?" he screeched.

"This young lady? Nothing. She fainted and I caught her so she wouldn't fall and hurt herself. That's all. What's your name?"

Still struggling and obviously intent on doing more bodily harm, the boy ignored the question. Looking past him, Taylor saw a slightly older child holding a toddler and standing next to the proprietor. Since none of the children was familiar to him, he called out, "Hey, Abe. Do you know this little rascal who's tryin' to take me apart?"

The old man nodded as he laid a hand on Luke's head and stroked his hair. "Aye. That's Mathias Reese, Miss Sara Beth's brother. So are these young gentlemen. This is Luke and the baby's Josiah."

"Then suppose you tell them I'm an innocent doctor, not a mugger?"

Mathias started to relax but his eyes looked suspiciously moist. "You're a doctor?"

Taylor lowered him carefully to the floor at his feet and released him before crouching to speak with him on his level. "That's right. And it's a good thing, too, because I think my ankle will need medical attention."

The child glanced out the door to where the crowd was still milling around the recently deceased threesome. "Can you fix my mama?"

Taylor's breath caught. Ah, so *that* was why the girl

had fainted. Little wonder. She and the boys were apparently part of a family that had just been devastated in a matter of minutes.

He laid a hand of consolation on the boy's thin shoulder before he said, "I'm sorry, son. I got here too late to help her."

"Papa?" Mathias whispered. His lower lip was trembling and he was clearly fighting to keep from weeping.

Instead of answering, Taylor swept the grieving child up in his arms and motioned to Abe to join him rather than leave the unconscious girl unattended.

"Both their parents?" Taylor asked quietly aside.

The old man nodded again. "Afraid so. I don't know what these poor little tykes'll do now."

"What about the other man. Who was he?"

"Can't say. I think I've seen him around but I never did catch his name. He's one of the regular dock workers is all I know. I didn't see everything that happened but I do know that Mrs. Reese managed to shoot their attacker before she fell, too."

"I suppose it was a robbery gone terribly wrong," the doctor said. "What I don't understand is why a refined couple like that was out wandering this neighborhood at night."

Behind him, the girl stirred and moaned. Taylor passed Mathias to Abe Warner and grasped her delicate hand. As her eyes fluttered open, he was struck by the flecks of golden color in her beautiful, green gaze.

She blinked, managed to focus, and tried immediately to sit up.

Taylor gently restrained her. "Lie still. You've had a bad shock and you need a few more moments to gather your wits before you try to stand."

Her eyes widened, misted. "Mama and Papa are both gone, aren't they?"

Taylor knew better than to lie to her. "Yes. I'm afraid so. Are you the eldest of their children?"

She continued to stare at the ceiling of the dimly lit room and act as if she hadn't comprehended.

"Miss?" Taylor chafed her wrist in his hands to help revive her. "Miss? Can you hear me?"

He saw her gather herself, mentally, before she answered, "Yes," and again endeavored to rise. This time he assisted her and carefully helped her down from the bar. She seemed steadier on her feet than he'd expected, so he released her.

To his surprise, she squared her shoulders, lifted her chin and addressed him boldly. "Thank you for your efforts on behalf of my parents, Doctor. I left home in a rush and neglected my reticule but perhaps my father's purse contains enough to satisfy your fee." She paused briefly then added, "Unless he has been robbed."

"Do you think that's what led to this?"

"Of course," she replied, yet there was something odd in her expression. Something that alerted the doctor to the possibility that she was hiding something.

"Would you like me to help you make final arrangements?" Taylor asked.

"Thank you, but that won't be necessary," Sara Beth answered. "I'm sure Mr. Warner can assist me."

"Well, please accept my condolences. If there is anything I can do for you in the future, feel free to call upon me. My office is located at the corner of California and Montgomery streets, above the Wells Fargo & Co. office." He withdrew a card from his vest pocket and presented it to her. "My name is Taylor Hayward."

For a brief moment, he thought she might refuse to take the card. Then, she pocketed it without comment.

The doctor turned to Abe Warner. "Can you handle everything in here for now?"

"We'll be fine." The apple-cheeked old man gave a wistful smile. "If I can manage my mischievous monkeys and all the birds and other critters in here, a few little boys won't cause me no trouble."

Taylor hoped Abe was right. He had an unsettled feeling about leaving the children in the elderly man's care, yet it looked as if their sister was old enough and wise enough to eventually provide a stable home for them.

She was an extraordinary young woman, he mused. Her fortitude in the face of disaster was not only unusual, it was inspiring. Most women he had encountered, of any age, were flighty and prone to getting the vapors over the littlest fright or disappointment. Miss Sara Beth Reese had fainted, yes, but for good reason. And she had quickly pulled herself together and regained her sensibilities in a way that truly amazed him.

Polite society required that he keep his distance unless summoned, of course, but he would nevertheless try to stay abreast of the little family's circumstances. Taylor had had the benefit of the support of both his parents all his life and he couldn't imagine how he'd have managed without his father's wise counsel and his mother's tempering gentleness and abiding Christian faith.

He glanced back at the Reese children as he stepped outside. They had gathered around their big sister and were clinging to her as if she were the only lifeline from a sinking ship. He hoped—and prayed—that that was not so. There were many opportunities in San Francisco these days, but there were also many pitfalls and dangers, especially for a young, pretty woman with no family elders to advise and cosset her.

As Sara Beth comforted the boys and dried their eyes, she wondered why she, too, was not weeping. She wanted to cry but the tears would not come. Perhaps that was because she still could not force herself to believe her mama and papa were gone forever. Oh, she believed in heaven. That wasn't the problem. Her question was how a benevolent Heavenly Father could have allowed her and the boys to be left so alone.

"I shall need to return home soon," she told Abe Warner. "Will you escort us?"

"I'd be obliged," he said, "but I can't leave my store with all these goings-on outside. There'll be the law to deal with and then—"

"Will you then arrange for a proper funeral?" Sara Beth asked. "I wouldn't know how to begin."

"Of course, of course. Your pastor should be notified, too. What church do you attend?"

"First Congregational," she said. "At least, Mama and I went and took the boys. Papa never seemed to have the time. He was always working."

"That reminds me," Abe said, frowning. "You'll need to make sure that that workshop of his is secure. Lock it up good and tight, if you know what I mean. There'll have to be an accounting and you wouldn't want to come up short."

"I don't know a thing about that, either," Sara Beth said. "Papa brought the gold dust samples home and assayed them all by himself. None of us were permitted to even watch from outside a window. What shall I do?"

"Leave everything just as it sits," Abe advised. "Whoever assigned him to do the assay work will surely contact you and make further arrangements." He shook his head pensively. "Always did seem a mite reckless to me, trusting outsiders to handle the dust—even a little of it. Then again, they say there wasn't room for the entire operation under one roof at the mint yet, and your papa was an honest man. He'd had that job ever since Moffat and Company sold to Curtis and Ward, hadn't he?"

"I—I think so." She rubbed her temples. "I'm sorry, Mr. Warner. I can't seem to concentrate at the moment."

"It's the shock, I reckon. You're right about needin' to get on home and take it easy. I'll arrange for someone to drive you."

"No, no. We can walk. I don't have the price of a private hack and I don't know when I'd be able to repay you."

"There's someone close by who has his own buggy. Never you fear. He won't charge a penny."

"But—"

"No argument, girl. I think he's still outside. I'll go talk to him and be back in two shakes of a lamb's tail."

Mathias tugged on her skirt to get her attention. "Are we goin' home, Sara Beth?"

"Yes, dear. As soon as we can."

"What about...?" His lower lip began to quiver as he gazed out the open door.

"Mr. Warner will take care of things for us here," she said, realizing that her real problems were only just beginning. "We need to get on home. I'll fix some nice pancakes. You'll feel better after you eat."

Although she knew that it now fell to her to hold the family together, she had absolutely no idea how she was going to accomplish that feat.

Yes, she knew how to keep house and do the same things her mother had always done, such as sew and prepare meals.

But those were the least of her worries, weren't they? With Papa gone, who would support them? Who would bring in the wages they'd need to survive, let alone flourish as they had been? Sara Beth had had only one serious suitor in the past year and repeatedly rejected his offers of marriage, with her mother's blessing.

Perhaps that was why Mama had specifically mentioned the Ladies' Protection and Relief Society, Sara Beth reminded herself. The benevolent organization had begun as a part of her home church and she already knew many of the members. Mama herself had once worked for some of those dear ladies as a seamstress, until she'd met and married Papa.

*Are my skills with needle and thread sufficient to do the same?* she wondered. Was there a chance she might find the kind of gainful employment that had once kept her and her widowed mother off the streets? She prayed so. For if not, she and her brothers were going to be in trouble. And soon.

Abe found the young doctor in the alley, awaiting the arrival of the sheriff. "You bring your buggy, Taylor?"

"Yes. I was just coming in from a call outside town so I already had the horse in harness. I wouldn't have stopped to hitch up otherwise."

"Good. I've got a favor to ask. Miss Sara Beth and her brothers need a ride home. I'd take 'em myself but I don't dare leave my emporium until the furor dies down a bit more. I figure I might as well open the bar and take care of the thirsty curiosity-seekers, too."

The doctor chuckled wryly. "That's what I'd have expected, you old reprobate. Don't you know that rotgut is bad for you?"

"It's a darned sight safer than the water we get from the water wagons," Abe countered. "That stuff's clear green sometimes, especially come summer."

"I can't argue with you there," Taylor replied. "All right. I'll bring my horse around and wait while you fetch the Reese children."

"One of 'em ain't exactly a child, if you get my drift. You okay with that?"

"I'm a doctor," Taylor said. "And we'll have the boys with us as chaperones. As long as Miss Sara Beth doesn't mind riding with me, I'm sure no one else will think twice about it."

The old man snorted cynically. "If you say so. Just keep your interest professional, you hear?"

"Have you taken it upon yourself to look out for the young lady's honor?"

"I wish I could," Abe answered, sobering. "An old codger like me is no good example for those boys, nor a fitting companion for a young woman of Sara Beth's upbringing."

"What do you think she'll do?"

Abe shrugged. "Don't know."

"Does she have grandparents? Aunts and uncles?"

"None, far as I know, although in a case like this

folks sometimes crawl out of the woodwork lookin' for a piece of the inheritance."

"Reese had money?"

"I reckon. They live in a pretty nice two-story house over on Pike. You'll see when you drive 'em home. Ol' Robert worked for the mint for a couple of years before he and another fella went into the assay business for themselves."

"Then that's good, right?"

"I ain't sure. Robert used to take lots of samples home with him. It was his job to double-check the official assay and he didn't like to work with a lot of other people watching. All I can see is trouble ahead."

"How so?"

"Can't say for certain. It just seems to me that if anybody was to take a notion to help himself to some of that gold dust, now's the time he'd prob'ly do it. Fetch the buggy. I'll go get your passengers."

Taylor mulled over the old man's opinions and concerns as he led his horse and compact rig into the alley. He supposed he should be thankful for the opportunity to help the orphaned children, but he had to admit that there was more to his interest than mere altruism.

Something about the lost look in Miss Sara Beth's eyes had touched him deeply, irrevocably. In an instant he had come to care about her far more than the circumstances called for. True, she was strong-willed, but she also reminded him of a lost sheep being circled by a pack of ravenous wolves. Given what Abe knew about the whole situation, it was little wonder the elderly man felt a fatherly bent toward the girl.

Taylor huffed and shook his head as his conscience kicked him in the gut. His personal feelings were far from paternal in regard to the lovely young woman. Her hair was the rich colors of autumn, spun into silk. And her eyes were jade gems, sparkling with the very flecks of gold her father had once tested. It was improper of him to notice such things, yet he had.

His outward behavior, of course, would always remain above reproach. He would never stoop to taking advantage of a woman, especially not one as innocent and needy as Miss Reese. He would, however, be more vigilant on her behalf than he would any of his other patients.

Taylor could already tell it was not going to be enough to simply check on her well-being via others. He was going to take a personal interest in the situation. There was no getting around it, no talking himself out of it.

As far as he was concerned, divine providence had placed him in this city on this night and had led him to make these particular acquaintances. It was therefore his duty to do all he could to help—with no thought of gain.

He had not become a doctor in order to get rich; he had chosen his profession because he truly wanted to benefit mankind. If he had wanted a more lucrative career, he would have followed in his father's footsteps and become a lawyer, or in his grandfather's as a judge.

Instead, he had studied medicine for nearly a year under the best minds at Massachusetts General Hospital, then had apprenticed for a while before he'd bid his family goodbye and headed west to practice.

More than half the time he wasn't remunerated for his efforts, and if he was, payment was likely to be a sack of potatoes or mealy flour or an occasional scrawny chicken. He had thought, with the discovery of gold and San Francisco's burgeoning economy, he'd easily find plenty of wealthy patients. Instead, he'd encountered more poverty and need than he'd imagined possible.

That was why he'd begun to donate his services at places like the city's two major orphan asylums and had been so adamant in his insistence that San Francisco needed a care facility devoted solely to the illnesses of children. As it stood now, the poor little things who could not be tended at home were carted off to the city and county hospitals, where they were then exposed to all sorts of nasty diseases and were in the constant presence of morbidity.

His horse nickered, disturbing his musings. Taylor looked up to see the approach of his passengers. He tipped his bowler to them. "Are you ready to go?"

Spine straight, shoulders squared beneath her fitted woolen coat, Sara Beth nodded. "Yes. Thank you, Dr. Hayward. If you will assist me, then hand me Josiah, I would be much obliged."

It worried Taylor to see her so apparently in control of her emotions. The boys seemed a bit sniffly, as children were wont to be anyway, but there wasn't a sign of tears in their sister's eyes.

As he offered his hand, he felt a strange hardness press into his palm. Pausing, he turned her hand over and saw what looked like the end of a smooth, thin stick. His puzzled glance caused her to falter ever so slightly.

"Oh. Forgive me," Sara Beth said, withdrawing the needle and displaying it for him with a trembling hand. "As I was leaving home I thought I might need some method of protection so I brought along one of Mother's knitting needles. I had forgotten about it until now."

"I hardly consider a sliver of bone a suitable defensive weapon," Taylor said. "You could have been hurt walking these streets alone at night."

He saw her countenance darken, her expression close. "Yes," she said, taking the baby and settling him in her lap where she could hold him close. "I might have been shot and killed, mightn't I?"

Without further comment he lifted the older boys into the crowded buggy, squeezed himself onto the single seat and took up the reins.

Perhaps he had overstepped propriety in his concern for the young woman, Taylor reasoned, but someone had to tell her she had behaved in a most foolish manner. If that decision to follow her parents into the dangers of the night was typical behavior, she wasn't nearly as mature and level-headed as he'd first thought. Nor was she likely to be able to properly care for what remained of her family by herself.

# Chapter Three

The steady, rhythmic echo of the horse's hooves on the cobblestone and brick-paved streets provided a soothing tempo until they had proceeded far enough from the busiest areas of the city to encounter hard-packed dirt dotted with muddy potholes.

To Sara Beth's relief, all the younger children had nodded off before the doctor's buggy had reached the portion of Pike Street where their home stood.

"This is it," she said, stifling a sigh and pointing. "That two-story, gray clapboard with the double porches. You can let us off in front."

As the doctor climbed down to hitch his horse to a cast-iron ring, he paused. Tensing, he held up his hand to stop her instead of continuing around to help her disembark. "Wait. Stay there."

"Why? What's wrong?"

"I think I see someone on your porch."

"That's silly. There can't be. Why would anyone…?" Peering at the house, she realized he was right. There was someone on her front porch. And another man on the upstairs porch that mirrored the structure at ground level. Judging by their shadowy forms, both men were carrying rifles.

Sara Beth remained in the buggy as she cupped her hands around her mouth and called out, "Who are you? What do you want?"

The gunman on the lower porch stepped off and started along the boarded walkway toward her. There was no mistaking the menace in his movements. She might have assumed she was overreacting but the buggy horse also seemed nervous, almost unseating her when it suddenly lurched backward to the end of its tether and stamped its hooves.

The man paused halfway to the street and struck a stalwart pose, his boots planted solidly apart, his rifle spanning his chest. "This house is off-limits," he said. "Sheriff's orders."

"But that's impossible. I live here," Sara Beth insisted.

"Not any more you don't. This property is sealed. No one can come or go," the guard replied.

"That's ridiculous. My father, Robert Reese, is the owner." The gunman's cynical chuckle chilled her to the bone.

"That's what you think, little lady. I have it on good authority that this property belongs to the U.S. government now."

"Who told you that? Who sent you?"

"I get my orders from Sheriff Scannell, like I said."

Sara Beth was not about to concede defeat. "Where did he get that authority?"

"From Judge Norton, I reckon."

The doctor had gotten back into his buggy and was again taking up the reins when Sara Beth noticed him.

"What are you doing? I'm not going anywhere. This is my home and I intend to claim it."

"Over their objection?" he asked. "I think that would be more than unwise, miss. I think it would be suicide."

"I'm not afraid of them, even if you are."

"Very noble, I'm sure. However, I have only a pistol and you are armed with a knitting needle. How do you propose we overwhelm at least two men with rifles and sidearms?"

"I don't know." Her voice rose. "They're in the wrong. We can't simply give in to such unfairness."

"We can retreat to fight another day," he said. "Hang on." He gave the lines a snap and the horse took off smartly, pushing Sara Beth back against the padded seat in spite of her efforts to lean forward.

She bit her lower lip and fought a swelling feeling of exasperation and powerlessness. This couldn't be happening! Everything she and her family owned was locked up in that house. She didn't even have a hairbrush or a change of clothing for herself or for the boys.

The doctor slowed the horse's pace when they were several blocks away. "Where to?" he asked.

"What?" She blinked rapidly to quell her tears of frustration.

"I can't very well take you home with me and I don't think the Cobweb Palace is a fit place, either. Do you have friends or family you could stay with until we get this mess sorted out?"

She noted his use of the pronoun "we," but chose to ignore the implication. "I have no family in San Francisco and Mother's friends are mostly affiliated with the Ladies' Protection and Relief Society."

Sighing, she said, "I had hoped to delay this decision, but I suppose I have no choice. We shall have to go straight to their orphan asylum. Do you know where it's located?"

She was relieved when he told her that he did. However, when he added, "I've had the sad duty of treating some of those poor little ones," her spirits plummeted. She and her brothers were now on a totally different social stratum, weren't they? In a matter of hours they had gone from being part of a middle-class family to being destitute, just like the dirty street urchins who begged along the piers and alleys down by the wharf.

Raising her chin and closing her eyes, Sara Beth vowed that as long as she had breath in her body, her remaining family would never have to beg. She would work somewhere, do something that generated an honest living, no matter how meager, God willing.

*And, please Lord, show me how to get our house and belongings back, too,* she prayed silently. She didn't know how she'd manage to accomplish that, but she would not give up trying, no matter what.

There was no need to hurry the horse along once they were in the clear, Taylor concluded. It was nearly morning. Although the city would soon be bustling with its usual daytime activities, there was probably at least an hour more before the keepers of the orphanage would rise and begin to prepare the first meal of the day.

Mulling over the plight of his passengers made him so angry he could barely contain his ire. It was fraud and abuses of the law such as these that had brought about the formation of the Vigilance Committee in the first place. The ballot boxes had been rigged, the honest votes nullified by internal corruption and the offices such as judge and sheriff sold to the highest bidders. Little wonder someone in power had had no trouble getting quick control of the Reese home and laboratory.

His own father and grandfather would have been astounded to hear of the despotism rampant in the city. Reform was urgently needed. And as far as he was concerned, men like him were charged, by their own innate sense of honor, to rise up and facilitate a change.

That was why he had joined the Vigilance Committee and why he was still an active member of the widespread secret society. He might not have been able to help Miss Sara Beth immediately, but he *would* help her. Someone was going to pay for turning her and her little brothers out into the night. He was going to see to it.

The horse ambled along the Montgomery block of hotels and up Sacramento Street past the four-story brick Rail Road House, a hotel that boasted accommodations for up to two hundred persons at one time, clean bedding and fresh water. The little figure of a locomotive atop its weather vane was said to anticipate San Francisco's eventual joining with the rest of the States by rail.

Taylor glanced at Sara Beth as he guided his horse up California Street and onto the sweeping, tree-lined drive that led to the orphanage. The building had been, and still was, a palatial private home, although living quarters for the host family were separate from the housing for the orphans and live-in staff. Ella McNeil, the matron, watched over her charges and managed the house with an iron hand. Unlike the Reese children, many of the other orphans had been living on the streets, unsupervised, for months or even years and were therefore in dire need of discipline and moral guidance.

"Miss?" Taylor said quietly. "We're here."

Sara Beth opened her eyes and nodded. "I know. I haven't been asleep."

"Would you like me to come in with you?"

"Yes, if you don't mind. I can manage Josiah, but I can't carry them all. And the older boys may be upset when they realize where we are."

"I understand."

He climbed down and circled the buggy to assist her. She passed him Josiah, then gently woke Mathias and Luke. "We need to get out here, boys."

Mathias rubbed his fists over his eyes and yawned. "Are we home?"

"Not exactly," Sara Beth said. "We'll be staying here for a bit while we get Papa's affairs settled."

Luke leaned past him to look. "What are we doing here? Where are we?"

"I wanna go home," Mathias began to wail.

"Give him to me," the doctor said. "I'll handle him. You, too, Luke." He held out his arms and took the boys from her one at a time, setting all but Josiah on the ground at his feet and offering Sara Beth his free hand.

When she placed her smaller, icy fingers in his, he felt an unexpected pang of pity. That would never do. A proud woman like her would surely take offense if she even suspected that he was feeling sorry for her.

She faltered once with a little stumble, causing him to reach to cup her elbow.

"I'm fine, thank you. I can manage," she said, righting herself and marching proudly up to the ornate front door of the stone-walled mansion. She rapped with the brass knocker and waited.

When the door swung open and the matron saw her,

she greeted her with open arms. "Oh, darlin', I heard what happened. It's awful. Plum awful. You come right in and make yourself at home. We're proud to have you."

As Taylor watched, the stalwart young woman became a child again. Catching back a sob, she fell into Mrs. McNeil's ample embrace. Taylor could see her shoulders shaking with silent weeping as the older woman patted her on the back. He didn't want her to suffer, but he knew that the sooner she began to properly grieve her enormous loss, the sooner she'd recover.

"Let's take the boys in and get them settled," he suggested as soon as the two women stepped apart.

Ella wiped her eyes with the corner of her starched, white apron. "Land sakes, yes. I'm forgettin' my manners. You come along, now," she said to Luke and Mathias. "We've got gobs of other boys for you two to meet and a bunk you can share." She glanced at Josiah in the doctor's arms. "Do you think the littlest one will be all right in there or shall we send him to stay with the infants?"

Before Taylor could reply, Sara Beth snatched up the baby and shook her head. Her tears were gone except for slight dampness on her cheeks. "Josiah stays with me. I won't have him put with strangers."

"Of course, of course." The matron rubbed the girl's shoulder through her coat. "It's been a long, trying night for all of you. We'll talk more about making permanent arrangements later."

No one had to tell Taylor what Sara Beth's reaction to that would be. He knew she'd resist before she opened her mouth.

"There's no need. We won't be staying. As soon as I get my father's business affairs settled I'll be going back home," she said flatly. "I did want to discuss possible employment for myself, though. Mother's needlework was finer than mine, of course, but she was my teacher and I promise to do my very best. Is there a chance I could work for you like Mother once did, Mrs. McNeil?"

Taylor could see that the matron was hesitant. He privately caught her eye and gave a silent, secret nod.

To his relief, she said, "I'm sure we can find something. Perhaps part-time in the kitchen. Would that suit?"

"Anything will do," Sara Beth said. "If you will show me where to place Josiah while he naps, I can start immediately."

"Nonsense," Ella said. "There'll be plenty of time for that. First, we need to get all of you settled and then fed. When you've rested, we'll talk further."

Sara Beth's deep sigh as a result was almost a shudder. "Thank you. I am weary. And there is so much on my mind right now I can hardly think."

"Little wonder," the doctor offered. "It's been a long night for all of us. Will you be all right if I take my leave?"

Whirling, she acted surprised that he was still there. "Of course. And thank you for looking after us."

"My pleasure," he said with a slight bow. He touched the brim of his bowler and smiled at the matron, too. "Ladies. If you'll excuse me?"

He managed to retain the smile until he had turned away and walked back outside. There was a deeply troubling wrong to right and no time to waste. If Abe Warner had been correct in his assumption about the gold samples kept in Reese's private assay office, it might already be too late to preserve their integrity.

Nevertheless, he had to try. And his first stop was going to be the Coleman house. William T. Coleman was the president of the Vigilance Committee, and although their roster was kept by number rather than by name, most of the members knew whose loyalty could be counted on in an emergency.

Taylor mounted his buggy and shouted to the horse as he snapped the reins. There was no time to waste. A helpless family was being mistreated and he was not going to stand idly by and watch it happen.

The middle-aged gentleman arrived on Pike Street in a cabriolet pulled by a matched pair of sorrel geldings and driven by a hireling in a frock coat and top hat.

As he disembarked in front of the two-story frame house, he grinned. This plan had come together even better than he'd anticipated. With Isabelle dead, too, there was no one left to stand in his way, no one who might know what Robert had discovered and thereby ruin his reputation. Or worse.

He strode up the front walk and onto the porch where he was met by the sheriff and two other rough-looking men.

"Sheriff Scannell," the gentleman said with a slight nod. He eyed the others with undisguised loathing and didn't offer to shake anyone's hand, though his own hands were gloved in pearl kidskin to match his cravat. "I see you're keeping company with the usual riffraff."

The sheriff laughed raucously and spit over the porch railing. "Meaning yourself, I suppose, Mr. Bein? You decide yet how you're goin' to explain all this?"

Bein grinned. "As long as the losses are credited to Reese instead of to me, I won't have anything to explain. Harazthy is so engrossed in that new vineyard of his, he barely notices what goes on around the mint."

"What about the Vigilance Committee? Ain't you worried about them?"

"Not in the least. I have it on the personal authority of Governor Johnson that Sherman is about to be made Major General of the second division of militia for San Francisco. He'll soon take care of the vigilantes."

Scannell shrugged and spat again before wiping his mustache with the back of his hand, "All right. If you say so. It's your funeral."

Leering cynically, William Bein snorted approval. "Not my funeral, gentlemen, my partner's, may he rest in peace."

He reached into his pocket and withdrew a handkerchief folded into the shape of a packet and monogrammed with the initials *R.R.* "Take this and see that it's placed in Reese's workshop, Sheriff. Don't make it too obvious, but be sure the gold shavings and dust are still in it when it's found. Do I make myself clear?"

"You think we'd steal from you?"

"In a heartbeat, if you thought you could get away with it," Bein answered. "Only this time you can't. We all need that gold to be discovered in Reese's possession. And since he and Isabelle are both dead, no one will be able to refute the charges against him."

"What about the girl? She came back here."

"What? You didn't let her in, did you?"

"No, sir. We sent her away. She never got out of the buggy."

His eyes narrowed below bushy, graying brows. "What buggy? Reese didn't even own a horse, let alone a rig."

"I think it was that doctor what brought her," Scannell said. "You know. The young one with the shingle on the second floor over the Wells Fargo office."

Bein cursed colorfully. "Oh, I know him, all right. He and Coleman are thick as thieves. He's sure to inform the Vigilance Committee."

"I thought you said you weren't worried about them."

"I'm not. I just don't want any further trouble over this." He glanced sideways at the hired thugs who were still standing guard at the corners of the broad porch. "If need be, we may have to eliminate the girl, too."

"Oh, now, I don't know as I like that idea," the sheriff said, edging away from the well-dressed man. "She's just a young thing. Pretty, too. It's bad enough her mama had to die the way she did."

"Only because she stuck her nose in where it didn't belong," Bein countered. "You lost one of yours in the gunfight, you know."

"I know. But Billy wasn't all that bright to start with. He never should of showed himself when he shot Reese." He was slowly shaking his head as he spoke. "Is it true that the woman got him?"

"That's my understanding," Bein answered. "Which should prove to you that her daughter may be someone to be reckoned with. I don't know about you, but I'm not going to go to jail just because some stupid woman points an accusing finger at me."

"I suppose you're right." Nodding soberly, Scannell perused the broad street. "All right. You look into it and get word to me if you need me to eliminate the girl, too. I won't like it, but I'll see that it's done."

"Good man. And keep your mouth shut about this," he added, eyeing the packet of gold the sheriff was about to deposit in Robert Reese's workroom. "Now, go get rid of that evidence like I told you to."

"What'll you be doing?" the sheriff asked.

"Offering my condolences to my partner's grieving family," Bein said with a self-satisfied smile. "As soon as I find out where the children went, their loving uncle Will is going to offer them a nice settlement and see that they have passage on the next ship back to Massachusetts, where their parents came from."

"You think they'll go? Just like that?"

"When they learn that this house and everything in it has legally passed to me upon the death of their father, I don't see what other choice those little brats will have, do you?"

## Chapter Four

The more time Sara Beth spent at the orphanage, the more she remembered about her early life there. Although she had been five when Mama had married Papa Robert, there were familiar smells and noises in that big old house that tugged at her consciousness and made her heart pound.

Friends she had made back then, children she fondly remembered, were, of course, long gone. Those who had come along later and replaced them, however, were so like the ones she recalled that she suddenly pictured herself as very young. And very scared.

Lucas and Mathias had quickly found other boys to interest them and had wandered off to explore the facility, while Josiah had fallen asleep in Sara Beth's arms. She didn't mind carrying him. Truth to tell, she was loath to even consider putting him down. It was as if she needed the little one's nearness to comfort her, rather than the other way around.

"Let's get you something to eat and a nice cup of hot tea," the matron said, ushering Sara Beth into the expansive kitchen where several other women were already hard at work.

The aroma from the pot of gruel bubbling on the top of the woodstove nearly turned Sara Beth's stomach. That was another of those old, pungent memories, this one best forgotten, she realized with the first whiff. Mama had never prepared that kind of breakfast for any of her family after they'd left the orphans' home, and Sara Beth assumed that memories of being destitute were at the heart of her mother's choices. That certainly made sense.

She blinked in the steamy atmosphere, hoping she was not going to disgrace herself by becoming ill. She knew Mrs. McNeil did her best to stretch the meager rations and was not to be faulted if their palatability suffered as a result. That conclusion, however, did little to relieve her unsettled stomach.

"Ladies, this is Miss Sara Beth Reese, an old friend and former resident," Ella told the other women. They looked up from their labors and she pointed to each in turn. "That's Mrs. Clara Nelson, our cook, and Mattie Coombs, her helper."

Sara Beth managed a wan smile. "How do you do?"

"Fair to middlin'," Clara said with an impish grin, made more amusing by her twinkling blue eyes, apple cheeks and snow-white hair. "You visitin' or stayin'?"

"Visiting. But I do want to make myself useful while I'm here. I'll be glad to help however I can."

Mattie snorted as if in disbelief, turning her thin wiry body back to the stove. Clara welcomed the offer. "You surely can," she said. "As soon as you've eaten a bite you can help me serve the boys while Mattie takes care of the girls."

"Oh, good. My brothers are here, too, and I'd like to look in on them."

Mattie huffed. "I knowed she was stayin'. She's got that look about her. Same as they all get."

Did she? Sara Beth supposed there was a lost quality to her demeanor, although she was not about to openly acknowledge it under the present circumstances. As soon as she had a chance to talk to Mrs. McNeil in private, however, she intended to tell her everything and ask for advice.

The more she pondered the situation, the more she felt there had to be a connection between what she'd overheard her parents discussing and their untimely deaths. Not that their conversation made much sense, even in retrospect.

For one thing, Papa had mentioned someone he worked with in a disparaging manner. The Reese family had treated his partner, William Bein, as part of their intimate circle, including him in social events and even asking the children to call him "Uncle Will." Surely he could not be responsible for anything that had happened.

But there certainly could be other nefarious forces at work, she reasoned. Papa had often expressed disdain for Sheriff Scannell, and that man was proving every bit as disreputable as rumor had painted him. Plus, there was the gold to consider. Anyone who knew that Papa worked for the new mint must also assume he would have samples of gold on hand in his lab. Sara Beth knew many a man had died for riches, especially in the years since 1849.

Reviewing the tragedy, her thoughts drifted to her new benefactor, Dr. Taylor Hayward. His was a difficult profession, one that rarely produced a better cure than most grannies could mix up from their favorite roots and berries. Men like him were an asset to the wounded in wartime, of course, but otherwise might just as well stay in their offices and let the citizenry treat themselves for the ague and such.

Chagrined, she felt empathy for the man. He had obviously attempted to help her parents, and for that effort alone she was grateful. His lack of ability was less his fault than the fact that doctors were little more than hand-holders and tonic dispensers—unless they had served on the battlefield or studied in one of those fancy hospitals back east. At least that was what Papa had always said when he'd gotten sick after spending long, tedious hours in his lab.

Dr. Hayward's presence at the scene of carnage on the wharf had been very comforting, she admitted. But then, so had Abe Warner's, and his calling was not in the healing arts.

Thoughts of the kindly old man brought a slight smile to her face. In a day or so, after she got her thoughts sorted out and decided what course to take, she'd have to walk over to the Cobweb Palace, thank Abe for everything and assure him that he needn't worry.

Taking a deep breath and releasing it as a sigh, Sara Beth realized that she had no certainty that her family would be all right. The way things looked, she would be fortunate to salvage their personal belongings, let alone reclaim the house on Pike Street. And if Papa Robert's laboratory was not safeguarded, there was no telling how much trouble the mint might cause her.

Surely they wouldn't expect her to be responsible, would they? The sheriff was the one who had moved in and posted guards. Therefore if there were any discrepancies, the explanation for those should lie at Scannell's doorstep.

Only that particular lawman's reputation was built on graft, not honor, according to the talk she'd overheard at church and in her own parlor. His election had been questioned from the beginning, and ballot boxes with false bottoms had been written about in the evening *Bulletin*. Its publisher, Mr. James King, had been crusading against corruption in San Francisco for months and had even withstood threats on his life in order to continue to print the truth.

"That's what I'll do," Sara Beth murmured, elated by her idea. "As soon as I have a chance, I'll pen a letter to the newspaper and ask for information about my parents' murders."

Would Mr. King print such a thing? Oh, yes. He was an honorable gentleman who stood firm against the riffraff and evildoers who lurked among the good people of the city. He would gladly print her missive. And then perhaps she'd see her parents avenged.

Thoughts of allies and admirable men brought Dr. Hayward to mind once again. Not only did he cut a fine figure, there had been benevolence and caring in his gaze. As soon as she was able, she planned to somehow repay his kindnesses. Until then, she would simply take each moment, each hour, each day, one at a time.

To sensibly contemplate the future, when her heart was breaking and her mind awhirl, was more than difficult. It was impossible.

The sun was rising and the city was coming to life as Taylor drove slowly down crowded Sacramento Street and past the What Cheer House. Hotels had proliferated in San Francisco until there were nearly sixty, although none quite as accommodating as the one R. B. Woodward ran, especially if a fellow wanted a warm, clean bath and a decent meal.

Freight wagons and vendors made up the bulk of the traffic to and from the docks. This was not the best time of day to be trying to squeeze a flimsy doctor's buggy through the main streets, wide though they were, so Taylor headed for the livery stable to leave his rig and complete his errands on foot.

There were times, like now, when he almost wished he were back studying at Massachusetts General Hospital. He had been happiest while learning his trade, always eager to follow successful medical men on their rounds and observe the latest techniques. Everyone agreed that the best teaching hospitals were in Germany but given the state of his purse, such a trip was impossible. Someday, perhaps, he'd manage to travel overseas to study. In the meantime, his place was right here in San Francisco.

"Helping Miss Reese," he added with conviction. He had not been in time to save her parents, but he was going to assist her in every way possible. It was the least he could do.

Leaving his horse and buggy, he made his way along the boarded walk to the Plaza on Portsmouth Square and passed the Hall of Records. As soon as he'd talked to Coleman he'd come back here and see if he could find out who owned the house in which Sara Beth and her family had lived. If, as the sheriff had claimed, it belonged to the government, then he didn't see how she'd ever win it back.

The thought of that sweet, innocent young woman having to take up permanent residence at the orphanage cut him to the quick. Yes, it was well-run. And, yes, it was useful as a temporary shelter. But that was where his approval ended. The place was too cramped, too crowded, and that meant that chances of sickness rose appreciably, especially when summer miasma engulfed the city.

He wasn't sure he believed the experts who claimed that the air itself caused illness, but he did know from experience that the more children who were housed together, the greater the chances that they would catch whatever diseases their companions suffered from. That was a given. And as long as the Reese children and their sister resided with the other orphans, they would be in mortal danger.

The day sped past. Sara Beth saw to it that her brothers were settled in the boys' dormitory and had gone with their fellows to afternoon classes at a nearby school. This new life seemed to suit them a lot better than it did her and Josiah. The little boy had fussed most of the day, wearing her patience thin until she had finally agreed to let him be taken to spend the daylight hours with the other babies under the age of three.

Their parting had brought tears to her eyes, especially when he had begun to sob and reach for her. "No, you need to go with Mrs. McNeil," Sara Beth had said firmly. "Sister has work to do and I can't do it if I'm toting you around." She'd patted his damp cheek in parting. "Be a good boy, now. I'll pick you up after I finish my evening chores. I promise."

Now, up to her elbows in dishwater, she started to

yearn for her former life, then stopped herself. "Don't," she said softly. "That's gone. Over. You have to make do. Mama did and you can, too."

"That's the spirit," Clara said as she added more soiled tin plates to the stack by the sink. "Never give up and you'll be much happier. I know I am."

"Have you worked here long?" Sara Beth asked.

"Since my Charlie passed on. Cholera got him right after we arrived. We was goin' to start a little restaurant and get our share of the gold dust the honest way." She sighed, her ample chest rising and falling noticeably with the effort. "I figure at least this way, my skills in the kitchen aren't going to waste."

"I wish I were talented in some special way," Sara Beth said. "Mama had been training me to keep a nice house, just as she did. Beyond that I know very little."

"You can read and write, can't you?"

"Yes. Of course. As a matter of fact, there is a letter I plan to pen as soon as I have a spare moment. Do you know where I can find paper and ink?"

"Ella can give you whatever you need," Clara said with a smile. "I swan, that woman could make a silk purse out of a sow's ear."

"She is amazing, isn't she? I don't know what I'd have done if she hadn't let me stay."

"What about your parents? Are they both gone?"

Sara Beth nodded solemnly. "Yes. I shall have to pay to have them buried and I haven't a cent."

"There's plenty of paupers' graves in Yerba Buena Cemetery. That's where my Charlie is laid to rest. The only thing that bothers me is not having a headstone. Practically no one does, so I guess that makes us all equal, rich and poor."

"I suppose so. Mr. Warner has promised to make the arrangements for me."

"Old Abe Warner? Then let him. He may live like poor folks but that saloon of his has to be rakin' in the gold dust by the bucketful. How'd you come to know him, a fine lady like you?"

That question amused Sara Beth. "Mama loved his menagerie. We used to take our constitutionals down by the waterfront and we'd often stop to feed the monkeys or those beautiful big birds he kept. I even saw a bear there once."

"I reckon he needs all those critters to clean up the garbage. From the looks of his place, he could use a few more, too." She chuckled, then added, "That's better. I know you could smile if you tried."

"I hate to. I mean, it seems wrong, somehow. My family has been decimated and we're in such dire straits we may never recover, yet part of me feels a sense of joy."

"That's the Lord tellin' you He's got the answers," Clara offered. "They may be a while in comin' and may not be the ones you asked for, but He'll look after his children. I've been sure of that ever since I walked through these doors and found my own place of refuge."

"Do you think it's ungrateful of me to wish to leave?" Sara Beth asked.

"No, dear, not at all. Just keep an open mind and heart and listen to God's leading."

"Even when I feel as if I'm spinning in circles?"

"Especially then," the cook said, pausing to give her a motherly hug. "Now, get to washin' them dishes so we can bank the stove and get ready for bed. I don't know about you, but I'm plum tuckered out."

Turning back to the pan of sudsy water, Sara Beth

gave silent thanks that Clara was such a wise woman. Now that Mama was gone she'd need friendly counsel like hers and Ella's in order to reform her life, plan her future.

Was it possible to decide anything this soon? she wondered absently. Not really. What she could do, however, was follow through on her idea to contact the *Bulletin* and see if they would champion her cause in regard to her home. They had often taken up the needs of the community and had revealed corruption in city government in spite of threats to their presses and persons. Surely, given this situation, Mr. King would take pity on her plight.

But first he must be properly informed, she added. Her jaw muscles clenched and she nodded to affirm her decision. As soon as she had brought Josiah to her cot in the girls' quarters and had gotten him settled for the night, she would begin to write to the newspaper.

Such a letter would require much thought and careful expression but she was capable. Her penmanship was beautiful and her mind keen. All she'd have to do was make certain she didn't alienate too many important people and yet stated her case in indisputable terms.

Such a goal seemed unattainable, yet Sara Beth was resolute. She could not hope to seize control of her assets by force so she would do it by her wits.

Finishing the dishes, she toted the heavy dishpan to the back door and threw the water onto the steps to clean them, too. At home, she might have tarried long enough to sweep the porch, but not tonight.

Tonight she had a letter to write. A letter that might very well be the most significant missive she had ever composed.

\* \* \*

Taylor Hayward had been disappointed in his earlier meeting with W. T. Coleman. The man had been too secretive to please him and had beat around the bush regarding what the Vigilance Committee might be able to do in respect to the contested Reese holdings.

"That's up to Bein," Coleman had insisted. "He was Reese's partner and as such has control of the assay office."

"Fine. But what about the family home at the same address? Surely we can't allow him to pitch the surviving family members out into the streets."

Coleman's thin shoulders shrugged and he blanched enough that his already pale skin whitened visibly. "It's not that simple. Not anymore. Governor Johnson is talking about putting that general, Sherman, in charge of the militia, and Mayor Van Ness agrees. If they do that, we're in trouble."

"I've never known you to back down from a fair fight," Taylor said.

"I didn't say I was backing down. I'm just telling you that it would be wiser to bide our time. All the newspapers except the *Herald* are already on our side."

"Which is to be expected since James Casey is running it and he's as crooked as they come," the doctor argued. "I'd heard that Casey was thrown out of the Drexel, Sather and Church building by Sherman himself over an editorial so full of lies that even a mule could have recognized its falseness."

"Doesn't matter. We still have to tread softly."

Taylor was beside himself. He paced across the office, then wheeled to face the man he had been counting on for aid. "Suppose there's more to it than what appears on the surface? Suppose Bein is trying to pull a fast one on the government? What then?"

"Then the sheriff should be in charge." Coleman raised his hands, palms out, as if prepared to physically defend himself. "I know, I know. Scannell bought the office for a whole lot more than he'll ever earn legally. That's common knowledge. But it doesn't change anything. We can't wrest control of the whole city from the hands of those criminals unless we're sure of major citizen support. That's all there is to it."

"What will it take to gain that?"

"I don't know," the obviously weary and worried businessman said. "But we can't continue this way for long. When the time is right, we will act, I promise you."

"What if it's too late for the Reese children?"

"That can't be helped." Coleman ran a slim finger beneath his starched collar as if his cravat were choking him. "I'm not looking forward to the bloodshed that may result."

"Neither am I," Taylor said soberly. "But someone has to do something before we're all slapped in jail or hanged for choosing the side of honor and justice."

"This Reese incident has really gotten you fired up, hasn't it, Doc? How did you get involved in the first place?"

"I was called to minister to the murder victims."

"And you didn't save them. I see. That is unfortunate. But it still doesn't explain why you're so adamant about the real estate."

"There were children left homeless," Taylor said. "I delivered them to the Ladies' Protection and Relief

Society. They don't belong there. They belong in the house Scannell is guarding."

"They're better off with Mrs. McNeil. Children couldn't manage alone, anyway."

It was the doctor's turn to loosen his tight collar. "There's—there's an older daughter to look after the little ones," he explained. "She seems quite capable."

"Ah." Coleman smiled. "And pretty, too?"

"That's beside the point."

"On the contrary, that is exactly the point, as I see it. You have developed some kind of connection to this young, helpless damsel and you're expecting me and my men to assist you in impressing her."

"Nonsense." With a deep, settling breath, Taylor had given up, bid his friend goodbye and left the office building.

In retrospect, he had known denial of his feelings was futile. He did care for Sara Beth Reese. And he could see no good reason for that reaction. There had been and still were, many other comely women in his acquaintance, so why was this one becoming so important to him? Was it her emerald eyes or that long, reddish hair that was so appealing? He had no earthly idea.

Later that day, as he closed his own office and started home to the What Cheer House, where he rented a room, he was still troubled. There had to be more to his burgeoning interest in that young woman and her kin. They had gotten under his skin so quickly it was truly astounding. He supposed Sara Beth's plight, having all those siblings to care for as well as herself, had touched a chord in his heart.

This was not the first time he had found himself caring too much about the welfare of his patients. According to his instructors at Massachusetts General, becoming overly involved in the lives of others was a flaw in his character that he needed to overcome in order to do his job efficiently.

Taylor's real problem, as he saw it, was that he didn't want to lose that touch of compassion that made him who he was. If it interfered with his medical practice, then so be it. He was not about to chastise himself for having feelings for the suffering and downtrodden.

And those poor Reese children were that, and more. For all he knew, they were the victims of the same greed and corruption that already poisoned much of San Francisco politics. If that was the case, they would be fortunate to reclaim anything that had once, by rights, been theirs.

Taylor clenched his fists as he walked, his boots clomping hollowly on the boarded walkway, their thuds lost among the other noises of the still bustling city.

"There has to be something I can do," he murmured in frustration.

Reaching the corner of Montgomery and Merchant streets, he paused, praying silently and then wondering if any of the churches had enough influence to help.

He glanced up and realized where he was standing. That was his answer. The *Bulletin* offices were here. It was the perfect solution. An exposé, written by a man with the solid reputation of James King might force Coleman to call the Vigilance Committee into action. It was certainly worth a try.

A lamp flickered on the second story.

Taylor pushed through the door and took the stairs two at a time.

## Chapter Five

Working late by the light of a kerosene lamp in the deserted parlor, Sara Beth labored that first evening and the next to phrase everything just right. Because both paper and ink were dear at the orphans' home, she took special care to make her first draft both concise and perfect.

Satisfied, she folded the sheet of paper several times, addressing the outside of the packet because she lacked an envelope. As soon as her morning chores were completed the next day she'd try to steal away long enough to deliver her written plea. If that wasn't possible, she'd have to entrust it to one of the older boys and hope he carried out her orders correctly.

Rising, she lifted the lamp to light her way back to the girls' area. When she looked ahead, a tall shadow was falling across the marble-floored entryway.

"Who...who is it?"

"Dr. Hayward."

The breath whooshed out of her and she noticed that she was trembling slightly. "What are you doing here? It must be very late."

"It is," Taylor said, approaching and relieving her of the glass lamp. "I was passing and I saw this light, so I stopped. Why have you not retired with the rest of the staff? Did the latest earthquake bother you?"

"No. I never even felt one happen. It must not have been very strong."

Sara Beth realized she was clutching her letter so tightly she was wrinkling it. Her first instinct was to tell the doctor everything. Then she realized that she really didn't know him, not as a personal friend, at any rate, and should therefore be prudent.

She slid the folded paper into her apron pocket to hide it. "I simply couldn't sleep."

"Would you like me to give you a powder to take? It would relax you."

"No. Thank you." She purposely lifted her chin to emphasize her decisiveness. "You should go. It isn't proper for us to be together like this. I don't want Mrs. McNeil to think I'm entertaining a gentleman in her absence."

The doctor bowed. "Of course. I'll go. Just let me see you to your quarters."

Instead, Sara Beth reached for the lamp and wrested it from his grasp. "That won't be necessary. I can take care of myself."

"Can you?" Taylor asked. "I wonder."

"What's that supposed to mean?"

"Only that I wish to be of service to you, Miss Reese. I assure you, I have no ulterior motives." He fell into step beside her as she started for the hallway. "I have already tried to assist you in getting your home back. Unfortunately, the head of the Vigilance Committee is not willing to act on your behalf."

"I'm not surprised," she replied.

"I was. But I had another idea and stopped by the newspaper to see if the editor wished to champion your cause."

That brought her up short. She whirled and held the lamp high to clearly observe his expression. "Which editor? Not James Casey, I hope."

"Of course not. He's too involved with Scannell and the others. I visited the offices of the *Bulletin*."

Sara Beth caught her breath. Was this the answer to her wish to have her letter safely delivered? It certainly appeared so.

"Do you know Mr. King?" she asked.

"Very well. And I think he'll print a story about you, if you want. All you have to do is tell him everything and leave the actual preparation of the article up to him."

Thinking, praying and rejoicing, all at the same time, she reached into her pocket and withdrew her letter. "I have already done so. Will you be so kind as to deliver these pages to him and extend my good wishes for his continued success? Papa didn't believe what was printed in any paper but his, and I have high hopes that that loyalty was not misplaced."

"It was not. And your trust in me is not, either," Taylor said soberly. He took the letter and slipped it into his inside coat pocket before touching the brim of his bowler and making a slight bow. "Good night, Miss Reese."

"Good night, Doctor. Will you try to find time to let me know how my words are received? I have done my best to explain my family's situation."

"I'm sure you have. I'll take this to King's home

tonight and leave it with him. Tomorrow is my day to check the wards here so you will see me again then."

"I look forward to it," Sara Beth said, struggling to hold the lamp steady and nearly succeeding. She had just placed the fates of herself and her siblings into the hands of a man she barely knew. If he delivered the letter to the editor, all would be well.

If, however, he chose to place it in the wrong hands, she could find herself in true jeopardy. There was only one way to find out and that would not happen until the publication of the story in the *Bulletin,* which would be tomorrow night at the earliest.

Until then, she would hope and pray and try to stay too busy to fret. If the doctor was not as forthright as he seemed, there was nothing she could do about it. Not now. While he had possession of her letter, he also held her fate in his hands. God willing, he would not betray her.

The nattily dressed gentleman stood back, smoking a thick cigar and leaning on his ebony-and-silver walking stick. Morning fog from the bay was thick and slightly hampered the official search of Robert Reese's workshop. As planned, however, one of the examiners easily located the monogrammed handkerchief containing particles of gold.

Bein stayed out of the furor until it quieted down, then made his way to the sheriff. "I see they have discovered proof that my partner was a thief," he said aside. "Tsk-tsk. How distressing. Once that news gets out, his good name will be tainted forever."

"What a cryin' shame." Scannell chuckled. "So, what

do you want me to do now? Shall I relieve my men or have them continue their guard duty?"

"Wait and see what the U.S. Marshal's office decides," Bein said. "A lot depends on whether Harazthy gets scared or not. His smelter has been refining for me on the sly and I don't want to ruin that deal."

"Last I heard he was too caught up in being a grape farmer to care one way or the other."

"True. And definitely to our advantage, Sheriff. As long as things are going so smoothly, I suspect you'll be free to be on your way soon. In the meantime, keep the guards right where they are and wait for my orders." He scowled at the taller man's expression of disgust. "Don't give me that look, not if you value your job. I have plenty of influence with the city council."

"Hey, I was elected, fair and square," Scannell insisted.

"You were elected, all right, but there was nothing fair about it and you know it."

"All right, all right. I get the point." He eyed the men who were carrying out boxes of assaying materials and records and loading them into a spring wagon. "What about the girl? Is she going to behave herself?"

"I'm sure she will. I've already booked passage for all those brats and I'm on my way to the Ladies' Protection Society right now to offer my condolences. Once they're on a boat headed for the east coast, we'll have nothing more to worry about."

"I hope you're right."

Bein laughed. "I'm *always* right."

Sara Beth was peeling potatoes in the kitchen when Clara tapped her on the shoulder. "You have a visitor."

"Who? Where?" Her fondest hope was that Dr. Hayward was bringing her word from the newspaper editor.

"Don't know him," Clara said, "but he looks mighty highfalutin for this place. He's waitin' in the parlor with Mrs. McNeil."

"Oh. All right. Thank you."

She was drying her hands on her apron as she hurried toward the front of the converted mansion. The moment she recognized her visitor her heart rejoiced. She ran to him and she threw her arms around his neck. "Uncle Will!"

He patted her on the back the way a parent would comfort a weeping child. "There, there, Sara Beth. Don't fret. I've come to take care of you."

"Are we going to get to go home?"

"Yes, dear," William Bein said. He stepped back and reached into his breast pocket to withdraw a stiff packet of papers. "Here are your tickets. I've arranged passage for you and the boys. You sail tomorrow morning."

She stepped back and frowned at him. "Passage? To where? We live here."

"Not anymore, I fear. The U.S. Marshal's office has taken possession of your father's workroom and the rest of the property will revert to me, as his partner, once the particulars have been worked out."

She backed away, aghast. "No! Papa would never have left our home to anyone else."

"Your mother would have inherited, of course, but since she's gone, too, it all comes to me."

When he smiled, Sara Beth noticed that the good humor did not reach his eyes. Suddenly, she was seeing the man in a different light. Gone was her kindly old uncle figure and in his place stood a ruthless businessman. A man who was pretending to be helpful while he banished orphans to goodness-knows-where.

"We will not be leaving San Francisco," she said flatly. "Our rightful home is here and it is here we will stay. The boys are happy and I am employed. We have no need of your charity, Mr. Bein." Nodding, she added, "Good day, sir," then wheeled, gathered her skirts and quickly left the room.

She heard Mrs. McNeil calling after her but *dear old Uncle Will* wasn't saying a word. Little wonder. His offer had not only been unfair, it had been transparent. He wanted their land, for whatever reason, and she and her brothers were standing in the way. Well, too bad. If it took her the rest of her life she was not going to cease trying to find a legal way to reclaim her rightful home. Situated next to Turner's store the way it was, it would make a decent boarding house or even a commercial establishment if she decided to take up dressmaking or millinery.

Truth to tell, she was far from certain that she was in the right in this instance, but something in her nature insisted that she stand firm. There had to be a point at which doing what was just triumphed over the letter of the law.

She tried to think of a scripture that would back up her conclusion and failed, although she did recall plenty about the trials of Job cited in the Old Testament.

Those thoughts and the conclusions they led to made Sara Beth shiver. A lot more could go wrong before the good Lord interceded to bring justice, couldn't it?

Her biggest concern was how she was going to withstand, let alone triumph over, whatever terrible, unknown trials still awaited her.

\* \* \*

It was late afternoon on the third day since the murders before Taylor was free to return to the orphanage. He immediately sought out Sara Beth and found her in the kitchen, as expected.

He removed his hat and greeted everyone. "Good day, ladies."

Clara was the first to speak. Grinning, she offered up a plate of freshly baked cookies. "Afternoon, Doctor, I think I have just the thing for whatever ails you."

"Umm. Thank you," Taylor said, returning her smile as he accepted the cookie plate but keeping his gaze fixed on Sara Beth. "I always know just when to arrive, don't I?"

"Pretty much," Clara said. "Looks to me like Miss Sara Beth needs a break. Why don't you two take these cookies into the parlor while I brew you up a pot of tea?"

"You needn't wait on us," Sara Beth said, blushing. "I have no desire for tea but I would like to speak to Dr. Hayward in private."

Taylor stepped aside to give her room to precede him. Instead of going to the parlor, however, she walked out onto the veranda and raised her face to the sun.

He followed. Young children were playing a game of hoops on the lawn while older girls jumped rope to a singsong chant, providing a perfect covering noise for their conversation.

"I delivered your letter to James King," Taylor told her.

She clasped her hands tightly together, her emerald eyes glistening. "What did he say?"

Although Taylor wanted to take her hands and offer physical comfort, he restrained himself. "The article will appear tomorrow. He didn't have time to get it written and set into print for this evening's edition."

"I suppose that will have to do."

"You seem more troubled than the last time we met," the doctor said. "Are your brothers all right?"

"They're fine. Even Josiah. He's the oldest one in the nursery, but he seems happy. And Mathias and Luke are already attending school, although I suspect that Lucas will soon have to find a job to help with our keep. I just hate to see him have to grow up so fast."

"I'll see what I can do to delay that." His brow knit. There was clearly more to the young woman's disquiet than concern for her brothers' fates. "What else is wrong?"

"How do you know something is wrong?"

"Because of the suffering in your eyes," Taylor said softly. "You don't have to confide in me, but you might feel better if you chose to do so. Have you had to arrange the burials? Is that it?"

She shook her head soberly. "No. Abe sent word that he has taken care of everything already. I saw no reason to expose the boys to more trauma by making them watch the interment, and I didn't think it was fair for me to go without them. I hope that was the right decision."

"Absolutely. Is that all?" He saw her jaw muscles clench and her chin jut forward.

"No. The rest is so unbelievable it's hard to fathom, let alone explain. William Bein, the man my father and mother trusted, has usurped our home and tried to ship us off to who knows where."

"Are you certain?"

"Positive. He showed me the packet of boat tickets he'd bought."

Laying aside his bowler and also placing the plate of cookies atop the broad stone railing that bordered the raised veranda, Taylor gave in to his instincts and grasped her hands. To his relief, she not only allowed his touch, she seemed to welcome it. "All right. Start from the beginning and tell me everything."

"There's not much to tell that I truly understand," Sara Beth said, tightening her grip on his fingers. "He and my father were partners in the assay business. Papa did the laboratory work and Uncle Will—I mean, Mr. Bein—handled the books and the safe transport of the ore."

"That might explain his connection to the workshop, but it should not mean he owns your house, too."

"That was my thought, exactly."

"Perhaps there's a way to convince him to split the two halves of the property."

She shook her head, her eyes misty. "Even if it were that easy, I doubt he'd listen to reason. I spoke with him, looked into his eyes. There is no Christian love in that man. Not a drop. I can't believe how taken in my father was by his perfidy."

Taylor was stroking the backs of her hands with his thumbs, when he realized it was inappropriate and quickly released her; he was stunned by how strongly he yearned to touch those soft hands again. Embarrassed, he cleared his throat. "Then we shall have to wait for the article in the *Bulletin* to create a groundswell of support for your cause. Once Bein realizes that his reputation is at stake, he should be more inclined to listen to reason."

"And if he doesn't?"

"If he doesn't, then I'll have to revisit my friends on the Vigilance Committee."

"Papa always insisted that we shouldn't take the law into our own hands."

"The law in this city is a travesty," Taylor said flatly. He handed the plate of uneaten cookies to her and squared his hat on his head. "I have to check on the health of the children before I leave. Take heart, Miss Reese. The hands of true justice may be slower than you and I would like, but they will triumph."

"I would like to see my brothers," she said. "May I accompany you on your rounds?"

He tipped his hat and offered his arm, delighted when she slipped her small hand into the crook of his elbow. "Please do."

Before they left the porch, Sara Beth handed the cookies to a nearby girl, instructing her to serve them to her playmates and return the plate to the kitchen.

"There. Now I have no good chores to keep me from accompanying you."

"I certainly don't want you to feel that I'm coercing you," the doctor said.

"It's not that." She lifted her hem slightly to step over the threshold. "It's the sadness I feel whenever I see all those poor, lonely children and realize that my family is now a part of that assembly."

"For the time being," he replied. "You will get your rightful inheritance. I'll see to it."

Her resulting smile and gaze of gratitude warmed his heart until he realized that there was a fair chance that he would fail. San Francisco politics were probably no worse than those anywhere else, but they were far from honest. Factions warred against each other until it was hard to tell who was really in the right. A man could be arrested for little cause, tried and hanged in the space of a day. There were many in power who would look the other way if Bein and his ilk had enough money to pay off the right people to get what they wanted.

Except for Coleman and the others on the secretive Vigilance Committee, there was no one Taylor could trust. No one. And so long as that was true, Taylor had to keep control of his instincts to protect Sara Beth and her brothers. It was one thing to help them now, but when this was over, Sara Beth would find a protector—a husband—who could provide better for her family than Taylor ever could. To help her meant keeping that lovely woman's best interests in mind and forming no attachment that would compromise her future happiness.

## *Chapter Six*

When Sara Beth got her hands on a copy of the *Bulletin* the following afternoon, she was astounded to find her story on the front page. The headline read, "Dastardly Deed! Local Couple Murdered in Cold Blood," and went on to detail her parents' demise.

As she read, she realized that Mr. King had dramatized her tale until it read more like an adventure serial in *Frank Leslie's Illustrated Weekly,* yet the facts remained.

Although reading the entire article made her heart ache, she forced herself to continue until she had taken it all in. Mr. King had not named names, but there was enough innuendo and oblique reference to leave little doubt as to which factions were in the wrong and who may have been responsible.

In truth, his account sounded far more plausible than her plain treatise had. The editor believed them to be neither random killings nor a robbery gone wrong. He inferred that they had been planned and were part of a larger, more sinister plot.

That thought caused Sara Beth's pulse to speed. Could it be so?

In an instant she was certain. Everything was starting to make more sense, especially since Mr. King had learned that her poor father was being blamed for the theft of gold he had been hired to assay.

She was about to crumple the newspaper in disgust when Taylor Hayward walked into the orphanage kitchen. He was clutching a copy of the *Bulletin* in one hand, his medical bag in the other.

"I can't believe this! Papa Robert did not have a crooked bone in his body," she blurted.

"We all know that," Taylor assured her, setting the black bag aside and approaching her. "That was the point James was trying to make when he wrote it that way. Anyone who knew your father will see that there's no truth to the accusations. I'm positive tomorrow's paper will follow up on that conclusion."

"How can anyone believe such lies about my father? And what about the others? Papa wasn't the only one handling that gold. There were smelters and refiners as well as the branch mint. He often said there was too much unexplained loss from the manufacturing of the coins and ingots, but he could never prove theft."

Suddenly she recalled the conversation she'd overheard the night of the murders. In her excitement, she grabbed the doctor's forearm through his coat sleeve. "Wait! I just remembered something else. Papa told Mama he was going to the wharf to meet someone he worked with and give that man a chance to repent. Do you suppose he finally did find proof of theft and was planning to face the person he felt was responsible?"

"Possibly. But who?"

"Who is profiting already? And who was in a position to frame my father for crimes committed by others?"

"William Bein."

"Precisely." Sara Beth began to pace and wave the newspaper for emphasis as she spoke. "I can't let this happen. Robert Reese rescued me and Mama from our struggles and gave us a wonderful home. He was the kindest, most forthright, Christian man I ever knew. I will not stand idly by and let his good name be ruined."

"What do you plan to do?"

"Write to Mr. King again and provide any other details I can recall, no matter how obscure. Now that I see what kind of exposé he plans, I can better tailor my words to fit his model."

"Are you sure that's wise?"

She arched her eyebrows and cocked her head. "Wise or foolish, I shall do it. No one can deter me. Don't even try."

Smiling slightly, Taylor raised his hands in mock surrender. "Far be it from me to stand between an angry woman and her goals." His grin spread. "I'll be glad to deliver any other notes you want to dispatch. In the meantime, would you like to visit the sick ones with me again? Your presence seemed to cheer them a lot yesterday." As he spoke he picked up his small satchel.

She turned to Clara. "Can you and Mattie spare me?"

"Of course, dear. You go with the doctor. We have everything in hand." Although she spoke plainly, there was an extra twinkle in her eyes and a knowing smile on her face that made Sara Beth a bit self-conscious.

Blushing, she left the kitchen. Clara was right, even if she had been teasing a bit. There wasn't enough work in the efficiently run kitchen to keep three women busy all day. Honestly, there was barely enough for two as long as they were both hard workers like Clara and Mattie.

As the doctor led the way down the hall toward the sickrooms at the rear of the mansion, Sara Beth's thoughts were racing. She almost had to run to keep up with his longer strides.

At the door, she grasped his arm to stop him. "Wait! I have an idea."

"All right. What is it?"

"I want to become your assistant. I don't mean a real nurse, just a helper. You know. Someone you can teach how to care for the sick little ones and be trusted to carry out your orders when you can't be here and the others are too busy looking after the healthy children."

His brow furrowed as he stared at her. "Why not become a real nurse? You're certainly intelligent enough."

"Thank you." Unsure of how he had come to that conclusion, Sara Beth waited for him to elaborate.

"I read the letter you wrote to the newspaper," Taylor said, beginning to smile. "It was quite impressive."

"Really?"

"Yes. Really." His grin widened. "On my next visit, I'll bring you some medical books to look at. Then, if you decide you can cope with all the trials we'll face, you may also become my amanuensis and help me keep proper records."

Her countenance sobered as she began to fully comprehend what he was saying. "The possible loss of life, you mean?"

"Yes. Medicine is not the science it may one day become. We're learning new things all the time. A few years ago, a doctor in Austria proposed that something as simple as hand washing might prevent hospital fever."

Intrigued, Sara Beth hung on his every word. "Really? How?"

"No one knows. Many doubt him, but the man has the statistics to back up his conclusion. I, for one, see no reason not to employ the technique. It certainly can't hurt."

"In that case, I'm thankful this property has its own well. That water the trucks deliver to most of the city is fetid, especially as the days warm in the summer."

"I've been using a diluted chlorine solution," Taylor said. "When a few drops are mixed with any water, everything clears, even odor, though I wouldn't recommend that anyone drink it." He displayed his palm. "It's hard on the skin if you don't wash it off, so it can't be good for the gut. Don't worry. You won't be actually touching any very ill patients, just writing down my findings for me."

"I'll do whatever you say. I want to make myself useful." His warm smile in reply blessed her.

"Then let's start by seeing how our little patients are doing today," Taylor said.

He held the door for her and Sara Beth walked boldly into the sickroom. Dealing with ill children was going to be harder than peeling potatoes or drawing well water to supply the kitchen, but at least here she'd feel needed.

One look at the wan, coughing child in the nearest bed, however, almost caused her to change her mind. Only a sincere desire to help the doctor and the children kept her steps steadfast.

"Have you seen this?" Bein shouted, throwing the crumpled sheets of the *Bulletin* onto James Casey's desk at the office of the *Herald*.

"Calm down, William. He's just stirring the pot. There's nothing he can prove."

"You wouldn't be so complacent if it were you he was slandering."

The younger, thinner man shrugged. "As a matter of fact, one of my spies tells me King is planning to do exactly that."

"You have skeletons in your closet?"

Casey guffawed. "You might say so. I was not always the upright businessman you see before you."

"There are no upright businessmen in this room," Bein countered. "Myself included. And proud of it, if you must know. Besides, you just got elected city supervisor. If he'd had anything on you, he'd surely have revealed it before the election."

"True. But one never knows what unwelcome information may yet surface. I was not exactly a model citizen of New York."

"Just because you spent some time in Sing Sing prison? Nobody's perfect."

"I'll be satisfied as long as we're not run out of town on a rail or tarred and feathered," Casey said, chuckling. "Now get out of here and forget about the *Bulletin*. There's nothing King or any other editor can do to us that we can't handle via my weekly."

"Except that you have to wait until Sunday to rebut."

"All the more time to plan an impressive response," Casey said. He arched a brow and eyed the newspaper his ally had brought in. "How much of that article is true, anyway?"

"All of it," Bein replied with a snide smile. "Why?"

The pile of books the doctor had delivered to Sara Beth weighed more than all her brothers put together. She had asked him to leave them in the parlor where she could choose one at a time rather than take them to the girls' ward and worry about the children being overly curious. Some of the illustrations had made her blush, but she kept reading, fascinated by her studies. The more she read, the more eager she was to learn, and the more she appreciated and revered her teacher.

When she saw Taylor Hayward the following day she was quick to tell him so. "I can't believe all you have to know," Sara Beth said, eyes wide. "Those medical books are amazing. I had no idea the subject was so complicated."

"You were able to understand the texts?"

"Most of them, yes," she replied, averting her gaze and blushing.

"I do apologize if some of the chapters upset you, Miss Reese. There was no way I could censor them to protect your refined sensibilities. I would have if I could."

She looked up and met his gaze. "I know that. I must admit that there were parts I skimmed rather than read every word. I thought, if it were necessary to know everything, I could always return to those chapters and study them then."

"Very wise." He smiled benevolently. "Truth to tell, most medical men refer to their textbooks often when making a diagnosis. No one could possibly remember every detail well enough to be certain."

Sighing, she, too, smiled. "Oh, thank goodness. I was afraid my poor mind was feeble."

That made Taylor laugh and Sara Beth felt her cheeks growing warmer as a result. "Well, I was," she insisted.

"I totally understand. In medical school I often felt that way."

"You went to a real school? Where?"

"Massachusetts General Hospital. Why do you ask?"

Embarrassed to have doubted him, she explained, "I had thought... I mean...the doctor who used to come by when Mama and I lived here had apprenticed under another man. I'm impressed that you actually attended a medical college."

"That's becoming more and more common these days," Taylor said, "although many practitioners of the healing arts are still given licenses after very little real study."

"Could I... I mean, might I do the same?"

"Become a *doctor?*"

Sara Beth could tell by his expression of astonishment and disbelief that he doubted her abilities and resolve. Nevertheless, she spoke her mind. "Why not? Surely there are many modest women who would rather be treated by someone like me. Someone who understands their reticence to put themselves in a man's hands." She felt her cheeks flame. "Figuratively speaking, of course."

"Of course."

It didn't assuage her embarrassment to see that the doctor was struggling to keep a straight face. She couldn't tell whether he thought her goal was silly or if he was merely amused at her rosy complexion and nervous manner.

Gathering her courage, she straightened and looked him in the eye, refusing to be cowed. "All I ask is that you give my idea some thought. According to the text I read this morning, there are many women who suffer needlessly because of their modesty. That is perfectly understandable, and if I can somehow assist them, I feel it is my duty to do so."

Taylor finally broke into a grin. "Bravo, Miss Reese. I applaud your ambition. But let's start with some simple nursing duties before you try to take over my job. All right?"

She didn't appreciate his laughing at her lofty goals, but she could nevertheless appreciate his opinion. Of course it would be a long time before she was ready to be a real doctor. In the meantime there was plenty to do and even more to learn by observing Dr. Hayward. As long as she applied herself and kept an open mind, she might eventually succeed beyond his or anyone else's wildest imagination.

Was that a foolish aspiration? She didn't think so. Not only did it give her a tangible goal for the future, it helped take her mind off seeking retribution.

She wasn't about to forget what had happened to her family. She simply needed something good to look forward to. Something that would perhaps give her life purpose and redirect her thoughts away from vengeance.

Surely, God was going to even the score, as the Good Book promised. The only question Sara Beth had in that regard was whether or not the Lord was leading her to assist. She was not the kind of person to sit back and let her world spin out of control if she could help it. The first chance she got, she would once again write to Mr. King, as she'd already planned.

What would she say? That answer came easily. She would tell him about William Bein's attempts to send her whole family away. Let the powers that be make of that what they would. She knew it was nothing but a shameful attempt to steal what rightfully belonged to her and her siblings. If *Uncle Will* thought he was going to get away with cheating them out of their inheritance, then he had another think coming.

She shivered, remembering the cold look in Bein's

eyes. If she never had to actually meet that man face-to-face again, she would count it a blessing.

*A doctor?* Taylor was still smiling to himself as he returned to his hotel for the night. Sara Beth was amazing in both her courage and her ambition. He supposed there were female doctors somewhere, although he had never personally met one. The notion was just so farfetched it amused him. He could envision the reactions of some of his stuffy professors if a young, pretty woman like Sara Beth Reese walked into the operating theater and wanted to observe, let alone begin to practice the healing arts on her own.

Entering the imposing What Cheer House, Taylor headed for the formal dining room. This was one of the most prestigious establishments in the city and also provided real baths in the basement, something most other hotels had not yet added to their amenities. Taking rooms there was his one extravagance and one he sincerely hoped he'd be able to afford to continue. It wasn't on par with eastern hotels, but it was one of the best available in San Francisco.

Gas-lighted chandeliers illuminated the separate dining area off the lobby. Crisp linen cloths draped the small tables, which were graced by only the finest china, silver and crystal goblets. Although no strong spirits were served, the hotel was nevertheless always crowded.

Waiting for a table, Taylor spotted W. T. Coleman, waved to him and was motioned over. He gladly obliged.

"Evening, W.T."

The wiry man offered a chair. "Join me?"

"Delighted. How goes it?"

"The raw oysters on the half-shell are delicious. I highly recommend them."

Taylor huffed and lowered his voice. "I had something other than food in mind when I asked. Any word on the problem you and I were discussing?"

Coleman shook his head, glancing from side to side as if expecting to be accosted any second. "No. And I don't want to discuss it in here. The walls have ears."

Waiting until a black-suited waiter had taken his order and departed, Taylor continued his query, albeit quietly. "Have you seen the latest issue of the *Bulletin?*"

"Yes. Do you think that's wise?"

"What? Printing the truth?" He unfolded his napkin and laid it across his lap.

"No. Letting King quote that girl. Do you have any idea how dangerous that may be for her?"

"I didn't notice any direct quotes," Taylor said, frowning. "Did he actually mention her by name?"

"Not in the article. Since I figured out where most of the information came from, others will, too. Where is she staying now that she has no home?"

"At the Ladies' Protection and Relief Society headquarters. She'll be safe there."

"Only if she keeps her head down and her mouth shut. A few more letters like the last one King printed and anything may happen."

Taken aback, Taylor leaned closer and grabbed his companion's wrist. "What do you mean, *printed?* He was supposed to build a feature on her letter, not run it."

Coleman nodded, looking decidedly uncomfortable. "Well, it's there. On page three. If all you read was the article, you missed the most important part of the paper."

"I'll stop and cancel my dinner order on my way out," Taylor said, standing and throwing his crumpled napkin across his place setting. Sara Beth fully intended to write again, this time making specific references to William Bein. Printing that letter would not only open her to a libel suit; it might endanger her just as W.T. had suggested, especially if she grew impatient and entrusted it to someone else to deliver instead of waiting until she saw him again.

"Where are you bound?"

"To head off a catastrophe, I hope."

"Good luck," his friend said.

"I'll need more than that," the doctor answered in passing. "I'll need divine intervention." He smiled over his shoulder. "Feel free to pray for us."

"Gladly," Coleman said. "Seems like I've done little else of late."

Taylor had also been praying almost constantly for the past week. Even when he didn't consciously realize he was doing it, he was often reminded that his thoughts had brought Sara Beth and her brothers before God.

The way he saw it, he had been put into their lives to guide them through these dark valleys. Yes, he knew it wasn't all up to him, yet he also believed that his wits and his friends would be of use in the long run.

Right now, however, his task was to stop her from having another letter published. If she insisted on writing it, as he assumed she would, he must convince her—and James King—to make the missive anonymous. Otherwise, she would place herself in even worse danger. If that were possible.

# Chapter Seven

Sara Beth's immediate concerns were temporarily set aside when she learned that Lucas had been causing trouble. Separating him from the other boys, she led him into the garden after supper.

The breeze off the Pacific was balmy and helped clear the air of the disagreeable odors drifting up the hill from the wharfs. Gulls soared overhead and squawked at each other like argumentative children.

Speaking of which, her brother was acting as if she were imposing upon him by asking him to accompany her outside for a private talk.

"You can't tell me what to do. You're not my mama," the boy grumbled, scuffing his feet on the grass that a few grazing sheep kept manicured.

His attitude cut her to the quick. "Of course I'm not Mother. No one will ever take her place. But we're family. We have to stick together, especially right now."

"Why? You don't care about us. You put Josiah in the nursery so you can go off with that doctor."

"That's not true. I've been working in the kitchen, too. I have to contribute to our keep. You know that."

"Fine. You can do what you want. I'm not staying here."

She frowned and grabbed his shoulders to force him to look at her instead of staring down at his toes. "Of course you are. We all are. Listen to me, Luke. This place is only temporary. As soon as I can get our house back we'll all go live there, just like we used to. I promise."

"Oh, sure. How are you going to do that?" His face started to show more than anger, as if he were struggling to keep from breaking down and weeping.

Sara Beth tried to embrace him and was rebuffed. Tearing free from her grasp, the eleven-year-old ran across the lawn and disappeared behind a hedge.

Rather than pursue him, she merely stood there, astounded and more than a little hurt. Lucas wasn't the only confused one in her family, was he? She was plenty upset herself, and poor Mathias had been moping around ever since he'd learned he was still expected to attend school. Only Josiah seemed to be content and that was because he didn't understand their dire straits.

Perhaps she should have made more effort to include her older brothers in her activities, she reasoned. If Luke felt needed, then maybe he'd be less likely to balk at every order he was given. There had to be some way to reach him and give him a task that made him feel important.

*Of course*! Encouraged, she called to him. "Lucas? Would you run an errand for me? I need someone trustworthy to carry a letter downtown."

His tousled head poked out from behind the bush. "Me? I get to go? Alone?"

"Yes," Sara Beth said, trying to sound nonchalant

when her stomach was churning and her heart racing. It was only slightly risky for the boy to be out and about this late in the day. If she intended to make him feel useful and a part of their quest, she had to let him participate, even if it did cause her slight concern.

Luke was slowly returning, hesitant but clearly intrigued. "What do I have to do?"

"Carry a letter to the newspaper building on the west side of Montgomery Street. Do you know where that is?"

He nodded. "Uh-huh."

"Good. When you get there, I want you to deliver my letter to Mr. James King, the editor. Give it to no one else. Understand?" Reaching into her pocket, she retrieved a folded piece of paper and offered it to the boy.

When he reached for it, she kept hold till she'd finished speaking. "This is a very important job, Lucas. For Mama and Papa. You have to follow my instructions precisely and get back here before dark."

"Okay." Grinning, he snatched the letter from her grasp and danced away, gamboling backward on the grass. "Can I have a penny for candy?"

"I don't have any money. I'm sorry. But someday I'll reward you, I promise."

Watching the boy dash off, clearly elated to have a job to do, she hoped she'd made the right choice. If Luke's new attitude was any indication, all would be well.

In her heart, however, she continued to harbor reservations. That boy had always been the quieter brother, but he had a stubborn streak a mile wide. Mathias would have simply joked about running away while Luke truly meant any threat he issued.

Sighing, she let herself drink in the beauty of the placid grounds, the blooming spring flowers, the distant calls of birds and the hum from the city that lay below the mansion on the hill. Under almost any other circumstances she would have been delighted to tarry in such a lovely place.

Now, however, try as she might, she could not seem to find respite from the cares that threatened to burden her beyond bearing. At times of introspection like this, she was always reminded of all she had lost and of how difficult it was going to be to triumph over the current adversity.

"Father," she whispered into the evening air, "what must I do? How can I possibly win?"

The only answer she received was a fleeting sense of peace. That was shattered almost immediately when a familiar buggy raced into the circular driveway and stopped in front of the orphanage.

Taylor Hayward disembarked. There was a frown on his face and his jaw was clenched. Sara Beth's first thought was that Luke had been injured and the doctor was bringing her the bad news.

She hurried to join him. "What is it? What's wrong?"

"Nothing, I hope," Taylor said, taking her hands. "I came to fetch your letter for the newspaper."

"Oh, that." Relieved, she smiled. "Don't worry about a thing. I've already sent it."

"You *what?*"

His outburst took her aback and she pulled away, confused and alarmed. "I—I gave it to my brother Luke a few minutes ago. He needed to feel useful and I thought—"

"Get in," Taylor ordered. "We have to overtake

him before he gets you into worse trouble than you already are."

"I don't understand." She let him assist her into the buggy and watched as he climbed into the driver's seat and grabbed the reins.

"King printed your letter."

"Of course. We knew that."

"No. I don't mean he used the facts you gave him. I mean he printed the whole thing, verbatim. I hadn't noticed it on a back page but it was there, all right, complete with your name at the bottom."

"So? I'm not ashamed of what I said. It was all true."

"Who else was privy to the conversation you heard your parents having?" He glared at her. "Never mind. I know you were the only one. This is as much my fault as it is yours. I should never have left your letter with King without stipulating that he keep your identity a secret."

"That's not sensible," Sara Beth argued. She had to hang on to the end armrest of the padded bench to keep from bouncing around and sliding into him on the corners. "My testimonial was needed to give the story credence."

"Not when you're the only witness who can accuse Bein," Taylor argued. "If something were to happen to you, he'd have no one else to fear."

That notion made her shiver. The doctor was right. As long as she continued to insist on justice and had the newspaper on her side, there was a chance that Bein would decide she was a danger to their plans, whatever they might be. If he and his men were as dishonest as she thought, they could easily decide to resort to more murders.

And right now her defenseless brother was walking the streets of the city, alone and bound for the very place that lay at the seat of the exposé. If anything bad happened to Luke because of her foolish choices, she'd never forgive herself.

Glancing at the stalwart man driving the buggy, she included him in her silent prayers for deliverance. Her heart was filled with gratitude and more. This virtual stranger had come into her life and, in the space of mere days, had become such an integral part of everything it was a wonderment.

Sara Beth knew that the doctor was merely a kind man who would have helped anyone in need. That wasn't the problem. As she saw it, her biggest obstacle was going to be remaining aloof in his presence when what she really wanted to do was throw her arms around him and thank him for his assistance from the bottom of her heart.

She would never be so bold, of course, but she couldn't help wondering if envisioning such an embrace was not as big a sin as actually acting on that desire. She certainly hoped not, because thoughts of being held in his arms refused to go away, no matter how hard she tried to stop entertaining them—especially when he was seated so close.


Taylor thought he spotted Luke trotting along the boardwalk that flanked Montgomery Street. He pointed. "There. Isn't that him?"

"Yes. Hurry!"

A slow-moving freight wagon was in their way. By the time it had passed and the doctor had maneuvered his buggy to the side of the road, the boy had disappeared.

"Where is he?" Sara Beth grabbed Taylor's forearm.

"I don't know. He can't have gotten as far as the *Bulletin* office this quickly."

Taylor jumped down, tied his horse to a hitching ring and circled the buggy to assist his passenger.

"Maybe he ducked into the mercantile," Sara Beth suggested as he lifted her down. "He said he wanted to buy penny candy. I didn't have any money to give him but he might have found some in the street."

Taylor arched his brows, trying to recall exactly who and what had been near the boy in the last moments before he'd vanished. The street had been crowded, as usual, with strolling couples, businessmen heading home and the usual loitering ruffians and lowlifes. Any of those people might have interfered with the boy's progress, although he figured that one of the latter was the most likely. It was even remotely possible that Luke had been shanghaied, although his small size was in his favor. Until he grew taller he wouldn't be useful on shipboard as anything but a cabin boy.

"You go that way and I'll go this," Sara Beth said.

Taylor grabbed her wrist and held tight. "No. We stay together. I don't want to lose you, too." The moment he spoke he knew that such a masterful attitude would not sit well with her. It didn't.

She dug in her heels and resisted, leaning the opposite direction. "Luke is my brother. It's my fault he's here. I'm going to find him."

"There's no time to argue. You're coming with me."

"I'll scream."

"Go ahead. The longer you stand there arguing, the farther away the boy will be." Taylor knew the moment she was ready to capitulate because her eyes grew misty and her shoulders slumped.

Without further discussion, he began to lead her toward the closest mercantile at a hurried pace. His heart was racing and his throat was dry. Their first task had to be locating the boy and making sure he was safe. After that, they'd go to the newspaper office and make certain that no more of Sara Beth's actual letters were printed.

She kept calling Luke's name to no avail. They checked the nearby stores, then proceeded along the street, peering into every doorway and down every alley.

By this time, Taylor had released her wrist and she had placed her slim hand in his, apparently unmindful of how their association might look to bystanders. He was glad, because it not only showed growing trust on her part, it pleased him greatly.

He hoped and prayed he would prove worthy of her confidence. If they didn't locate the missing boy soon, he would have to solicit outside help. Alerting Sheriff Scannell was out of the question, which left only the Vigilance Committee as his other option. He wasn't looking forward to asking W.T. for another favor, but in this case, he'd do whatever it took to succeed.

They *would* succeed, Taylor promised himself. They had to. This poor young woman could not stand to lose another loved one. The notion was unthinkable.

Covering the few blocks between where they had seen Luke and the *Bulletin* office took only minutes. Taylor squeezed Sara Beth's hand to offer moral support before he said, "Here we are. Let's go in and talk to James. Maybe Luke has already been here."

"You go," she said with a deep, telling sigh. "I'll wait out here and watch for Luke."

Taylor could tell she had to make an effort to give him a wan smile.

"Really," she went on when he hesitated. "I'll stand right here while you go see Mr. King."

"You won't leave? You promise?"

She made an *X* on her chest with one finger. "Cross my heart."

"All right. I'll be right back."

It was hard to take his leave. He scaled the stairs leading up to King's office two at a time. He burst through the door, startling his friend, and found himself looking down the barrel of the editor's pistol.

"Whoa!" Taylor raised his hands. "It's just me."

"Sorry. I've been receiving death threats and it pays to be ready." Stowing the gun in his desk, the editor asked, "What brings you here? You look agitated."

"I am. Have you seen a boy about this high?" He held out his hand. "Miss Reese sent her brother to bring you another letter and we can't locate him."

"No." Frowning, King strode to the window and scanned the street below. "No boy has been here today. What was in the letter?"

"More proof of criminal activity and details about what has happened to the Reese family since we last spoke."

"Does the child know what he's carrying?"

"I doubt it," Taylor replied. "His sister didn't think it risky to send him and he hasn't been gone long. We nearly overtook him until he vanished about a block away. Being only eleven, it's possible he got distracted."

King huffed. "In a city as colorful as this, a grown

man might. I'll keep my eye out for him. He may arrive yet."

"If he doesn't, I'm going to need help searching. Can I count on you?"

"Of course. How about the others on the committee? Have you asked them to help?"

"Not yet. I was hoping Luke had been here already and we'd just missed seeing him." Backing toward the door, Taylor said, "I left Miss Reese keeping watch downstairs. I'd best go back to her."

"You left her there? Alone?"

"Yes." He frowned. "Why not? This is a good neighborhood."

"Normally it is," his friend said. "Trouble is, I can never tell who or what may be lurking out there, just waiting for me to make a mistake."

"You really are scared, aren't you?"

King shrugged and seemed to relax. "Yes and no. The Good Book says we have a certain amount of time allotted. I just don't want to waste mine recovering from a beating. Or worse." He pulled his top hat from a hall tree, donned it and joined Taylor. "Let's go see this girl and settle the problem of her lost brother."

"You're sure you want to come? Don't you have work to do here?"

"It will wait. I have today's paper printing in the basement and nothing pressing at the moment." He smiled. "Besides, if Miss Reese wants to, she can tell me her story in person as we search for the boy."

"All right. But you have to promise you won't print her name the way you did the last time."

"I have to prove my allegations," the editor argued. "The whole story revolves around her family."

"I know." He led the way down the stairs. "Just be as discreet as you can."

"I am always the soul of discretion, dear boy." King was grinning as he stepped out into the waning sunshine. "Now, where is this young woman with the fantastic story?"

Taylor swiveled right and left. There were plenty of folks jamming the street and boardwalk but there was no sign of Sara Beth Reese. Nor of Luke.

"I left her right here. I swear it." Shading his eyes, he peered into the distance, hoping against hope that he would spot her yellow gingham skirt among the plethora of springlike colors adorning other women.

There was a flash of brightness here and there but nothing definitive enough to spur him to action. Taylor's heart lodged in his throat. She had promised she'd stay put. Only one thing might have drawn her away— the sight of her brother.

*Which way? Dear God, where?*

Frantic, he grabbed James King's arm. "Her hair is reddish and her eyes are green. The boy's, too, I assume. We left in a hurry so she wasn't wearing her bonnet or shawl."

"All right," the older man said. "Calm down. We'll find her. Don't worry. It's me the villains are after, not Miss Reese."

Taylor's eyes met his as he said soberly, "I sure hope you're right."

# Chapter Eight

Sara Beth was breathless, frightened beyond belief. Not only had she spied Luke, she had seen that he was being held by the wrist and dragged along the opposite side of the street. The boy was struggling to get free, as she would have expected, but he and the surly-looking man who had hold of him were being summarily ignored by the passing gentry. Only the hooligans seemed to be taking notice and all they did was cheer the man's efforts to control the unruly child.

She started to call out, then changed her mind. If she didn't alert anyone to her presence she'd have a better chance of overtaking Luke unobserved. At least she hoped so. What action she might take when she did face her brother's captor was another matter.

Empty-handed and defenseless, she knew she had only her wits on which to rely. "Such as they are," she murmured, disgusted at herself for leaving the orphanage without so much as her reticule. What on earth was she going to do?

That didn't matter. All that counted was getting her brother back. Lifting her skirts to keep them out of the foul mud as she crossed the street, she began to zigzag around wagons and horses. Luke must not get away again. She would not allow it.

*Please, God, please*, she whispered to herself. *Help me.*

The closest freight wagon stopped, blocking her path. Sara Beth deftly dodged around the rear of it, barely escaping being run down by a buggy and team headed in the opposite direction. That driver shook his fist and cursed at her. She ignored him. Every effort was focused on Luke and the burly, filthy man who was still holding him hostage.

Closer. She was drawing closer. Just twenty yards more and she'd be able to lay hands on the boy, to wrest him from his captor.

Panicky and frantic, she gasped as a painful stitch in her side nearly doubled her over. She didn't think she had cried out until she saw the man pause, wheel back and stare at her.

Luke spotted her at the same time. "Sara Beth! Help!"

"Let my brother go," she demanded loudly.

The surly, middle-aged man merely chortled and spit into the street.

Sara Beth resorted to the only weapon she had—her voice. Screaming, "Kidnapper!" at the top of her lungs, she screeched so loudly that every person within earshot stopped and stared. "He's kidnapping my brother," she yelled, pointing. "Stop him! Somebody help us. Please."

No one stepped forward. In the intervening seconds of indecisiveness, however, Luke managed to break free. Weeping and wailing, he dashed to Sara Beth and fell into her arms.

She embraced him tightly. When she looked up, expecting an attack, the man had melted into the crowd and disappeared.

Suddenly, all the strength and resolve that had sustained her during her wild pursuit was gone. In its place was overwhelming fatigue. And tears of gratitude.

Cupping Luke's cheeks, she raised his face to hers. "What happened, honey? Tell me."

"He—he just grabbed me for no reason," the boy stuttered.

"Are you sure that was all there was to it?"

"I'm sure," Luke insisted.

"All right." She dashed away her tears and took his hand. "Come on. We have to get back to the newspaper office. Dr. Hayward will be looking for us."

To her surprise, Luke dragged his feet. "No. I don't wanna go back there."

"Why? Is that where you were taken from?"

He nodded, sniffling. "I—I was just going in the door when somebody grabbed me."

"All right. We'll stand across the street and watch the office from there. We can call to the doctor when he comes out."

"By the mercantile?" Luke asked, his tears all but forgotten.

The quick change in his mood was off-putting. "Yes. Why?"

"'Cause I want some candy."

"I already told you, I don't have any money."

"That's okay," the boy said, reaching into his pocket and fisting a coin. "I do."

Sara Beth drew him to a bench along the walkway and forcibly sat him down. Leaning over so she could stare into his face, she asked, "Where did you get money?"

"I found it."

"Luke, no lies. I want the truth. Who gave you that coin?"

When no answer was forthcoming, she guessed and saw the truth revealed in her brother's guilty expression. "That bad man gave it to you, didn't he?"

"No. No, I found it on the street."

"What did he want you to do for the money?"

"Just go with him. But I changed my mind. You saw."

A disquieting thought suddenly occurred to her. "Where is my letter, Luke?"

The boy looked away, refusing to meet her inquiring gaze. "I dunno. Maybe I lost it."

"Or you *sold* it," she said, her heart racing and her thoughts awhirl. "That's what really happened, isn't it? Oh, Luke, how could you *do* that?"

"It was just an old letter. Who cares? You can write another one."

"I have never understood the scripture 'Spare the rod and spoil the child' until now," Sara Beth said. "If Papa Robert were here he'd whale you good." She gritted her teeth. "And you'd deserve every lick of it."

"You can't spank me," Luke said defiantly.

"I could, but I won't," she replied. "The damage is already done. If that letter falls into the wrong hands, all of us may be in terrible trouble."

"You can't scare me. I ain't scared of nothing."

"Of anything," she corrected. "You looked pretty frightened to me when that ugly man was hauling you down the street."

"I wasn't scared. Not really."

She shook her head in resignation as she plopped down on the bench beside the boy and sighed. "You may not be afraid, little brother, but personally, I'm terrified."

By the time Taylor spotted Sara Beth and Luke, his patience was more than worn thin, it was nonexistent.

"Where were you?" he demanded before he noticed the tears in her eyes and the distress in her expression.

Instead of answering him she stood, slipped her arms around his waist and stepped into his embrace, totally banishing his righteous anger. Taylor felt her shaking with silent sobs and his heart melted.

He gently patted her upper back through the fabric of her dress. "Take it easy. You're safe now. And I see you found Luke all by yourself."

All she did was nod against his shoulder.

"Then everything is fine, right?"

"No," Sara Beth answered. "It's awful. Luke sold my letter to some stranger."

"What?" Furious, he glared down at the cowering boy. "Who? Who did he sell it to and why?"

"For money, of course." She recovered her composure and stepped away far enough for Taylor to see her face. "The man wasn't satisfied, though. He tried to kidnap Luke, too."

"So that was where you went. I figured it had to be really important to make you break your promise to wait for me." He stared into her emerald gaze. "Do you have any idea how worried I was?"

"Yes. And I'm sorry. I just saw them for an instant and I was afraid if I waited for you to come back it would be too late. Luke would be gone for good."

"That's probably true. What did the man look like?"

Sara Beth shrugged. "Like every dock worker around here. He was big and burly and dirty. And when he leered at me I think I saw some of his front teeth missing, although I can't be positive. I was more concerned about getting him to release Luke."

"Of course. Other details may come to you later, after you've rested and had a chance to think calmly."

With a hand at her back, he gently guided her toward the newspaper office, noting that all he'd had to do was cast one threatening glance at the boy and he'd fallen into line behind them. At this point, that derogatory letter could be in anyone's hands. The thief was likely one of Bein's henchmen, which was all the more reason to worry, Taylor told himself.

"I want you to come back to the *Bulletin* with me and speak to James King. He was helping me search for you and went back inside when I spotted you. These streets have become dangerous for him since he printed your first letter. You can tell him the rest of the story and let him decide how best to proceed. Will you do that?"

Sara Beth nodded. "Yes. Of course. We should also inform Mrs. McNeil of where we are. She's bound to miss us and worry, too."

"I'll send a runner." He frowned at Luke. "A trustworthy one this time."

"He's been through a lot in the past week," said Sara Beth. "I should have explained how important the letter was to us all."

"No," Taylor countered. "He should have done as he was told and not allowed himself to be bribed."

"I just wanted some candy," Luke grumbled. "Mama always bought me candy when we went for a walk."

At that, the child's voice broke and Taylor's heart softened toward him. Even adults made mistakes and at only eleven, the boy had little practical experience on which to draw. He'd learn. He was probably already a lot wiser than he'd been an hour ago.

The question that continued to vex the doctor was who had sent the kidnapper for Luke? Who now possessed Sara Beth's letter, and what might he do after he had read it?

That unspoken question sent a shiver zinging up his spine and prickled the hair on the back of his neck.

Sara Beth perched on the edge of one of the captain's chairs in King's office, her fingers laced together in her lap, her spine stiff. The editor cut an imposing figure with his dark hair and eyes and the beard and mustache that outlined his thin mouth. He had been staring at her and Luke for what seemed like an eternity before he nodded, apparently in agreement with all she and the doctor had revealed.

"I believe I may have discovered a connection between your nemesis and mine," King said. "Casey has been seen in the company of William Bein, not to mention Sheriff Scannell. They make strange bedfellows."

"Agreed," Taylor said, pacing the small office. "The question is, what can any of us do about it?"

"First things first." King smiled over at Sara Beth. "Miss Reese's story will appear next week, without any mention of this interview, although I imagine that whoever was behind the attempted abduction of her brother is probably having this office watched day and night."

"Then they know I'm here." She took a shaky breath.

"Undoubtedly. If they didn't see you enter this time,

they have your letter, at the very least. That is unfortunate." Glaring at Luke, King nevertheless refrained from verbal chastisement.

She was not so inclined. "My brother understands that what he did was very wrong. He will not make a similar mistake in the future. What I wonder is how there can be a connection between William Bein and this Mr. Casey? They travel in totally different social circles, don't they?"

Taylor nodded and spoke up. "Yes and no. Both are deeply involved in the politics of the city and both have a monetary stake in how it is run. That alone would make them allies."

"And I have the two of you," she said, standing and beginning to smile. "I would not trade either of you for the whole gang of those horrid men." She offered her hand to the editor and he shook it briefly.

"I plan to live up to your high opinion of me," King said with a slight bow. "And I know Dr. Hayward feels likewise."

Sara Beth didn't have to look over her shoulder to know that Taylor had stepped closer and was now directly behind her. She could feel his presence the same way she felt the rays of the summer sun or the radiant warmth of a hearth in the winter. It was an awareness she had not sought, yet she craved its comfort and the unspoken support she felt every time he drew near.

"We should be getting back to the orphanage," Taylor said softly. "It will be dark soon."

She turned and gave him a most thankful look. "Are you offering Lucas and me a ride in your wonderful buggy?"

"It will be my pleasure." He squared his hat on his head and crooked his arm. "Shall we go?"

Slipping her small hand through the bend of his elbow, Sara Beth felt as if she were being escorted to a fancy dress ball on the arm of a true prince, just like the story of Cinderella. Taylor Hayward was that, and more, to her. If he had not come along and taken such a personal interest in her cause, she didn't know what she would have done. How she would have coped.

Oh, there was Ella McNeil and the other women who supported the work of the Ladies' Protection and Relief Society. But those dear ladies had homes and families of their own to worry about. They could not, should not, be asked to cope with the serious problems that the surviving Reeses were facing. That was a job for the honest men of San Francisco, assuming Mr. King could find any who would stand with him.

Sara Beth knew her cynicism was misplaced. She had listened to enough of her parents' conversations to be certain that there was an underground element ready to insist upon justice. If and when the right time came, they would band together and act on the side of right, no matter what corrupt government officials said. She didn't look forward to vigilante justice but if that was the only kind offered, she would accept it.

Making her way to the waiting buggy, she held tight to Taylor's arm and scanned the crowd that thronged the street and nearby business establishments. Somewhere in that multitude was the man who had tried to steal her brother, and surely he hadn't acted alone. Were they connected to William Bein? Or was that too simplistic a notion?

Shivering in spite of the balmy evening, Sara Beth

stumbled and had to lean on the doctor's arm to keep her balance.

He laid his hand over hers where she had grasped his arm. "Are you all right?"

"No," she said honestly, fighting the tears that brimmed and threatened to slide down her cheeks. "I am far from all right. I feel scared and lost and nearly at the end of my endurance."

"Little wonder."

She saw the doctor cast a disparaging glance at Luke as the boy clambered into the buggy ahead of her and took a seat on the floor, legs crossed.

"It's not just because of what my brother did," she insisted, letting her protector assist her in climbing aboard. "It's everything. I feel as if there are villains lurking everywhere, ready to pounce. It's very disconcerting."

"You'll be safe enough once we get you home and inside those stone walls where you're among friends."

"The orphanage is more like a prison than a home," Sara Beth told him as he joined her and took up the reins. "I know I shouldn't feel that way. Perhaps it seems worse because I dare not leave. If I did, I'd always be jumping at shadows and wondering who is plotting to harm me or my brothers."

"This, too, will pass," Taylor said. "Be patient."

She knew he was right. And wise. And privy to much more inside information than he had chosen to share with her. Still, she was adrift in her current situation because she didn't know enough details about those who stood against her.

Would old Abe Warner know anything useful? she

wondered. She was overdue for a visit with him and there was no time like the present.

"I'd like to swing by the Cobweb Palace on the way home, if you don't mind," Sara Beth said. Before the doctor could object she added, "I owe Mr. Warner for taking care of my parents' final arrangements, and I'd like to make sure everything is in order."

Sighing, the doctor nodded. "All right. It's not far. Just promise me you won't go running off again."

Sara Beth placed a hand on her brother's shoulder and answered, "We will stay together and remain beside you at all times. Won't we, Luke?"

Although he merely mumbled, he did deign to nod so she was satisfied. The boy had to be suffering and confused. Although he did not have to shoulder the full responsibility for everyone else in the family the way she did, he was still to be pitied. They all were.

Which was another reason why she wanted to see Abe. He had gone beyond normal kindness in order to assist her. She wanted him to know how much she appreciated his efforts as well as demonstrate that she was happy and well cared for at present. He was like the grandfather she had never known.

That thought made her smile wistfully. Abe Warner was not only a colorful character; he was quite unlike the real grandparents her mother had spoken of so fondly. However, since those dear ones had gone to Glory long before Mama and Papa, she had no one else. Her fondness for Abe had grown as she had, with maturity bringing understanding. He was a lonely old man whose animals were his only real family and whose business served as his social circle, such it was.

She and Mama had both tried to get him to come to

church with them, but he had always begged off. That was probably just as well, since he didn't exactly smell like a rose. His heart, however, was as pure as the very gold her father was accused of stealing.

"I will clear your good name, Papa," she whispered. "I will. I swear it."

Beside her, she felt Taylor tense and sensed that he was looking at her so she forced a smile for his sake.

"That's more like it," he said, returning her grin. "I'm glad to see you're feeling better."

*Better? Perhaps,* she reasoned. Then again, maybe she was merely getting to the point where she could accept what had happened and move forward. There was certainly no option of going back. Her days as the cosseted daughter of a trusted assayer and a member of polite society were over.

Sara Beth, Lucas, Mathias and Josiah Reese were now nothing more than numbers on the books of the Protection Society.

Still, she reminded herself, she should be doubly thankful for Ella's kindness in taking them all in when she and Luke were technically beyond the ages specified in the society's charter. He was a year older than was generally allowed for boys, and she was not at all qualified because she was neither an unwed mother nor a widow with small children to support.

*Thank You, Father, that they bent the rules this time,* Sara Beth thought, amazed that it had taken her this long to realize how truly blessed she was.

The buggy stopped in the dusky alleyway next to Meigg's wharf. She shivered, remembering the last time she had been there and hating the fact that she'd have to pass the place where the bodies of her poor parents had lain so recently.

Taylor reached over and covered her hand. "Are you sure you want to go through with this? I can take a message to Abe for you instead."

"No. I'm going to go speak with him, to thank him in person. I owe him that, and more."

She watched him climb down, circle the buggy and offer her his assistance. As she placed her hand in his, she was struck once again by his warmth, his gentleness. He had long, tapering fingers, skillful surgeon's fingers, she noted, just as the medical texts had described.

Right now, however, it was not the doctor's medical expertise she was appreciating. It was his caring expression and the slight smile he was bestowing upon her. If she lived a hundred more years she didn't think she'd ever see a kinder look in anyone's eyes.

That thought, and the one that followed, made her falter. Taylor caught her by the waist and lowered her feet carefully to the ground.

"What's wrong?" he asked, frowning.

Sara Beth was not about to tell him what tricks her mind was playing on her. When she had thought of having many years of life ahead of her, her imagination had immediately countered with the notion that this next breath might be her last.

She had wobbled when she had realized how real that possibility might be. The man who had slain Mama and Papa had died, too, but if he had not been working alone the threat of assassination was still there. Still lurking in some black-hearted knave like William Bein who might easily hire another scoundrel to slay her. Or her whole family.

## Chapter Nine

The Cobweb Palace was not an establishment Taylor would have chosen for Sara Beth or her impressionable brother to visit, particularly at this time in the evening. Dock workers and others had bellied up to its bar till there was no room for one more man to squeeze in. Raucous laughter echoed from the celebrants enjoying French brandy, Spanish wine or English ale, and the aroma of hot food mingling with that of the old man's menagerie was anything but appetizing.

Sara Beth shrank back in the doorway. "Maybe this was a mistake. I've been here with Mama many times and it was never like this."

"That's probably because you came on a Sunday afternoon. A saloon is a saloon, even if there is enough stuff crammed in here to make it a museum or a zoo."

Spotting the top-hatted old man behind the bar, Taylor motioned him over. As soon as Abe recognized Sara Beth, a grin lifted his whiskered cheeks.

She greeted him tearfully and gave him her hand. He patted it affectionately, sending a twinge of jealousy through Taylor and leaving him shocked by his untoward reaction. The young woman had intimated that she thought of Abe as a grandfatherly figure, so why did his innocent attention to her seem so off-putting? Might he covet the easy affection between the two despite his vow to keep his feelings out of it?

"I—I just wanted to thank you in person," she told Abe, watching as Luke played with a monkey that was chained atop a keg at the rear of the room.

"Nothing to thank me for," he said. "Have you been to the cemetery yet?"

The doctor saw her glance at her brother before she said, "No. I know Mama and Papa are in heaven. There's no need for me to see their earthly resting places."

"Well, I put up a marker for them anyway," Abe told her. "It's just temporary till I can get one carved proper."

"I will repay you, somehow, someday," Sara Beth vowed.

"Ain't no need for that. None at all." He gestured to-ward the bar. "These fine gentlemen ponied up plenty for the graves and there's enough left over for a nice headstone."

"I thought stone markers weren't allowed at Yerba Buena."

"It ain't that. It's the way the sand hills drift over the graves that hide 'em. But don't you fret, Miss Sara Beth. I'll see to it that the plots are kept clean so you can find 'em when you're ready to go pay your respects."

"Thank you." She leaned close enough to kiss the old man's cheek. "And God bless you."

"He has, He has," Abe said with a chortle. "I'm a happy man with a place of my own and plenty of good company. Couldn't ask for more."

Taylor snorted in the background, drawing Abe's attention.

"We can't all be highfalutin like the doc here. I'm just glad he's taken such a shine to you, little girl. Your Mama and Papa would be pleased."

Before Taylor could deny any personal interest, Sara Beth did it for him.

"We are just acquaintances," she insisted. "However, he is going to teach me all about medicine so I can work with him at the orphanage. Isn't that wonderful?"

Abe looked surprised, then started to roar with laughter, tightly clasping his sides as if he were about to shake them apart. When he recovered enough to speak he said, "You? A doc? That'll be the day. Imagine. A woman doctor? Might as well move right into my collection. I can put you up next to the sea monkey or the mermaid. Yes, sirree."

She looked to Taylor. "I think it's time we left."

"I couldn't agree more." He had noticed that their presence was attracting far too much attention, especially since Abe had begun hooting and hollering, and he wanted to take her away before things got further out of hand.

"Luke," the doctor shouted. "Come on. We're leaving."

The boy came slowly, scuffing his feet on the dusty floorboards. "Aw. Do we hafta?"

"Yes," Sara Beth said firmly. "We have to."

In Taylor's opinion the boy was far from being as reformed as his sister seemed to believe. There might be hesitant compliance in his actions but he retained a defiant look, a posture that indicated he was inches from outright refusal.

Now was not the time to bring that up, of course, but Luke would bear watching. His young mind had obviously not yet grasped the gravity of the situation and he was still a danger to everyone. Any boy who would take money for betraying his sister was not going to change his ways after only one good talking-to. Nor was he likely to think things through himself and decide to do right in the future.

*No,* Taylor decided easily. That boy was trouble. All he had to do was figure out how to warn Sara Beth without alienating her completely. He would have felt a lot better about the situation if he'd had a clue how he should proceed.

*Well, one problem at a time,* he told himself as he escorted her and the boy back to his buggy. The sun was already so low over the bay that twilight was upon them. The sooner his charges got back to the orphanage the better.

Once he saw Sara Beth and Luke safely inside, he'd finish his rounds of patients in town and quit for the day. His practice had suffered greatly since he'd become so involved with the Reese family. Nevertheless, he was going to persevere until things were settled properly, although their modest estate might not be worth much by the time Bein got through milking it and they overcame the additional problem of government involvement.

None of that mattered in the grand scheme of things. There were some events over which man had little or no control, just like the flurries of earthquakes that kept shaking up the city. Taylor knew that. He also knew at this point there was nothing he could do to stop caring too much about what happened to Sara Beth and her siblings for his own good. It was as if he had been designated her protector without any option to decline.

Unfortunately, that task seemed to suit him so well he no longer had any desire to quit.

Ella McNeil was beside herself when Sara Beth and Luke finally arrived with the doctor. She pulled both her charges into her ample embrace as if they had been away for months. "Land sakes. I thought you'd never get back. What on earth is going on?"

"It's a long story. We're fine. Really, we are," Sara Beth assured her as Luke extricated himself and edged away. "Dr. Hayward has been escorting us."

"Fine kettle of fish." She glared at Taylor. "Don't you have a lick of sense? These poor things missed supper and evening devotions already."

Sara Beth noted that he had already politely removed his bowler and was trying to look suitably contrite. He was also failing miserably. She came to his defense.

"Actually, it was Luke who left first, on an errand for me, and if the doctor had not taken me down the hill to search for him, things might have turned out for the worse."

"Mercy me." Ella fanned herself with fluttery hands. "What happened?"

Choosing her words carefully, Sara Beth explained in detail while her brother sulked. When she was finished, she sighed. "Do you suppose Clara would mind if we looked for a bite to eat? I know I'm probably too late to help with the dishes and I don't want her to think ill of me."

"Of course she won't mind. You all just go out there and have whatever's left. Nobody will mind a bit."

"Come with us?" Sara Beth asked, addressing the doctor. "You haven't eaten either, have you?"

"No. I almost did. I had to leave the table before I was served."

Although he was smiling, she realized everything was her fault. "I'm so sorry. Let me fry you some eggs and side pork to make up for it."

"I'd love to stay, but duty calls," Taylor told her, making a slight bow before he put his hat back on his head. "I'll be by tomorrow and we'll look in on the children together."

"You haven't changed your mind about letting me help?" Her cheeks warmed. "I wondered, after the way Abe Warner acted."

Taylor smiled and Sara Beth felt extremely blessed by his beneficent expression.

"Abe has no idea how intelligent you are, Miss Reese. If he did, he wouldn't have laughed." He sobered. "I know it hurt your feelings. Just remember, there may come a day when your understanding of the practice of medicine will prove your mettle."

"I sincerely hope so." She offered her hand to him. "God's speed, Doctor. Be careful out there. The world is a far more unfriendly place than I had dreamed."

She stood in the half-open doorway as Taylor took his leave, climbed into his buggy and drove away. Her last statement kept echoing in her mind and heart. *Unfriendly?* More like perilous. And fearsome. And volatile beyond reason.

Sara Beth momentarily closed her eyes, offering up a silent prayer for the doctor's protection. He was so kind. So helpful. So...dear, her heart insisted.

Her eyes popped open and she stared into the dimness of the garden, not seeing any of what lay before her. Instead, her mind's eye was focused on the handsome doctor and all he had done for her, even agreeing to teach her the art of healing when so many other men would have laughed the same way Abe Warner had.

Dr. Hayward, *Taylor* in her heart, was more than her benefactor. He was special beyond words, beyond thoughts. It was probably a terrible sin to covet his presence and think so highly of him, but she couldn't help herself. The only thing she truly looked forward to was seeing him again. Listening to the timbre of his voice as it sent shivers up her spine. Perhaps even holding his hand the way she had that very evening.

She blinked, trying to clear her head. It was no use. She was besotted. Smitten. A hopeless romantic caught up in a tangle of intrigue and beginning to care less about her current trials than she did about one special gentleman.

"This will never do," Sara Beth insisted, taking a quick step backward and preparing to secure the heavy door for the night.

As it swung closed she heard a loud noise. It wasn't until she glanced up at the edge of the mahogany door and saw a splintered hole that she realized she had just been shot at!

"Well, did you get her?"

Scannell shook his head. "Naw. She ducked at the last minute and my man missed."

Bein cursed.

"Simmer down. We'll fix her. We fetched you her letter, didn't we?"

"A fat lot of good that does when she spent an hour talking to King at the *Bulletin*."

"He can be dealt with, too, you know."

The stylish businessman shook his head as he brushed invisible dust off the cuff of his jacket. "Not yet. We don't want to call too much attention to him or to his paper, especially not when the governor has sent Sherman to take over as major general of the second division of militia."

Chuckling, the sheriff snorted. "I wouldn't worry about Sherman. He'll be hamstrung by General Wool and maybe Farragut, too, if he asks the Navy for help. We're the Law and Order Party, remember?"

"Yes. And we have Governor Johnson hoodwinked. I just don't trust everyone to continue to act in my best interests. Neither should you."

"I don't see why you're so worried about one newspaperman. King doesn't control all the press."

"No, but he's influential with the right people. Remember, he was a banker until he lost his own fortune in the panic of '54. He made plenty of friends among the rich when he was one of them."

"So? He bleeds like every other man."

"I hope it won't come to that," Bein said. "Eliminating my partner was bad enough. Having poor Isabelle caught in the crossfire was inexcusable."

"Did you have a soft spot in your heart for her?" Scannell asked.

"None of your business. Just see that I'm kept abreast of any new developments and guard the Reese property until I tell you different."

"Yes, sir." He smiled slyly. "What about the girl?

She's trouble and you know it. Do you want us to try for her again?"

"Not yet. Let's give it a few days and see what else happens. I'm curious about what King's actually planning to print and I don't want anyone to have reason to blame me for your sloppy work."

"Well, it's pretty confusin' and that's a fact. I can't hardly tell who's on our side and who's not."

"As long as you continue to take orders from me you'll be fine. Don't even think of selling out to the other side or you won't live long enough to spend whatever they pay you. Understand?"

"Yeah, yeah. You can trust me, Mr. Bein."

He lit a cheroot and blew smoke before he smiled and said, "I don't trust anybody but myself. Never have and never will. That was my late, lamented partner's problem. He trusted the wrong people." He chuckled. "And look what it got him."

Taylor arrived at the orphanage late the following afternoon and entered through the kitchen with the express goal of seeing Sara Beth. He wasn't disappointed.

Squealing with delight, she ran straight to him, stopping just inches from being in his arms once again.

He could tell from the expression on her face that she was embarrassed to have shown so much emotion. He could sympathize. When she'd raced across the room to greet him he had nearly acted on instinct and swept her into his embrace. *That* would have given Clara and Mattie plenty to gossip about, wouldn't it?

"How are you today, Miss Reese?" Taylor asked.

She gave a slight curtsey. "Fine, thank you, Doctor."

"I trust you slept well."

As he spoke he was peeking past Sara Beth at the older women, and it was clear to him that they were not fooled one bit. They both looked dreamy-eyed, as if they were watching a courtship rather than the conversation of two casual friends, as he'd intended.

"No. Not really," Sara Beth said, sobering and lightly touching his forearm. "Come with me. I want to show you something."

Puzzled, Taylor frowned. "Show me what? What's the matter?"

"You'll see." She led him to the heavy front door and slowly opened it, staying behind its bulk as she did so. "Don't stand in the open. Step back here, closer to me."

"I really don't think that's wise, do you?" he said, smiling and feeling decidedly ill at ease. The lovely young woman might not realize how her presence had begun to affect him, but that did not excuse him from behaving properly.

She grabbed his sleeve and pulled him aside. "I am not about to let your stubborn nature get you killed." Pointing, she added, "Look."

Aghast, he stared at the splintered wood. "Is that what I think it is?"

"If you guessed a bullet hole, then yes. It happened last night, after I bid you goodbye. Thankfully, the shot missed."

That was too much for Taylor. He drew her into his arms and held her close, oblivious to the lack of propriety. "Dear Lord. You might have been killed."

"Like my father and mother were," Sara Beth murmured. "I didn't see anyone out there. Maybe it was merely an accidental discharge of a firearm and I happened to be in the wrong place at the wrong time."

"Whatever the reason, you're not going outside again. Not until we figure out who is behind all this."

Instead of agreeing as he had hoped, she pushed him away and stepped back. "Don't be ridiculous. You can't be certain anyone was shooting at me. Besides, I attended church this morning with the others. We walked all the way and nothing bad happened."

That thought chilled Taylor to the bone. He grasped her shoulders to keep her facing him. "Do you believe you're safe merely because you're on your way to worship service? That's idiotic. Oo is assuming that the shot last night was an accident."

He took a deep breath, warring within himself to control his impulse to embrace her again. "If you didn't agree, you wouldn't have warned me to stand behind the door."

"Okay. So maybe I do think it was an attack. That still doesn't mean I have to live like a prisoner in a dungeon."

At the end of his patience and so worried he could hardly keep from trying to shake some sense into her, he dropped his arms to his sides, turned and walked away. "I'm going to make my rounds. Are you coming?"

He heard her soft footsteps and the rustle of her skirts behind him. What was he going to do with her? How was he going to convince her that she was in mortal danger? Surely she must not fully realize the gravity of the situation or she wouldn't be behaving so irrationally.

Not that he was any more sane, he told himself. Ever since he had first encountered Sara Beth Reese he had been acting as addled and erratic as a Sunday-dinner chicken with its neck wrung.

That colorful analogy did nothing to calm his fears.

Neither did the way Sara Beth was acting. To look at her, a person would think she hadn't a care in the world.

He, on the other hand, was worried enough for both of them. If she continued to insist on going out, there was nothing he could do to protect her. Absolutely nothing.

# Chapter Ten

The *Bulletin* had remained silent about the Reese situation for the past week. Each day, Sara Beth had eagerly scanned the evening edition and each time she had been disappointed

Only Dr. Hayward's continuing encouragement and pleasing presence buoyed her spirits. He had taken to visiting the orphanage at least twice every day and she was delighted to see him, no matter what news he carried.

"I don't understand why your friend hasn't printed my story yet," she remarked as they tended to ailing children and administered a spoonful of Clara's home-made horehound cough elixir to each one.

"He'll get around to it," Taylor assured her. "Right now he's in the middle of a series about corruption and is focusing on James Casey. I told you about Casey. He owns the *Herald*."

"Can't Mr. King cover more than one topic at a time?"

"The way he explained it, he figures it will be advantageous to clear the city of Casey's negative influence and then proceed with cleaning up the rest of the crooks who are in power, including Bein and his cohorts."

"Are his facts accurate?" She made a face that mimicked the expression of the child who had just tasted the cough cure. Truth to tell, the sinful atmosphere of the city was far more revolting to her than any bitter medicine. Just thinking about the dirty politics was enough to turn her stomach.

"Of course they are. James King is the most honest, careful editor in San Francisco. We're lucky to have him on our side."

She nodded, her expression grim. "Until I was wronged, I had never paid much attention to what went on at City Hall. I suppose many citizens are the same. We're too content to let sleeping dogs lie."

"These so-called dogs may well be rabid," Taylor countered. "Did you read any of the exposé on Casey?"

"Most of it. I can hardly believe that he was a convicted criminal who served prison time in New York. He was elected city supervisor here by a landslide. That's incredible."

"I'd agree, if I didn't believe that the election was rigged like so many others have been." Washing his hands, Taylor dried them on a small towel before packing up his medical bag. "I told King he'd better be careful. A hardened criminal like Casey can be dangerous, especially if he's convinced he has nothing more to lose."

"What can he do? Surely the newspaper articles are not considered defamatory as long as they're true."

Taylor set his jaw. "He's threatened retribution in front of witnesses, for one thing. I wish I could get King to take the threats seriously. He's carrying his pistol with him at all times and watching where he goes and with whom, but that may not be enough."

"I disagree," Sara Beth said. "Casey wouldn't dare harm him, especially not after issuing public threats. He'd be blamed immediately and probably hung."

"Would he?" The doctor arched his eyebrows. "Even if Scannell arrested him, I doubt they could find a fair judge and jury for a trial. Casey would have half the town in his vest pocket to start with."

Sara Beth did not want to believe there was so much evil all around her, yet the more she learned, the less she believed that she and her family would ever obtain justice.

Praise the Lord for a man like James King who believed her. "Do you suppose it would help if you and I visited the *Bulletin* office again?"

The look Taylor sent her was anything but supportive. "Don't be silly."

"I'm not anything of the kind," Sara Beth argued. "I'd like to talk with Mr. King again, that's all."

"And say what?"

"I don't know. I just feel so helpless, acting as if I'm in hiding. I need to get out, do something, even if it's futile. Can you understand that?"

"I understand it but that doesn't mean I think it's a sensible idea."

"Sensible or not, I want to go. I will go. With or without you."

Taylor sighed and nodded slowly. "All right. We're finished here. Go tell Mrs. McNeil we're going downtown. I'll drive you so you don't have to walk. The less time you're out on the streets, the better."

Her spirits soared. "Oh, thank you! I've felt so

cooped up and frustrated staying inside. And it's a lovely, sunny afternoon. Perfect weather for a drive." She didn't care that she was grinning foolishly. "I'll get my shawl and meet you at the buggy."

*We're going for a ride. Together.* Sara Beth's heart was practically singing and her feet felt as if they barely touched the floor as she hurried to the small chest that held her personal things. She had managed to obtain a second presentable dress and Clara had loaned her several aprons to keep her clothing clean while she worked. Other than that, she had only her coat, a shawl, mother's reticule and...

That thought focused and brought Sara Beth up short. She had not looked inside her mother's purse since that awful night when some kindly stranger had handed it to her at the wharf. Mama had been carrying a small, single-shot pistol. If it was still there, as she hoped, it would provide a little extra protection.

True, it had not helped Mama. Not enough anyway. But any weapon of self-defense was better than being totally vulnerable.

The reticule lay in the bottom of the small storage chest, just where she'd stashed it. Sara Beth's heart pounded as she eased the drawstrings, opened the velvet-lined bag, then gingerly lifted the pistol to study it. To her dismay, it was not loaded.

*Because Mama shot the attacker.* Of course. That one bullet had found its mark and had served its purpose well.

The trouble was, she had no idea how to reload safely or where she would find ammunition if she did know how to fit a ball and powder properly into the tiny pistol. As it was, it was about as useful for defense as a hand-size rock would be.

Nevertheless, she slipped the gun into her pocket. Later, after she and the doctor had visited the newspaper office, she'd ask him about ammunition and enlist his expertise. Perhaps they could get it loaded tonight because without a suitable weapon, she *was as useless as that unloaded pistol*.

James King was not a foolish man. Nor was he fearful. He'd always been able to talk his way out of trouble, even in the face of apparently insurmountable odds.

Closing his editorial office, he checked his pocket watch as he descended the stairway on the west side of Montgomery Street. It was just past five. Mist from the bay was starting to roll in and the mournful sound of foghorns echoed off the tall, brick buildings of the business district as well as the surrounding hills.

The hair on the back of his neck suddenly prickled. He whirled. His eyes widened when he saw who was approaching. "What are you doing here?"

"I told you I'd kill you if I saw you," Casey said. He was pointing a revolver.

King held up his hands, palms out. It was too late to draw his own pistol. If he hoped to survive, he'd have to argue his way out of this. "Take it easy. I didn't print anything that wasn't true. It was only a matter of time until the whole story came out. You know that."

"All I know is that you've ruined everything," Casey said. He was eyeing the other man's bulging coat pocket. "Go ahead. Go for your pistol. I'm willing to shoot it out right here and now."

"Well, I'm not," King said, beginning to perspire beneath his top hat. "Be sensible, man."

At the last second, when he saw his adversary's eyes narrow and his flushed face tighten in a sneer, he knew he had underestimated Casey. The gun fired. King dropped, hit squarely in the left shoulder.

Before he lost consciousness he was briefly aware that his attacker was approaching. He could only hope and pray that the man did not intend to fire again and finish him where he lay.

Taylor and Sara Beth were almost to the intersection of Montgomery and Merchant streets when they heard a commotion.

She grasped the doctor's arm. "Was that a shot?"

"Sounded like it." He pulled the buggy to the side of the road, passed her the reins and jumped out. "Stay here. I'll go check."

Before he disappeared around the corner of the nearby hotel, she had already made up her mind. She was not about to just sit there idle when he might need her help.

Unmindful of danger to her own person, she shed her shawl, carefully gathered her skirts and eased herself down by way of the small metal step at the side of the buggy. In his haste, Taylor had left without his medical bag. That provided a perfect excuse. She would deliver it to him.

What she encountered on Montgomery Street was utter chaos. Dozens of people were milling about. Women wept. Men cursed or shouted or laughed maniacally.

She stared. Her heart pounded and she was barely able to catch her breath. *Taylor. Where is Taylor?*

There! In the midst of the throng. That had to be him. Frantic, she pushed through the crowd and immediately saw the full effect of the carnage. The doctor was crouching next to the body of a well-dressed, middle-aged man. Off to the side, another man was being wrestled to a standstill by passersby. She didn't recognize the second person, but the victim was definitely James King from the *Bulletin*.

The whole scenario was an agonizing reminder of the way her parents had died. For an instant she relived their demise as if she were seeing it again. Would she never have peace? Would the terrible pain and sense of loss never fade?

Forcing herself to focus, Sara Beth blinked to clear her head. She must act. She would act. She willed her feet to carry her closer to the doctor and saw, to her great relief, that the victim, Mr. King, was still moving, although he was groaning and bleeding badly.

She thrust the medical bag at Taylor. "Here. You forgot this."

The swift look he gave her was chastening in spite of his obvious need of the instruments. "Thank you."

"You're welcome." This was the first time Sara Beth had been present when her mentor was doing anything other than taking temperatures or handing out doses of elixir. She was so fascinated by his deft movements that she momentarily forgot her own distress.

He pressed a thick pad against the patient's shoulder, then gestured to a couple of men loitering nearby. "We need to get him inside and into bed. Help me carry him to the closest hotel. You take his feet," he told the first. "And you and I will support his shoulders," he said, pointing to the second man. "I'll handle the injured side."

Following Taylor inside, toting his medical bag once again, Sara Beth wondered if she could have risen to the occasion as he had. Easing the discomfort of a child with a cold was one thing. Stopping a man from bleeding to death was quite another. Maybe Abe had been right to laugh at her lofty aspirations. Maybe she wasn't cut out to become a doctor.

Then again, although she had felt her stomach clench at the grisly sight and had momentarily relived the worst time of her life, she had not swooned the way some of the other women in the crowd had. On the contrary, she might be a bit shaky, but she was nonetheless alert and ready to do whatever Taylor told her to do—other than stay behind in the buggy.

She realized she was as stubborn as her brother—and as stubborn as her mother had been. The thought surprised her and she forced herself to focus on the situation at hand.

As the men struggled to carry their limp burden up the stairway and place him in a hotel room, Sara Beth hung back and studied the crowd. Some of those present seemed distressed over the editor's shooting. Many, however, were smiling and apparently enjoying the excitement. Worse, those who had captured the assailant had already released him and were behaving as if he had done nothing wrong! James Casey was hiding behind Sheriff Scannell as if the lawman was his personal shield.

Perhaps that was what Taylor had meant when he'd said they would have trouble finding a fair judge and jury. If such a panel were chosen from the men she observed here, there would be a very good chance that King's foe would be exonerated.

Her feet felt leaden and so did her heart as she finally proceeded up the stairs, pausing at the landing. This was wrong, so wrong. And yet it was happening right in front of her eyes. A good, honest man was injured and might be dying while his attacker had been released and was now standing with his cronies in the hotel lobby below, laughing, talking and smoking a cigar as if nothing untoward had occurred.

Her breath caught. In the rear of that throng, near the door, stood the smug-looking figure of William Bein. And he was leering at her.

Taylor was afraid for his friend. As soon as Sara Beth joined him with his medical bag, he held out a hand. "It's the subclavian artery. Give me the large hemostats. They're made like scissors only they clamp instead of cutting."

"I know what they look like."

She was not only quick to respond; she seemed quite calm amidst all the bedlam, further impressing Taylor with her bravery and fortitude.

As he worked to stem the bleeding and failed repeatedly to locate and clamp the damaged ends of the artery, he wondered how long poor James could last. It didn't look good. Not good at all. And there was little anyone could do.

Other doctors, older medical men, had been summoned. They shoved Taylor away and took his place. He would have fought for position if he had not already done all he could. Nuttall and Toland were good men, as surgeons went. Perhaps they would have more success by working as a team.

"Why are you backing off and letting those men tend to him?" Sara Beth asked, frowning as she handed Taylor a damp towel from the washstand so he could wipe his hands.

"Because there's nothing more I can do. I'd let old Abe Warner himself try if I thought it would help."

"I'm so sorry."

"Don't give up on him yet," Taylor insisted. Though he knew his friend probably didn't have much longer to live, he also knew that even while unconscious, James could likely hear and understand what was being said. Many a professor had impressed that fact upon him in medical school, citing instances where dying patients had rallied at the last instant and had later been irate at the conversations they had overheard during their supposed passing.

Leading her aside, Taylor spoke privately. "I need to get you back home but I can't leave James."

"Of course you can't. I wouldn't ask it of you. Besides, there may be some way we can assist those other doctors."

"Perhaps. Perhaps not." Even from where he and Sara Beth stood they could hear the others loudly discussing treatment. Nuttall was suggesting that they plug the wound with a sponge, much to Taylor's dismay.

"You can't do that," he insisted, stepping closer. "He'll die of infection. Haven't you read Semmelweis's papers?"

The others ignored him. Starting to turn away, he suddenly heard his friend moan and call his name.

"James?" Taylor pushed through and fell to his knees by the side of the bed. "I'm right here."

"Don't leave me," King pleaded, grasping Taylor's fingers so tightly the grip was painful. "In the name of all that's Holy, Hayward, don't leave me to these butchers."

"I've done all I can to stem the flow. We should let them try."

"I'm already a dead man. I know that," King said in a low, shaky voice. "Promise you'll see that Casey pays for murdering me."

Nodding, Taylor vowed that he would. In seconds, the other man was once again unconscious and had loosened his grip.

The young doctor rose and returned to Sara Beth. "When we came in, I think I spotted W. T. Coleman with some of the other men from the Vigilance Committee. If I can locate him, I'll have him take you home in my buggy."

"I should stay with you," she said, eyeing the pompous other doctors. "You might need moral support, and besides, William Bein was downstairs the last time I looked."

"All the more reason for you to take advantage of the distraction provided by the crowd. I may be here for a long time. There's no sense both of us holding vigil."

"All right. Whatever you think is best."

"Thank you for understanding," Taylor said, gently taking both her hands and holding them. "If I don't have your safety to worry about I'll be better able to think, to help look after James properly."

"I heard him say he thought he was dying," she whispered. "Isn't that a bad attitude to foster?"

"Not if it's true." Taylor released her and started to turn toward the closed door that led into the hallway. "I'd much rather see a man prepare himself to meet his Maker than die suddenly and not have a chance to repent."

The moment those words were spoken he rued them. Sara Beth's mother and father might have faced exactly that fate and, judging by the pained expression on her face, she had reached the same conclusion.

"I'm sorry. I didn't mean—"

"I know. And I agree. No man can predict when his time is near. I know Mama's soul was right with God and I can't imagine divine providence separating two people who loved each other as dearly as she and Papa Robert did."

"All right. Stay up here with James and the others where you'll be safe. I'll locate W.T. or one of his trustworthy men and arrange an escort."

"I don't suppose you'd consider just letting me walk home?"

"Not in a million years," the doctor said flatly.

He was not a bit surprised when Sara Beth answered, "That's what I thought."

## Chapter Eleven

As far as Sara Beth was concerned, she was not in need of cosseting. However, given the stress Taylor Hayward was currently under, she figured it would be best to go along with his ideas and allow Mr. Coleman to see her home.

The only off-putting element was the degree of nervousness and mental distraction the middle-aged businessman was displaying as he drove. To look at his pale skin, perspiring brow and glassy eyes, a person would think he was the one who had just been shot instead of James King.

He brought the doctor's buggy to a stop in front of the orphanage without comment, leaving Sara Beth wondering if he had even noticed where they were.

She offered her hand. When he seemed to ignore the friendly gesture, she simply gathered her skirts and climbed out of the buggy unassisted before saying, "Thank you for bringing me home, sir. Will you be returning to the hotel now?"

"What? Oh, I suppose so." His hand was trembling as he touched the brim of his hat politely. "Evening, miss."

Watching the familiar buggy drive away, Sara Beth realized that she was not lamenting its departure the way she usually did, which was, of course, because Mr. Coleman was driving instead of Taylor Hayward.

Her heart ached for the young doctor. How difficult it must be to tend to a close friend and be unable to help him. Since the very thought of being in that untenable position caused her anguish, how must Taylor feel to be facing it in reality?

How long would poor James King linger? she wondered as she entered the orphanage. He had endured so much suffering already that she was almost prepared to pray the Lord took him home soon, before he had to bear more. In that respect, she supposed her parents had been blessed, if one could imagine death being a positive event. How unbelievers coped with such a loss was unimaginable. No wonder so many folks, like Abe Warner, for instance, professed faith even if they chose not to attend church.

Entering the kitchen, she smiled at Clara. "I'm back. Is there anything I can do to help you and Mattie?"

"There's always somethin'," the heavyset woman answered soberly. "But I think you should check with Ella first."

Clara's lack of joviality took Sara Beth aback. "Why? What's wrong?"

"You'd best talk to Ella. I don't want to be carrying tales, if you know what I mean."

"No, I don't know what you mean," Sara Beth said. "Tell me. Please?"

Sighing, the cook dried her hands on her apron and nodded. "All right. It's that brother of yours. Luke. He snuck off right after you left and hasn't come back."

"Oh, dear!"

She wheeled and ran for the front of the mansion. Luke was gone. And chances were good that if he'd made it all the way into the city, he'd heard the rumors and had done what so many others had. He'd followed the crowds to the scene of the shooting to see for himself what all the excitement was about.

Locating Mrs. McNeil in the parlor, Sara Beth immediately grasped her hand. "What happened to Luke? When did he leave? How long has he been gone?"

Just then, a mild tremor shook the house, making the chandelier sway. Sara Beth was so used to the shaking and rumbling of the earth beneath the city that she barely took notice.

Ella McNeil, however, gave a little shriek and froze, listening and waiting for more. "Mercy. I hate it when that happens."

"It's over," Sara Beth insisted. "What about Luke?"

"Yes, Luke." The matron made a sour face. "I don't know what we're going to do about that boy. I tried to reason with him, but I might as well have been talking to the garden wall."

"What did he say? Clara told me he left right after I went with the doctor."

"That's right. He insisted that if you could leave, he could, too. He said he wanted to go home. I tried to explain that your old house was all shut up and guarded but he refused to listen to me."

"Is that where he was headed? Are you sure?"

"I reckon so." She held tight to Sara Beth's hand when the younger woman tried to pull away. "I've sent one of the men from the Vigilance Committee to look for him. Luke will be fine. I don't want you running off to find him, you hear?"

"Who did you send? Does the man even know what Luke looks like? Does he?" She knew her voice was rising and her tone panicked but she couldn't help it. "I have to go. Don't you see? Luke will listen to me."

In her deepest heart she hoped that conclusion was correct. She realized that she had erred when she'd failed to inform the two oldest boys of William Bein's treachery. As far as Luke and Mathias knew, *Uncle Will* was still to be trusted. Given that fact, there was every chance that if they chanced to meet, Luke would go willingly with that appalling man.

And then what? she asked herself, her eyes growing misty. Someone had already tried to kidnap Luke once. If anything like that happened again and she wasn't around to rescue him, what would become of her poor brother?

She knew she should be furious at Luke for disobeying and leaving the orphanage grounds, yet she could sympathize with his urge to return to their once happy home. If that was all he did, and if he was not spotted by the guards the sheriff had placed at the property, then perhaps he would return unscathed.

Tears brimmed and slipped down her cheeks. She had promised Taylor that she would stay on the grounds of the Ladies' Protection and Relief Society for refuge. Like it or not, she was going to have to break that vow. She must track down her brother and see him safely back to the orphanage. There was no other sensible option.

She paused. Her eyes widened. In all the confusion and drama surrounding the assassination attempt, she had neglected to find out how to load her mother's pistol or obtain the means to do so. Once again, she would be making the journey down the hill unarmed.

King had lapsed into unconsciousness and stayed there, even after Dr. Nuttall's sponge had stanched the bleeding. If Taylor had been in charge he would not have risked the onset of sepsis by using that method, but he had to admit that, for the moment, his friend was still breathing.

With the unconscious man fading, and the other doctors clearly in charge, Taylor decided to leave long enough to check with Coleman and make sure Sara Beth had arrived safely at the orphanage.

Coleman was not in his office. Taylor found the head of the Vigilance Committee leading a rally at the Turn Verein Hall on Bush Street.

Taylor had just reached the hall when another party arrived, led by Governor Johnson and a wiry military man he soon realized was Major General Sherman. While their entourage was made to wait, Taylor was ushered inside to see Coleman.

The meeting room was filled with men who were risking their lives and their businesses by gathering this way, even though the roster of the committee was kept by number rather than given name.

"Did you get her home?" Taylor asked.

"What?"

"The girl. Miss Reese. Is she safe?"

Coleman took out a monogrammed handkerchief and mopped his brow. "Safer than any of us are. Did you see who's waiting to interview me?"

"Yes. So? You're not doing anything wrong. None of us are. There's no law against holding a meeting."

"There is if you're planning vigilante justice," Coleman said in a low voice. "How's King?"

"Near death. It won't be long."

"That's what I was afraid of."

Taylor eyed the throng. Many were watching their conversation with grim expressions. It looked to him as if Coleman was about to lose control of the mob.

"Aren't you going to go see what the governor wants?" the doctor asked.

"I suppose I have no choice. What if he orders us to disband? I'll never be able to convince these men that they shouldn't act, especially if King dies."

"One thing at a time," Taylor said, clapping him on the back. "Come on. I'll go with you to beard the lions. I can tell them about King's condition and his declaration that Casey shot him."

"Think it will matter?"

"I certainly hope so. I'd hate to be stuck between justice and the law."

"Scannell, you mean?"

"Him and Judge Norton. I don't trust either of them, even though the judge does have a good reputation."

"At least the grand jury is in session. We may be able to convince them to indict Casey quickly and avoid a riot."

"It'll have to be fast," Coleman replied. "These men are at the end of their ropes and I can't say I blame them."

The afternoon wind off the Pacific was chilling, making Sara Beth wish she had remembered to grab her shawl from the buggy. She hugged herself, wrapping her arms tight to ward off the shivers. It was not only the temperature and the breeze that were making her cold; it was also thoughts of her brother. Luke was not a bad person; he was simply naive. All the Reese children, herself included, had been sheltered from reality and were therefore unprepared to discern evil and properly deal with it.

How was she going to help Luke if he got into trouble again? She didn't have a plan, but she would take advantage of the fact that she was young and female and would attract far less attention than a grown man, particularly if she kept her eyes downcast and didn't get in anyone's way. Such subservient behavior was contrary to her nature. That didn't matter. Not now. Not when Luke was out there somewhere, alone and probably courting danger once again.

She hurried along the boarded walkway that led to her former home on Pike Street, darting behind a tree as soon as she had the place in sight. From that vantage point she could see most of the property, at least the front and one side. It looked deserted. Then again, the guards might be inside, sitting in Papa's chair, propping their dirty boots on Mama's needlepoint-covered footstool and spitting tobacco juice on the floor.

"That's so wrong," she murmured as those vivid imaginings whirled in her mind. "No one has a right to desecrate our family home. If my brothers and I don't get it back, no one should have it." She gritted her teeth. "Especially not William Bein."

Long minutes passed. There was no sign of life at the house or the laboratory that made up one wing. Not only were there apparently no guards, there was also no sign of Luke, which could be good news or bad, depending on whether he had come here at all.

Stepping out from behind the tree, Sara Beth started to inch closer. A flash of movement in the bushes caught her eye. She froze, staring and praying that she had not alerted a hidden adversary.

The crouching figure moved. It was small. Too small to be one of the sheriff's men.

It was Luke! He was trying to pry open a window near Papa's assay office.

Rather than call out and startle him or call attention to either of them, she hiked her skirts above her toes and raced across the intervening distance. The boy was just lifting the sash when she clamped a hand on his shoulder.

He screamed like a frightened girl.

"Hush," she ordered in a hoarse whisper as she pressed her free hand over his mouth. "It's me. Sara Beth."

Instead of listening, Luke tried to bite her palm.

"Stop that!"

The boy was panting and wide-eyed in panic when she let him go. To her shock and disappointment, he started to curse a blue streak.

"Where did you learn such terrible language?"

"What do you care?"

"I care enough to have followed you here," she said flatly. "Now come with me. We're going home."

"I am home," Luke said, pouting. "I want my things. I'm going to go get them. You can't stop me."

She grabbed him and pulled him down into the bushes beside her just as a shadow crossed in front of the window. "Quiet. I didn't spot any guards on the porch but I just saw something inside. Unless you want to be kidnapped again and hauled off to goodness knows where, I suggest you button your lip."

"I don't see nobody."

"Anybody," she corrected. "I don't now either. Let's go check some of the other windows."

To her relief, the boy seemed agreeable. "Okay. You go that way and I'll—"

"Oh, no, you don't," Sara Beth said. "We're staying together. If you're right and there's no one inside, then I'll help you get your personal belongings. I'd like some of mine, too. And clothing for the others. But if we see guards we're leaving. Is that clear?"

"I guess."

"Good. And while I'm thinking about this whole situation, I need to tell you a few things about *Uncle Will*." As she watched her brother's expression she found his apparent lack of concern surprising. Luke had always acted as if he worshipped that man, so why was he now apparently feigning disinterest?

"William Bein is the reason why we can't live here," Sara Beth said. "He told me he owns the house and everything in it. He's the one who's responsible for the sheriff keeping a guard on it."

"I don't believe you."

"I had trouble accepting it, too," she said, nodding and looking directly into his wide-eyed gaze. "But it's true. All of it. Mama and Papa trusted him and he betrayed them." She hesitated, weighing her words before she added, "I even suspect that he may somehow be responsible for their murders."

"No!"

"Yes. He even tried to ship us back east. I saw the boat tickets with my own eyes."

Weeping, the boy tore himself from her grasp and ran. The only reason she didn't immediately race after him was that he had headed back the way they'd come, in the direction of the orphanage.

All she had to do was follow and hope that no one with nefarious connections spotted her or Luke on the street, alone and unprotected.

She sighed. Gone was her joy in living, her sense of belonging in the city by the bay. Her childhood had been one of gladness, even before Papa Robert had married Mama, thanks to the benevolence of the Ladies' Protection Society. As an adult, however, she saw what her mother had seen. The orphanage was not a place where she would choose to stay if she had any other options. It was shelter, yes, but it would never be a real home.

Shivering, she once again folded her arms and began to trudge up the hill. In the distance, the mournful sounds of foghorns blended into a gloomy symphony that suited her mood perfectly.

Shadows were deepening, heralding a dismal end of the formerly lovely day. At the base of the hill, she heard a fuss. Men were shouting. Many were cursing at the top of their lungs, much to her dismay. What in the world could be wrong?

She heard someone shouting about the *Bulletin* and surmised that the ruckus stemmed from the shooting of its editor. Pausing to look back, she watched the crowd grow, saw torches, heard guns firing and hoped they were being shot into the air rather than into other men.

Frissons of terror gripped her as more and more people ran past her and joined the mob. She was jostled.

Shoved out of the way and off the walk into the muddy street.

Struggling to keep her balance and also dodge the passing throng, she felt herself falter. Someone gallantly righted her. She turned to offer thanks. Her jaw dropped.

Sheriff Scannell had hold of her arm and was grinning like a naughty little boy with a frog caught on his gigging fork.

"Let me go," Sara Beth demanded.

The sheriff laughed. "You're going all right. You're going with me to jail."

"Why? I haven't done anything wrong."

"Breaking into a house that belongs to the government and trying to steal gold ain't nothing, little lady. Don't try to deny it. I seen you with my own eyes."

# Chapter Twelve

"Where is she? Where has she gone?" Taylor shouted. "How could you let her leave like that?"

Ella was near tears and wringing her hands. "I didn't *let* her. She went after the boy. What could I do?"

"Which way was she headed?"

"Toward their old house, I reckon. At least that's what she said."

"All right. If I don't find her and she comes back by herself, keep her here. There's trouble brewing and I don't want her caught in it."

"What kind of trouble?"

He figured it was better to frighten the matron with the truth than to let her blunder into danger due to ignorance. "Mob justice," he said. "The Vigilance Committee is planning to issue an official proclamation and try to take this city back from the powers of corruption. In the meantime, I suspect there will be violence."

"Mercy. Miss Sara Beth might be caught in the middle."

"My conclusion exactly," the doctor said.

He dashed out the door and vaulted into his buggy.

The horse seemed to sense his anxiety. It pranced and pawed at the ground. Taylor eschewed the use of a whip in most cases, but this time he cracked it in the air above the horse's back and shouted, "Get up!"

The buggy careened out of the drive and into the street. Wagon traffic was unusually light, due, he surmised, to the turmoil closer to the city center. The number of citizens filling the wide streets multiplied as he traveled west until he could barely steer a safe path through the pedestrians.

It was all he could do to keep himself from plunging his rig into the crowd and trying to part it the way Moses had parted the Red Sea. Such a radical move was against the oath he had taken as a healer. He couldn't bring himself to chance harming anyone, yet he saw no way to get closer and hopefully locate Sara Beth if he didn't forge ahead.

Standing in the buggy, he scanned the thronging masses. His nervous horse wanted to run but he held him in check. Most of the people in the street were men. That should make finding her easier. That, and the fact that she had no hat or bonnet and therefore her reddish hair would stand out.

He was about to give up and climb down when he saw her. "Sara Beth! Over here," he shouted.

She turned her head, but instead of stopping and coming to him she continued to press on in the opposite direction.

In seconds, Taylor understood why. She was being held prisoner! Sheriff Scannell was dragging her away by the arm.

The buggy whip was in Taylor's hand. His grip tightened. Urging the horse forward, he cracked the whip repeatedly to clear a path. "Out of my way. Move," he yelled.

The tactic was successful enough to bring him within whipping distance of the sheriff. Giving no thought to his own culpability, he reached out and stung Scannell on his ear.

With a shout, the burly sheriff clapped a hand over that side of his face and raised his other arm to fend off more lashing. That was enough to give Sara Beth a chance to escape. She ran straight for the doctor's buggy.

Taylor gave her a hand up and pushed her into the seat, then flicked the whip one more time to keep Scannell occupied before he snapped the reins and gave the fractious horse its head.

"Hang on!"

"How did you find me?"

"Divine providence," Taylor shouted. "Keep your head down."

His wasn't the only rig racing through the city streets. Bedlam reigned. Women screamed. Men scuffled and cursed. Mayor Van Ness had promised that troops under Sherman would contain this trouble, but it was clear that the army didn't have nearly enough men on hand to keep the peace, no matter what orders the general gave.

As far as Taylor was concerned, that meant only one thing. The revolt had begun. And the only safe place nearby would be Vigilance Committee headquarters on Clay Street. There, a makeshift fortification was being constructed out of sandbags in preparation for standing off the troops, if necessary, not to mention the so-called Law and Order party that the sheriff represented.

"Where are we going?" Sara Beth screamed.

"The closest safe place."

"What about Luke?"

Taylor did his best to contain his fury, but he could tell she was sensing it in spite of his best efforts because she didn't argue when he looked her in the eye and said sternly, "Believe me, Luke is the least of our worries right now."

Sara Beth had never seen the city in such an uproar, not even during one of the mild earthquakes that so often shook its citizens. This was different. This sense of disaster would not abate as soon as some worrisome tremors stopped.

She hung tightly to the edge of the buggy seat and braced herself. Their trip consisted of periods of breakneck speed interspersed with zigzagging around other wagons, an occasional omnibus and men on horseback as well as people on foot. It looked as if every one of San Francisco's eight thousand citizens was on the street at the same time. Some of the Chinese had even strayed from their usual section of the city and were mingling without censure, much to her surprise.

It was as if the entire city had gone mad and she was trapped amidst the mass hysteria. Praise God that the doctor had come after her, or there was no telling what the sheriff might have done, especially since there seemed to be no real law left.

She tensed as Taylor turned onto Clay Street and reined in at an opening in a row of sandbags piled as high as a man's shoulders.

"You get off here," he said.

"Why? Where are you going?"

"To check on King and then go look for your brother."

She reached for his arm and held tight. "Please don't leave me. Not now. Not when this is happening."

"You'll be safe in there with the Vigilance Committee," Taylor told her, pointing.

Her heart gave a sharp jolt and her already speeding pulse increased as he suddenly opened his arms and drew her into his embrace. She laid her head on his shoulder. "This is all my fault. I never should have gone after Luke. I just didn't know what else to do."

"You're responsible for him. I understand why you went looking. I just wish you'd gotten off the streets before this situation exploded."

"What's going on, anyway? Why are the people so upset?"

"This has been brewing for a long time," he said. "It was the shooting of King that brought it to a head."

"Is he dead?" Sara Beth hoped it was not so because that would mean that Taylor had lost a good friend.

"Probably," he answered softly. "Either way, if Casey doesn't have to stand trial, there will be more bloodshed." He gave her a brief squeeze. "I'll be back for you as soon as I can. There may be a curfew tonight. If there is, we'll have to figure out another way to get you back to the orphanage."

He climbed down and reached for her. Sara Beth placed her hands on his shoulders and let him lift her by the waist, setting her on the walkway in front of the vigilante headquarters.

"Take care of her," he told one of the nearby men. "W.T. knows who she is and why she needs to be here."

Her eyes filled with tears and she choked back a sob as she watched her rescuer climb back into his buggy and drive off. She cared for him. Deeply. And she had never even spoken his first name aloud, let alone confessed her burgeoning affection. When Taylor returned she would do so, she vowed as the strange man took her arm and escorted her inside the building.

In her heart she couldn't help adding, *If he returned.*

Taylor located Luke hanging around the docks in the company of some older, tough-looking youths, made certain the boy was once again confined at the orphanage, then headed back to claim Sara Beth.

She greeted him with so much overt emotion he hardly knew how to respond. As she clung to him and wept, he gently enfolded her in his embrace. Was she truly so enamored of him, he wondered, or was she simply reacting to the fright she had experienced?

He didn't know, nor was he sure he should press her about it. They had only been acquainted for a few weeks and although they had worked well together, he still couldn't accept anything more. He had his work. And she had her family's welfare to consider. The little he earned from his practice wouldn't come close to supporting her and her brothers in a proper manner.

Finally, she dried her eyes on the handkerchief he offered and apologized. "I'm sorry. I was just worried sick about you."

"I'm fine. And so is your brother. I gave him another good scolding and left him under Mrs. McNeil's watchful eye. She's locked him in the boys' ward. He won't get away again."

"Oh, dear." Sniffling, she shook her head. "I'm afraid Luke will see that as a challenge and double his efforts to escape. I don't know what to do with him."

"One crisis at a time," Taylor said, taking her hand and smiling. "The mob in the street has dispersed since they heard that King is still breathing and Casey has been hauled off to jail, mostly for his own safety, I assume. Things have quieted down enough that I can drive you home."

"All right. If you say so."

"I should be angry with you, you know."

I know," Sara Beth said, averting her gaze. "But you're not, are you? Not really."

There was no way Taylor could overlook the sweetness of her smile or the blush on her fair cheeks. Her hair had become mussed during her ordeal and the loose curls made her look like an endearing moppet. "No," he said. "I'm not."

Her grin spread and her green eyes twinkled mischievously. "Good. I'd be terribly sad if you were."

"Sad enough to behave and stay safely away from the city center for a while?"

"Well…"

Her soft drawl and the way she was gazing into his eyes made him melt inside like butter on a summer's day. This amazing young woman had led a sheltered life until mere weeks ago, yet she had coped and had blossomed in spite of the trials she'd been forced to endure. Many a man would have folded under less pressure.

His gut twisted as she laughed lightly. "Don't look so worried. I promise I shall behave as well as is sensible."

"That's what worries me," he quipped. When she reached up and gently caressed his cheek his knees nearly buckled.

"Sweet, sweet man," Sara Beth said. "You are so very dear to me."

"You're just overwrought," Taylor told her. "After things settle down and we get your inheritance back, you won't feel that way."

The crestfallen look that came over her cut him to the quick and affirmed his suspicion that she was growing far too fond of him. That would never do. Once she was again part of the landed gentry of the city, she would have her choice of many suitors who could add to her holdings and support her properly.

"Is there no swain waiting for you?" he asked.

"Papa was asked for my hand in marriage recently," she said, squaring her shoulders and lifting her chin to look at him with pride. "I refused the proposal."

"Why? Was the man unsuitable?"

"I suppose not," she replied. "I simply didn't love him."

"Perhaps you should reconsider."

He could tell by the misty look in her eyes that she not only did not think his idea had merit, she was hurt by the suggestion. That meant only one thing. Sara Beth Reese had set her cap for him.

Unfortunately, that distressing conclusion also warmed his heart and made him feel even more attracted to her than he had before.

The ensuing few days seemed to creep by for Sara Beth. Tom King, James's brother, had taken over the publication of the *Bulletin* and its editorials stirred up more unrest than they had before the shooting, especially once James King passed away.

The poor man had lingered at death's door longer than anyone had imagined he would, and in the interim a tenuous peace had returned to the city. In the end, his demise was caused, as Taylor had feared, by a raging infection.

According to the current stories in the newspapers, Casey's defense attorney was claiming that the death was brought about by the improper actions of King's doctors, not by the initial shooting.

That made Sara Beth furious. She could see no way that any judge or jury would believe such nonsense. If the bullet had not been fired in the first place, there would have been no wound to get infected.

She said as much when Taylor Hayward finally returned to the orphanage. He had been conspicuously absent since she had confessed her tender feelings toward him, leading her to conclude that he did not share them as she had hoped. Nevertheless, she still wanted to assist him, so she proceeded to do so, behaving as if her heart had not been broken.

"What's the word on the Casey trial?" she asked, following him down the hall and hoping that making small talk would relieve some of the tension she felt between them.

"Nothing new. Dr. Toland took the stand and swore under oath that it was that sponge in the wound that killed King, not the shooting."

"That's a ridiculous conclusion."

"I agree," Taylor said. "Hopefully the judge will, too."

"What about my house? Now that the *Bulletin* is only concerned with the King murder, what are my chances of getting justice?"

"I don't know. Word on the street is that Bein is being investigated for a theft originally blamed only on your father. If they can pin any part of the crime on him, you should have a better chance to eventually lay claim to your property."

"What about Papa Robert's good name? I can't just stand by and let him be vilified."

"I don't see how you'd ever prove his innocence. Not unless Bein confessed and exonerated him."

"Then that's what I shall pray for," she said flatly, keeping the rest of her thoughts to herself. There had to be some way she could help, something she could do. But what? And how could she be of any use as long as she was cooped up like a prisoner in this stone fortress of a mansion?

If Taylor hadn't been so deeply involved in the Vigilance Committee, she might have petitioned them to champion her cause. As things stood, however, she was certain he would intercept her plea and tell the others that it was a hopeless situation.

Sighing, she realized that was probably a correct conclusion. It was a useless fight. She was barely old enough to be listened to, even if she had been a man, and since she was only a woman she had zero chance of being taken seriously.

*One more letter,* she decided. She would pen one more letter, this time to Tom King, and hope he listened half as well as his elder brother had. If she could tie her problems to those of the rest of the city, perhaps he would print what she had to say.

And this time she would not ask Taylor Hayward to deliver the letter. Nor would she trust Luke.

This time, she would take it to the editor herself, even if she had to wear a disguise and sneak in his back door to do so.

## Chapter Thirteen

The temporary fortification surrounding the building on Clay Street was made up of stacks of sandbags, planks, overturned wagons and anything else the vigilantes could lay their hands on. They had even managed to appropriate a cannon and place it conspicuously at the corner near Front Street, a further demonstration of their power.

Before the buttressing was half completed it had already been nicknamed "Fort Gunnybags," much to the amusement of its builders.

Some of the men involved had served in the California militia and had assisted Fremont during the Mexican War. It was they who had formed the vigilantes into platoons and marched them through the streets like regular troops.

Taylor Hayward didn't choose to train with them, but he did begin to stockpile bandages and medicine in preparation for the battle he was certain would ensue, especially since W.T.'s command had been usurped by a younger, less levelheaded man named Seymour.

It was he who brought the bad news. "It's over, boys. Time to march," Seymour shouted as he burst into the hall.

Listening, Taylor felt his blood run cold.

"Casey got off scot-free," the excited courier explained, cursing. "They ruled with Toland that it was the use of the sponge that killed James King."

As Taylor listened to the grumbling all around him it became clear that this was not going to be an occasion for negotiation. These men were irate. As long as they had each other for moral support there would be no reasoning with them. Nevertheless, he tried.

"It's the law, boys. We may not like it but it's legal."

"Only if we stand here jabbering and don't act," Seymour shouted. He raised his fist and gave a rallying cry. "Justice for our brother!"

"Justice. Justice," echoed from the walls and rattled the windows. Taylor knew better than to intercede further. Not only had he lost a great friend, San Francisco had lost a champion for true equality. He wasn't going to take part in a lynching but he wasn't fool enough to stand in the way of such a volatile throng, either.

Stepping aside, he watched the members of the Vigilance Committee crowd out the door, spill into the streets and form ranks. They could very well be marching to their deaths, yet they stepped boldly. James King had tried to clean up the city with his words. These men were determined to do so with their guns. Who was to say that either way was totally wrong? Being a pacifist had certainly not done the editor any good. Yet Taylor couldn't agree that taking the law into their own hands was right, either.

"Casey is guilty," he reminded himself, hoping that the vigilantes would at least hold another trial. A fair one. If Coleman had still been in charge that was exactly what would have happened. Unfortunately, that man's reluctance to wage war had been his undoing and he was now relegated to the background and being summarily ignored.

As Taylor climbed to the rooftop to gain a better vantage point, he was thankful that he had gotten Sara Beth out of the committee headquarters long before all this had come to a head. It was highly unlikely that the violence would spread beyond these few blocks near the city center and endanger the orphanage. Once the posse felt that justice had been served, the furor would die down. At least he hoped it would. If the riots continued long enough, Sherman might have time to join with General Wool in Benecia and actually muster enough armed men to physically put down the uprising. Then more men would die needlessly.

The ranks of armed volunteers were marching up Broadway in orderly fashion, heading toward the jail. Crowds of onlookers had already gathered in the lower streets and all the way up Telegraph Hill, as if they'd known what would occur once Casey was acquitted.

To the doctor's amazement, the scene was far less chaotic than it had been before. It was a stunning sight. The citizens may as well have been lining up to view a parade. Some waved handkerchiefs while others held bear flags of California or the Stars and Stripes.

He looked down, peering over the edge of the roof. Someone had already thrown a knotted rope across a beam that jutted from the front of the building.

It was tied in the shape of a noose.

Although Sara Beth was awed by the size of the crowd, she felt no fear. Not only was she wearing Ella's copious cloak and hood to hide her identity, these people were behaving in a far more orderly fashion than the previous mob had.

They were all moving along briskly, yet not pushing or acting angry. On the contrary, many looked relieved and expectant. She had heard that King's funeral had taken place the previous Sunday, so she couldn't imagine what would have brought all these folks into the streets at once.

Curious, she spoke to a nearby woman. "What's going on? What's happened?"

"There's gonna finally be a hangin'," the woman said, smiling. "Imagine that."

"A hanging? Today? Did they judge Casey guilty?"

"Naw. Leastwise not in court. But our brave boys will take care of that shameful mistake."

A knot of fear formed in Sara Beth's stomach. That news could mean only one thing. The law had failed and the Vigilance Committee had gone into action.

Hesitating, she stepped aside to think. If she proceeded to the newspaper office at a time like this there would probably be no one there to talk to, let alone receive her letter. All the reporters and everyone else would be in the streets, watching and waiting to see what happened.

To her dismay and disappointment she, too, wanted to watch. Perhaps it was a flaw in her character or a lack within her Christian walk, she mused. Then again, maybe she was just like everyone else. She wanted to see justice done for a change.

Looking right and left, Sara Beth realized that no one was paying the least attention to her since she'd donned that dark, worn cape and hood. Wearing it made her feel a hundred years old but she didn't care as long as it kept her safe while she was out and about.

Did she dare proceed with the others? She sighed, undecided. The sensible thing to do would be to return to the orphanage and wait for Taylor to bring news of the hanging. Would he? She had her doubts. He had been acting so distant lately she wasn't sure he'd bother to inform her, even if he were free to do so.

And he might need her help, she reasoned, her mind made up. If there were wounded, which there were likely to be, she could assist him as his nurse.

"He's definitely going to need me," Sara Beth said firmly as she stepped out and rejoined the throng. "I belong at his side."

To her chagrin she immediately remembered the promise she had made to him. She was supposed to stay out of the city. She was bound to the orphanage by her vows. If she didn't go back and do as he'd told her to, he might be very angry.

She shook her head, her lips pressed into a thin line. "No. I have to go on. Taylor needs me."

*And I need to be with him,* she added silently, ruefully. She craved the doctor's presence the way a drowning person longs for a gulp of air.

That realization shook her to the core. In the space of a few weeks he had become so much a part of her that it was impossible to banish him from her thoughts. She knew, no matter what happened, she would never be the same person she'd been before meeting him.

And in her heart of hearts she also knew that their chances of finding happiness together were slim. When the current crises were past, there would be no need for him to watch over her. And perhaps there would also be no need for her to remain at the orphanage, where she encountered him so often.

That was the saddest thing of all. Attaining her goals for herself and her brothers would mean letting go of her dreams of working with the doctor and eventually becoming a nurse—or even a full-fledged doctor. She could not hope to support a household without income. Thinking of practicing medicine had been a lovely reverie, but it was no more than that. She knew where she ultimately belonged.

Right now, however, she was needed at the Vigilance Committee headquarters. And it was there she would go. As the Good Book said, "The cares of the day are sufficient." She would worry about her future at a later date.

The crowd in the street parted to make way for a commandeered freight wagon containing the prisoners. James Casey had been liberated from the sheriff and was accompanied by a man named Charles Cora, another murderer who was awaiting retrial for killing a U.S. marshal.

Taylor had been praying silently that no innocent people would be injured and, as far as he could tell, his pleas had been answered.

The wagon stopped just outside the sandbagged fortifications and the guards admitted their fellows as well as the two prisoners.

He could hear shouting and could tell that there was a kangaroo court convening below. It didn't take long for a unanimous verdict.

"Guilty. Hang 'em," the crowd shouted.

"Where's the doc?" someone yelled. "We need him to tell us when they're good and dead."

Others disagreed loudly, much to Taylor's relief. It was his job to save life, not take it, and he didn't want any part of the hangings. Yes, he knew the men were guilty. And yes, he wanted justice. Desperately. He simply wasn't willing to dish it out without official sanction.

Turning, he started down the stairs. Others met him on the landing.

"C'mon, Doc. We're gettin' ready."

"I know. Are you sure about this?"

The vigilante sneered at him. "King was your friend. Don't you care that his murderer was gonna go free?"

"Of course I care. I'd just like to see this done lawfully, that's all. What about turning the prisoners over to the army?"

One of the men laughed and cursed, then elbowed his companion. "Let's go. He's got no stomach for justice."

*They're right in this instance,* Taylor thought as he stood there and watched them hurry back outside. *I can't believe God wants me to take a life when I've spent so many years trying to save them.*

*And speaking of saving lives, I have the orphan children to think of. They need me, too. If I'm arrested for being a part of all this, who will look after them?*

Huffing, he called himself a fool as many ways as he could think of. It wasn't the children he was truly worried about; it was one young woman. Sara Beth Reese. She was the focus of most of his concern. He needed to stay out of trouble so he could continue to work on her behalf.

With a sigh and a nod, Taylor proceeded down the

stairs. He was almost to the ground floor when he heard a commotion at the side door. One of the guards was scuffling with someone who seemed very determined to get inside.

The person was clad in a dark cloak. That alone made the hackles on the back of the doctor's neck rise. It was a warm, sunny afternoon. People were dressed for summer weather. So why would anyone wear a cape like that unless they were bent on skulking around and causing trouble?

He hurried to assist the guards. The hood fell back. Taylor's jaw dropped. "You!"

"I came to help," Sara Beth said, her cheeks rosy, her eyes bright.

"Help? You need to be locked up like your brother," Taylor said, making no attempt to hide his temper.

"Well, I'm here." She threw off the cloak and lifted her chin with obvious pride. "If you can't put me to work, then perhaps I should go back outside and see if I can assist someone else."

He took her arm, led her into an anteroom where they could talk privately and closed the door. "Do you have any idea what you've walked into? Do you? There's about to be a lynching."

"I gathered as much when I passed the men rigging the nooses. It looked as if they were planning to hang two men."

"They are. Two murderers."

"Then what's the problem?"

Frustrated and so angry he could barely remain civil, Taylor stared at her. "The problem is that vigilante justice is frowned upon by the powers that be. Every one of these men can be arrested and tried for murder, and judging by the way this city has been run so far, they're likely to be convicted."

"Surely not all of them."

"Why not? And by being here, you're an accessory to their crimes."

He saw her green eyes widen with understanding as she looked at him. "Then so are you."

"Unfortunately, yes. I tried to talk them into waiting for martial law, but they wouldn't listen."

"What about your friend Mr. Coleman? Where's he?"

"Last I heard he was still trying to regain control of his former command. I don't hold out much hope for his success. He's too mild-mannered."

"What shall we do, then?"

Taylor threw up his hands and paced away from her. "How should I know? You're the one who thinks she has all the answers."

Sara Beth nodded. She had blundered into a terrible situation and had made things worse for Taylor—and for herself. So what should she do? What could either of them do?

"I came down the hill to take one last letter to the *Bulletin*," she said. "Suppose you and I go try to deliver it? That way we'll surely have witnesses that we weren't directly involved with the hangings and you'll still be close enough to render aid if any of your friends are hurt."

She could tell by the expression on his handsome face that he was at least considering her idea. When he finally agreed, she was both relieved and thrilled. He had listened to her. He truly *did* value her opinion!

"I think I saw Tom King at the rear of the crowd directly across the street," Taylor said. "If we sneak out the back and circle around, we may be able to locate him without too much difficulty."

"And he'll swear that you and I are innocent bystanders," she added, encouraged.

"Hopefully. I don't know him as well as I knew his brother, but judging by the editorials he's been writing, he's sympathetic to our cause."

"I thought so, too. That's why I decided to write one last letter and see if I couldn't get him to speak out on my behalf. You can understand that, can't you?"

Taylor nodded slowly, pensively. "Yes. It's your timing I take exception to, not your lofty goals."

"I need to get my cloak before we go," Sara Beth said, starting for the door.

He touched her arm and stopped her. "What am I going to do with you?"

"Accept me as I am?" she said with a slight smile.

Sighing, he opened his arms and welcomed her into his embrace, holding her as if he never intended to let go.

She was thrilled. And sad. And carefree, all at the same time. In his arms was where she found more solace, more peace and more joy than anywhere else. His presence fulfilled her, uplifted her spirits beyond imagining. Given a choice, she would gladly have stood in the doctor's embrace ad infinitum.

Finally he released her, set her away and said, "I'm sorry. I shouldn't have done that."

"Yes, you should," she insisted. "Whether you like it or not, you and I are part of each other's lives. We belong together."

"Don't be ridiculous. You're just confused because

I've been trying to help you. We may be friends but there is nothing more to our relationship."

Soberly, Sara Beth shook her head. "I'm sorry to hear you say that, Taylor, because I've fallen in love with you and I don't have the slightest idea how to overcome those feelings and go back to the way things used to be before we met. Do you?"

Instead of insisting that she was wrong, he moaned and put his arms around her once again. She tilted her head back and raised her face to his.

Other young men had tried to steal a kiss in the past, but she had always managed to thwart their efforts. This time, however, she was more than ready to accept whatever Taylor chose to do. Yes, it was inappropriate. And, yes, she might be sorry later. But right now, right here, there was nothing she wanted more.

His breath was warm on her face. She closed her eyes.

And, wonder of wonders, he did kiss her.

*You're a fool,* he told himself. Yet there seemed to be nothing he could do to stop the way he felt, the way he was acting. In any other situation he would have been in total control, but not where Sara Beth Reese was concerned. She was the dearest person in his life and it was time she knew it, even though there was no chance they would be able to attain marital bliss.

The way she melted in his arms was nothing compared to the sweetness of her kiss or the surety he had that she was far from experienced in such things. That was enough to cause him to push her away, although he did keep hold of her hands.

"I should not have done that, Miss Reese. Please forgive me."

"No. I will not," she said, beginning to smile. "There is nothing to forgive. I was as much a party to what just happened as you were."

"I can tell that you do not make a practice of letting a man kiss you."

"Does that make a difference?"

"Yes," Taylor said solemnly. "It makes a great deal of difference. I would never do anything that might harm your reputation."

"Then I guess you will have to marry me," she said lightly.

"That's impossible."

"Why? I may not be as worldly as you are, but I sense that you care for me as much as I care for you. What is the problem?"

He released her, wheeled and paced away. "It's not that simple. You have no idea."

"Then enlighten me. Please?"

"I'm not ready to marry. And there's your family to consider." The moment those words were out of his mouth he was certain he had erred. "Your brothers, I mean."

Watching her expression change and harden, he knew she was hurt. Until she spoke, however, he wasn't sure why.

"My brothers? I think not. You cannot bear to risk your reputation by choosing the daughter of a man who is suspected of theft. You don't believe my father is innocent and you're worried that his supposed sins will reflect badly on you."

"Don't be ridiculous."

"Ridiculous? Hardly," she said with a catch in her voice. "I have seen how these things work. You want a wife who can bring honor and prestige to your name and your medical practice. Someone whose family can bolster your standing in San Francisco society and see to it that you draw the richest patients."

"I don't believe you're saying that." Taylor stared at her, his jaw agape. "Don't I volunteer at the orphanage?"

"Yes, and its rich patrons are exactly the kind of women whose influence will assist you in climbing the social ladder."

She wheeled and walked briskly toward the door. "I'm going to get my cloak and then go looking for Tom King. Are you coming or not?"

Taylor was so shocked he almost couldn't make his feet move. She was so wrong about him that it was almost comical. He did not aspire to that kind of life, nor was he giving of his time and expertise to gain influence among the supporters of the orphanage.

Or was he? That notion brought him instant anguish. If there was even a slight chance that Sara Beth was right, he'd have to rethink his motives until he was certain they were pure.

In the meantime, he had to follow her no matter what she thought. She needed him. It was as simple as that.

# Chapter Fourteen

Sara Beth was fighting to focus through her unshed tears. "I will not cry. I will not cry," she insisted under her breath. The press of the crowd helped distract her. She didn't know whether she was angry or sad or both. One thing was certain. She had been sorely disappointed in the one person she'd admired above all others.

Reaching the opposite side of Clay Street, she suddenly realized that she hadn't any idea what Tom King looked like. She would have recognized his brother in an instant, but unless the younger man was the spitting image of James there was no way she could be sure which of the nearby men he might be.

Taylor arrived moments later.

"Do you see him?" she asked, taking great pains to avoid actually looking at the doctor.

"I think so. Follow me."

As they weaved their way through the mass of people, Sara Beth let Taylor take the lead and shoulder a path, almost making the error of instinctively grabbing his hand to keep from being separated from him.

*What a mistake that would be!* The man already believed she was pursuing him and had made it crystal clear that he was not interested in her tender feelings. The last thing she wanted to do was to appear emotionally needy.

A roar was building. The crowd cheered. One quick glance told her that the first of the prisoners had just been hanged. He kicked for a few seconds before his body went limp.

Bitter gorge rose in Sara Beth's throat. How could she have ever imagined that she'd want to witness such a horrid spectacle? A life had ended. The crowd should be mourning the possible loss of the killer's eternal soul, not celebrating his death.

Taylor's voice drew her back to the task at hand. "This is Tom King," he said. "Tom, I'd like you to meet Miss Reese. She was acquainted with your late brother."

Looking up at the taller man, Sara Beth was surprised at how young he seemed. She smiled as he tipped his hat. "How do you do, Mr. King?"

"Fine, thank you. Especially now," the slim, sharply-dressed editor said, inclining his head toward the scene of the execution. "How may I help you, Miss Reese?"

She produced the letter she had written and solemnly handed it to him. "This will explain everything. Your brother had already broached the subject of the troubles connected with my home and family before his passing. I trust you will see how my dilemma coincides with the articles you have printed of late."

"Indeed?"

"Yes. If you have any questions, feel free to call upon me. I'm staying at the Ladies' Protection and Relief Society home on Franklin Street."

The editor touched the brim of his hat with the folded letter. "I look forward to reading this," he said.

Before she could respond, Taylor interrupted. "Don't print your source, whatever you do."

With a snort, Tom King shook his head. "No promises. I will write whatever seems best for my paper and for San Francisco."

Sobering, Sara Beth laid her hand lightly on the man's sleeve. "Do what you must. There are already evil forces set against me. God will be my refuge."

"I trust He will," King answered. "If you're staying in town to watch the rest of this spectacle, perhaps we can talk more later."

"Sorry, no," she said firmly. "I'm not needed here and I have chores waiting at the orphanage." Although that was not exactly true, she hoped the Lord would forgive her exaggeration. There were always jobs that needed doing at the home and she was adept at most of them. There would be plenty to keep her occupied. And by leaving, she would no longer have to face Taylor Hayward and see the rejection in his expression.

The way she viewed her situation, the less she had to do with the doctor from now on, the better.

In her deepest heart, however, she felt as if she herself had just died. Her spirit certainly had.

There was nothing more that Taylor could say. He'd already said far too much, and in the wrong way. The best thing to do at this point, he reasoned, was to let Sara Beth cool off before he tried to explain further.

"Do you want me to see you home?" he asked as they elbowed their way to the fringes of the throng.

"That will not be necessary." Her chin jutted out and

her lips were pressed into a thin line. "I managed to get here by myself. I can get home as well."

"I'd offer to drive you, but my buggy is at the livery. I was afraid the horse might spook if there was a lot of shooting."

"Do you think there will be?"

"Probably not now. Later, if the army tries to capture our headquarters, perhaps. That was why I didn't want you to be there."

"Of course." Her voice was flat, almost expressionless, as if she was merely reciting words rather than feeling them.

"How will I know you're safe if I don't come along?"

"Suit yourself," Sara Beth said. "If you believe you need to establish further proof that you were not involved in the lynching, then accompany me. I'm sure Mrs. McNeil will gladly vouch for your integrity."

Taylor opened his mouth to refute her opinion of him, then closed it without speaking. When Sara Beth was in a mood like this there was little chance she'd be swayed by any explanation. Not that he knew what he should ultimately say. If he became too apologetic, she might think it was because he actually did want to court her. If he was too matter-of-fact, she'd assume he wasn't fond of her at all.

Sadly, that would be a blatant untruth. He did care. More than he could put into words. And he did want to marry her despite everything. It was only for her sake and the sake of her brothers that he would hold his tongue and encourage her to look for a husband who was more able to give her the finer things in life, like a home and expensive clothes and maybe even her own town buggy. That was the kind of easy life Sara Beth deserved. The life of a lady.

Sighing, he stayed several paces behind as he followed her. The sway of her cape hid her from view, but his imagination still saw her as clearly as ever. Her reddish hair was silky as a kitten's fur, her complexion clear and fair, her eyes bright like precious emeralds. The dusting of freckles across the bridge of her nose was icing on the cake. She was, she was… *Perfect,* his thoughts insisted. Taylor didn't argue. He knew it was true.

*Okay, I love her,* he finally admitted. *And she hates me because she thinks I'm ashamed of her family.* If she continued to believe that, perhaps she'd be more likely to seek a more suitable husband.

That notion stuck in his throat and left a bad taste in his mouth. Unless he or Sara Beth Reese left San Francisco and went somewhere where they'd never encounter each other again, he was liable to spend the rest of his life in agony. Every time they accidentally met on the street or, heaven forbid, she came to him for medical treatment, he'd suffer this sense of loss all over again.

There was only one honorable thing to do, one course to plot for himself. As soon as her estate was properly settled he'd board a steamer—any steamer—and leave the city.

Where he would go was unimportant. Escaping was the only way to cope. His heart insisted.

It wasn't the trudge up the hill that had tired Sara Beth so much. It was the knowledge that Taylor Hayward had remained so close by the whole time—near enough to turn and touch.

She didn't do so, of course. She had her pride. And she had grown so weary of doing battle with her emotions she'd simply shut them down as best she could. That had left her worn and weary and dreadfully demoralized but it had still been better than weeping and throwing herself at the poor man the way she'd yearned to.

Unfortunately, now that he had taken his leave, she couldn't seem to concentrate enough to complete any task. Clara had gotten so frustrated with her that she'd sent her out of the kitchen and told her to sweep the porches. Even that seemed beyond Sara Beth's current capabilities. When she had turned to admire her efforts she had realized what a poor job she'd done.

"I can't even wield a broom anymore," she muttered, thoroughly disgusted with herself. "I hope my talent with a pen is better than my household skills these days."

She'd wanted to linger downtown until the new editor had had a chance to look over her letter. If the doctor had not insisted on standing right there, she might have done so. However, since she'd had to struggle so hard to control her emotions in his presence, she had decided that heading home was the wisest choice. At least that way if she lost control and burst into tears, she'd be doing it where no one could see her suffering. Especially not Taylor.

Plopping into a chair on the porch, she released a sigh and waited for the tears to start flowing. They did not. Instead of weeping as she had expected, she simply felt empty, as if all her emotions had vanished into the fog that was now rising up from the bay. Soon the lush gardens would be shrouded in mist and the setting sun would be hidden. That kind of weather was the main reason why San Francisco remained so temperate year-round, and it suited her current mood perfectly.

Sara Beth felt as colorless as the dreary day, as cold as the fog in winter, as bereft as the mournful cries of the gulls. At this moment, she didn't care about anything. Not herself, not her stolen estate, not anything. Her heart was as icy as the wind that was rising off the sea and chilling her to the bone.

Shivering, she wrapped her arms around herself and went back inside, determined to think about something uplifting. To seek out company.

The first person who came to mind was baby Josiah. She had made it a point to visit with him in the nursery as often as possible and show him plenty of love. In another year he'd be old enough to join the other boys in the regular wards and then it would be much easier for her to keep track of his welfare.

*In another year?* Sara Beth shivered. Would she still be living here then? Most likely. And although Mathias could also remain there with her, it would be past the time when Luke had to leave because he was too old. Poor Luke. What would become of him? How would he survive on the streets? And how, dear Lord, was she going to see that he grew into a fine man like Papa Robert?

Seeking solace, she decided to gather all her brothers and talk to them. The older ones would be comforted by her efforts on behalf of the family. And having them all together would be a mutual morale boost. At least she hoped it would.

"Are you sure the Reese boy understands what to do?" Bein asked. "We have to hurry. I'm expecting to be arrested any moment and once that happens I may not be able to pay you—or your men—easily."

Scannell nodded. "It's all set. When we get his signal it means he's ready to open the door and let one of his so-called friends inside."

"There won't be any slipups? You're certain?"

"Positive. I arranged for him to get involved with a local gang that listens to me. He trusts them."

"Are they old enough to carry out your orders?"

"The young man I'm sending is. I have plenty on him already. He'll do whatever I say because he knows he'll rot in jail if he fails."

"Even murder?" Bein was smirking.

"It won't be his first killing," Scannell replied with a wry chuckle. "That's why I know he'll cooperate."

"All right. Then get it over with so I don't have to worry about that irksome girl stirring up more trouble. I can handle everything else, just as I've planned, as long as there are no witnesses to testify against me."

"What about Harazthy?"

"I plan to sacrifice him under the wheels of the ore wagon, so to speak. After all, he's in charge of the mint operations and the late, lamented Robert Reese was his chief assayer. They can both take the blame."

Bein paused and cursed under his breath. "I don't care what I have to do. I am *not* going to prison."

Taylor was surprised to find that the crowds had dispersed quickly after the hangings. He had expected more celebrating and violence. Down by the docks there was a rowdy atmosphere, of course, but that was normal.

He decided to end his usual evening patient rounds at

Abe Warner's Cobweb Palace. He didn't often frequent that place, or any like it. It was information in the form of gossip that he sought and he was not disappointed.

"Yup, I heard plenty," Abe said, grinning behind his silvery beard and mustache. "That Vigilance Committee is sure kickin' up its heels."

"I meant about the Reese family," Taylor said. "What's the word on the street regarding the investigation of theft from the mint?"

"Not much is new." The old man tilted his trademark top hat back by poking the brim with one gnarled finger. "Government men are all over the city, snoopin' into things that don't concern 'em. You know how it is."

"I'm afraid I do. Have they found any evidence besides those bits of scrap gold that were discovered at Reese's place?"

"I'm thinkin' yes. Leastwise, that's how it looks to me. Last I heard, they were fixin' to arrest his partner."

That news made Taylor's heart race and his breathing quicken. He grabbed the old man's forearm. "William Bein? The man who's trying to steal Sara Beth's house?"

Abe chuckled and winked at his companion. "The very same. Now, suppose you tell me a few things."

"Such as?" Taylor didn't like the twinkle in the old man's eyes or the lift of his mouth, especially since he assumed the amusement was a result of his questions.

"Such as, since when does a gentleman like you call a lady by her first name? What's been goin' on up at that orphanage, anyways?"

"Nothing illicit or immoral," the doctor answered soberly. "I have, however, become far too attached to Miss Reese."

"You could do worse. She's a mite comely little thing. Smart, too."

"I know."

"Then why the long face? She turn you down?"

"No. There was no proposal to turn down. I've told her she'd be wise to find a suitable swain and marry well, for the sake of her brothers and her estate."

"That why you're so all-fired determined to get that house back for her?"

"That's part of it, yes. The property is rightfully theirs and Bein's claim to it is not honorable, even if it may be legal."

"That still don't explain why you ain't interested in courtin' her. Does she like you?"

"Apparently. We get along fine. That's not the problem. There's simply no way a man in my position can adequately provide for her and her brothers." He made a derisive noise in his throat. "I'm lucky to collect enough fees to keep my office rent paid, let alone establish a home and start a family."

"You tell her that, did you?"

"Yes. Of course."

"In so many words?"

Taylor shrugged and arched his eyebrows. "I don't recall exactly what I said. I do know that she mistakenly assumed I was hesitant because of her father's tarnished reputation."

"Were you?"

"Of course not! I hadn't even considered that until she got upset and brought it up."

Abe began to laugh. "Sounds to me like a couple of children squabbling over a toy."

"I hardly consider affairs of the heart to be childish,"

Taylor countered. "I truly do care for her. I just refuse to saddle her with a husband who cannot properly provide for her and her family."

Sobering and getting a wistful look in his rheumy old eyes, Abe sighed audibly. "I had a gal once. A pretty one she was, too. Man, could she cook."

"I didn't know you'd ever been married."

"I haven't. That's what I'm tryin' to tell you. I wanted to sow my wild oats before I settled down, so I put to sea for a couple of years. When I came back, she'd got tired of waitin' and married another man." He gestured at the cluttered, crowded saloon. "Since then, it's been just me and this place and my menagerie."

"Surely you've had other opportunities to find a wife. This city has far more men than women, but still…"

"Never wanted any other gal," Abe said flatly. "Once you've tasted a rare steak, you don't want to settle for a pot of cold mush."

That analogy struck Taylor funny. He chuckled. "Believe me, I'm simply trying to do what's best for Miss Reese and her family."

"Then tell her so and let her make up her own mind. Because if you don't, you may never find another woman who takes your fancy the way that one has."

In his heart, Taylor knew Abe was right. His conscience, however, put up such a strong fight that he was at a loss as to which course to take.

Finally, he left the Cobweb Palace and stood on the boardwalk outside, listening to the foghorns in the distance and peering, unseeing, into the mist that was rolling in off the bay like waves of seawater at high tide.

The musty salt air smelled of all the sundry things that made the wharf a successful business enterprise, including the garbage from numerous restaurants and the offal from the fishing boats moored nearby.

There was blurred movement within the mist from time to time. Groups of men talked or laughed or cursed as they passed by. Some revelers were already so drunk they could hardly stand. Others were sneaking around as if waiting to lift purses from hapless sots and pitch their victims off the docks into the drink if they dared resist.

Taylor huffed. Half his patients would be suffering from combat wounds or hangovers after this weekend, not to mention the dangerous days to come. The worst was not over. Until the official law became trustworthy, no one would really be safe.

Suddenly, all he could think about was seeing Sara Beth again. Making sure she was all right. Telling her how he truly felt.

And if he bared his soul and she rejected him? Then he would consider her choice to be directed by the Heavenly Father they both worshipped and would stop dreaming of a happy time when they could be together.

Could he end those dreams by sheer force of will? He doubted it. Oh, he might be able to bid her a polite farewell and walk away, but his heart would be as scarred for life as old Abe Warner's.

Taylor realized he was as smitten as a schoolboy with his first crush and as committed as an old man who had spent a lifetime devoted to the same woman. If he and Sara Beth did not somehow find the path to marital bliss, he did not know how he would survive. The more he thought about her, the more he came to realize that she was the only one for him.

He didn't know how he could possibly toil any harder

than he already was, but he would find a way. He'd scrimp and save and hoard every spare penny until he was able to offer her a real home.

Would she wait? he wondered. Abe's beloved had not done so, yet perhaps that was because Abe had gone to sea. Taylor intended to stay right here where he could keep an eye on Sara Beth. Keep her safe.

Pondering such things, he shivered and started to walk briskly toward Franklin Street. The urge to see and talk to her—to confess his love—was so intense, so demanding, he almost broke into a run.

## Chapter Fifteen

The temblor began as Sara Beth was assembling her brothers in the otherwise empty parlor. It shook the sturdy house briefly, causing the teardrop crystal pendants on the kerosene lamp bases to sway in unison and the fringe on the silk piano scarf to ripple.

Already bouncing on Sara Beth's knees, Josiah paid the shaking no mind, but both Mathias and Luke looked to their sister.

"It's nothing," she assured them. "I can't count the number of earthquakes I've noticed in the nearly eighteen years I've lived around here. Pay it no mind."

She continued bouncing the two-year-old on her lap and grinning at him while the older boys sat on the floor at her feet. "What I wanted to talk about is our plans for the future."

To her delight, Mathias's eyes widened expectantly. Luke, however, started to frown.

"Hear me out, please," Sara Beth said firmly. "I have been writing to the newspapers in the hopes their editorials will embarrass Uncle William enough to make him do right by us."

"He'd help us if you'd ask him nice and polite," Luke muttered.

"No. He would not." Sara Beth concentrated on her oldest brother while speaking to include them all. "William Bein has laid claim to Papa Robert's estate by virtue of their business partnership and refuses to listen to reason. He wants it all. He has told me this directly to my face."

Tears glistened in Mathias's eyes. She reached down to pat him on the head. "Don't worry, darling. As long as we have each other, we'll be fine. And I promise I'll keep us all together, somehow, no matter what I have to do."

"That's okay for you," Luke countered in a squeaky, breaking voice. "I'm the one who's gonna be pitched out into the streets any minute."

"We can work something out to stop that from happening. I know we can," she insisted. "All I'm asking is that you boys be patient and give me a chance. Mrs. McNeil has allowed us all to stay in spite of the rules against keeping boys once they've reached Luke's age. I don't really qualify either, since I'm not your mama."

"See?" Luke looked as if he was about to cry.

"Don't fret. I know she's not going to make us do anything else for a while."

"Yeah, right." Sniffling, the eleven-year-old scrambled to his feet and stormed out of the room.

Sara Beth chose to let him go and concentrate on her other siblings. She hugged the toddler close. "Don't worry about him, boys. Luke is just having trouble adjusting to living here. He'll get better as time passes."

*At least, I hope he will,* she added to herself. Luke's attitude troubled her greatly. He had always been the willing one, the sensible brother. Mathias had been the imp. And Josiah? He was his usual, cheerful, cherubic self, ever ready to grin and always eager to be held and babied.

That would change with age, of course. Luke had been a wonderfully sweet babe. So had Mathias, when he wasn't squalling for food or demanding more attention.

Thinking back on the boys' childhoods, she was struck that she had often played the part of their mother while Mama was busy with other chores. There had been times when it had seemed burdensome to do so, but in retrospect it had been for the best. She desperately needed her brothers to accept her authority.

Especially Luke.

Especially now.

Luke lit a candle and moved its flame across in front of the glass of a rear window. Then he waited.

The knock on the kitchen side door was so faint he would have missed hearing it if he had not been standing right there. His palms were clammy. He wiped first one, then the other on his pants before he held the candle high and reached for the latch.

"Who—who is it?"

"You know."

He did. And he was prepared to do anything he had to in order to fit in with the older boys who held his shaky future in their hands. There was nothing left for him but a life on the streets and he knew it.

Easing open the door, he admitted the shabbily dressed young man, noting as he passed that there was a foul, dank odor about him.

Everything stunk in his life, including his friends,

Luke mused, disgusted. Papa had always preached honesty and Mama cleanliness and Godliness. What good had that done them?

"Where is everybody?" the interloper asked.

"Mostly in bed. My sister was in the parlor with my brothers last time I saw her so you should probably start in one of the other rooms."

"Start?"

"Stealing stuff," Luke said, frowning with puzzlement.

"Right. Stealing." He shrugged. "Forgot to bring a sack. Think you can scrounge me one? Pillowcases are good."

"Sure. Wait here. I'll be right back."

"Take your time," the would-be assassin said as the younger boy shielded the flickering candle with his cupped hand and left the kitchen. "Take all the time you need."

He inched closer to the hallway Luke had entered. He wasn't sure of the layout of the house, but he had a rough idea from talking to a few previous residents. That should suffice.

Pausing, he looked left, then right, letting his eyes adjust to the dimness. He'd begin where Luke had last seen his sister. And if she wasn't in the parlor, he'd come back to the kitchen and wait for her stupid brother to lead him straight to her. If luck was with him, he'd be finished and gone before anybody else even realized he'd been there.

He opened the small knife he had concealed in his hand and stepped forward.

Taylor had arrived on the grounds of the orphanage just as the moon was rising. Its reflection off the mist appeared to thicken the atmosphere until he could barely distinguish the house, let alone see well enough to tell what was going on inside.

He'd intended simply to knock on the front door and ask to speak with Sara Beth, but no lights continued to burn. That was a problem. Assuming the matron and her staff were already abed, his social call would seem quite odd.

Being thought inconsiderate was the last thing he wanted. If he hoped to eventually win over Sara Beth, he would need Mrs. McNeil's support as well as the goodwill of sensible matrons like Clara and Mattie. Rousing the household after all the lights were out was not the way to make a favorable impression.

Hesitating, he tried to decide how best to proceed. It wasn't that he believed that Sara Beth was in danger the way she had been earlier, he assured himself, yet there was a nagging insistence in the back of his mind that he must speak with her. *Tonight.* His mission would not wait till tomorrow. His heart would not let it.

The closer he got to the house, the more sinister and shadowy it appeared, giving him pause. That was an unnerving, totally abnormal reaction, particularly considering all the times he'd been summoned to the bedside of a sick child during the night and had responded to that call without a twinge of apprehension.

"Guess I'm a lot more overwrought than I thought," he whispered into the mist, mostly to hear his own voice.

"I'm also standing here babbling to myself," he added, beginning to smile and shake his head. "What would my patients think if they could see me now?"

*That I'm praying,* Taylor said, deciding easily that

that was exactly what he should have been doing all along. When he momentarily closed his eyes and attempted to talk to God, all he was able to do was picture the love of his life and worry about her safety.

He managed a heartfelt, "Bless her and keep her, Father," before he gave up entirely and moved on.

Slowly circling the house, he kept an eye open for any indication that someone was still up. A lighted candle moved near one of the rear windows. Perhaps a child had taken sick and Sara Beth was fetching a dose of tonic?

The same candle cast a sliver of light into the swirling fog as the door was opened. A shadowy figure, not too large, passed in front of the flame and quickly slipped inside the building.

Taylor froze, his heart in his throat, his mouth suddenly dry. It wasn't the presence of someone at the door, or the fact that they were being admitted that bothered him. It was the stealth of movement and the obvious sense that one or more people did not want to be seen entering.

His pulse pounded in his temples. Sara Beth was inside that house. And now, so was someone who most likely did not belong there.

That was enough for him. He jogged up to the same portal, intending to demand admittance. He didn't have to. The door was not only unlocked, it stood ajar.

Taylor pushed it open and stepped inside.

The hair on the back of his neck prickled. Something was terribly wrong.

For Sara Beth, the evening had been nearly as tedious as the entire day. She was exhausted, yet she'd taken the time to walk Mathias back to his bed before returning sleepy Josiah to the nursery. Thankfully, both boys had behaved beautifully. She was not up to an argument after Luke's tantrum. What bothered her most was the chance that his bad attitude might influence Mathias.

Well, that couldn't be helped. Considering all the other boys who lived there, Luke's problems were truly insignificant. Not to him, of course, but given the rigors of surviving on the streets or going to bed hungry night after night, Luke had led a blessedly easy life. If only she could make him realize it.

"Father, help me," Sara Beth said as she lifted the kerosene lamp in one hand, her skirts in the other, and started up the staircase to bed.

A sudden shimmying of the pendants drew her attention to the lamp. The liquid fuel inside the glass base was trembling as if she had just shaken it. Only she had not.

She released her skirt and grabbed the banister for balance. There was a low, sustained rumble, as if the house was protesting being disturbed.

Waiting, she listened. In seconds, the noise of a few whimpering, frightened children was all she could hear. The earthquake was over quickly, as usual.

This spate of shaking had seemed harder and a bit more sustained, yet she doubted that there was anything to worry about. After all, the city experienced so many earthquakes that only the worst were even mentioned in the newspapers, and then only if there was no other interesting news to print that same   day.

The last big temblor of any note had caused a few fires, however, so Sara Beth doused her lamp for safety. Better to eliminate the chance of a catastrophe than to accidentally drop the glass lamp and perhaps set the whole orphanage ablaze.

That thought gave her the shivers. So did being alone in the dark. Her vision adjusted slowly. She could discern little more than fuzzy shadows of the stairway and its newel posts. That was enough to allow her to proceed.

She took each step with caution, hiking a bit of skirt in the same hand as the dark lamp, leaving her other hand free to grasp the banister in case she lost her footing. The path up the stairs was as recognizable to her as the rest of the enormous house, yet she still took her time, slowly counting each step.

"Seventeen, eighteen, nineteen," she murmured, coming to the landing. Something made her pause there. Listen. Tense. "Luke? Is that you?"

Silence and darkness enveloped her. The atmosphere seemed suddenly dank, as if the whole house was in desperate need of airing. "Luke?"

When she held her breath and waited for a reply, she thought she heard someone else breathing. Panting. The stairs below her gave a familiar creak. Which riser always did that? Number four or five, if she remembered correctly. That meant that whoever was sneaking up behind her still had a ways to go. If she fled…

Whirling, Sara Beth raced up the last tier of the stairway as though she could see clearly. She tripped, regained her footing and continued. As soon as she reached the second floor she thrust the unlit lamp into a corner to keep it safe from an accidental spill, grabbed her skirt in both hands and ran for all she was worth.

She rushed past the rooms where others slept, thinking of sleeping innocents within. Instead of taking immediate refuge, she headed straight for the door leading to the old servants' quarters at the end of the hall. Her hand closed on the brass knob. It turned!

The narrow door gave with a noisy squeak of its hinges. "Unlocked. Thank You, God," she whispered, jerking it all the way open and pivoting through so she could slam and lock it behind her.

It wouldn't close tight! Sara Beth panicked and slammed it again. The bang of the wood smacking the door frame echoed hollowly, sounding muted as if...

A tug on her skirt told her all she needed to know. She eased her grip enough to extricate her clothing from the space and jerked the door closed again, just as someone crashed into it from the opposite side.

Sara Beth staggered. "No!" she screeched. "No."

Her heels were hard against the hidden stairway that led to the servants' quarters. She gripped the inside knob with both hands and pulled as hard as she could.

She felt the tarnished brass orb start to turn, then stop. Was she safe? Had it really been that easy?

Moments later she realized that whoever had been outside the door had ceased trying to gain entrance to her hiding place. Nevertheless, she continued to hold tight to the knob, waiting for another attempt.

None came. Quiet descended. All she could hear was the sound of her own heavy breathing and the pounding of her heart.

This was too easy. Too unbelievable. Perhaps her imagination had simply been working overtime and no one was actually out there. Or maybe Luke was playing a very unfunny joke to get even for whatever supposed slights she had committed.

She relaxed enough to press her ear to the door. "Luke? Is that you? Because if it is, I am not amused."

Someone chuckled. Someone whose voice was unfamiliar.

Although Sara Beth recoiled, she kept her hands on the knob. She didn't know how long her strength would prevail, but she was not going to let go and simply give a stranger the upper hand. No, sir. Not her. She had been through enough in the past weeks to prove her mettle, at least to her own satisfaction, and she was not a quitter.

On the other side of the door the soft, snide laughing continued. It would fade for a few seconds, then return. Something hard banged against the door, startling her.

"Please, God," she prayed aloud, "help me keep this closed."

"You won't have any trouble doing that," the voice in the hallway said. "Matter of fact, I'd like to see you try to open it."

It was a trick. It had to be.

"No way. Leave me alone."

"Gladly," her pursuer said. "I'm done here." He chortled with sinister glee. "Well, almost, anyways."

The voice sounded young to Sara Beth, perhaps a bit older than Luke, but not nearly as mature as Taylor. Meaning that she may have surprised one of the other boys, or a former resident, and he had merely reacted the way any misbehaving child might. He had tried to frighten her so she wouldn't tell Mrs. McNeil that he'd been prowling around at night when he shouldn't have been.

Beginning to catch her breath and calm down, she nevertheless delayed leaving the stairway alcove. It was dark as a tomb in there, yet comforting enough that she had no problem convincing herself to wait a little longer before venturing out. A few more minutes would suffice. And then she would do what was right, even if Luke had been involved in the prank. She would tell Ella everything.

She sighed. Poor Luke. Everything he did seemed to turn out badly. That was partly because of his disobedience, of course. That, and his hostile attitude. It was no wonder he hadn't made friends there the way she and Mathias had. Luke was not the kind of boon companion anyone would want—except perhaps one of the ruffians who hung around the wharf and begged for food or stole what he needed.

"That must never happen to Luke," Sara Beth told herself. "He deserves the kind of life he would have had if Papa and Mama were here."

Only they weren't. She was all the parent her brothers had left and she was sorely lacking, especially in matters of finances.

"Well, one problem at a time," she said, placing her hand on the knob and slowly starting to turn it.

The brass knob moved, as expected, but the door did not budge. She tried again. Still it refused to open. She pushed her shoulder against it. The wood rattled, only giving a fraction of an inch.

Wide-eyed, Sara Beth stared into the blackness. It couldn't be locked, could it? She felt for a keyhole and found none. Therefore, there had to be another reason why she was apparently trapped in the stairwell.

*Of course!* That unusual banging noise she had heard would explain everything. Someone had crammed the wooden back of a chair from the hallway under the knob. That was what was interfering with the door's path.

She sank back on the lower steps and just sat there, thinking. If she raised a ruckus someone would surely hear, eventually, and rescue her. Shouting was a great idea—as long as her original pursuer was truly gone.

And as long as he was as innocent as she had imagined, she added. The notion that there might be real danger lurking in a place like this would never have occurred to her a few weeks ago. Now, however, she seemed to be seeing bogeymen behind every velvet drape and inside every ward.

"That is preposterous," Sara Beth insisted aloud. "Patently false. I am as safe here as I was in my own home."

Shivers shot up her spine when she pictured that home and the man who now laid claim to it. Panic began to well up within her and cause her to tremble.

She grabbed the knob and shook the barred door as hard as she could. It was only then that she realized there was more shaking going on than what she was causing. San Francisco was having another earthquake.

And this one was no trifle.

## *Chapter Sixteen*

Taylor would have called out a greeting as he entered the orphanage if he hadn't been relatively certain mischief was afoot. Truth to tell, he hoped that that was all it was. Given the events of late, there was no telling what was actually going on inside the dark house.

He knew the floor plan by heart, making it easy for him to wend his way through the kitchen and check out the other rooms on the ground floor. Nothing seemed amiss until he rounded a corner into the hall and ran smack into someone.

Instinct made him grab for the smaller figure. "Whoa. Hold on. I'm not going to hurt you," Taylor assured him. "What's going on?"

"None of your business," the boy said, struggling to free himself.

Taylor was certain he recognized that voice. "Settle down, Luke. All I want to know is why you're up and about when everybody else seems to have gone to bed."

"Let me go."

"Not until you talk to me." He hesitated, bracing

himself as he felt a tremor beneath his feet. "Did the earthquakes scare you? Is that it?"

"Uh, right."

"Where's your sister?"

"How should I know? It's not my job to take care of her."

Although Taylor couldn't see the boy's face as more than a shadow, he could hear the contempt in his tone. "You should be thankful she doesn't feel that way about you."

"I don't care. I can take care of myself."

With that, Luke gave a quick jerk and managed to twist out of Taylor's grip. In an instant he had ducked beneath the doctor's outstretched arms and fled.

Something white on the floor at his feet caught Taylor's attention. He bent and picked it up. It was an empty pillowcase.

Puzzlement quickly gave way to anger. Evidently, Luke had been planning to fill the linen bag with booty and then leave the orphanage, just as many unmanageable boys had done in the past. It took a special kind of person, a truly forgiving soul, to keep the doors of the home open to all those in need when so many took advantage of the kindness.

Troubled by his conclusions, Taylor sighed. He would have to inform the matron, of course, and then tell Sara Beth. Such painful honesty would probably do his personal cause little good, but he had no choice. If the boy was on the wrong path it was up to them all to try to turn him around.

He smiled slightly. His own youth had not exactly been misspent, but he had come close to making a few bad decisions, for which he would still be paying if a kindly church deacon had not befriended him. There was hope for Luke. Especially if they could keep him from taking that first step into a life of crime.

Fisting the pillowcase, Taylor started up the stairs. He would rouse some of the adults within the household and enlist their help in searching for Luke and trying to talk sense into him. Perhaps Mrs. McNeil would also notify Sara Beth. No matter what else occurred, Taylor was determined to follow through on his plans to speak with her. To ask her to consider him as a beau.

If he had been paying more attention to his path instead of musing about Sara Beth, he might have avoided a collision with another person galloping down the stairs.

The wiry youth crashed into Taylor's shoulder as he bolted past, almost knocking him off his feet.

"Hey! Watch out," the doctor shouted, wheeling and grabbing the banister.

The youth didn't slow. Nor did he answer except to curse colorfully. Taylor didn't recognize his voice or his stature, although there were a few residents who may have been nearly that tall. In the dark and on the stairway, it was hard to judge size accurately.

Pausing to stare after the fleeing figure, he had decided to return to the kitchen for a candle or a lamp when he noticed a faint glow coming from the upper story. Was someone else awake after all?

Light reflection moved and increased as he watched, beginning to shimmer on the walls and ceiling. It looked like the effects of a lamp, yet…

He sniffed as the air began to thicken. *Smoke?* His heart leaped. For a few seconds he was speechless.

Then, he recovered enough to begin to run up the stairs, two at a time.

His eyes burned and watered. The most important task was rousing the household and getting everyone out. He made a fist and started down the hall, banging on each bedroom door in turn and shouting, *"Fire!"*

Sara Beth had not wasted time pushing on the blocked door. Instead, she had followed the closed-in stairway with the hope of finding an alternate exit.

The abandoned servants' quarters at the top of the stairs were stuffy. One window at the end of the narrow attic room admitted just enough moonlight to allow her to see shadows and shapes in spite of the fog.

Arms extended, she cautiously worked her way around the room, sliding her feet along the dusty floor so she wouldn't trip. There was a table, a bedstead and a rickety ladder-back chair, which she found the hard way by almost falling over it. Other than that, the place seemed totally abandoned.

Thankfully, its small dimensions allowed her to quickly examine the wainscoted walls, looking for an exterior door. At this point she didn't care where it led as long as it eventually brought freedom.

The moment she touched the edge of the jamb and realized she'd found what she'd sought, she reacted with thankfulness. Unshed tears welled.

She kept repeating, "Praise the Lord," while her fingers explored the rectangular jamb. Like the entrance from which she had emerged, this portal was narrow and fitted with a brass knob.

She grabbed it. Twisted. Unfortunately, this door remained firmly in place. "No, no, no," she whispered. "Please, Jesus, let me get out."

Still exploring by touch, Sara Beth found that this door, unlike the one at the bottom of the stairs, did have a keyhole. To her dismay, however, there was no key in evidence.

Dropping onto her hands and knees she began to feel along the dusty floor, hoping against hope that a key had simply fallen out and was lying there waiting for her to pick it up. There was nothing but dirt.

Frustrated, she huffed in self-disgust. This was a fine kettle of fish, wasn't it? Morning might come before anyone missed her, let alone heard her cries for help and either located the right key with which to let her out or removed the chair from the door on the floor below.

"Well, at least if I can't get out, no one can get in this way to harm me," she told herself, starting to worry more about the others in the mansion, especially the innocent children, and realizing that there wasn't a thing she could do about it.

Looking for diversion, she edged carefully toward the narrow window and gazed at the city below. Normally, with the weather as foggy as this, she would not have been able to see much.

Her hand flew to her throat. Not only could she see plenty, she could tell that this most recent quake had done the same thing that had happened in the past. It had started fires.

She could only spot two places aglow through the thick, moist air, but there might be more. There probably were. And that meant that the volunteer fire brigades would be out in force, risking their own well-being while trying to save life and property.

Prayer was her only recourse, the only way she could hope to help. She folded her hands and closed her eyes. "Please, Father, help them. Help them all. And keep the firemen safe from harm, too."

Her prayer then expanded to include her friends and family, especially Taylor Hayward. He would undoubtedly be out and about, too, offering care and doing all he could to ease suffering. That was the kind of man he was. Stalwart. Sacrificing. Admirable beyond words.

"And I love him, Father," Sara Beth said aloud. "He's ashamed of my family but I can't help myself. I love him so much it hurts. I just don't know how to stop myself."

Opening her eyes, she caught a glimpse of white objects moving on the lawn below like tiny flower petals blowing in the wind. Nightshirts? Yes! Lots of them. Myriad children were scurrying around the expansive gardens and it looked as if plenty of adults were with them, shooing them hither and yon like gaggles of geese.

Had there been earthquake damage to this building, too? she wondered. It seemed sturdy enough to her. Then again, she wasn't privy to the whole structure.

It suddenly occurred to her that this had been the answer to her prayer for the children. As long as they were awake and in the company of their caretakers, they would be safer than sleeping in their beds with a stranger prowling the halls.

And, perhaps, when all the excitement from the shaking died down, someone would miss her and start a search.

She smiled. Maybe, since God was already answering her pleas, the person who came looking for her would be Taylor Hayward! There was no one she would rather it be. She could hardly wait.

"Where are the Reese boys?" the doctor shouted. "I don't see them."

Mrs. McNeil pointed. "Over there. With their ward caretakers. We got everybody out safely, thanks to you."

"What about the baby?"

"The people from the nursery are all out in the back garden. I'm sure he's fine."

"What about Sara Beth?"

The matron's eyes saucered. "I don't know. She must be here somewhere. She's probably helping with the littlest ones. I know the staff checked each ward carefully before leaving."

Taylor wasn't satisfied. Until he saw the love of his life with his own eyes, he was going to keep looking. The fire was still small enough that he could reenter the orphanage if he had to. And if he could not quickly locate Sara Beth, that was exactly what he was going to do.

Running, he rounded the corner by the kitchen and ran smack into Luke. "Where's your sister?"

The boy's expression was unreadable.

"Answer me." He shook Luke by the shoulders. "Tell me. Where is she?"

"I—I don't know."

"Where did you last see her?"

"In—in the parlor. I told you."

"That was half an hour ago. Have you seen her since?" He gave the boy another shake. "Well?"

Luke lowered his head until his mop of hair masked his face, but Taylor could tell plenty by his body language. The boy was clearly hiding something. And as long as Sara Beth was unaccounted for, he was not going to let him get away with any subterfuge.

"Look, son, I don't care what else you were up to tonight. Understand? I just want to make sure your sister is all right."

"Why?"

"Because I care about her—and so should you," Taylor said. "She's the glue that's holding your family together and she's risked her life to do it."

"Oh, really?"

"Really." Taylor would have liked to turn the boy over his knee and give him a proper education with a hickory switch the way a few of his teachers had enlightened him when he was a child, but he didn't have time to waste.

"So, what were you and your friend up to tonight?"

Luke cringed beneath the man's grasp. "I don't know what you're talking about."

"Yes, you do. Who was he and what were you two planning? I found the sack where you dropped it. Was he going to make you a member of his gang if you helped him rob this place?"

His head snapped up. "How did you know?"

"Because I was young and stupid once, too. And because I think I may have recognized the fellow who ran into me right after you did. I couldn't place him at first but now that I think about it—"

"We never took a thing," Luke insisted.

"Only because a fire started and you had to get out with everybody else."

Wide-eyed, the boy swiveled his neck and stared at the mansion. "Do you think Sara Beth…?"

There was a glow behind the front door and smoke was billowing from several open upstairs windows. Taylor figured the building was still salvageable, assuming one of the fire brigades arrived fairly soon.

"I don't know," Taylor said. "You go find Mathias and then both of you wait with Josiah. If she's in there, I'll find her."

"Let me go, too."

"And have to spend my time tracking you down again when you're already safe out here? No way. For once in your life, do as you're told."

Expecting an argument, Taylor was astounded when the teary-eyed boy merely nodded and said, "Yes, sir."

"Is she dead?"

"As good as." The assassin held out his hand. "Where's my money?"

"I expected you to use the loot from the orphanage to pay yourself," Bein said, laughing wryly.

"I had to leave in a hurry. I didn't get nothing."

"That's hardly my fault."

"If you don't pay me I'll—"

"You'll what? Talk? Blame me? I hardly think so. Not when the sheriff tells me you have another murder hanging over your head." He scowled. "Did you make sure she was dead?"

"She will be. I left her trapped in a closet and set the hall outside it on fire. She'll bake like a loaf of bread in an oven."

"She'd better. What about all the others in that big house? What if they die, too?"

"That's none of my concern," the assassin said. "I don't owe nobody there a thing. They turned me away after my ma died and my pa took off for the gold fields. Said I was too old."

"I hope you were old enough and smart enough to handle this job."

"I was." He brandished the knife that he'd intended to use on Sara Beth before his plans had changed. "Now, let's you and me talk about money."

# Chapter Seventeen

The stuffiness of the tiny upper room was growing unbearable. Sara Beth tried to open the small window. It had apparently been closed for so long that it was stuck tight, because no matter how hard she strained it wouldn't budge.

She sighed, wishing she were down on the lawn in the fresh air with the children. Patience had never been one of her virtues, as she was being constantly reminded. She might have many pleasing traits such as kindness, forbearance, love, joy in adversity, forgiveness…

The instant she had that particular thought, she was penitent. She was not forgiving. Not the way the Good Book said she should be. She was holding a grudge against the man whom she believed had had her parents killed and she didn't see any way to stop hating him for the horrible things he had done.

That was probably the key, she reasoned. It was all right to hate evil acts, but not to hate the person who carried them out. Sadly, she could not manage that either.

She immediately visualized William Bein. He may

not have been directly responsible for Papa Robert's and Mama's deaths, but he had certainly taken advantage of them. And who was to say for certain that he had not been the evil force behind everything? Papa had visited the wharf that night to speak with someone he had caught cheating. Who fit that description better than dear old Uncle William?

Taking a deep breath and releasing it as a sigh, Sara Beth was surprised to catch a whiff of a strange, acrid odor. She frowned. In the dimness of the moonlit garret she couldn't spot any source of such a smell, yet...

She sniffed. Followed her nose. It took her to the stairwell she had climbed to gain access to the abandoned room. Continuing to inhale slowly, thoughtfully, she made up her mind.

*Smoke*. It was smoke she was smelling. It was drifting up the stairway and starting to infiltrate the tiny room. That was why all the children had been taken outside. The orphanage was on fire!

Heart pounding, she spun in a circle, trying to decide what to do. There was no way out that she could see. Her one best hope was probably staying as far from the flames as she could until someone rescued her.

"Only no one knows where I am," she lamented. "No one but God." Her eyes widened as she noted the smell of burning wood increasing.

One thing was certain. The same Heavenly Father who had given her a useful intellect would expect her to use it rather than simply sit there and become a victim of her own lack of initiative. But what could she do? And how long might it be before someone found her?

Determined to isolate herself from the acrid air as much as possible, she whipped off her petticoats and hurried down the stairs to stuff them at the base of the door. That would buy a little time. So would finding a source of breathable air.

It took her only a moment to decide to break out the stuck window. Grabbing the chair, she struck the glass with its ladder-shaped back. Once. Twice. Nothing happened.

Finally frantic enough to use her full strength, she managed to crack the heavy glass. It shattered in a starburst pattern that she was then able to break away from the frame. Leaning out, she took deep, cleansing breaths. Night air from the bay had never smelled better.

Now that there was nothing but open space between Sara Beth and the people on the lawn, she began to shout. "Help! Up here. I'm trapped!"

To her dismay, there was so much racket and mayhem going on below, no one even looked up.

She tried again and again. Nothing.

"Father, what shall I do?" she prayed, panicking.

*The chair!* That was it. If she could throw it out the window, perhaps someone would figure out where it came from and send aid.

Hefting it once more, she tried to fit it through the narrow sash. It was no use. The window frame was at least three inches narrower than the seat of the old chair. And it was the smallest thing in the nearly empty room.

"What else? Think," she murmured, thoroughly frustrated and at a loss as to how to help herself. This was maddening. She felt like screaming, like kicking the wall, like smashing everything in sight.

"That's it!"

Reaching for the chair once again she drew back and swung it the way she would have a wire rug beater. It met the sturdy bed frame with a crack and started to splinter. Two more hard whacks and the back parted from the seat.

Sara Beth raced to the window. She could see a man-drawn fire wagon being tugged up the driveway by countless firemen and volunteers. Soon they would be in place to start battling the blaze.

But would they have it under control in time to save her life? She didn't know. All she could do at this point was start flinging parts of the broken chair out the window in the hopes that someone would notice.

That, and screech at the top of her lungs. Given the level of noise below, she knew her efforts in that regard would probably be futile. Nevertheless, she tried.

"Help! I'm up here. Look, somebody. Look at me!"

Taylor was back inside the building, searching from room to room the way he had before the fire had started. He couldn't take the chance that Sara Beth had made it downstairs, only to lose consciousness.

That thought chilled him to the bone. She had to be all right. She had to be. He couldn't lose her.

"Sara Beth," he shouted. "Where are you? Answer me."

Most of the smoke had stayed on the upper floors, the same way it rose up a chimney, and it lay like bay fog in a cloud that extended halfway to the landing on the main stairwell. If he was going to move toward that, he'd need to cover his mouth and nose.

Dashing to the kitchen, he whipped off his coat and shoved it into a pail of water that was awaiting the cooks. It wasn't much, but it would have to do, he reasoned, quickly soaking the jacket.

He pressed the wet wool cloth to his face like a mask and returned to the stairs. Sara Beth was obviously not on the ground floor. There was only one thing to do. He had to enter the fire zone to search. No other plan was acceptable.

The chair back was the first to go. It sailed out over the mansard roof and dropped out of sight. "Help," Sara Beth screeched. "Up here. Help!"

She followed with the spindle legs, then stomped on the seat to try to break it more. When it refused to crack, she upended it and heaved it out the window vertically. It was, unfortunately, so heavy that it didn't clear the edge of the roof.

Turning, hoping to find some other object she might have overlooked, she was stunned to see that there was now a lot of smoke rising from the stairwell. As it reached the main room it headed straight for the open window.

By breaking the glass she had evidently created an updraft that was going to suck the fire right to her!

As Taylor crested the stairs, he could tell that the fire's origin was at the far end of the hallway. Thankfully, it seemed confined to an area where there were no bedrooms so the children had been able to escape. If it had started mid-hallway instead, there would surely have been numerous victims trapped.

Peering at the blaze, he was taken by the fact that it seemed so isolated. There was really no fuel in that area other than the walls and floor, yet it was burning with a high, hot flame. The kind of flame that the oil from a dropped lamp might produce.

He paused for the length of a heartbeat to assess the situation. If the firemen didn't get water on this conflagration soon, it could easily claim the whole building. He lowered his wet coat and thought about trying to beat out the fire with it, then concluded that that effort would be futile.

An object within the flames caught his eye. It looked for all the world as if a fancy side chair had been placed in the middle of the inferno. Why in the world would a chair be parked in front of a door like that?

He racked his memory. Where did that door lead? He didn't recall ever opening it, yet it must have been of some use, at least in the days when the mansion had been a private home. He supposed it could be a closet, but if that were the case, then why prop a chair at such an awkward angle in front of it?

There was no way Taylor could find out without breaching the worst of the fire, and he was not about to do something so reckless.

His first instinct was to continue checking the bedrooms, but since Mrs. McNeil had assured him that that had already been done, perhaps he'd be wasting his time.

He hesitated, thinking, wondering, praying. If he wanted to ask about that strange door he was going to have to return to the lawn and find someone who knew. He didn't understand why the urge to do so was so compelling. He could not seem to shake it no matter how much he argued with himself.

"Sara Beth needs me," he kept insisting.

*Yes, she does,* his heart answered. *And if she's truly trapped behind that door, she may already be dead.*

That was more than Taylor could take. Giving no

thought to his own well-being, he wrapped his wet coat around his forearm, held it up like a shield against the heat and charged at the burning chair.

The heat was intense. The flames singed his hair and eyebrows. He kicked the remains of the chair away with his boot and tried to grab the knob. It made his hand sizzle.

Shouting in agony, he sheathed his palm in a piece of the coat and tried to twist the handle once again. He was already nauseated by the pain. If he didn't get the door open this time he was going to have to give up or risk collapsing where he stood.

"What was that?" Coughing, Sara Beth strained to listen. By now, the crackle and roar of the fire was so loud she wasn't positive she'd actually heard a shout.

Nevertheless, she screamed again. "Help! Help me."

A mighty whoosh of air carried billowing smoke clouds up the stairway. *Oh, no!* The door must have burned away and now there was no barrier between her and the blaze.

She backed toward the window, wondering if it would be possible to squeeze through such a small opening. Probably not, she decided, although trying to do so was starting to look like her only chance of surviving.

The black smoke whirled. Eddied. Sara Beth's eyes burned. Her throat felt as though it was closing. She gasped and coughed so hard it doubled her over.

Suddenly, strong arms grabbed her and for an instant she wondered if she had died and was being taken to heaven in the arms of an angel. Then, she realized that her prayers had been answered in the best way. Taylor Hayward was beside her.

She threw her arms around his neck and held on for dear life.

"How did you get up here?" he asked, gasping and hacking worse than she was.

"Somebody was chasing me. They blocked the door."

"I saw. If he hadn't done it with a chair I might not have found you in time."

Her eyes were watering from the smoke and she was weeping with joy at the same time. "That other door," she said, pointing. "It's locked."

Taylor kept an arm around her as he shepherded her across the room. He didn't even pause to try the knob. He simply kicked the door with the sole of his boot and it sprang open.

In mere seconds they were on their way down an outside stairway and headed for the garden. Sara Beth was doubly thankful that he had not let go of her because she wasn't sure how steady she'd be if he did.

As far as she was concerned, if Taylor never left her side again it would be just fine with her.

# Chapter Eighteen

They emerged into a small, secluded side garden that was hemmed on three sides by manicured hedges. There was plenty of shouting and other noise in the background, but they were temporarily alone.

Sara Beth faltered, coughing and gasping for breath as they made their way to a stone bench.

She sat first. Taylor plopped down beside her. He was also struggling to get enough air.

"The children…are they…safe?" she asked, wheezing.

He nodded. "Yes. The staff got them all out. Everybody was on the lawn, except you."

"How…how did you find me?"

He coughed again, then managed a smile. There was moisture glistening in his eyes that she hoped was not simply an adverse reaction to the smoke.

"Divine providence again, I guess." He took her hand. "I was puzzled by that chair in front of the door in the hallway. There was just something about it that didn't look right. I don't know why I felt so strongly except that perhaps the Good Lord was guiding my thoughts."

"That sounds good to me," she replied. The tender, loving expression on his face touched her deeply. She reached across to caress his cheek and felt the coarseness of a beginning stubble. "You need a shave, Doctor."

"No," Taylor said as he covered her hand with his own. "What I need is you."

She was thunderstruck. Was he saying what she thought he was? Could it be? Nothing in her personal life had changed for the better. She was still responsible for her brothers and Papa Robert's reputation was still under a cloud.

"Close your pretty mouth," he said, starting to grin. "You're gaping at me."

"Little wonder. You aren't making sense. Did the fire unhinge you?"

"If that was what it took to wake us up to our true feelings for each other, then it was for the best. Whoever set that blaze did us a favor."

"He did?"

"Yes. He did," Taylor said as he enfolded her in his embrace. "I had come here tonight to explain myself and to beg you to forgive me. To grant me the chance to court you."

"I think it's already too late for that," Sara Beth said, leaning her cheek against his strong shoulder. She felt as if she could hear the rapid pounding of both their hearts. She could certainly feel the racing of her own.

"Then I suppose I shall have to do the right thing and ask for your hand in marriage," he said. "Since you lack parental guidance, perhaps Mrs. McNeil will suffice."

"Or old Abe Warner," Sara Beth offered. "I can just hear him laughing at the both of us over it."

Taylor sobered. "We will have to wait to actually marry, of course."

Her brow furrowed and she leaned away to look at his face. "Why?"

"Because I can't properly provide for you and your family yet. I promise I'll do my best to save for the day when I can."

"Oh." The joy of his proposal remained. The excitement of becoming his bride, however, quickly faded. "I suppose that is sensible."

"Very."

"It's also too bad. I really do want to leave this place and have a real home again." The moment she'd spoken she realized that he might misunderstand.

"Is that why you're agreeing to marry me?"

"No. Of course not. No more than you were hesitant to ask because of my father's reputation. I can see that now. We've both been trying so hard to behave properly in a difficult situation that we've lost sight of how we feel about each other. That's the most important thing."

Pausing and gazing into his eyes, she swallowed hard before she added, "I love you, Taylor. I have for ages."

This time, there was no doubt in Sara Beth's mind that he was touched. When he said, "I love you, too," his eyes glistened with unshed tears and there was so much affection in his expression that it stole her breath and made her giddy.

Sara Beth suddenly understood that this was the kind of overwhelming love and devotion Mama had found with Papa Robert, the kind that had made her follow him to the wharf and willingly sacrifice her life to try to save his.

And she could finally forgive her mother for leaving her family the way she had. It was a shock to realize that she had blamed her parents for the decisions that had ended their lives so early. But she had. And that had led her to question God, as well.

Yet here she sat, looking forward to the future and a whole new life with Taylor Hayward. Who knew? Perhaps she would continue to learn medicine at his side and someday fulfill that dream, too.

The way she saw it, at this point in her life, the future held nothing but possibilities and opportunities.

Cuddling closer, she closed her eyes and thanked her Heavenly Father for bringing her and her loved ones through the fire. Literally.

Taylor soon led Sara Beth back to the front lawn and reunited her with Mrs. McNeil, then wrapped a loose bandage around his burned hand before he went to fetch the boys. He intended to suggest that they welcome their sister and celebrate survival with her. To his relief and delight, even Luke seemed amenable to the idea.

"Is she okay?" the eleven-year-old asked. He and Mathias were tagging along while Taylor carried Josiah.

"She breathed a lot of smoke, but she'll be fine."

"Are you okay?" The boy was eyeing his bandaged hand.

"Yes. It's not as bad as it looks."

"How did the fire start?"

"How?" Taylor gave him a withering glance and stayed stern in spite of the obvious fact that the boy was worried. "Suppose you tell me."

"I didn't do it!"

"No, but I suspect your friend did. What happened to him, anyway? Where did he go? I haven't seen him since he crashed into me on the stairs. That was just about the time I first saw the flames."

"Why would he do that?"

"I don't know. Maybe he was supposed to."

"That doesn't make any sense," Luke argued. "If the house was on fire he wouldn't have time…"

"Right. To steal anything. I had that part already figured out, assuming that was his goal. Where did you meet him, anyway?"

"Down by the docks. You saw."

"*That's* where I remember him from. You're right. I did see you two together." He hesitated, mulling over what he knew. "That gang of rowdies just came up to you and took you in? Is that what you're telling me?"

"Yes. So?"

"So, it doesn't make sense unless they knew who you were and where you were living."

"They wanted to rob the orphanage?"

Taylor was slowly shaking his head. "I thought so at first, but now I'm not so sure. Think back. When you met them, did they ask you anything about your family, your sister in particular?"

Judging by the way the color drained out of the boy's face, Taylor assumed he was onto something. "They did, didn't they? What did they want to know?"

"Nothing much. Just what her name was and where she was staying. I thought they were worried that my parents would wonder where I was and wanted to make sure I didn't have any."

"Did they ask about your brothers? The rest of your family?"

Luke was trembling and wide-eyed when he answered, "No."

Firemen had not been able to draft through their hand pumper at the orphanage the way they did from the city's cisterns, so they had formed a bucket brigade to keep the reservoir full. They were already manning the hose and getting the worst of the fire under control by the time Sara Beth saw Taylor returning with the boys.

She opened her arms to Josiah and was a bit chagrined when he recoiled.

"I think you and I are too dirty and smoky for his taste," Taylor explained. "He wasn't thrilled when I picked him up, either."

"Of course." She grimaced at her sooty hands and used the back of her wrist to push loose hair off her forehead. "I must look a fright."

The doctor laughed. "You are the most beautiful sight I have ever seen, Miss Sara Beth."

"And you are prejudiced."

"Decidedly so." Passing Josiah to Mrs. McNeil, he grinned. "I suppose I should speak my piece since there will probably never be a better time."

She glanced briefly toward her elder brothers. They were standing back as if they sensed something significant was about to happen. "You haven't thought about all this and changed your mind, have you? It is a lot to take on."

"I would adopt a hundred children if it pleased you," Taylor said, continuing to grin widely. He turned to the matron. "Mrs. McNeil, it is my desire to have this young lady's hand in marriage. May I have your blessing?"

Giggling, Ella blushed and nearly jumped up and down with glee. Sara Beth suspected she might have done so if she had not been toting Josiah on her hip. "Mercy sakes, yes. I thought you two young people would never see the light. I was running out of ways to throw you together."

Stepping closer to Taylor, Sara Beth was not at all surprised to feel his arm encircle her shoulders once again. This was life as it should be, she mused. All else paled in comparison to her feelings for her beloved.

The way she saw the situation, there was only one more obstacle to their happiness. They needed to clear her stepfather's name and regain possession of the house on Pike Street. Taylor might not have thought of it yet, but that building was the perfect location. She would use the house for business as she had once planned, only it would not house a millinery, it would become a doctor's office. Taylor Hayward's office.

She began to smile. Let him try to postpone their wedding then.


The *Bulletin* printed a string of revealing articles over the course of the next few months that led to a rapid shakeup in San Francisco politics.

Taylor had been initially worried about repercussions, but by July the Vigilance Committee had hanged several more miscreants and had driven Chief Justice Terry out of town. Then they had quietly disbanded. General Sherman had resigned in frustration and had been replaced by General Volney Hayes, a lawyer and former member of congress from Texas, so things were finally getting back to normal.

It was Taylor's pleasure to bring news of William Bein's arrest for embezzlement. He found Sara Beth in the kitchen garden, digging onions.

"Hello there."

Grinning, she whirled and dusted off her hands. "Taylor! I'm so glad to see you. If I had known you were coming I would have washed up and put on a pretty frock."

"You look beautiful to me," he said, ignoring the dirt and taking her hands. "I brought news."

"What?"

"Your nemesis has been arrested for robbing the U.S. Mint. The investigators watched him till they caught him red-handed. He even admitted the theft."

"Really? Oh, my. What about Papa Robert? Did Bein's confession clear him?"

"It looks like it may. According to Tom King, the United States Grand Jury is planning to indict their boss, Augustin Harazthy. Once that happens, the whole truth should come out."

The look of relief on her face was so immeasurable he didn't know what else to say. Instead of more words, he decided to let his actions speak for him.

Tilting her chin up with one finger, he placed a gentle kiss on the lips he had yearned to kiss again for literally months. When she melted against him, he was astounded by how perfect she was. How lovely. How dear.

He stepped back, staggered by the effect of that one simple kiss.

Sara Beth's eyes held a dreamy look and her lips began to lift in the whisper of a smile. She sighed before she said, "I thought you would never get around to doing that again." The smile spread to include her eyes, her rosy cheeks. "It was even better than the first time."

"Perhaps you're learning," Taylor teased.

"Or you are," she countered, laughing. "Let's just promise to keep practicing till we're sure it's perfect."

"You are already so perfect it takes my breath away," he confessed. "I don't know how much longer I can continue to be the kind of gentleman you deserve."

"Then I suggest you stop stalling and marry me," Sara Beth said boldly. She took him by the hand. "Come. I have something special to show you."

Although he knew he wasn't financially ready to take a bride, he also knew it was not fair to Sara Beth to keep delaying. She was a good woman. She deserved a proper wedding and a suitable home. He had saved some money but not nearly enough to set up housekeeping. What could he do? What should he do?

She led him into the kitchen and pointed to the table. "Sit there."

"Yes, ma'am," he said, much to Clara's—and Sara Beth's—obvious amusement.

"I had not heard about William Bein's arrest, but I did receive an official document from the court this morning." She reached into her apron pocket and unfolded a piece of paper. "It says that the title to the family house and property is mine."

Taylor started to rise, intending to give her a congratulatory hug. She stopped him with an upraised hand. "Wait. There's more."

"More? What else was there?"

"Just this," she said as she reached into a cupboard beneath the sink and pulled out a slab of wood. "I had it made from the mahogany that was salvaged from the upstairs hall after the fire. I couldn't think of a better source, and I wanted it as a memento, too."

Flipping the board around, she proudly displayed it.

Taylor was afraid he was going to disgrace himself by weeping. He blinked as he struggled to control his emotions. It was a new shingle. A sign that declared, "Doctor Taylor Hayward" in gilt letters. Below that was the address on Pike Street.

It took him several seconds to see what she was getting at. "How could you have known to do that?"

"I didn't," Sara Beth said. "It was just a dream I had and I figured it was best to act as if I were positive it would come true." Grinning, she handed him the sign. "We'll not only have a place to live, you'll be able to stop paying rent on a separate office and we'll have plenty of extra money."

Laughing, he laid aside the sign and stood to embrace her. "When you get your mind set on something you don't give up, do you?"

"No, I don't. You should be delighted because that means I'm never going to stop loving you."

"And I will always be totally yours," Taylor vowed. "Set a date. We're getting married just as soon as we can."

# Epilogue

Sara Beth had not asked her brothers to call her "Mama"; it had simply happened naturally after she and Taylor had had a son of their own.

Luke was currently apprenticed to a saddle maker in Benecia while Mathias continued his schooling back east. Josiah, now nearly ten, had no recollection of Isabella or Robert Reese, so the transition had been easiest on him.

"Mama, there's a man here who says you're needed," Josiah called from the front of the house.

Quickly removing her apron, Sara Beth hurried to the parlor and found a harried husband, pacing, hat in hand. "Is it time?" she asked him.

"Yes'm. She says so."

"Well, it's her fourth baby, so we have to assume she knows," Sara Beth said. She turned to Josiah. "Watch your brother for me till your papa gets home, will you? He was making the circuit to Mission Dolores today, so he shouldn't be very late getting back. Supper's on the stove and there are cookies you can share if you get hungry before then."

"Yes, ma'am."

"And tell your father that he won't be needed unless I send for him." The look on the boy's face made her smile.

"I have been a midwife for longer than he had been a doctor when we met," she said. "My patients and I will be fine."

Swinging a shawl over her shoulders, she picked up a black bag that was identical in size and shape to the one Taylor carried. He never seemed to tire of telling her how much he admired her and her work. That, and having a chance to help other women, was enough for Sara Beth.

She smiled as she turned to the expectant father. "Let's be going. Babies don't wait for anything and I can hardly wait to greet your newest family member."

\* \* \* \* \*

**Allie Pleiter**, an award-winning author and RITA® Award finalist, writes both fiction and nonfiction. Her passion for knitting shows up in many of her books and all over her life. Entirely too fond of French macarons and lemon meringue pie, Allie spends her days writing books and avoiding housework. Allie grew up in Connecticut, holds a BS in speech from Northwestern University and lives near Chicago, Illinois.

### Books by Allie Pleiter

### Love Inspired

#### *Matrimony Valley*

*His Surprise Son*
*Snowbound with the Best Man*
*Wander Canyon Courtship*

#### *Blue Thorn Ranch*

*The Texas Rancher's Return*
*Coming Home to Texas*
*The Texan's Second Chance*
*The Bull Rider's Homecoming*
*The Texas Rancher's New Family*

#### *Lone Star Cowboy League: Boys Ranch*

*The Rancher's Texas Twins*

#### *Lone Star Cowboy League*

*A Ranger for the Holidays*

Visit the Author Profile page
at Harlequin.com for more titles.

# MISSION OF HOPE

## Allie Pleiter

Being confident of this very thing,
that he which hath begun a good work in you
will perform it until the day of Jesus Christ.
—*Philippians* 1:6

For Nora
May your future always be the best of adventures

## Acknowledgments

One does not tackle the great San Francisco earthquake and fire of 1906 without backup. And while people look at you sideways when you get on an airplane with a dozen disaster books, I am grateful to all the fine texts out there that made my research complete. Thanks galore to historian and general good sport Eileen Keremitsis for enduring questions, finding obscure facts and graciously unearthing errors. Any historical errors in this book can only be laid at my own stubborn and ignorant feet, certainly not at hers. Special thanks go to my local and national buddies from American Christian Fiction Writers for befriending me despite my many oddities. Krista Stroever continues to be the finest editor God ever gave me, and I could never have survived this cyclone of a publishing career without the careful guidance of my agent Karen Solem. And you, my dear readers; God bless you all.

# *Prologue*

*San Francisco, July 1906*

The world rumbled and heaved. Screams and moans pierced the thundering roar, the staccato breaking and snapping, drowning out her own cries for help as the earth swallowed her up like a hungry beast. Nora Longstreet grasped for any hold she could reach, but everything dissolved at her touch so that nothing stopped her fall.

Something soft smothered her face, and she shot upright, clawing at the thing. "Annette!" she screamed for her cousin who'd been beside her just moments before. "Annette!" The monster was eating her, devouring her.

A hand clasped her shoulder. "Hush, Nora. Wake up, love, and be still."

Nora opened her eyes to find no beast, no rumbling, no danger. "I…"

"We're safe. We're at Aunt Julia's and we're safe. Breathe now, there's nothing to harm you." Mama pulled a handkerchief from the sleeve of her nightshift and dabbed at Nora's brow.

"Oh, Mama, she was there. Right beside me, asleep, I could hear her breathing. And then…"

Why must she live that horrible morning over and over when she closed her eyes? Nora moaned and leaned back against her pallet in the parlor of her aunt's Lafayette Park home where she'd been camped since the earthquake. She was soaked with sweat, and although it was nearly dawn, she felt as if she had not slept at all. Still, she couldn't let that stop her. Today was too important a day. Nora swung her legs over the edge of the cot and raked her fingers through her hair. "I'm going to the rally," she said to her mother. "I think Papa needs me."

# Chapter One

It was her. It had to be. It was the eyes that made him certain, even from this distance.

Quinn Freeman stared harder at the young woman—not much more than twenty from the look of it—sitting uncomfortably onstage. She was trying to pay attention to the long rally speeches honoring the city's recovery, but not quite succeeding. And the speeches were surely long. Politicians fought banks who fought insurance companies and everyone nursed a grudge over how things had been handled. The most eloquent speech on God's green earth couldn't explain how one man was still alive while another's life had come to an end. The uncertainty of everything made for chaos.

Still, she was here. By some astounding act of God, she was here. And what a sight she was. Even in the gray light of this cloudy morning, she looked clean and pretty, and he hadn't seen anything clean and pretty in days.

It was the eyes, really, that captured his attention. Round and wide, framed with golden lashes. Even in the brown tint of the charred photo he'd found, he'd somehow known they were an unusual color. Something between a blue and a violet, now that he saw them. The color of the irises Ma was fond of in one of the city gardens.

Quinn fished into his pocket for the battered locket he'd found last week as he walked home from yet another insufferably long bread line. He'd seen it glint in the corner of a rubble pile just south of Nob Hill, a tiny sparkle in a pile of black and brown timber. Usually, Quinn was looking up; he was always looking up at the buildings—or parts of buildings—still standing, admiring how they'd survived with so much rubble marking where others had fallen. It wasn't as if bits of lives couldn't still be found all over the city—even months out as it was, Quinn was forever picking up one shoe or a bit of a cup or a chipped doorknob.

This was different. There was something amazing about the fact that the locket was still shut, and that despite the soot and dents, there were still two tiny photographs inside. Two young women about his own age. Sisters? Cousins? He kept the charm in his pocket, making up a dozen stories as he worked or walked or waited, because everything now took hours longer than it had before. Yes, it was dirty and dented and the chain was broken, but the faces inside had survived an earthquake and a fire. And now he knew the people had, as well. Or at least one of them. Quinn just couldn't ignore the hope in that.

Reverend Bauers never called anything a coincidence. No one was ever "lucky" to Reverend Bauers—they were "called" or "blessed." Quinn had survived the earthquake and the fire. His mother had, too. But he was beginning to wonder if he'd survive the next two months. A few months ago he'd been just another grunt down at the printing press, scratching out a living, trying to hang on to his big dreams. Then the world shook and fell over. He'd survived, but why had God kept him alive while scores of others died?

"God does not deal in luck or happenstance," Bauers always said to Quinn when something went their way or a need miraculously became met. "He directs, He provides and He is very fond of surprising His children." The saying rang in Quinn's ears when he saw the familiar face on the stage this morning. And he knew, even before he pulled the locket from his pocket and squinted as he held it up to her profile, that it was her. *Well, Lord, I'm surprised, I'll grant You that.*

When that pretty woman saw him hold up the locket, her eyes wide with amazement, he made the decision right there and then to do whatever it took to return the locket to her, to bring *one thing* home.

The man fished something out of his pocket and held it up, comparing it to the face—her face—before him.

Annette's locket. With the elongated heart shape that was so unusual, the one Annette had picked out for her birthday last year, it just *had* to be. He had Annette's locket!

It took forever for the rally to end. The moment she could, Nora swept off her chair in search of the fastest way into the crowd. He couldn't have missed her intent given how hard he seemed to be staring at her. Surely he would wait, perhaps even make his way toward the stage.

The crowd milled exasperatingly thick, and Nora began to fear the man would be lost to her forever—

and that last piece of Annette with him. Nora pushed as fiercely as she dared through the clusters of people, dodging around shoulders and darting through gaps.

She could not find him. Her throat tight and one hand holding her hat to the mass of blond waves that was her unruly hair, she turned in circles, straining to see over one large man's shoulders and finding no one.

"This is you, isn't it?" came a voice from behind her, and she turned with such a start that she nearly knocked the man over. He held up the locket. Nora let out a small gasp—it was so battered now that she saw it up close. The delicate gold heart was dented on one side, black soot scars still clinging to the fancy engraving and the broken chain.

*Soot.* A fire seemed such a terrible, awful way to die. Nora clutched at the locket with both hands, her grief not allowing any thought for manners. The two halves of the dented heart had already been opened, revealing the remains of a pair of tiny photographs—one of her, the other of Annette. Nora put her finger to the image of Annette and thought she would cry. "Yes," she said unsteadily, "that's me, and that's my cousin, Annette. However did you get this?"

The man pushed back his hat, and a shock of straw-colored hair splashed across his forehead. "I found it last week. I've been looking for either one of you since then, but I didn't really think I'd find you. I just about fell over when you walked onto the stage this morning, Miss... Longstreet, was it? The postmaster's daughter?"

Nora suddenly remembered her manners. "Nora Longstreet. I'm so very pleased to meet you. And so very pleased to have this back...although it isn't...actually mine." She felt her throat tighten up, and paused for a moment. "It's Annette's, and she isn't…she's isn't here. Anymore." She pulled in a shaky breath. "She died…in it."

"I'm sorry. Seems like everybody lost someone, doesn't it?" He tipped the corner of his hat. "Quinn Freeman."

"Thank you for finding this, Mr. Freeman. It means a great deal to me."

Quinn tucked his hands in his pockets. He wore a simple white shirt, brown pants that had seen considerable wear and scuffed shoes, but someone had taken care to make sure they were all still clean and in the best repair possible given the circumstances. "I'm sure she would have wanted you to have it, seeing as it's you in there and all."

"I'm sure my father would be happy to give you some kind of reward for returning it. Come meet him, why don't you?"

Quinn smiled—a slanted, humble grin that confirmed the charm his eyes conveyed—and shrugged. "I couldn't take anything for it. I'm just glad it found its way home. Too many people lost too much not to see something back where it belongs."

Nora ran her thumb across the scratched surface of the locket. "Surely I can give you some reward for your kindness."

He stared at her again. The gaze was unnerving from up on the stage, but it was tenfold more standing mere feet from him. "You just did. It's nice to see someone so happy. A pretty smile is a fine thing to take home." He stared for a long moment more before tipping his hat. "G'mornin', Miss Longstreet. It's been a pleasure."

"Thank you, Mr. Freeman. Thank you again." Nora

clutched the locket to her chest and dashed off to find
her father.

She found him near the stage, talking with a cluster
of men in dark coats and serious expressions. "Papa!"
She caught his elbow as he pulled himself from the
conversation. "The most extraordinary thing has happened!"

"Where have you been? You shouldn't have dashed
off like that."

"Oh, Papa, I've survived an earthquake and a fire.
What could possibly happen to me now?"

"A great deal more than I'd care to consider." He
scowled at her, but there was a glint of teasing in his
eye. She was glad to see it—he hadn't had much humor
about him lately.

She held up the battered charm. "Look! Can you believe it? I thought it lost forever."

Her father took the locket from Nora's hand and held
it up, turning it to examine it. "Is this Annette's locket?
That's astounding! However did you find it?"

"A man gave it to me, just now. He said he recognized me from the photo inside. The photographs hadn't
fully burned. Can you imagine? I knew there was a reason I needed to come with you this morning. I knew I
should be beside you up there. Now I know why!" Right
now that dented piece of gold was just about the most
precious thing in all the world. The moment she fixed
the broken chain, she'd never take it off ever again.

"Well, where is this man?" Her father looked over
her shoulder. "I'd say we owe him a debt of thanks."

"I tried to get him to come over and meet you—he
knew who I was and who you were—but he said he
didn't need any thanks." She left out the bit about her

smile. *Oh, thank You, Lord,* Nora prayed as she took the locket back from her father. *Thank You so much!*

"Did you at least get his name?"

"Freeman," Nora said, thinking about the bold stare he'd given her at first, "Quinn Freeman."

# Chapter Two

The mail had always been mundane to Nora. A perfunctory business. Hardly the stuff of heroes and lifesaving deeds. Papa had told her stories of how they'd soaked mailbags in water and beaten back the fire to save the post office. And now, the mail had become just that—lifesaving. Thanks to Papa's promise to deliver all kinds of mail—postage or no postage—mail had become the one constant. The only thing that still worked the way it had worked before. It was amazing how people clung to that.

No one, however, could have foreseen what "all kinds of mail" would be: sticks, wood, shirt cuffs and collars, tiles and margins of salvaged books or newspaper had been pressed into service as writing paper. Each morning Papa would take her to the edge of an "official" refugee camp—for several questionable "unofficial" camps had sprung up—and they would take in the mail. Standing on an older mail cart now pressed into heavy service, Nora took in heart-wrenching messages such as "We're alive" or "Eddie is gone" or "Send anything" and piled them into bags headed back to the post office.

Nora—and any other female—could only *accept* mail, for mail delivery had become a dangerous task. Arriving mail consisted of packages of food or clothes or whatever supplies could be sent quickly, and that made it highly desirable. The massive logistics of distributing such things had necessitated army escorts in order to keep the peace. Even after months of relief, so much was still missing, so much was still needed, and San Francisco was discovering just how impossible it was to sprout a city from scratch. The nearly three months of continual scrounging, loss and pain turned civil people angry, and there had even been a few close scrapes for Nora in the simple act of accepting mail. Those incidents usually made her father nervous, but today they made Nora all the more determined to help. Someone had delivered something precious to her, and she would do the same. It was not her fault the postmaster had not been blessed with a son who could better face the danger. If God had given Postmaster Longstreet a daughter, then God would have to work through a daughter. Father had always said, "We do what we can with what we have." What better time or place to put that belief into practice?

"Please," a young boy pleaded as he pressed a strip of cloth into Nora's hand. Its author had scrawled a message and rolled up a shirtsleeve like a scroll, tied with what looked like the remnants of a shoelace. "Martin Lovejoy, Applewood, Wisconsin" was printed on the outside. "All we got is the clothes we're wearing," the lad said, "but Uncle Martin can send more."

"Is your tent number on the scroll? Your uncle Martin needs to know where to send the clothes."

"Don't know," the boy said, turning the scroll over

in his hands. He held it up to Nora again. "I don't read. Is it?"

The scroll held none of its sender's information. "What's your tent number?"

The tiny lip trembled. "It's over there."

The boy pointed across the street to the very large "unofficial" encampment that had taken over Dolores Park. Nora bent down and took the boy's hand. "Which…" she hesitated to even use the word in front of him, "…shack is yours?"

He pointed to a line of slapped-together shelters just across the street. "There."

The shack stood near the edge of the camp, but still, he was so small to be here by himself. Nora looked around for someone to send back with him—the unofficial camp was not a safe place to go—but everyone was engrossed in their own tasks. The little boy looked completely helpless and more than a little desperate. It was by the edge, not forty feet away, and perhaps it wasn't as dangerous as Papa made it out to be. Taking a deep breath, Nora made a decision and hopped down off the wagon. Five minutes to help one little boy couldn't possibly put her in any danger, and her father looked too busy to even notice her absence. Nora held out her hand. "Let's walk back together and we'll sort it out. We can ask your mama to help us."

The little boy looked away and swiped his eye bravely with the back of his other hand. "Mama's gone," he said in an unsteady voice. "My daddy wrote it."

Nora gripped the little hand tighter. "All the more reason that note should get through. We'll do what it takes to reach your uncle. It'll be all right, I promise. What's your name?"

"Sam." The boy headed into a small alleyway of sorts between two of the shelters.

The official refugee camps were surprisingly orderly. Straight rows of identical tents, laid out with military precision in specific parts of the city. Pairs of white muslin boxes faced each other like tiny grassy streets.

The sights and sounds of another world rose up, though, as Nora crossed the street into the unofficial camp. An older man to her left coughed violently into a scrap of bandage he held to his mouth in place of a handkerchief. The thin material was already red-brown with blood. He looked up at her clean clothes with a weary glare. Even though the blouse she wore was three days old and the hem of her skirt was caked with dirt, she looked nothing like the people she passed. The scents—so full of smoke and char everywhere else— were also different here. Intensely, almost violently human smells: food, filth, sweat. A hundred other odors came at her with such force that she wondered how she had not smelled them from the other side of the street. She realized, with a clarity that was almost a physical shock, that her concept of how bad things were paled in comparison to *how bad things actually were*. Nora felt a powerful urge to run. To retreat back to the official, orderly camp and its neat rows of tents before the depth of the unofficial squalor overtook her like the beast in her nightmares. This felt too close to the awful hours of that first morning.

It wasn't as if Nora didn't understand the scope of the catastrophe before. She did. But she'd somehow never grasped the sheer quantity of lives destroyed. Walking down this "alley," the real-life details pushed her into awareness. The air seemed to choke her. Her clothes felt hot and tight.

The lad pointed to what passed for his front door, saying, "It's just there."

Nora's brain shook itself to attention just enough to notice a small crowd had gathered at her appearance. It was not a friendly-feeling crowd—it had an air that made the hairs on the back of her neck stand on end—and she understood all too clearly why her father had not allowed her to venture off the cart before.

A young man to her right fitted scraps of cardboard into the holed soles of his shoes. Sam rattled off a list as he pointed to the surrounding shelters. "Elliot went for bread, Mrs. Watkins for bandages, Papa for water and me for mail." It seemed an awful lot to manage at his young age, but he spoke the list with such an everyday dryness that Nora's heart twisted to hear it.

"Papa!" Sam ducked into the shack, calling for his father. It left Nora standing in the aisle alone, listening to the shuffle of feet come to a stop behind her. "Papa!" Sam cried again from inside the shack, but no one answered.

A man came out from the next shelter. "He went back for more water, Sam." He eyed Nora, his expression confirming how out of place she already felt. His eyes fell to the scroll in her hand.

"I need Sam's tent number so I can add it to his father's letter."

"Who're you? The postmaster?" It was more a hollow joke than any kind of inquiry. The man took a step closer while two more even shadier characters came out from between two battered structures on the other side of the alley.

"My father's office is doing everything they can." She had to work to keep a calm voice.

"He is, is he? And how about *you*?" A skinny, greasy-looking young man smiled as he wandered closer. "You doin' all you can?"

"Of course," Nora answered, until the glint in his eyes turned the question into something she didn't want to answer. The wind picked up and made a shiver chase down her neck.

The man twisted a piece of string around his fingers in a fidgety gesture. "Really?" He stretched out the word in a most unsavory way. "You sure?"

"I am," came a deep voice from behind Nora. She spun around to see Quinn Freeman step solidly between her and the leering man. He hoisted a large piece of steel in one hand with a defensive air. "I'm really sure, Ollie. Want to find out how sure I am?"

"Charity's a virtue, Freeman." Ollie grinned, but it was more of a sneer.

"Just make sure it's virtue you got in mind. Miss Longstreet was just helping out, I imagine, and I'll make sure she gets back to the mail wagon safe and sound, don't you worry." Quinn nodded at Nora, taking the scroll from her as if to personally see to its security.

"You do that." Ollie kicked a stone in his path and started walking back down the alley. "You just go ahead and do that."

With Ollie's retreat, Nora felt the rest of the gathered crowd sink back to wherever they had come from. She let out the breath she had been holding. "It seems I owe you yet another debt, Mr. Freeman."

He put down the piece of steel and handed her back Sam's scroll. "I'm not so sure it was a smart idea for you to wander over here like that. Even to help Sam. Things can get a little…rough around here if you're not careful."

"My father would agree heartily. He'll probably be rather sore at me for trying. I hadn't realized…thank you again. First the locket, and now this. Surely there's some way to thank you."

He smiled the engaging grin he'd shown her back at the rally. His eyes were a light brown, an almost golden color that picked up the straw shades of his hair. He had a strong, square jaw that framed his easy grin—the sort of face at home with a frequent smile. "Like I said, Miss Longstreet, I was happy to see *something* find its way home." The sadness in the edge of his voice—the sadness that caught the edge of so many voices all around her—undercut the cheer of his words. "But there is something I'd like to show you. Something you ought to see before you leave with Ollie's version of how things are in here."

"Do you live nearby?" She realized what a ludicrous question that was, as if he had a house just up the street instead of a shack somewhere in this makeshift camp.

He tucked his hands into his pockets and nodded over his left shoulder. "Two rows down. The charming cottage on the left." When Nora blushed, feeling like an insensitive clod for asking such a useless question, he merely chuckled. "It's okay, really. I've seen worse. My uncle Mike says we might get back into a house next month. Just come see this and I'll walk you back across the street before your papa begins to worry."

He led Nora through one more row of shacks to where a cluster of children gathered. The gaggle of tots surged toward Quinn when they saw him, parting the crowd to reveal a rough-hewn teeter-totter pieced together out of scrap and an old barrel. She knew, instantly, that the makeshift toy had been Quinn's doing.

"Mister Kin, Mister Kin!" a chubby blond-haired girl greeted. Nora guessed it to be her approximation of Mr. Freeman's given name. "It works!"

Quinn hunched down and tenderly touched the tot's nose. "Told you it would." Nora smiled. How long had it been since she had heard children's laughter?

The girl giggled. "You're smart."

"Only just. Go ahead and take another turn, then. It'll be time to get on back to your ma soon, anyway."

Nora stood awed for a moment. Quinn Freeman had handed her the smallest patch of happiness, but it did the trick. "Thank you." She looked up at him, for he was a good foot taller than she if only a few years older, and thought that he was indeed clever to recognize a slapped-together toy would do so much good. "I did need to see this—you were right."

"Most people are afraid to really build anything here, thinking it'll make it feel like we'll be here forever, but even I know lads with nothing to do usually find something bad to fill their time."

"You'll be here another month?" Many families were talking of pulling up stakes and starting over somewhere else just as soon as circumstances would allow. Others refused to even think past their next meal.

"That's my guess. Don't pay much to peer too far into the future these days. God's got His hands full in the present, I'd say."

"He does." And he talks about God. In a *calm* way. Many people—her own family pastor Reverend Mansfield included—were shouting about the awful judgment God had "sent down" upon the sinful city of San Francisco. It wasn't so hard a thought to hold. With dust and destruction everywhere, it was easy to wonder if the Lord Almighty hadn't indeed turned His head away.

By this time they'd reached the mail wagon, and Papa was standing with a sour and alarmed look on his face. "Thank heavens you're all right. Just what do you think…?"

"I've seen her back safely, Mr. Longstreet, and told her not to venture over here like that again," Quinn cut in.

"Papa, this is Mr. Freeman. The man who returned Annette's locket. Now you can thank him in person."

The announcement took the wind out of Papa's scorn. Her father stepped down off the mail wagon and extended a hand to Quinn. "Seems I owe you."

The two men shook hands. "You don't owe me a thing. I was glad to help."

Papa looked at Nora. "Don't you go needing help again. I'll not let you come back if you wander off like that again. It's only by God's grace that Mr. Freeman was here to keep you from any trouble."

"Grace indeed," Quinn said, shooting a sideways smile at Nora as he tipped his hat at Papa. "Don't let it happen again, Miss Longstreet." As he turned, he added quietly over Nora's shoulder, "At least not until tomorrow around two."

Nora climbed back on the wagon to join her father. Perhaps the mail would not be so perfunctory from now on.

## Chapter Three

Ah, but she was a beauty.

Quinn stood mesmerized by the way she held her ground. Tall and proud, with defiant lines he wanted to catch from every angle.

Quinn was vaguely aware of an elbow to his ribs. "Nephew, ya look foolish just standing there like that."

Rough hands grabbed his face on both sides and pulled his gaze to the dusty, whiskered sight of his uncle Michael. "There's something wrong with you, man. It ain't natural, the way you look at buildings."

"Architecture. It's called architecture. I'd give anything to study."

Uncle Mike snorted. "You need a wife."

Quinn shifted his sore feet as his mind catapulted back to the rows of tiny black buttons that ran up the sides of Nora Longstreet's boots. He'd stared then, too, liking their lines as much if not more. "I need to *learn*," he said impatiently to his uncle, who simply rolled his eyes at the speech he'd heard every day even before the earthquake. "Apprentice an architect. Only there's no time to learn anymore. We need loads of builders, but we need them *now*." Everything took so much time these days. *Lord Jesus, You know I'm thankful to be alive, but this bread line feels two thousand miles long. I'm in no mood to learn no more patience, if You please.* He felt he'd die if he wasn't back at the camp edge by two. He had to see her again. Had to see that dented locket that he just knew would be polished up and hanging around her neck. He'd miss half a week's worth of bread to make sure he caught that sight—even if it meant he'd catch a whole lot more from his ma for returning without bread.

By the time the sun was high in the sky and the police officer on the corner said it was one-fifteen, Quinn still was looking at forty or so people in line in front of him. Without so much as an explanation, Quinn nudged his uncle and said, "I'm off."

"And just what do you think you're doin'?" the man balked as Quinn strode off in the direction of home, his feet no longer feeling the holes that burst through his shoes yesterday.

"I ain't sure yet," Quinn replied with a grin, tipping his hat as his uncle stood slack-jawed, "but I'll let you know."

Nora sat beside her father in the mail cart, her heart thumping like the hooves of the horse in front of them. Since the earthquake, she'd barely looked forward to anything or been excited about anything.

She wanted to see him. To feel that tug on her pulse when he caught sight of her. He seemed so *happy* to see her. She knew, just by the tilt of his head, that she brightened his day. There was a deep satisfaction in that; something that went beyond filling a hungry belly.

Still, that hadn't stopped her from bringing a loaf of bread she'd charmed out of the cook this morning.

He was a very clever man. He stood on the other side of the street, far enough from the cart to be unobtrusive, near enough to make sure she caught sight of him almost immediately. His eyes held the same fixation they had at the ceremony, and Nora felt a bit on display as she went about her duties.

He watched her. His gaze was almost a physical sensation, like heat or wind. He made no attempts to hide his attentions, and the frank honesty of his stare rattled her a bit, but not the way that man Ollie's stare had. She might be all of twenty-two, but Nora had lived long enough to judge when a man's intentions were not what they should be. Simply put, Quinn looked exceedingly glad to see her again. And there was something wonderful about that.

"You'll stay by the cart today," Quinn said, walking across the street when the line finally thinned out. "Mind your papa and all."

"I should," she admitted. "However, I would like very much to see the teeter-totter again. It seemed a very clever thing to do, and I wonder if there aren't some things back at my aunt's house that we could add to your contraption."

A bright grin swept over his face. "My contraption. I like that a far sight better than *that thing Quinn built*." He pushed his hat back on his head as he looked up at her, squinting in the sunlight. It gave Nora an excuse to settle herself down on the cart, bringing her closer to eye level with the man. "A contraption sounds important. I'll have to build another just to say I am a man of contraptions."

They held each other's gaze for a moment, and Nora felt it rush down her spine. It was powerful stuff these days to see someone happy—they'd barely left misery behind, and there was so much yet to endure ahead of them. She'd taken the streetcars completely for granted before. Now, everyone's shoes—and feet—had suffered far too much walking. She imagined his smile would be striking anywhere, but here and now, it was dashing.

"Still," he said, "it's best we don't wander off today. I wouldn't want your papa thinking poorly of me."

"Oh, I'm sure he couldn't do that." Nora fingered the locket now fastened around her neck. Something flickered in his eyes when she touched it. "You brought me back Annette's locket, and that was a fine thing to do."

"The pleasure's mostly mine, Miss. I think it made me as happy as it made you. And good news is as hard to come by as good food these days."

"Oh," Nora shot to her feet, remembering the loaf of bread tucked away behind her. "That reminds me. I know you said you didn't need a reward, but I just didn't feel right without doing something." She pulled out the loaf, wrapped in an old napkin. "Cook makes the best bread, even missing half her kitchen." She held it out.

"Glory," Quinn said, his grin getting wider, "You can't imagine how glad I am to see a loaf of bread. Especially today."

"Aren't you able to get any?"

She thought she saw him wink. "That's a long story. Just know you couldn't have picked a better day to give me a loaf of bread."

That felt simply grand, to know she'd done something he appreciated so much. "I'm glad, then. We're even."

"Hardly," he said, settling his hat down on to his head again. "I'm still ahead of you, Miss Longstreet. By miles." He bent his nose to the bread and sniffed. "I'd best get this home before it gets all shared away. Thank you, Miss Longstreet. Thank you very much."

"My pleasure," Nora said, meaning it. Taking a deep breath, she bolstered her courage and offered, "Tomorrow?"

"Absolutely."

The only sad thing about the entire exchange was that three months ago, Nora would have rushed home to tell every little detail to Annette. Today, she didn't mind the trickle of mail customers that still came to the wagon, for there was only Mama waiting at home. Nora laid her hand across the locket, hoping her thoughts could soar to where Annette could hear them. Is heaven lovely? I miss you so much.

Reverend Bauers tried to lift the large dusty box, but couldn't budge the heavy load at his advanced years. He huffed, batted at the resulting cloud of dust that had wafted up around him and threw Quinn a disgusted glance. "I'm too old for this."

Quinn wiped his brow with his shirtsleeve. It was stale and dusty down here in the Grace Mission House basement, and he'd already had a long day's work, but he'd be hanged if he'd let Reverend Bauers attempt cleaning up the rubble on his own. The man was nearly eighty, and although he showed little signs of slowing down his service to God, his body occasionally reminded him of the truth in "the spirit is willing but the flesh is weak."

"Didn't I just get through telling you the very same

thing? Reverend, I don't think when God spared you and Grace House through the earthquake and the fire that He did it all to have you collapse in the basement. You've got to slow down. You'll do no good to anyone if you hurt yourself."

His long and fast friendship with the pastor—since boyhood, going on twenty years now—had given him leave to speak freely with Reverend Bauers, but even Quinn knew when too far was too far. And even if the reverend's insistence on ordering the Grace House basement was a bit misguided, Quinn wasn't entirely sure he should be the soul to point it out. People reacted in funny ways to the overwhelming scale of destruction. His own ma bent over her tatting every night, even though Quinn was certain there'd be little use for lace in the coming months. Many people focused on ordering one little segment of their lives, because they could and because so much of the rest of their lives was spinning in chaos.

"I can't seem to stay away," Reverend Bauers said, giving a look that was part understanding, part defiance. "I keep getting nudges to tidy up down here, and you know I make it a policy not to ignore nudges." Reverend Bauers was forever getting "nudges" from God. And Quinn believed God did indeed nudge the portly old German—he'd seen far too much evidence of it to dismiss the man's connection with The Almighty. Only no one else ever just got "nudged." God seemed to be shouting at everyone else—or so they said. People were talking everywhere about God's judgment on San Francisco or claiming they'd heard God's command to destroy the city—and/or rebuild it, depending on who you talked to.

Only, after twenty-six years, God had yet to nudge or shout at Quinn. Reverend Bauers was always going on about purpose and providence and such, and he'd so vehemently declared that God had spared Quinn for some great reason that Quinn mostly believed him. The reason just hadn't shown itself yet, nor had any of God's nudges.

Quinn sighed as Bauers slid yet another box out of his way, poking through the cluttered basement. "There must be something down here," Bauers said, almost to himself. "Over there, perhaps." He pointed to a stack of shelving that had toppled over in the far corner of the room and motioned for Quinn to clear a path.

It took nearly ten minutes, and Quinn was tempted to offer up a nudge of his own to God about how dinner might be soon, when suddenly Bauers went still.

Quinn looked up from the shelf he was righting to see the reverend staring intently at an upended chest. "Oh, my," Bauers said in the most peculiar tone of voice. "Goodness. I hadn't even remembered this was down here."

"What?" Quinn cleared a path to it.

"That's it, isn't it? And there should be another one—a long, narrow one—right beside it somewhere."

Quinn stared from Bauers to the pair of chests, his heart thumping as he recognized the shape of the long narrow box. He must have been, what, twelve? Surely not much older. He caught Bauers's gaze, the old man's eyes crinkling up when he read Quinn's expression.

"Mr. Covington's things." Quinn began tearing through the boxes, bags and beams between him and the pair of chests. "Those are Mr. Covington's…"

"No, man, not just Mr. Covington's, and you know that. Those belong to the Bandit."

Quinn had reached the chests, fingering the latch on the longer box. He remembered what was inside now. He remembered thinking that that sword and that whip were the most powerful weapons on earth. He blew the dust off the box and set it atop a crate. "Do you think it lasted?"

"I see no scorch marks or dents. I'd venture to say it's in perfect shape." He picked his way quickly through the room until he stood next to Quinn. "But we'll not know a thing until you open it."

## Chapter Four

With a deep breath, Quinn undid the pair of latches on either side of the long wooden box. Inside, carefully nestled in their places on a bed of still amazingly blue velvet, lay a pair of swords. Even with the patina of twenty years, they gleamed in the basement's faint light. "His swords," Quinn remarked, not hiding his amazement. "The Bandit's swords."

Reverend Bauers's hand came to rest on Quinn's shoulder. "So many years. Such a long time ago—for both of us."

Quinn could hear the smile in Reverend Bauers's voice, sure it matched his own as he remembered the daring heroic feats of the Black Bandit that had once captured his young imagination. A dark hero who roamed the streets at night, offering aid to those who had none, supplying food to needy families, even sending money once to fix Grace House. The Black Bandit legend had woven its way into San Francisco's history—everyone's mother and grandmother had a Black Bandit story—but Quinn and the reverend were two of the only four people in the world who knew Matthew Covington had been the man behind the mask. He cocked his head in the clergyman's direction. "Wouldn't we like to have our Bandit back now, hmm?"

Quinn picked up the sword, turning it to catch the light. When he was twelve, this sword had seemed enormous. Too heavy and long for a slight boy. Time and trials had done their work on Quinn, however, and he was a tall man of considerable strength. He wondered, for a moment, if he remembered any of the moves Mr. Covington had taught him. "Do you remember that day, Reverend?"

There was no need to explain "that day." Bauers would know Quinn was referring to the day he met— and marred—the noble English businessman. Bauers's smile and nod confirmed his understanding. "Evidently, I've remembered it better than you. You, who have the most reason of all to remember that day."

Quinn's introduction to Matthew Covington had been, in fact, by injury. He'd taken a knife to Covington's arm as the Englishman tried to stop a robbery. A crime Quinn and his buddy were attempting—stealing from Grace House. It was amusing, in a sad sort of way, to think they'd thought times hard enough to steal from a church back then. Those times were nothing compared to what they were now.

Still, Quinn was young, impressionable and desperate for decent food. His father's love of the whiskey bottle hadn't made for much of a steady home life. Trying to steal from Grace House Mission—an organization bent on helping his impoverished neighborhood—had been the low point of his life.

It had also been the turning point. Back in that garden, watching Matthew Covington bleed, Quinn had realized he had two choices in life: up or down. Dark or light. Hard or easy. And, when it came right down to it, destruction or redemption. That day Quinn chose to climb his way out of the mess his young life had become, and Reverend Bauers had been the first to recognize it. That troublesome day, and the tense ones that followed it, marked the beginning of Quinn's unusually close relationship with the reverend. Uncle Mike had been known to say that Bauers was the real father Quinn never had; and it was true.

Quinn swung the sword in a gentle arc. It felt so light now. "Do you think he knows? Everything that's happened here?"

Bauers smiled. "Matthew and Georgia wired money last week and asked that we wire back a list of needed supplies. His own son is fifteen now."

Quinn tilted the sword again, admiring it. Even though Bauers had only been able to secure him a year or two of fencing lessons, he knew it was an outstanding weapon. It had a graceful balance and tremendous strength.

As wondrous as the sword was, it wasn't the weapon most people associated with the Black Bandit. Catching Bauers's eye, Quinn flipped open the second chest. There it lay, on top, carefully coiled; the Bandit's leather whip. His mind wandered back to the summer afternoons where Quinn would swish a length of rope around the Grace House garden, pretending at the Bandit's skill with his whip. Quinn lifted it carefully—it hadn't survived the years as well as the swords. Bits of leather disintegrated with every flex, and the rich black braids were a stiff and crackled gray. He found himself afraid to uncoil it, simply moving it to the side to gain access to the rest of the chest's contents. It contained exactly what he knew it would: a pair of black boots with a small silver B imbedded in each calf, a trio of dark gray shirts—voluminous, almost piratelike in appearance—and a black hat with the remnants of a white feather beside it.

And there, at the bottom of the chest, lay the mask. An ingenious thing, the Bandit's mask was almost a leather helmet with a strip that could either come down over the eyes or fold up into the hat. Covington had let him try the mask on once, and the thing had nearly slid off his head. Quinn raised the mask into the light, inspecting it. It had held up much better than the whip, still surprisingly supple even after so much time. He couldn't help but smile at the memory of the Bandit's myriad of adventures. "Mr. Covington should have kept these."

The reverend's expression changed. "I don't think that was the plan. He gave those to *you*. And Matthew Covington did everything for a very good reason."

That made Quinn laugh. "I've not much use for a sword and whip, now do I? Although I could put the boots to good use."

Reverend Bauers leaned his heavy frame against a dusty chest of drawers. "It makes one wonder."

"What?"

"What else you could put to good use."

It took Quinn a full ten seconds to gain the man's meaning, at which point he dropped the mask. "You're not serious."

The sparkle in Reverend Bauers's eye was unmistakable. "Why not?"

Quinn squared off at the man. "I'm a bit old for adventure stories. And times are a mite harder now."

Bauers folded his arms across his chest. It was a gesture Quinn knew all too well, and he did not like the look of it.

"Matthew was close to your age when it all started. And it all started with a story." He caught Quinn's glare. "Stories are meant to be told. And *retold*."

"I'm not Matthew Covington," he said, because it needed saying. Covington was a clever, wealthy man who'd done remarkable things.

"No, Quinn. You're *you*. Matthew knew that, too. What if you are exactly the man we need? Do you really think we're down here digging in the basement for no reason at all?"

Quinn sank down on a crate. "I hardly think God brought me down to your cellar to ask me to be the Black Bandit."

It was a long moment before Bauers answered simply, "How do you know?"

"Because it's insane. I've barely enough food to eat, my shoes have twelve holes in them, the city's barely getting through the day, I've no money, no influence and barely a spare hour to think."

Bauers's face split into a satisfied grin. "But you found enough time to help an old man go through his cellar. You found enough time to build those little ones that toy you told me about. You know what I always say—there's always enough time to do God's will."

Even as the mail cart bounced its way a block from Aunt Julia's house, Nora could tell something was happening. The house seemed almost bustling, with Mama

and Aunt Julia scurrying around the yard and porch
with a speed and energy Nora hadn't seen in a while.
A gracious table—or as gracious a table as one could
manage these days—was set up on the porch.

Tea. Mama and Julia were setting out afternoon tea.
And while afternoon tea had recently meant cups and
saucers on mismatched plates with whatever crackers
could be managed, this tea was different. It took a moment for Nora to realize what Mama and Aunt Julia
were actually doing; they were entertaining.

"There you are," said Mama hurriedly as the cart rattled its way into the drive. "Goodness, I thought you'd
miss it altogether. Run upstairs, find whichever dress
is the most clean and put it on. She'll be here soon."

"Who?" Nora and her father asked at the same time.

"Mrs. Hastings."

"Dorothy Hastings? Here?" Papa asked. "I didn't
think she was still in town."

"She's returned." Mama said it almost victoriously,
as if it were as significant a societal achievement as the
streetcar lines coming back into service. "And she's
coming *here*."

The Hastings family was a social pillar of San Francisco. Mr. Hastings was on the Committee of Fifty—
the emergency governing body that Papa served. Mrs.
Hastings, like many of the city's finer families, had
removed herself from the city to safer environs. Why
she was in town at all, much less at Aunt Julia's house,
Nora could only guess. Still, it was clear her visit was
important to Mama. Perhaps even more than that, the
opportunity to host someone, especially someone so
important, seemed to light a spark in Mama and Aunt
Julia that had been gone since the earthquake. A spark,

when Nora was honest with herself, she hadn't been sure would return. That relief made Nora practically dance up the stairs to find whatever dress seemed the least tattered.

She found a frock—a deep rose that hid dust and dirt especially well and whose neckline showed off the locket to particular advantage—and a small pink flower that had fallen off a hatpin to tuck into her hair. It did feel wonderful to "dress up," even just this small bit. She had no idea how Mama and Aunt Julia could pull together any kind of tea under the circumstances, but they were highly motivated and resourceful women. And the combined skills of the two household cooks had managed some wondrous meals given the lack of foodstuffs. Half of Nora understood her father's amused scowl at the whole thing. She was sure Papa found the whole exercise to be simply a diversion for his wife. Even if Mr. Hastings was in charge of city services, tea seemed rather pointless.

Still, the other half of Nora understood how valuable it could be right now. To engage in something—anything—for the mere pleasure of it seemed a dear luxury. A tiny, beautiful shield against the endless, tiresome obstacles of rebuilding. Not unlike, she realized as she fixed the small flower into the corner of her chignon, Quinn's teeter-totter. Papa might consider that a pointless diversion as well, and yet she recognized the plaything's value.

Nora was just dusting off her skirts a second time when Mama entered the room. The *real* Mama, not the wisp of a woman who had seemed to occupy Mama's skin for the last few months. She'd been praying nightly for God to return the light to Mama's eyes. Today, those prayers had been answered.

For days after the earthquake, Mama had carried all her good jewelry around in a pocket tied inside her skirts. There was no safe place to put anything, and no one knew, as the fires ate up more and more of the city in an arsenal hunger no one could quite believe, when a hasty exit might be required. Over and over again during those first weeks, Nora had watched her mama lay her hand over the lump in her skirts. Checking to be sure it was still there or perhaps just shielding the trinkets from the horrors of the outside world. Eventually, Uncle Lawrence had produced a lockbox for Mama and Papa, and their valuables went in there. Nora thought it was far too tiny a thing to hold a life's valued possessions, but then again, Nora had had to rethink a lot about life's valued possessions in recent weeks.

Today, Mama had her pearls around her neck. And Grandmama's pearl ring—a piece that belonged to Mama and Aunt Julia's own mother—graced her right hand. It wasn't the beauty of the jewelry that made Nora smile, it was the way Mama carried herself when she wore it.

Mama came over and readjusted a curling tendril that fell from Nora's chignon. "You look lovely," Mama said. "But I think," she said delicately, "that it would be kindest to tuck the locket inside your dress."

Nora's hand came up to touch the locket. She'd already been gratefully amazed that Aunt Julia let her keep it. In her joy over recovering the locket, she hadn't even considered that Aunt Julia might want her lost daughter's necklace for herself until Papa brought it up on the ride home. He'd gone with Nora to show the locket to Aunt Julia, and it had taken every ounce of will Nora had not to beg Aunt Julia to let her keep it. It would be wrong to deny a grieving woman any remnant of her daughter, but the necklace couldn't come close to meaning to Aunt Julia what it meant to Nora. She *needed* to have it. Needed to feel the only tangible evidence of that sweet friendship around her neck, close to her heart.

Aunt Julia had clutched the locket for a long moment that made everyone in the room hold their breath. Papa kept his hand on Nora's shoulder, as if to say, *be strong*, but said nothing. After a hollow-sounding breath, Aunt Julia let it slide back into Nora's hand. "You keep it, dear," she said with an unnatural calm. Nora and Papa waited there for a moment, thinking she meant to say something else, perhaps to cry or to say how glad she was to have the locket found, but she never said anything else. She just straightened her shoulders, touched Nora's cheek in a way that made her shiver and walked on to the porch to sit staring out over the city.

Nora went after her to thank her, but Papa's hand held her back. "Let her be," Papa said quietly. "It is a terrible thing to bury a daughter. And it is a far more terrible thing to not have a daughter to bury."

Of course Nora would tuck the locket out of sight. And Mama was right—it was by far the kindest thing to do.

# Chapter Five

"It's hopeless." Quinn's ma stood at the opening of their shack and rewound her graying red hair up into the ever-present knot at the base of her neck. "You can't expect children to run around such filth all day long without shoes and not cut their feet to ribbons." She looked up and saw Uncle Mike coming up the path. "Did you find any, Michael?"

"It's just as I thought, Mary. Only the sisters in the other camp have any iodine left."

His mother blew out a breath. "The sisters. Well, that's all well and good for them, but we're on the wrong side of the street to get much of that, aren't we?"

"And they don't come over here 'til Thursday."

Quinn watched his ma look at poor Sam. He'd cut his foot yesterday morning on a nail, and it was an angry red this afternoon—a bad sign. "It hurts you, don't it, boy?"

Sam, smart enough to see the bad news in Ma's eyes, put on a brave face. "Not so much."

Quinn sat down next to the boy. "Your limp says different, Sam. If it hurts a lot, my ma should know. Ma's are smart that way, besides. No use fooling them about things like this."

Sam swallowed hard. "It hurts a lot," he admitted.

"I reckon it does," Ma said, her smile softening. "You've got a man-sized wound in your foot, and you're just a tiny one, you are." She put Sam's foot back into the bucket, which was really just a large tin Uncle Mike had found and washed, and motioned for Quinn to stand.

"I'll take it you'd know where to find a shot or two of whiskey," she asked.

Quinn raised an eyebrow at his mother. Given the damage alcohol had done in this household, he knew his mother's disapproval of drinking. "For the *wound*," she clarified in an exasperated tone. "Iodine would be better, but we can hardly get persnickety now, can we?"

Uncle Mike put his hands into his pockets while Ma reached for the small pine box she kept under her trunk. Quinn knew they were searching for a coin or two—the man at the far corner of Dolores Park, who'd opened an undercover tavern, brooked no charity whatsoever. Even if he carried Sam bleeding and screaming in pain to the man, Quinn doubted the profiteer would spare a table-spoon for medicinal purposes. "I've got one," Quinn said, producing the silver coin he'd found under a beam two days ago. He'd had his eye on a pair of hose for his mother—her fifty-first birthday was next week—but Sam seemed a more pressing cause.

Ma sighed. "That'd buy a whole bottle of iodine be-fore."

*"Before."* Quinn echoed her sigh, tucking the coin back in his pocket and tussling Sam's hair. "Before" didn't even need words around it anymore. It had be-

come an expression unto itself. Everybody knew what you meant when you said "before," especially when you said it that way. As he walked out of the tent toward the rowdier edge of the camp, Quinn wondered if the time would come when someone said "before" like it was a bad thing. Like things were so much better now. *That day will come, won't it, Lord?*

As he picked his way through the moonlit alleys—lamps or any other open flames were scarce and outlawed after sundown besides—Quinn was almost sorry he'd said that prayer. It kept ricocheting back to him somehow, as if the answer to it lay within his own reach. He was one man, barely able to scrape up enough whiskey to treat a boy's wound, much less make things better than before. Right now, with the wind rousting up an uncomfortable chill, San Francisco was a problem that felt even too big for God, and Reverend Bauers would surely scold him for thinking that way.

Reverend Bauers.

Quinn thought of the boxes they'd discovered in the Grace House cellar. Did he even dare think one man could make things better?

Bauers would undoubtedly argue that Quinn did know one man who had made things better than before. Quinn shrugged and pulled his thin coat tighter around him. Had he really? Or was he just remembering the daring Black Bandit exploits with the easily impressionable eyes of youth? He'd thought the Bandit's weapons giant-sized, but they weren't when he held them yesterday. Matthew Covington was clever, yet hadn't Nora Longstreet called him clever to realize the children needed playthings?

*Am I clever enough, Lord?* The question seemed to

shoot right through him, like an electric current. Donated medical supplies were supposedly pouring into the city. They had to be going somewhere. Perhaps a clever man need only help get such things from one place to another. And these days, with as few people watching as possible. That, Quinn surmised with a low churning in his chest, was most definitely the job for one clever man.

Quinn Freeman couldn't really be the Black Bandit. That was fine, however, because San Francisco didn't need a Bandit. It needed a messenger. An invisible transporter, getting things from those who sent them to those who needed them. He could do that.

I can do that. Quinn had to stop for a moment, reeling from the weight of the idea. Actually, he reeled from the *lightness* of the idea. Quinn had just answered the question burning in the corner of his heart since the fires. The question everyone asked but no one dared to voice. The thing niggling at him, keeping him up nights, making him stare off into space for hours instead of sleeping: *Why am I still here?*

"That's why I'm still here?" His chest began to lift as he said the words aloud to himself. It made perfect, ridiculous sense. He knew the streets in a way a wealthier man never could. He had size and speed and the kind of wit that can get a man from one point to another without being seen. He had weapons to defend himself and the unfaltering faith of Reverend Bauers at his back.

And he'd been chosen. Decades ago. By the one man most qualified to choose.

That's why I'm still here. That's why I survived. That's why the chest survived and why we found it again yesterday. Quinn could almost feel God's eyes looking down on him, waiting with a stare twenty years long. Poised to launch him into an unimaginable adventure.

Quinn looked quickly around, somehow sure he'd changed physically, that those around could see the earth-shattering moment that just took place.

The world shuffled by dark and unawares. There seemed no other words to use. Quinn squeezed his eyes tight and prayed. *Here I am, Lord, send me.*


Nora examined Sam's injured foot as he poked it toward her. An angry red gash ran down the soft pink flesh; far too large a cut for such a fidgety, innocent foot. And to call it clean was a bit of a stretch, given the grime on the rest of the boy. She had no doubt Mrs. Freeman struggled to get the boy as clean as he was. "They make me sit here all the time," he pouted. With youth's astounding flexibility, Sam pulled the foot up practically to his nose and squinted at it. Nora's hip joints hurt just watching the contortion.

Comically, Sam sniffed at his foot and wiggled his toes. "Smells fine," he pronounced, giving the tiny jar of whiskey on Mrs. Freeman's trunk a suspicious glare. "I'm okay now." He put the foot down, stuffing it back into the single enormous sock—one of Quinn's, Nora supposed. Mrs. Freeman had tried to make Sam wear it in a last-ditch effort to keep out the constant dust.

He made to stand up, until Quinn's hand came down on his shoulder. "I thought you said you wanted a visit from Miss Longstreet here. It took a fair amount of promises and convincing to get her to come over here." Quinn pulled the huge sock back off Sam's foot. "You can't just up and leave now that she's been nice enough to come and call, now can you?"

Sam's wiggles suggested that he intended to do just that, and Nora wondered if her visit had been meant to distract Quinn, not Sam himself. "Oh, no, Sam, I came to see you." Nora paid careful attention not to catch Quinn's eyes as she spoke that last bit. "I wanted to make sure you were all right. After all, you've entrusted your mail into my care, and that means we're friends now."

"It was fine of your father to let you come." Mrs. Freeman nodded toward Sam, who didn't relax until she put the jar of alcohol away back inside the trunk. She handed Nora a roll of makeshift bandages, much like the strips of sheets and cloth Nora had made with her mother and Aunt Julia nearly every week since the earthquake. Nora's family—and most of San Francisco's female population—was down to one petticoat in the name of bandage making. "He was just a bit less wild with the promise of a visit from you." She shook her head and motioned for Nora to begin wrapping Sam's foot. "'Tis a crime to be treating lads with whiskey." She spoke sharply as she slammed the trunk shut. "But I suppose we should say a prayer of thanks that we've got anything at all." Mama might have taken Mrs. Freeman's sharp tone as an accusation, but Nora could see it was just frustration at how slow relief seemed to be moving. Everyone—Nora included—had thought things would be so much more settled by now. Mrs. Freeman turned to Sam with a mother's piercing glare. "You say a prayer of thanks, young Sam, that Miss Longstreet brought you those fine sweets to suck on while we tended your foot."

"I did," Sam replied quickly. Under Mrs. Freeman's suspiciously raised eyebrow, he added, "Sort of."

Quinn hunkered down to Sam's height as Nora tied off the end of Sam's new bandage. "I'd change that 'sort of' into a 'thank You, Father God' tonight, if I were you. My ma talks to God all the time, so she'll know if you don't."

Sam nodded.

"You've still no real bandages?" Nora asked, straightening up. She'd caught sight of Quinn staring at her hands as she wrapped Sam's foot. Even though it was a quick glance out of the corner of her eye, she found it unnerving. That man watched things far too intensely. "No things to treat wounds? My father said supplies like that are coming in from the army all the time." She handed back the bandage roll while Quinn tied the enormous sock in place with a piece of string. The makeshift footwear looked absurd, the toe of the sock flopping about as Sam jiggled his foot.

"Your father would know that more than I, miss, and it may be true." Mrs. Freeman opened the trunk once more, tucking the roll of cloth strips inside. "The nuns and the official camps have supplies, surely, but they only come over here once a week. You can't very well ask people to only cut themselves on Wednesdays, now can you?"

"It's just iodine," Nora said, amazed. "There must be bottles and bottles of it at the other camps by now. Papa says crates of supplies come through his office every day."

"And you can see how much of it makes its way to us out here." She softened her hard stare. "We can't all fit into the official camps, no matter what those men in suits say. But that's none of your doing, Miss Longstreet. I've not meant to grouse at you. I don't know where they expect us to go or how they expect us to get by. So much making do and doing without wears on a soul."

Obviously cued by Quinn, Sam stood up straight and extended a chubby hand. "Thanks for my licorice, Miss Longstreet. And for coming."

Nora shook Sam's hand with grand formality. "You're welcome, young master Sam. And thank you for the invitation. I do hope you're feeling better soon."

Sam was evidently feeling better now, for he tumbled through the door as soon as Quinn's hand released his shoulder. A limping tumble, but an energetic one just the same. Nora watched him go. "What else do you need? I have to think there is something I or my family can do."

Mrs. Freeman planted her hands on her hips. "What *don't* folks need? We need everything. Bandages, iodine, wood, water, socks, pins, string… I could rattle on for days."

"Wait a minute." Nora fished into her pockets for the bits of paper and the stub of a pencil she'd begun keeping in there during her mail cart visits. "Let me write this down." Mrs. Freeman rattled off the surprisingly long list of basic items needed in the makeshift camps. Many of these things showed up regularly in the official camps. How had things become so segregated?— everyone suffered. It made no sense. Two or three of the items she could provide from her own household. Surely in the name of Christian mercy Mama and Aunt Julia—with a little help from Mrs. Hastings, perhaps— might scour up the rest.

"Could you make another copy of that list?" Quinn asked, holding out his hand. "Reverend Bauers could put one to good use, I'd guess."

"Of course." Nora found another scrap of paper— this one a page torn out of a cookery book—and copied down the list.

Quinn folded it carefully and tucked it into a pocket of his shirt. He had the most peculiar smile on his face, as if he'd just learned a great secret. "I should get you back, Miss Longstreet, before your father worries."

Quinn stared at the list. Miss Longstreet did a funny, curvy thing with the dots on her *i*'s. A delicate little backward slant. He ran his fingers across the writing again, careful not to smudge it.

He had his first challenge. A list of basic supplies.

It was in her handwriting. That shouldn't have mattered much, but it did. There was a generosity about her that stuck in the back of his mind. She was kind to Sam, but not out of pity—the sort that he had seen far too much of lately. That version—a superior, ingratiating sort of assistance—bred the hopelessness that was already running rampant in the camp. Nora's kind of help was respectful. She grasped the truth that made so many people uncomfortable in this disaster: fire was no respecter of privilege. Those now without homes had done nothing but live on the wrong street corner at the wrong time. The firestorm and the earthquake destroyed nice homes as eagerly as they consumed shanties. Bricks fell just as hard on good men as they did on criminals. Certain people had begun to sort victims into worthy and unworthy categories. Official camp refugees and squatters. Implying reasons why the refugees were in the positions they were. It was, Quinn supposed, a perfectly human reaction to death and destruction's random natures. A desire to seek order amidst chaos.

It was just very irritating to be on the receiving end. And Quinn, like most of Dolores Park's residents, had come to see it a mile off.

Nora wasn't like that. And yes, he had come to think of her as Nora, even though he'd always address her as "Miss Longstreet," of course. Quinn felt as if he could read all her thoughts in those violet eyes. It seemed such a cliché to say "there was something about her," but he could get no more specific than that—something about her tugged at his imagination constantly. Little details, like the gentleness of how she bandaged Sam's foot. The delicacy of her handwriting or the way her fingers fluttered over the locket when she was thinking.

He could no longer lie to himself: Nora Longstreet had caught his eye.

# *Chapter Six*

"I've laid it all out in my head, Reverend. It wouldn't be that hard, actually."

Reverend Bauers sat back in his chair, ready to listen. Quinn had once loved the meticulous order of the reverend's study—it had seemed to him like an enormous library, although he'd never actually seen a true library. Today, Bauers reclined between tall stacks of linens and a tottering tower of pots and pans. The neatness of his study had been overthrown by the new demands on the Grace House kitchen, which had suffered damage in the earthquake but now had even more mouths to feed. As such, the study now doubled as an extra pantry, so the books shared their shelves with tins of tomatoes, jars of syrup, and whatever foodstuffs Bauers had managed to find to feed his flock.

"I expected as much, Quinn."

Quinn again had the sensation of being the center of a story that had begun before he arrived. As if everyone around him knew more of his own future than he himself did. It was the kind of thoughts that could make a man edgy. And bold. "If we could get them from the army or the hospital, it'd be easy as pie."

Reverend Bauers frowned. "If you could get them easily from those places, you'd have them already."

Quinn leaned one shoulder against the wall. "You're right. And that's wrong. Even I can see we can't fit in those official camps. Why bother to divide us at all unless someone wants the groups to start fighting each other?"

"Just to make things clear here, man, stealing will not be an option. I admit we might have to stretch our definition of 'procurement,' but there will be no taking of supplies against the will of those who have them. You must become an agent of expediting, not a thief."

Quinn furrowed a brow at the long word. "Expediting?"

"The art of expediting is the art of getting things where they need to go quickly. Efficiently. And, I've no doubt in this case, rather creatively. You possess the creativity in spades. We just need someone very well-connected. And, you'll be happy to know, God has been kind enough to present us with an ally. Can you be at Fort Mason tomorrow afternoon at two?"

Quinn winced. There was only one place he ever wanted to be at two in the afternoon, and it wasn't anywhere near the army base. "I've got someplace to be at two, but make it three and I'll be there."

"Two minutes after three," said a dark-haired man in uniform with a precise mustache and an even more precise snap of his pocket watch. "He's punctual, at least. That's something." Quinn found himself nose to nose with a meticulously dressed man with dark, sharp eyes.

"I'm told you run fast." The man pocketed his watch.

"I do."

"Have you a steady hand?"

Quinn wasn't entirely sure where this was heading. "So they tell me."

"Quinn Freeman," Reverend Bauers cut in, "may I present Army Major Albert Simon. Major Simon, this is Quinn Freeman, the man I've been telling you about."

Major Simon walked around him, appraising him as if he were buying a horse. "Tall, strong, good reach, I'd expect." He turned to Bauers. "He's had some training in fencing?"

"Two years," Quinn stepped in, not liking the idea of Bauers and Simon talking about him as if he weren't in the room. "It was a long time ago, but I still remember most of it."

Simon stroked one hand down either tip of his mustache. "Ever shot a pistol, Freeman?"

"I've been fired at," Quinn offered, "but I don't own a gun."

"It's harder than you think."

"So is a lot of life, Major. Especially now."

"Which is why we're here," Bauers declared. "Major Simon," he said in a lower tone, "has agreed to be in on our little scheme."

Quinn looked at the man. He was fit but a bit on the heavy side, somewhere in his late thirties from the looks of it and alarmingly serious. He didn't seem at all like the scheming type. "The Bandit—"

"Is not a name I'd mention in loud tones around here," the major cut in sharply. "Not everyone in the army is a fan of such…resourceful measures."

"I think you'll find Major Simon a most extraordinary fellow." Reverend Bauers walked over to a large sack Quinn only just then realized sat on a table in the center of the room. "With some very considerable resources." He pulled open the drawstring and tilted the top for Quinn to peer inside.

The sack held half of what had been on his list. On Nora's list, that is. Bandages, iodine, salt, a few tins of meat, needles and thread and half a dozen other various supplies. Major Simon went up a few notches in Quinn's book, to be sure. More than a few.

"Where'd you get all that?"

"No need for you to know," Simon said slyly.

"You stole it. Why else would you answer like that?"

"Would you take it no matter where it came from?"

"I'm smarter than that. I don't know you, even if Reverend Bauers does."

"They were 'procured,' perhaps, or more precisely, 'diverted,' but ready for you to put to good use." Simon pulled the string shut, placing the sack into a crate that sat under the table. "And no, you don't know me. Yet."

"The major has arranged a discreet drop-off point," Bauers said, clearly enjoying the adventure of it all. With that look in his eye, Quinn could easily imagine the days when Reverend Bauers had been the Black Bandit's trusted accomplice. He seemed delighted to step into those shoes again. "You're to return tonight and get it back to camp by…well…whatever means you find necessary."

His first mission. It hummed through Quinn's veins. Suddenly, he couldn't get the Bandit's old gray shirt on fast enough. He longed to strap on the sword and take the world by storm. Now.

"You have a fire in your eye, Freeman," Major Simon

said to him. "I've found our friend the reverend is rarely wrong on such things. But you'll need far more than good intentions if you really want to do what you say. You'll need training and cunning and several very particular skills. Skills I've offered to teach you. But you'll have to be both patient and discreet."

"I am."

"You don't strike me as patient in the least."

"Would you be patient if your family didn't have enough to eat or a real roof over their heads?"

Simon chuckled and clapped Quinn hard on the back. "Bold as brass. You're right, Bauers, he's just the man for the job. If he doesn't get himself killed first."

"You've no idea where all this came from?" Nora asked as she peered at the supplies that had appeared overnight at the Freeman shack.

Mrs. Freeman squinted at the cut on Sam's foot, paused, and then dabbed it with a bit more iodine. "None at all," she said over the resulting protests from Sam. "Quinn said he'd put the list up on a fence post across the street last night, asking for help. That's all we know." She turned to the boy. "Hush, lad, it'll hurt far more than that if it don't heal properly." Her words were harsh, but her eyes were kind.

"It is amazing, isn't it?" Nora examined the items again, grateful her father had allowed her to come over to Dolores Park to inspect this surprise package—provided, of course, that she was properly escorted, which wasn't at all an unpleasant requirement. Nora turned over the tins of meats, looking for any clue. She'd shown the list to several people, and obviously someone else had now seen the list, but still no one seemed to know who'd found the rare items and delivered them to camp. It was a feat. As common as the items were, Nora could only manage to scare up two needles and three spools of thread. Before the earthquake, it might have taken her all of fifteen minutes to secure the entire list. How scarce life's necessities had become.

"You'd best listen to my ma," Quinn said, planting himself down on the chest next to a squirming Sam, whose bottom lip threatened tears at any moment. "You strike me as a smart lad. And a brave one. We'll need you fit and strong to help out. You'll be no use to me limping around like a goat, now will you?"

"I'll need you to escort me," Nora whispered to Sam, grinning. "I shouldn't trouble Mr. Freeman much longer. He's a busy man and he's likely to tire of leading me to and fro."

Quinn applied a mock frown, but his eyes told a far different story. While he'd refused her any details, she knew he'd gone to great lengths to meet the two o'clock mail run yesterday. When they were late because one of the cart's finicky wheels had jammed, she'd found him practically pacing the street in a state she could only describe as panic. And while he'd walked calmly— perhaps it wasn't too much of an exaggeration to say he swaggered slightly—back to the edge of the camp, she'd noticed he broke into a flat-out run once he turned the corner. Yes, sir, Quinn Freeman was very late for something yesterday, and she could not deny what his tarrying had done to that sparkling spot just above her stomach. He looked at her as if she were the best part of his day, and she was not at all certain she hid her own pleasure at seeing him.

"She's far too much work, this one," Quinn said. The

sour notes in his voice were no match at all for the spark in his eyes. "Take her off my hands as fast as you can, man." He ruffled Sam's moppish hair.

Mrs. Freeman gave the quickest of glances back and forth between her son and Nora. "When the foot's ready, and not a moment before. Iodine and bandages are too rare to go wasting with foolishness. Put that sock back on, young man, and mind you stay out of the dust as best you can. Come back tomorrow and I'll have a look at it again."

"Yep," said Sam, sliding off the trunk.

Quinn snagged the boy's elbow as he went to leave. "Yes, *ma'am,* and say thank you."

"Thanks, ma'am." Sam punctuated his attempt at manners by wiping his nose on his sleeve.

Mrs. Freeman moaned. "I'm climbin' uphill both ways to keep anything clean here." She rubbed the back of her neck with her hand and sighed. "What I wouldn't give for a true sink and a clean set of sheets."

Quinn gave his mother a quick peck on the cheek. "You've worked wonders as it is, Ma." He pointed to the stock of supplies. "And somebody's taken notice."

"And wouldn't I like to know who?" his mother said, smiling. "And what else they've got. Father Christmas coming in July. Who'd have thought?" She wiped her hands on her apron and began loading the supplies back into the trunk. "Get her back now, Quinn, before her father starts to worrying about where she is."

Quinn shrugged his coat back on as they walked. "So your father's office didn't deliver that package? I thought surely you'd done it. You had the list, after all."

"So did you," Nora replied. "And you posted it. Someone with the things must have seen the one you tacked up. Still, what showed up didn't really match up to the list we'd made."

"It's a mystery, to be sure." He went to do the button on his coat, found no button to do, and gave out a little *hrrmph* as he was forced to let it hang open. "I may have to beg Ma for a little of that thread, won't I?" They walked on, and Nora made a note to dig through her father's coats for a sparc button tonight. "Everyone needs everything, it seems," Quinn sighed. "Reverend Bauers at Grace House can be a resourceful man, but he needs all of those things as much as we do, if not more."

"I've heard stories about Grace House. Is it still standing?

"It is," Quinn replied. "The building next door fell to the ground, but Grace House is mostly fine."

Nora let out a long sigh. "It's hard not to wonder how He's let all this happen and why. I can't get my mind around anything that makes sense, no matter how many prayers I say."

"No sense to be made, if you ask me. Some things just are. You could stand around all day trying to figure out why, and it still won't find you dinner or get your house rebuilt. It's not the *why*s we need to worry about now, Miss Longstreet, it's the *how*s that matter most."

"*How,* then, do you think those things found their way to your mother?"

He stuffed his hands in his pockets and shrugged his shoulders. "Don't rightly know."

"Someone, somewhere, has played the hero. I think it's perfectly grand. I hope everyone hears about it and twenty other people do the same. What a wonderful thing that would be, don't you think?"

Quinn laughed. He had a very delightful, forthright

laugh. "I think you're getting ahead of yourself, miss. It's not smart to make so much of one good deed."

"One good deed like a teeter-totter? Oh, I think you know the power of one good deed far more than you let on." She didn't hide the broad smile that crept up from somewhere near her heart.

"Grace House does the important work, not me. But even they're busting under the load right now, or so Reverend Bauers says. He's got a few benefactors who can help out, you know, friends in high places and all, but not nearly enough."

Why hadn't she thought of it before now? "I can help with that."

He raised an eyebrow. "I think you're helping as much as you can now. Your pa'll be sore at your being gone as long as you have, if not worse."

"No, I mean with the benefactors. I know someone who can help. We had a wealthy woman named Mrs. Hastings to tea at the house the other day. She's wanted to see the ruined city but her husband won't let her come any farther than our house." Nora looked at Quinn. "What if we could get Mrs. Hastings to tour Grace House? Surely her husband couldn't object to something like that? Then she could meet people. She could meet Reverend Bauers. I've heard so much about him, even *I'd* like to meet Reverend Bauers. It's the perfect solution."

Quinn stopped walking and looked at her. "You've never met Reverend Bauers?"

He made it sound as if her social upbringing lacked a crucial element. "Well, of course I've shaken his hand at some city ceremony at some time or another, but I don't really know him. I only know of him. Papa knows him, I think, but not socially."

Those words came out wrong. As if people like Papa didn't socialize with people like Reverend Bauers. It was true, in some ways, but not in the way her words made it sound. Quinn had noticed. He stood up straighter, started walking again, and the set of his jaw hardened just enough for her to notice.

Nora reached out and caught his elbow. "I didn't mean it like that."

"No one ever does." The edge in his voice betrayed the wound her words had caused.

"No, really. It was a horrid way to put it. I just meant…" What did she just mean? She'd said it without thinking, without consideration, of what Mama would have called "their differences in station." Why consider some great foolish gulf between them—especially now, when all that seemed to matter so very little? She dropped her hand. "I don't know what I meant. But I've not met Reverend Bauers and I would very much like to. And I want to help. I believe Mrs. Hastings will want to help, too, if we can show her Grace House. Please. I know she will."

"If she honestly *wants* to help, and not just gawk at other folks' hardship. I've seen those types. Riding in carriages around the edge of our camp with hankies pressed to their noses. As if we're all some odd entertainment."

"Mrs. Hastings can be a bit stuffy, but I think she truly does want to help. She just doesn't know how. Or maybe just where to start. I know something good would come of it if we could just make the arrangements." Suddenly, it had become the most urgent thing in the world. Something large and important she could do to make things better. And surely, once she'd been to Grace House with Mrs. Hastings, Papa might let her do more than just sit around and wind bandages. Mrs. Hastings had loads of friends with all sorts of connections. Even Mama would be delighted to work on projects with someone of the Hastingses' stature. It was the most perfect of ideas.

Quinn's expression softened. "I'll see what I can do."

# Chapter Seven

"You've left your side unprotected," Major Simon warned. "I could have run you through four minutes ago."

"So you said," Quinn panted as he wiped the sweat from his forehead with his sleeve. Major Simon was proving to be a merciless teacher. Just a moment ago he'd planted the tip of his sword over Quinn's pounding heart and declared with an annoying calm that in a *real* duel, Quinn's life would have come to an abrupt end. Something in his eyes made Quinn believe he could do it. Part of him suspected the major had taken more than one life—in battle or otherwise—but the wiser part of him decided he didn't really want to know.

"Die? Right here?" Quinn challenged as he regained his footing. It was useful to discover he didn't at all like being on what Mr. Covington had once called "the business end" of a sword. Quinn vowed to remember the unpleasant sensation of having a blade planted gingerly on his chest—and vowed it would never happen again.

"Hardly sporting of me, I know," Simon pronounced as he flicked the blade away.

"Speaking of sporting..." With a swift move, Quinn

skidded down and forward, making sure his tattered boot collided with Major Simon's foot, sending the stocky officer off balance. With another kick, he knocked Simon's remaining knee sideways so that the major came down to the floor in a crash of weapons.

He shot Quinn a nasty look, then laughed. "One does not kick in fencing!"

Quinn held out a hand, telling himself it would be unsporting to enjoy the moment but enjoying it immensely. Simon had kept the upper hand for most of the hour, anyway. "Were we fencing?"

Simon took Quinn's extended hand and pulled himself to his feet. "That was entirely uncalled for. And downright clever. An old general of mine used to say that the best use for rules was knowing when to break them." He slid the foil into the holder at his hip. "I dare say it's a lesson you already know."

"Life can be a good teacher of some things."

"And not others. You kicked me because you were angry, not because it was a good strategy. It worked this time. It won't the next." He pointed a finger at Quinn as he pulled a handkerchief from his pocket. "You fight with too much emotion, Freeman. We'll have to work to cool that temper of yours. Give me your hand." He held out his hand to shake Quinn's.

Matthew Covington had insisted they shake hands at the end of every fencing lesson or duel as well. Quinn pulled off his glove and held out his hand.

At which point Simon grabbed it, held it, and before Quinn could even blink, had produced a short dagger from his boot and dragged it sharply down Quinn's forearm.

"Ouch!" Quinn yelled as a thick line of blood pooled where Simon had scratched—no, sliced him. He just barely bit back a retort that would have made Ma's ears burn. "What the…"

"No broken rule goes without consequences. Every knife hurts, especially the one you didn't see coming." Simon handed Quinn the handkerchief. "Next time you face me, you'll think twice. A small price to pay for wisdom."

Quinn stood, staring at the man, unable to piece together the gentleman with the savage who'd just calmly cut him.

"It's but a scratch," Simon said, "and the first lesson I give all my best students."

"Some compliment," Quinn muttered. "What will happen to me if you really like me?"

Simon looked him straight in the eye. "You'll live."

As he stood in Reverend Bauers's study that afternoon, wincing at the excess of iodine the pastor dabbed over his forearm, Quinn recounted the major's painful lesson.

"I can't say I care for his methods, but Simon makes an important point." The reverend smiled. "No pun intended."

Quinn thought about the tip of Simon's foil skewered into his chest. "He's a wild sort, he is. Dangerous."

"No, I think that Major Simon is just a man aware of how dangerous a game we aim to play here. The moment you forget yourself in the name of playing hero, that's the moment any fool could come out of the shadows and take you." He put a clean bandage over the wound. "How'll you explain that cut to your ma?"

"I'll worry about that later." Quinn looked at the reverend. "Are you saying I shouldn't be doing this now? Changing your mind?"

"Not at all. I'm only saying we can't be too careful. 'Wise as serpents,' the Bible says. Taking on evil— even with the best of intentions—is always a dangerous endeavor."

Quinn muttered a thing or two about the snakelike nature of a certain army major as Bauers bound off the bandage. The wound smarted for a dozen different reasons, only half of which could be attributed to Reverend Bauers's enthusiastic doctoring.

"Think of it as a repayment," Bauers said, raising a disapproving eyebrow to Quinn's muttered insults. "You do remember the very nasty gash you gave Mr. Covington on your first meeting? The cut you lads gave Matthew was much bigger and twice as deep. All for his noble effort to try and stop you two hooligans from stealing from Grace House. Why, I stitched up his arm in the very next room. After twenty-odd years, has a bit of balance to it, don't you think?"

"No, I don't." Quinn flexed his arm. "And this hurts."

"Good. Now—" Bauers changed his tone as he put the medical supplies back in their box "—have you given thought to the message system?"

"It'll go up just before dark tonight," Quinn replied. "If I've got both arms to use by then. I found the wood yesterday, and with a bit of help I can have the post up in an hour. Right across the street from where the mail cart comes in."

Bauers smiled. "By the mail cart. What an extraordinary coincidence."

When the mail cart pulled up the next day, Nora noticed a large square post had been erected across the street. A sort of column made from pieced-together planks of wood now stood in the passageway between two shacks. People crowded around it, and it was a minute or so before Nora realized small pieces of paper and scraps of wood and material were stuck to the thing.

She'd heard about a fountain downtown that had become a message board of sorts. People fastened messages or notices or sad notes like "Can't find Erin Gray since Tuesday" on Lotta's fountain at Kearny and Market streets. It had become a vital communication place, a gathering spot for the lost and those who had been found. Logistically and emotionally the center point of town. Someone—someone very clever—had thought to do the same here.

When Nora looked out over the crowd, her suspicions proved correct, for her one raised eyebrow of silent inquiry was met with Quinn Freeman's grinning nod.

"The mail can't all be headed out of town," he said when he ambled across the street. "Folks here need to send messages of a smaller sort, too. Took all of an hour, once I found the wood."

She noticed he had a bandage on his right forearm. "It took a bit more than that, it seems," she said, pointing to the wound. "That wasn't there yesterday."

From behind her at the mail cart, Nora heard her father make a grumbling sort of noise, as if he wasn't much fond of his daughter noticing the state of some man's forearms. When she turned, he shot a look of warning between them, as if telling her to stay on the cart while he climbed down to hoist another mailbag off.

"A fencing injury," he said, pleased at her concern. "I won the duel, anyway."

What a wit he had. "Now, Mr. Freeman, what sort of man has time for fencing these days?"

"You'd be surprised." His eyes fairly sparkled. He had the most extraordinary vitality about him. An energy, an inner source of power that stood out like the noonday sun in such a sea of weary souls. And when he looked at her like that, a spark of that power lit up inside her own soul. It was at once thrilling and dangerous.

Nora hid the blush she felt creeping up her face by changing subjects. "How is Sam?" she said brightly, fiddling with a stack of mail. "All healed?"

"Soon enough. He was asking to come over here this morning, but Ma held him off one more day. Fairly bursting to run around, he is. Ma threatened to put him on a leash yesterday afternoon after you left."

"How resilient children are," she sighed, sitting down on the edge of the cart. "I think they've fared the best of all of us." Mrs. Hastings's visit had cheered Mother and Aunt Julia for a little while after, but the dark melancholy had returned within a few days.

"We do fine. Well, as much as we can. You should come over and look at the post. There's happy news there, as well as the sad news." He pointed toward the wooden column and extended a hand to help her out of the cart.

Her father didn't look pleased, but neither did he voice an open objection—that would have to do for now. Nora took Quinn's hand, forgetting she'd removed her gloves, for it was nearly impossible to handle stacks of paper and the other odd forms of mail with gloves on. He clasped her hand, stunning her with the touch of his rough palms. They were working hands, large and calloused, yet strong and steady. Warm. Something unnamed shot through her, something far more alarming than what his eyes had done. Nora tried to brush it off as something from a dime-store novel, a juvenile thrill, but it felt so…important.

*A touch.* Quinn Freeman had touched her. Papa was undoubtedly cross, even though it was something as genteel as helping her out of the wagon. Still, she wasn't the least bit sorry she wasn't wearing gloves.

He winced, and she realized he had helped her out of the wagon with his injured arm. "Goodness," she said, "You really are injured there."

"Only just," he said, still smiling. "I'll be fine." She knew by the way he looked at her that he was as aware of their touch as she was. He held her hand for a fraction of a second longer than was necessary before letting it go and motioning toward the post. She felt that tiny linger—a trembling sensation in her hand—as if her palm would somehow be able to retain the feeling. Nora felt as if she would look at her hand an hour from now and find it physically changed.

She saw, out of the corner of her eye, that Quinn ran his thumb along the tip of each finger. He felt it, too. They walked quietly toward the post, each of them a little bit stunned, pretending at normalcy when nothing at all seemed normal.

Notes of every description, on every kind of material, had begun to cover the post, tacked and pinned or stuffed into cracks. One small corner of a newspaper held the message "Looking for Robert Morris." Another read "A.D.—I'm fine—M.T." One heart-wrenching note read "Josiah Edwards born Tuesday morning." Nora hadn't even thought about the fact that babies were still arriving. It was cheering to know life went on, but what sort of anguish gripped a mother bringing a precious new life into the wake of catastrophe?

Quinn noticed her eyes on the announcement and nodded at her. "I saw little Josiah yesterday morning. Fine and healthy and hungry as any baby ever was. He's hurting for a few necessities, but I gather he'll make out just fine."

Nora thought of all the soft, clean pampering that surrounded the last baby she'd seen. Babies should never know hardship—it was just wrong. "What's he missing?"

Adjusting his hat, Quinn pursed his lips in thought. "The usual things—diapers, cloths, jumpers and such. Soap, too, I suppose." Getting an idea, he began to walk around the post, one hand roaming over the fluttering papers. "Oh, here's one. 'Baby arrived. Need sheets, shirts, cloths and pins.' You know, that sort of thing. Ma found a clean pillowcase they cut down for Josiah to wear and a pair of little socks from a doll somewhere, so things find their way."

Nora began to look all over the post now, scanning for any requests like the baby's. There were half a dozen, maybe more, and the post had only been up one day. "I want to write these down, like I did the others. Surely we can find some of these things."

"Could you make me a copy, like you did before?"

"Of course I could. Do you have any ideas where we might find some of this?" The "we" had slipped out of her mouth unawares.

"I've a few thoughts," he replied. His eyes glowed again, and Nora felt surely Papa would storm across the street this very second and plant her back on the cart.

"Let me get a page from Papa's ledger," she said, needing to turn away from the way Quinn smiled at her, trying to wipe the smile from her own face as well.

Nora could barely keep her eyes on the page as she copied down the posted needs Quinn read out. There was an enthralling partnership in this, as though she were grafting herself into something far bigger than her own tiny problems. Here was something—something concrete and important—that she could do. The first list had been just a product of her being in the same tent as Sam and Mrs. Freeman. This felt more deliberate. *Help me, Lord,* she prayed as she worked the pencil and paper. *I'll move Heaven and earth to get these things to these people.*

Her plan hadn't worked. Quinn knew just by the set of her shoulders when the cart pulled into sight a day or so later. He'd feared as much, suspected that Nora Longstreet hadn't yet realized just how hard supplies still were to come by. And while a huge chunk of him wanted her to wheel in here victorious, his practical side knew she had always stood a far bigger chance of wheeling in here sad and frustrated.

She was even prettier when she pouted. Her delicate frown whipped up something fierce inside him, some heroic urge to see her smile again and to do whatever it took to produce that smile. She didn't know he had the means to do it. She didn't know how much he'd stared at his hand yesterday, trying to recall the softness of her palm and the distractingly soapy scent that seemed to float around her.

She didn't know her father was standing over her shoulder looking straight at Quinn, as if to say there'd be no wandering across the street today. That was fine—Quinn had another strategy to restore Nora's smile, and that strategy was currently tugging impatiently on his good arm. He didn't mind at all that Sam wouldn't take no for an answer in coming to see Nora.

The moment Quinn finally let go of his hand, Sam scrambled across the street and up onto the cart to give Nora an enthusiastic hug. Her laugh at Sam's exuberant, nearly tackling welcome made Quinn smile. Those two were a pair from the first moment.

He stayed back while Nora went through her usual business with the mail, which was hampered by Sam for most of her visit. Sam had obviously declared himself her assistant, and Quinn couldn't help but laugh as Sam's "assistance" made Nora's tasks that much more complicated. Every once in a while she would look up, catching Quinn's eye. Even at this distance—as they had at the rally not so long ago—her eyes could dazzle him. He could tell she was disappointed at not being able to provide the items they'd listed. He admired how important helping out had become to her, mostly because he shared the same urgency.

When her mail was dutifully received and Sam had been thanked, rethanked and thanked again for his "invaluable assistance," Nora tugged a small box from the back of the cart and then handed it to Sam while she climbed down. Quinn wanted to sprint over there and help her down again, if only to buy himself the fraction of a second it gave him to hold her soft hand, but he decided restraint was the better choice. No one used to say restraint was a characteristic of Quinn Freeman, but maybe the stinging cut on his right forearm was sinking the virtues of discretion into his thick skull.

After producing a piece of licorice for Sam from her pocket, Nora waved Quinn over. He forced himself to walk casually to the cart.

"Here. It isn't much, I'm afraid." She held out the box to him with a handful of bandage rolls and half a dozen dish towels inside. "I think the dish towels will make fine diapers if they're cut in half."

"Don't say it's not much," Quinn replied to the frustration in her voice. He took the box from her, resisting the urge to find a way to make sure their hands touched when he did. "Every bit helps out here. You're doing so much already. Josiah's ma will be thrilled."

The wind stole a lock of hair out from underneath her hat, and she reached up to push it back off her face. "There's just so much to do."

"Reverend Bauers says all we can really do is the bit God puts in front of us. With all he faces, I think he might know a thing or two about big problems."

"The post has twice as many messages as yesterday," she assessed, squinting across the street. "It was such a splendid idea. You really should be proud of yourself."

Quinn shrugged, hiding his pleasure at how obviously she wanted to go over and inspect his creation. "I just copied the fountain. Anyone could have done it."

Her eyes told him she thought otherwise, and he liked that very much.

She stared harder. "The post looks nearly full."

"And I need to talk to you about that." Quinn leaned in as close as propriety would allow. "I know someone. If we could write all these down, I could get the list to him and he might…help out."

"Someone? Who can find these things?" Her eyes grew wide, and he feared he'd blurt out his secret any second.

"Could be. A bit early to tell, but it's worth trying."

"Really? How wonderful."

"We'll have to be quiet about it. Careful. Things might get out of hand otherwise, there being so much need and all. Will you help?"

He had expected her to hesitate, to worry about the clandestine nature of it all. She didn't. "Absolutely," she said, taking in a breath. "How could I not?" Looking over her shoulder at her father, who was thankfully otherwise occupied, Nora asked, "But why do you need me?"

He hadn't thought about that. He'd just wanted to make sure she was involved. With clever moment's inspiration, he held up the bandaged right arm. "Hurts still. Besides, you've got more access to decent paper than I do." He'd thank Major Simon at tomorrow's lesson. Maybe.

"Oh, of course. I should make two copies again, like we did with your mother. That way I can look while your...friend...does his own looking." Resolutely, she brushed off her skirts and nodded back toward the mail cart. "I'll just go fetch another piece of Papa's ledger. I'm sure he won't mind."

"You mind your pa, now. Don't give him any reason to decide it's not wise for you to be coming here anymore." Quinn didn't even want to think about how he'd endure the days if two o'clock didn't mean seeing Miss Nora Longstreet anymore.

"I'll mind." Her smile was as warm as sunshine. He had a partner. Actually, if Major Simon and Reverend Bauers counted, he had a tiny army. Quinn felt like he could take on the world if God asked him to do so.

Quinn felt himself grinning like a fool the entire time Nora ventured across the street and wrote down items from the post. She slipped him a conspiratorial smile as she climbed back aboard the mail cart and handed him his copy of the list. "Do you really think this will work?"

"No harm trying. Oh, by the way, I'm meeting with Revered Bauers to set up that tour you asked for."

"That's wonderful. I think Mrs. Hastings could be a grand patroness if she chose. And I imagine Reverend Bauers can be most persuasive. I do hope it will be all right with them that I come along."

Quinn wouldn't have it any other way.

## Chapter Eight

As it turned out, Reverend Bauers was already familiar both with the Longstreets and the Hastingses, and it took little convincing to arrange a tour. The hardest part about it turned out to be accommodating Mrs. Hastings's packed social schedule and her limited visits to town. How anyone managed to do so much socializing in the wake of an earthquake, Quinn didn't know. That world was as foreign to him as the hatch-mark signs that used to hang in the Chinese quarter of town. And while Ma raised an eyebrow when Quinn asked if there was anything close to a clean, pressed shirt in the camp, she'd long learned to expect strange things from Quinn's association with Grace House. She'd only looked at him for a quizzical second when she handed him a surprisingly tidy shirt on the appointed day.

"There simply isn't enough space," Reverend Bauers said as he pointed the tiny tour group down the hallway. "With the camp right next to us in Dolores Park, the needs have been enormous. The army is doing a commendable job with the official camp, of course, but I think we can all see how much more help is still needed. He pointed to a row of long, narrow tables that now filled what used to be the front parlor. "We already feed sixty or so at a time at these standing tables. With a little help, we might be able to add benches, but that seems a long way off for now."

"Gracious," said Mrs. Hastings, gripping the hankie that had been her constant companion for the visit. "Eating standing?"

"When one is thankful to eat at all, sitting or standing hardly seems to matter," replied Reverend Bauers.

"It is an amazing thing," Nora said as they walked down the hallway. "You'd think feeding all those people would be chaos. But it seems quite orderly. People seem grateful and very kind."

"I suppose," Mrs. Hastings said, "that might depend on your definition of order. And they certainly ought to be grateful. Free hot meals." Her phrases were kind, her tone was not. Quinn bit back the retort he would have liked to offer.

Surprisingly, Nora stepped in where he'd been silent. "I think they'd much rather be paying customers, earning their own keep," she said. "They're no happier to be out of their homes and out of their jobs than Mama and Papa would be. They weren't even given tents like at the other camps. That's hardly their fault. Everyone has suffered."

Quinn wondered if Nora was as aware of Mrs. Hastings's expression as he was. The woman bore a look Quinn had come to recognize over the time since the earthquake. The unspoken theory that folks had brought the earthquake down upon themselves. It made no sense, of course, for the Grace House kitchen fell down just as fast as a brothel kitchen half a mile away.

Reverend Bauers said those society types had "hoarded their grace and left none for anyone else," and looking at the sharp angle of Mrs. Hastings's eyebrows as she surveyed the Grace House pantries, Quinn thought the description fit. He was trying not to judge, but it was mighty hard.

Reverend Bauers pointed to the near-empty pantry shelves. "Our need is great, as you can see. Even the staples are hard to come by."

"But I hear food and goods are pouring in from all over the country. They tell us the camps are in fine shape. Money has been donated," Mrs. Hastings argued.

"The official camps are indeed doing well, and it gladdens my heart to see it. But too many are struggling in places like Dolores Park, and we can't turn our backs on those souls. Distribution to those in need is still nowhere near fast enough."

Yet, Quinn's mind silently added. He had Nora's second list from the message post, and he had an appointment with Major Simon late this afternoon.

"Things have been finding their way, Mrs. Hastings," Nora offered. "Just this week I learned of some medical supplies finding their way into Dolores Park to help a little boy. Little miracles happen every day as people help each other out." She turned her smile full force to the woman, and Quinn felt a twinge of ridiculous hope that her charming smile would one day be turned to him. "Can you see the good a woman of your compassion and influence might be able to achieve? I just know you could work wonders." She reached into her pocket and pulled out the piece of her father's ledger. "There's a post in Dolores Park. People have been tacking up requests on it, and I've copied them down."

She handed Mrs. Hastings the list. "See? It's nothing so hard to get. Everyday things."

"I'm flattered you hold me in such high regard, Miss Longstreet. And ladies have been shredding petticoats into bandages since the first day. I'm not at all convinced there's that much to go around. And Dolores Park is…" The woman stopped short of the remark she was obviously thinking.

Nora simply stood in front of the lady, hands folded, silent. Quinn, trying not to get his back up over Mrs. Hastings's judgmental attitude, would have handed Nora the shirt off that very back were she to turn that look on *him*.

"But what kind of Christian woman would I be to turn down such a thoughtful request?" Mrs. Hastings took the list from Nora and tucked it into her fine silk handbag. "I shall see what I can do."

"Splendid!" said Reverend Bauers, clasping his hands. "I've no doubt you will indeed work wonders. Praise God for bringing you across our threshold, my dear madam. God will smile kindly on your charity."

Major Simon sheathed his sword with narrowed eyes. "The post was a brilliant idea. I'm not sure if I should be impressed or rather worried. You've too much a talent at deceit for my taste."

"Deceit?" Quinn asked, trying not to pant as he spoke. The major had just taken him through an exhausting series of exercises and Quinn was certain his arm—and lots of other parts of him—would be hurting in the morning. "I'm not trying to trick anyone. I'm keeping quiet in order to do what I think needs doing. I needed a way for folks to make their needs known that wasn't obviously attached to me. It's not like everyone can come tell me what they need." He took the towel Simon offered and wiped the sweat off his brow. "Besides, I didn't even think it up on my own. I just copied what I saw happening on the fountain downtown."

"Smart men don't bother rethinking good ideas. They just borrow them for their own use." The major took a drink from one of the glasses of water that had been set on a table at the side of the room, gesturing with his hand to the bandage that still wrapped Quinn's right forearm. "I stole that move from a particularly successful, if rather nasty general in the southern states. And I noticed you were far more thoughtful with your attacks this afternoon."

Quinn had to admit it had worked; the fact that his arm stung every time he thrust it forward made him more deliberate in his choice of offensive moves. Was it sheer pain or a learned lesson that had reined in his impulsive nature? Mostly, it seemed as if Major Simon wasn't out to get his goat today the way he'd been at first. Either Quinn was growing used to the major's larger-than-life persona, or Simon wasn't going out of his way to provoke him. It was for the best either way. "Lesson learned, Major. But I'd rather have done it without the blood, thanks."

Simon put down the glass. "Nonsense. Blood's a necessary part of the thing. And I imagine a clever fellow like yourself could squeeze a little sympathy out of a kind lady with that bandage...*if* you were so inclined."

Quinn might, under certain circumstances, have admitted to being pleased at the attention his wound seemed to garner from Nora, but neither here nor now.

"I manage," he said with what he hoped was an enigmatic grin.

Simon grinned back. It was times like this that Quinn could almost muster an older brother kinship with the man. A tentative friendship was forming between them despite Quinn's first impressions. "I imagine you do," Simon said with something almost like a wink. "And you've remembered more of your fencing than Reverend Bauers led me to believe. We may be able to start next week."

And start the next week they did. Major Simon had come through with flying colors. His supplies, along with some of Quinn's old connections to dockworkers and the men in the rail yards, had produced half the list of items requested on the post. The deliveries began. It had taken most of the night to quietly ferry the items from the secret storage location to the shacks in question, but the next day Quinn knew.

It was worth every risk. The look on folks' faces, the way they chattered around the post the next morning, the jolt of it all, was worth a month of sleepless nights. And the look Nora shot him as Sam rattled on about "the most amazin' thing that happened"? Well, that would have kept him up a week straight with ease.

"…and Missus Barker, she got soap, and some other lady got things for her baby, and no one knows how."

Unbidden, Quinn's memory brought back the morning he'd been sent to socialite Georgia Waterhouse's mansion by Reverend Bauers. He'd been assigned to fetch her back to Grace House the morning everyone discovered the Bandit's first delivery. The Bandit—whom Quinn would later learn was both the invention

of Miss Waterhouse and the surprising new alter ego
of Matthew Covington (although neither knew the other's involvement at the time)—had nailed actual dollars to the top of Grace House's doorjamb. It was more
money than anyone had seen in years in one place, and
Reverend Bauers stretched those dollars as far as the
eye could see. By his first gift of funds—and the many
gifts of all kinds the Bandit gave after that—Quinn had
watched one man spark a tidal wave of optimism and
good deeds.

And now, it was Quinn's turn. This morning, standing among the folks' astonished buzz, Quinn felt the
legend come full circle, as if he'd been there way back
when just so he'd be ready to be here right now. As if
God really had lined it all up in perfect harmony just
the way Reverend Bauers always said He did. Quinn
felt the power Matthew Covington had spoken of, the
limitless energizing from knowing he'd ignited the rarest and most powerful resource known to man: hope.
He knew now how Matthew Covington had forgone
sleep, ignored pain, defied odds and sometimes even
gravity to complete the Black Bandit's missions. He
felt it himself.

"It is extraordinary, Sam. A wonderful thing indeed."
Nora smiled. "We should all be very happy and very
grateful, don't you think?"

"Extra-extraordinary!" Sam's small mouth could
barely make its way around the large word.

There was a second, a sun-gilt moment when Nora's
eyes caught Quinn's overtop of Sam's continued chattering. She looked at Quinn as though he'd done something monumental. As though the world spun on his
command. No one, not even his ma, had ever looked

at him like that. The look she'd given him when he returned the locket had near stopped his heart, but this, this was even more stunning. It fired through his chest like a lightning bolt. A very addictive lightning bolt.

He stared at her for a moment, feeling the weight of the moment drive him to memorize its details. She had a splash of freckles starting on her cheeks, as though she'd spent too much time without her hat. He knew proper ladies weren't supposed to sport freckles, but he found them hopelessly endearing. They lent a naturalness to her grace and breeding. He had the feeling he'd remember the slant of the sun and the particular scent on the breeze for years to come.

"Your post has done a world of good, Mr. Freeman," she said. Her words were pleasant and ordinary, but Quinn felt the world tilt and whirl like a shiny top all around him. She smiled, inclining her head in the direction of his earlier contraption. "It's as clever as your teeter-totter, I think. Maybe more. You've a talent for simple things that accomplish great feats."

Her compliment swelled in his chest. "I just see what needs doing. Maybe clearer than most, but not by much."

"Seeing clearly is a great gift. Papa says if there's anything San Francisco needs right now, it's men with clear vision." She shrugged her shoulders. "Things have been difficult for him at the post office lately. Everyone seems to argue about everything and nothing gets done. But you, you see clearly enough to make a post and put it in the ground and look at all that gets done."

"No one is fencing me in with a load of rules or bickering about whether or not I can be trusted. Most men would have a time of it if they had to work the way your papa has to. Everybody's breathing down everybody else's backs these days. It's a wonder anything gets done at all."

Nora leaned in a bit. "Speaking of getting things done, I've managed a small bit myself." She produced a small parcel from her pocket and held it out to him. "There's some tea in there. It's not much, but Mama was saying there are days when her only luxury in life is a cup of tea with sugar, and I thought maybe you know someone who might need the same."

He'd almost grown used to choking down the concoction Ma liked to pretend was coffee each morning. And as for what passed for tea, well, it stretched the imagination, that's for sure. "Ma's birthday is this Friday," he said, "and she's been missing a decent cup of tea something fierce. I'll tell her you sent it."

"No, don't," Nora said. "Give it to her from yourself, not from me. A son should be able to give his mother a present on her birthday. If I made that happen, then that's thanks enough for me. Unless you had a gift already planned."

Quinn shrugged, trying to hide the surge of gratitude that was threatening to make him do something silly. "I haven't had a moment to sleep lately, much less scour up a birthday present for Ma. She'll feel like a queen having a real cup of tea with real sugar." He unfolded the handkerchief to see the little cache of tea and sugar. "There's enough here for a regular tea party I suppose."

She laughed. The sound of it fluttered through him like the flocks of birds that swirled around Union Square, perching somewhere just above his heart. "What's the world coming to when four spoonfuls of tea and two lumps of sugar constitute a tea party?"

"Nothing bad. Nothing bad at all." He held her gaze for as long as he dared, which was a lot longer than he ought to have.

After a flustered second, she reached into her pocket to produce another slip of ledger sheet and her pencil. "Well, should we make another list of what's on the post today?" She froze for a moment, as if a thought struck her. "Goodness, who'd have thought?"

"Thought what?"

"Well, now San Francisco has two kinds of 'post'— the kind you send and the kind you tack your needs to. Both are messages. It's really quite witty, when you think about it. Mr. Freeman, there simply is no end to your surprises."

# *Chapter Nine*

You're being a loon, Nora chided herself after making that ridiculous remark about "posts." He must think her the most vapid creature to say such a thing. It wasn't even close to funny, and yet he laughed and smiled as though she'd made charming conversation. He'd made far too much of her tiny gift—surely a handful of tea and some coarse sugar weren't that handsome a present.

But oh, there was something handsome about him today. Yes, handsome was the word, even if she'd never speak it aloud to anyone. There was a confidence in him she'd not seen at Grace House. Something in the surety of his steps, even though his boots looked worse than ever. Mama would say something curt about the glint in his eye, but Nora saw it more as a spark, an energy that was so different than the weary glaze most men wore nowadays. "There's a new one over here," she said, pointing to a bit of shirt collar that had "hammer and nails" written on it with a name scratched alongside.

They went on for a minute or two, Quinn sorting through the messages and she recording what they found. Without ever really discussing it, they'd crafted a partnership of sorts, and she liked the feeling of camaraderie that rose up as they worked their way around the post. When she helped with the mail wagon, Nora was always aware of her "assistant" status. Always cognizant that Papa could deem it too dangerous or no longer necessary and end her involvement there and then. But here, she was an equal. They worked together, each contributing important skills to the task.

She heard Quinn's breath catch as he squatted down to look at a little strip of blue cloth tacked down low on the far side of the post. "Isn't that the oddest thing ever?" he said, motioning for her to peer down and look.

In an unsteady script was the heartbreaking question, "Can I have a doll again?"

Nora felt a lump in the back of her throat. The little girl had dared to ask for a doll, but put her request on a tiny slip at the very bottom of the post as if she hadn't the right to ask for something so frivolous. But as Quinn's teeter-totter had proven, sometimes the frivolous things were the most important for survival. Her locket had proven that. She raised an eyebrow in silent question, and he nodded. "I'll take care of this one," she said, not even needing to write it down.

Quinn squinted at the name. "Edwina Walters. She had a baby sister. Died three days after the fires. They had a little funeral, and her mama cried something horrible. Little Edwina just stared all quiet and numb. Broke your heart to see her blank little face with all those folks sobbing around her."

Nora ventured a look into Quinn's eyes as they stood over the brave request, and she saw the same compassion in his face that welled in her heart. She'd grown too old for dolls, but she'd ransack every scrap of material in the house tonight to sew up a doll for little Edwina. Even if she had to cut up her own dress to do it.

"I could say a thing or two about simple things that accomplish great feats, Miss Longstreet," he said with a sad smile. "But I'm guessing you already know."

Nora tore the two duplicate lists apart and handed one to Quinn. "I'm learning. I have a gifted teacher, Mr. Freeman."

He took the paper with that thing Mama would call a glint in his eye again. "Is that so?"

"Miss Nora." Nora heard her father's voice call from behind her. He had been watching the two of them. "Best not to dally, your mother will be waiting."

Quinn's quick glance spoke volumes. Did he anticipate their daily meetings as much as she? "You'd better mind your pa," he said. "Everyone will be sorry if you can't come back." Nora was almost certain there was a meaning to the way he said "everyone." She hoped there was. Quinn tipped his hat, that breathtaking smile sweeping across his face, and said goodbye.

Two days later, Nora clutched the handmade doll to her chest as she scanned the rows of shacks for Edwina's. Papa had been called into an important meeting this afternoon, forcing a last-minute schedule change to the mail run, and she'd barely finished Edwina's little doll in time. She'd stayed up half the night sewing the crude doll, finding yarn for hair and embroidering a simple face. It was no masterpiece by any standards, but she was proud of it and prayed it would be sufficient to cheer young Edwina.

Which was, despite the dozens of reasons why she shouldn't, why Nora found herself not at Grace House as she'd told her mother, but several blocks away, wandering alone into the unofficial camp. She was looking for Edwina's family shelter. As it was well before two, Quinn was not there to meet her. Papa wasn't even sure he'd make a mail run at all today, given this meeting he was attending, so Nora had asked to be driven to Grace House, thinking it would be easy to make it to Dolores Park and back without incident while her father was otherwise occupied. She could have waited until two for Quinn, or try to find him now, but it seemed presumptuous to assume he had nothing better to do with his time than escort her around on missions of mercy. He had devoted a great deal to accompanying her as it was—it would be both improper and inconsiderate to demand yet more.

Then again, it wasn't particularly prudent to be wandering Dolores Park alone, either. Yes, one little girl could easily wait for a doll she didn't even know was coming, but something about this entire process pulled at Nora so strongly that she couldn't rest until Edwina had her doll. And there had to be something behind that sense of urgency, didn't there?

*Lord,* Nora prayed as she walked down what she hoped was the final aisle, *I believe that urgency is from You. Am I wrong? Is this just me being willful? Please, don't let me regret this kindness. Guide my steps and don't give Papa reason to be angry with my foolishness.* A few minutes later, she found the shelter someone had described. "Hello, I'm looking for Edwina," she called, knocking on the broken shutter that served as an entrance.

"Why?" The sharpness of the male voice from inside the shack caught Nora off guard. It still astounded her how suspicion had become the order of the day all over the city.

"I...have a gift for her."

A thin old man—too old to be Edwina's father, Nora guessed—slid aside the shutter. He peered suspiciously at Nora. "It ain't Christmas."

"No, it isn't. But I'd still like to give her this." Nora held up the doll. "Is she here?"

The man's countenance softened. "Edwina's asleep over by her cousin's. We put the little ones all together so they can nap. Her daddy's in the work lines and my daughter—her mama—well, she ain't been right since the little one passed."

"I'm sorry about your granddaughter," Nora said. "Edwina put up a little note on the message post that she'd like another doll."

The old man shook his head. "And here I was thinkin' that was just plain foolishness to let her put that up."

Nora held out the doll. "I'm afraid it's not much, but I hope this will do."

His eyes moved from the doll to Nora's face as he took the toy with careful hands. "And who're you?"

Nora shrugged her shoulders. "Just someone who could help. I got back something I lost, so I thought I'd do the same when I saw Edwina's note."

"Edie misses her baby sister," he said wistfully. "This'll help for sure. That's mighty kind of you. Thank you. I bet Edie'll want to thank you, too—how will she find you?"

Nora wasn't sure why, but she liked the idea of staying anonymous. Perhaps some part of her thought the mystery would make the doll's appearance more wondrous for the girl. On impulse, she said, "Do you know Quinn Freeman?"

"Shamus's son? Tall, sandy-haired, built that thing for the young'uns over on the other side of camp?"

"That's him. Tell Edwina she can thank Mr. Freeman if she wants to thank someone. He made the post that let Edwina ask for what she wanted."

He squinted at Nora as the sun pierced the afternoon clouds. He had the appearance of a once-strong man who had fallen on hard times. A weary, unshaven look that hung uncomfortably on his straight frame. "That don't make sense. She ought to thank *you*."

"I don't need it. Perhaps it will help your daughter to know that people care about what's happened to your family. I'm sorry for the terrible loss." Nora felt her hand stray to the locket around her neck. "I lost my cousin. And her mama, my aunt? Well, she hasn't been right since, either. It feels good just to know I helped, you understand?"

The man's face melted into a sad smile. "Well, what do you know? The world ain't entirely shot to pieces, now is it?" He held out a hand, and Nora noticed he was missing half a finger on his right hand. It was a recent wound, still bandaged. "Thank you kindly, miss. Edwina will be right pleased. Like I said, I didn't think it was such a good idea to write that note. When Edie asked her aunt to write it, I tried to stop her. And my daughter just cried and told her no one could care about one little girl's doll in all this disaster." He looked at Nora with such a tender heart that Nora felt as if she'd just received all the gratitude she'd ever need to make a dozen dolls. "I've never been so happy to see my daughter so wrong. I hope it helps the both of them."

He managed a wider grin and put his hand on his chest. "Lightens my heart, that's for sure."

Nora nodded toward the wounded hand. "Is your finger healing? Do you need a doctor?"

The grandfather looked down at his bandaged hand and wiggled his fingers. "Me? I need a good steak more than I need a doctor. Who needs all ten fingers anyways? Don't hurt much anymore." It was as if he had transformed in front of her. His face had changed from the harsh man who opened the shutter to a fatherly man who thought it wasn't much to lose a finger. It made Nora wonder how many other people's faces would change with an act of kindness. It had been worth whatever risk she'd taken to be here now, delivering the doll. She wished the man well and smiled broadly as she made her way up the row of shacks out of the park. Despite the long walk, her feet hardly felt the ground.

Until she turned the corner.

She hadn't seen Ollie since the day he'd leered at her in front of Sam's shack, but she recognized him instantly. His eyes had a lazy, sinister quality one didn't easily forget.

"It's the pretty mail lady doin' her bit for charity again." He grinned and looked around them. "Way in here. You sure do get around, missy."

Nora felt her anger rise. She hated to have the satisfaction of her trip undercut by the nasty look in his eyes. "I've no business with you, so I'll thank you to leave me alone." She began walking faster toward the park's edge.

He followed. "But you're such a kindly type. There's *all kinds* of need in here. All kinds." His voice hinted at the kinds no one associated with charity. How foolish she'd been to think it would be all right to go this far into the park alone. She made her feet move as fast as they could. The way Ollie was following, she'd never make it as far as the street. Looking up, however, she spied the teeter-totter that told her Quinn's family's shelter was only a handful of rows away.

"C'mon, miss mail lady, there's no need to rush." He began closing the distance between them.

"Stop it!" Nora broke out into a run despite the tangle of her skirts. "Leave me alone." Praying for protection, she headed straight for the teeter-totter and the knot of children gathered around it, hoping even someone as awful as Ollie wouldn't lay a hand on her in front of children.

"Come on back here and…" Ollie managed to grab one elbow as Nora attempted to turn the corner at a run. She twisted out of his grasp and kept running. Angered, he came after her faster, not caring about the group of shocked young faces who now watched.

Just as they passed Quinn's contraption, Ollie caught her shoulder and tried to spin her around. With dread, Nora felt the chain of her locket tangle up in his fingers and snap off from around her neck. She grasped at it as it sailed through the air to land in the dust a few feet away. Nora lunged for it, ducking out of Ollie's outstretched arm.

"Leave her alone!" Sam's voice came out of the crowd, and running at Ollie full tilt, he knocked the startled man backward a few paces. "You're nothin' but a mean old goat."

Startled, Ollie backed off and let out a string of curses that made Nora wince and one of the younger girls start to cry. Nora was near tears herself, and she scrambled in the dust for the locket she couldn't bear to lose a second time.

"Get out of here. Pa! Danny! Missus Freeman!" Sam began howling a list of adult names in an effort to get one—or all of them—on the scene.

The locket was broken. It had come unhinged in the fall, and the tiny ovals of glass that held the pictures had slipped out. Nora's fingers tried to push the charred photos back in place, but they were too cracked and damaged to stay intact without the glass to hold them together. Annette's image, barely visible as it was, seemed to disintegrate under her touch. "No," Nora sighed, unable to hold back tears of fear and fury. "No, stay together, don't…"

It was useless. The photo crumbled into tiny black flakes that scattered into the dust at her skirts. Her last image of Annette, her locket photograph, was gone.

"Oliver McDonough, ye nasty excuse for a man, so help me if you don't get out of here this very minute…" Mrs. Freeman's sharp brogue cut through the gaggle of children's voices.

Nora felt the woman's strong hand on her shoulder as she bent down. "Miss Longstreet? Is that you? Did Ollie touch you? Hurt you in any way?"

Nora could barely even think about what Ollie had done in the heartache of losing Annette's image. The broken locket hurt much worse than any bruise Ollie had left by grabbing her. "I'm not hurt," she said as the tears overcame her. "He grabbed me and it…broke the locket." A small breeze stirred up the dust, setting the flakes flying and setting a panic in Nora's heart. It was somehow like losing Annette all over again. Desperately, she grasped at the tiny charred pieces before the wind took them forever, but it was impossible to do. "No," she cried, feeling helpless and foolish and startlingly wounded.

"Come now, hon, let's get you up." Mrs. Freeman crouched down beside Nora and took her by both shoulders. "There's nothing to be done about your bauble now." Nora let herself be pulled up, even though she felt as if she couldn't stand on her own. All the previous joy was gone—and then some, for she felt worse than ever to have lost the locket a second time. "You've gotten your fine dress all dirty now, but you don't look hurt. Ollie's a brute. Let's get you inside, Nora, dear. I just happen to have the makings of a cup of tea, and I think we both could use one."

The generosity—especially knowing Mrs. Freeman's fondness for tea and the scarcity of it—made everything worse. "Oh, no," Nora cried, the tears still coming down despite her efforts to stop them, "you couldn't use your birthday tea for this."

Mrs. Freeman stopped for a moment and looked at Nora before she pulled open the flap of leather that served as a door and steered Nora to the one chair inside. "And how is it that you know about my birthday tea, missy?" Her tone wasn't a suspicious inquisition, it was more of an amused curiosity. She began gathering things for tea, only taking her eyes off Nora for a few seconds here and there.

"Your son told me." Nora had to choose her words carefully for she didn't want Mrs. Freeman to know the tea had come from her. "He was delighted to find some tea to give you." The tears ebbed, giving way to a huge, shuddering sigh as Nora felt the panic subside. She brushed the worst of the dirt off her skirts—she would have some explaining to do when she got home. "He told me how much you loved tea and missed it."

Having sent Sam off to fetch hot water from a common fire pit down the way, Mrs. Freeman hunched down to assess Nora's condition with a mother's experienced eye. "You'll have a bruise where that knee hit, but I think that's the worst of it. On the outside, that is. Ollie get fresh with you, did he? He's all bark and no bite that one, but he can surely bark. He was no good before the earthquake, and now he seems to have plenty of chances to show us what a louse he can be." She pulled a cloth from her pocket. "Here, love, wipe your face. You've had a good scare, but thank the Lord it's no more than that."

It was much more than that, but Nora thought if she tried to explain she'd only end up flooding the shack with tears. And these people had endured losses so much worse than hers. It felt selfish to go to pieces over, as Mrs. Freeman put it, "a bauble."

Sam returned, and as Mrs. Freeman tended to her teapot, Nora wiped her face and then used the cloth to wipe the dust from the remains of the locket. It lay open and empty on her lap, as forlorn a sight as she'd ever seen. Both photos gone, glass gone, chain broken; it made her want to start crying all over again. Mrs. Freeman came back in, "I'll just tell Sam to run and get…" She stopped and looked around the shelter, one hand flying to her chest. "Mercy! Where's Sam? He was just here a second ago… *Sam!*" She pushed her head out of the shack and called "Where'd ya go, lad? Oh!" Nora couldn't see whatever it was that Mrs. Freeman saw, only watch her spine stiffen with the sight—whatever it was. "Glory! What happened to you?"

## Chapter Ten

Quinn ducked into the shack a moment later, Sam ahead of him. Quinn's right hand was bruised and bloodied. He ignored his mother, heading straight to squat down in front of Nora. "Are you hurt, Miss Longstreet?"

Sam tugged on Mrs. Freeman's skirts. "Ollie sure is."

Mrs. Freeman rolled her eyes. "Oh, son, you didn't."

Nora felt Quinn's eyes lock on to hers. "Did he hurt you in any way?" he said angrily. "Any way at all?"

"He knocked me down, that's all." She tried to sound as calm as possible.

Quinn's intensity eased—until he saw the locket that lay broken in her hands. He returned his gaze to her eyes, and his simmering anger deepened into a look that held more sorrow and understanding than Nora thought her heart could hold. He, of all people, knew the significance of that "bauble." He seemed to know it was an almost unspeakable pain for her, for while he saw her own heartbreak reflected in the golden brown of his eyes, he said nothing. Were they alone, Nora felt she would have flung herself into his arms and cried for hours.

"Sam fetched more than water just now, did he? So you went and found Ollie," Mrs. Freeman said with an exasperated air. "And you let your fist say a thing or two on the matter?" She shook her head as she rummaged through that enormous trunk of hers for yet more bandages.

Quinn stood up. "Surely you didn't expect me to stand there and wag a finger at him. He had it coming, Ma. He's had it coming for a while."

"Oh, and that's *just* what we need in these parts," Mrs. Freeman scolded, "Grown men beating each other up in front of young lads."

"He had it comin'," Sam piped up, sticking his brave little chin out. "No one gets to hurt Miss Nora."

Mrs. Freeman leveled a "now look what you've gone and done" glare at her son and showed him precious little mercy with the stinging iodine. Quinn only sucked in a great deal of air between his teeth, winced and glared right back. "Ouch, Ma."

"I hope it stings 'til Sunday, ye great oaf." Anger thickened her brogue. Nora had to give Mrs. Freeman credit; Quinn had almost a foot on her, yet she held her ground fiercely. Of course, she had a bottle of nasty iodine to back her up, but Nora doubted that tipped the scales much.

"Are you badly hurt, Mr. Freeman?" Nora asked, mostly to change the subject. He'd defended her. Brutally, yes, but with such a ferocious loyalty that she felt it lodge deep in her chest and stay there. What a powerful thing it was to know he'd roared out as her champion like that.

"I'll be fine," Quinn said, flexing his fingers. From the look of things, his bleeding knuckles stung fiercely. "I only hit him twice." He looked up at Nora, the slightest hint of a smirk tugging at one corner of his mouth. "He deserved more."

"Enough in front of the lad," Mrs. Freeman said over her son's shoulder in a low monotone threat. "Now," she planted her hands on her hips, "this was hardly the tea party I had in mind, but since you're all here, have a cup and then we'll get Miss Longstreet back to her father before yet another man loses his temper in this place."

"I don't know who'll be more angry—your papa or my ma," Quinn said as he accompanied Nora on the long walk to her Lafayette Park home after tea. It had been the most ridiculous "tea party" in history—Ma seething and him all stinging and bandaged up so he could hardly hold the cup and Sam chattering and Nora so quiet. Quinn couldn't get out of there fast enough. Not to mention his insistent desire to steal a few moments alone with poor Nora so they could talk about the locket. Every time he thought about what Ollie had done, the urge to go find that snake and pummel him again surged up within him. Major Simon was right— his impulsive nature would lead him to trouble again and again. And trouble—even the righteous kind— was still trouble. He'd be no good to anyone locked up for brawling.

Nora nodded toward Quinn's hand. With his knuckles wrapped up just below the bandage still on his forearm from Major Simon's "lesson," his right hand was looking mighty worse for wear. "Perhaps Ollie is the most mad. It would certainly feel better to think he is."

"Whatever made you think it'd be wise to find Edwina on your own? I'd have come if you asked—you know that. I *should've* come—and you know that, too."

Nora looked up at him with a tender smile. "Oh, and you've nothing to attend to all day but my whims? I've no right to ask you to be at my beck and call."

She had every right, but Quinn wasn't sure that was a safe thing to say.

Nora fussed with the dark smudge of dirt on her skirt. "It was a foolish thing to do, I know. But I couldn't seem to stop myself. I just kept thinking of poor Edwina. It was like I was choking on her wish until I could get that doll to her." She looked up at Quinn again. "And I met her grandfather. If you could have seen the way he changed—the way he literally changed in front of me when I told him why I was there. I felt like I was doing just what God wanted me to be doing. At just the moment He wanted me doing it. I don't know that I can explain it any other way. When I was walking back home, it was like I was walking on air."

He knew that feeling. He'd felt it walking back from his "delivery," wide-awake and deliriously satisfied even though it was two o'clock in the morning. He'd felt it as he drove that message post into the ground, full of energy even though it was blazing hot and he ought to have been exhausted. Reverend Bauers quoted that scripture about "soaring on eagle's wings," when he talked about feelings like that, and although Quinn found the description rather fussy, it did fit.

"'Til Ollie knocked you right off that air. I'm sorry that happened. Seems a double sin to take away someone's joy like that."

Nora's hand went to her throat, as it had done so

many times since he'd given her the locket, and found only her neckline. "It feels awful to have lost her again like that. I know it's silly but it…hurts so much."

Her voice trembled again, cutting through Quinn. Without thinking, or perhaps it was more precise to say without caring, Quinn reached out and took her hand. He had intended it to be a light, momentary touch, but when she settled her hand into his he felt it ignite his heart.

"I'm going to fix that locket, just like I said. And mind you, don't go off like that without me again," he said. He hoped his voice didn't betray the storm going off inside him, but from the look on her face he knew it had. "We have to be careful," he felt compelled to add, meaning more than just her traveling safety. He was going to have to be very careful about her. She could drive him to impulses that were miles beyond unwise.

She pulled her hand from his, but gave it a squeeze before she did. "I know." He watched her run one hand across the other, and he knew her hand tingled the way his currently did. She did feel something. He knew he couldn't be the only one. There was too much between them to miss it.

There was *so much* between them. When they crossed Market Street, Quinn had the uncomfortable feeling that they'd shifted from his world to hers. Funny how life had made him feel like a trespasser in parts of his own city.

She felt it, too, for her steps became more determined. "Papa gave me a speech yesterday." She crossed her arms over her chest. "He went on about how the world wasn't the same anymore and how I ought to be sensible."

Quinn tucked his hand in his pocket. "I've never been one much for sensible myself. But he's your pa, that's his job." As they started up the hill toward the nicer part of town, Quinn tried to make a mental list of all the reasons he shouldn't be sweet on Nora Longstreet. He failed.

They walked on in a companionable silence for several blocks, looking up once or twice to catch each other's eye and offer a smile. More than once he had to stop himself from reaching out and taking her hand again. Impulsive as he was, he knew that would invite a host of trouble out here in her world.

A block before her house, Nora stopped and drew herself up straight. "Despite what happened today, I don't want to stop at Edwina. I don't think I'm *supposed* to stop at Edwina. I think there are more of these requests I can fill, but I don't know how it's all going to work just yet. I just know it's got to, and I suppose the 'how' will have to be God's problem."

Quinn thought he could not find her more endearing. Before today he would not have said something like tender bravery could exist, but it stood before him, her unsteady smile stealing his affections. "Well, then, you leave me no choice. I've got to help. I'm good with impossible problems. So consider me your partner."

"How?"

"Well, like you said, the 'how' may just have to be God's problem."

Her gaze held his eyes. "That would mean I am your partner as well, Mr. Freeman."

It was a step too far. It was not at all the proper thing to say, but none of that mattered. "My partners call me

Quinn." Suddenly, it was the most important thing in the world to hear her say his name.

The smile on her face reached up into the violet depths of her eyes. "Quinn. But very quietly and when no one else is around."

"It'll do." It would, but probably not for long.

Quinn thumped the list of requests he'd written down over the last day onto the table in front of Major Simon. "How many of these can you get?"

Simon peered at the list. "Are these from that post in Dolores Park? The one you put up?"

"It started with just messages, but then people began posting the things they need. It's perfect. They know I built the post, but they don't realize they're telling *me* what they need."

"Unless they watch you taking down notes every day," Simon cautioned.

"I make sure no one sees me take things down."

"You better be."

Quinn nodded impatiently toward the pile. "So tell me how much of this we can get."

"After you tell me how you got *that?*" He pointed to the bandage covering Quinn's knuckles.

Quinn told as fast a version of the story of Ollie and Nora as he could manage. "He deserved more. Mad as I was, he's lucky I stopped at two."

Simon let out a chuckle. "You should have stopped at one. Or none at all." The major planted his hands on the table between them. "Freeman, there are better ways to deal with louts like that. Think before you act. Rein in your impulses or you'll be no good to anyone."

Quinn scooped up the list in frustration, stuffing it

back in his pocket with a loud grunt. "I'm in no mood to improve my character while things get much worse out there."

The major crossed his arms over his chest. "So get out your sword."

Quinn said nothing, just gave Simon the darkest look he could manage.

"Fight me now, while you're good and angry." With that, the major picked up a sword and readied his stance. He was so annoyingly calm and careful. Quinn wanted to take his sword and slash something to pieces—preferably the major's crisp, clean jacket laying across the back of a chair in the corner of the room. A warm coat had been one of the things on those notes—San Francisco's night winds could be freezing, even in July. Did fine, upstanding Major Simon even know what it was like to need a coat? To be so cold you thought you couldn't ever be warm again or so hot you thought you'd drop over? Quinn snapped open the box that held his swords.

"See if you can channel that anger. Make it a focus instead of a distraction. Fight smart, Quinn, not hard. *En garde!*"

Quinn took a set of lunges at the major, but Simon blocked his thrusts as easily as if he'd known which blows were coming when. "You're an imaginative sort, don't be so obvious."

Simon pointed the tip of his sword directly at Quinn's neck. "Stop," he said in a commanding tone. "Take a breath and look at me. Think about what I'm expecting, and then plan the opposite. Plan. Don't react, Freeman, *plan*."

Quinn took a deep breath, willing the anger to settle

down into something closer to resolve. He started off by moving toward the side but ducked around at the last minute to land a blow so hard to Major Simon's chest that it knocked him to the ground. The satisfaction of a calculated victory sung through his veins. He pulled off his glove to help the major up, only to find his knuckles and other wounds bleeding from the force of the blow he'd just struck. Smiling, he offered his left hand to the major, who took it with an equal grin.

"I haven't been knocked off my feet in five years. My only mistake, it seems, was to underestimate how fast you learn."

They went through several other lessons, the hour passing by so swiftly that it seemed neither of them had a moment to catch their breath. Wiping his brow, Major Simon snapped his pocket watch shut and pointed to Quinn's pocket. "Shall we have a look at that list again?"

Quinn put the list back on the table. His hand was still bleeding, and a corner of the list had a swath of blood across one side. "Go tend to that," the major said. "I'll look through these and see what I can do."

As he walked over to the side table and wet a handkerchief, Quinn hid his smile. "And not just that list. Anything and everything will help," Quinn offered. "If you've got it, I can find someone who needs it."

"You know a great deal of people, Mr. Freeman, of the good and the bad variety it seems. Miss Longstreet should be grateful for such a champion." Simon looked up and caught Quinn's eye with those last words.

"Ollie had no right to trouble her like that." Quinn tried to keep any hint of his affections for Nora out of his voice. "Or any other lady just trying to help," he added for good measure.

"Seems to me Miss Longstreet should well know the dangers of wandering around Dolores Park unescorted. It was a foolish thing to do."

"Some might say helping out a stranger is always a foolish thing to do, Major Simon. I'm fixing to do something mighty foolish, but you're fixing to help anyways, aren't you?"

Simon laughed. "You've a future in politics. You lack eloquence, but you've all the other tricks required. Still, I would advise Miss Longstreet to be more prudent in her efforts. I'll not say anything when I'm at dinner tomorrow night. As you seem to be friends, I hope you'll impress upon her to show more caution when you're not around to save the day."

Quinn evidently showed more shock than he would have liked, for the major nodded to his unspoken question.

"I've been invited to dinner at the Longstreet home tomorrow night. Mr. Longstreet seems intent on getting Miss Nora more involved in the ministries at Grace House and invited the reverend to dine. Bauers and I had a dinner planned, so he very kindly secured me an invitation as well. I must say I'm looking forward to it. Eugene Longstreet has quite the earthquake tale to tell, I hear, and I'd hardly object to a better acquaintance with Miss Nora. Can't say I wouldn't wallop a brute or two in her defense myself, Freeman. She's a fine woman, don't you think?"

Quinn said nothing and pretended to busy himself with the details of cleaning his cuts. He bristled at the idea of Simon having such access to Nora when he had to limit his visits to her the way he did.

When he turned his attention back to the table,

Simon had written all over the list. "These," he said, pointing to circled items, "I can have ready for you tonight. I'll leave them in the same place. Make sure you come well after midnight or there'll be too many men rummaging around. These," he went on, pointing to ones with check marks, "may take a little doing. I may have one or two of them tonight, but the rest will take a few days at least. And these—" he pointed to three or four with dashes in front of them "—are near impossible. Be less bold Quinn. I'd hate to see 'shoot the messenger' come into play here."

## Chapter Eleven

The evening reminded everyone that summer in San Francisco could feel far too much like winter by kicking up a stiff breeze and a good, heavy fog. *No one should shiver in July,* Quinn complained toward Heaven, flattening himself against one of the fort's walls as he waited for the last of a group to pass. Shaking off the cold, he reminded himself that one of the items he'd be delivering tonight was a blanket for a child.

The men walked into another building, the wedge of light that had spilled out into the alley disappearing behind the shut door. Quinn counted to twenty-five, just to be safe, then slipped in through the hatchway Major Simon had shown him. Following the instructions Reverend Bauers had passed down from his time working as the Bandit's accomplice, Quinn tied a dark bandanna over his sandy hair with a dark hat to obscure his face. He wore one of the Bandit's dark shirts, along with the many-pocketed trousers and the black boots left to him in the Bandit's chest. It felt ungrateful to cut off the tops of the boots, but they were too high for Quinn's liking and the silver *B*'s imbedded in the calf had a nasty habit of catching the light. They were about half a size too small, but since they lacked holes in the soles, they were still better than his everyday shoes by a mile.

Not that crawling on his hands and knees through a musty tunnel that led to the hidden spot where Simon left his "booty" was particularly heroic, but he doubted the shivering little boy would care how his blanket got delivered.

Quietly, Quinn loaded the items into his pack—a large drawstring contraption he'd devised out of an army duffel he'd darkened with ink and hot water. Slung over one shoulder, it held a lot—even bulkier things like tins of meat and such—but still gave him mobility. This time the pack was stuffed so full he had to pull it along behind him in the tunnel, making for an especially clumsy and undashing exit. No riding off into the sunset for this messenger—Quinn felt he'd spend most of his heroic efforts creeping in and out of shadows. Still, this messenger could creep mighty fast, and the entire trip into and back out of the hiding spot was accomplished in less than a quarter of an hour. Now for the more adventurous task of getting his goods into Dolores Park without notice.

All was going well until the last two blocks, when Quinn ran into a loud, drunken fellow brandishing a bottle in one hand and a gun in the other. Quinn made the mistake of thinking the fellow too far gone into his liquor to be very observant, but the man wheeled around as Quinn snuck behind him, waving the gun entirely too close to Quinn's head.

"Who're you? And what'cha got there, mister?"

"Laundry," improvised Quinn, lowering his voice.

"You're clackin'. Laundry don't clack." The man narrowed an unsteady eye at Quinn. "You've got food in there, don't you?"

Technically, Quinn was redirecting relief supplies, but he hardly thought this was the kind of man to quibble over semantics. "Nah," he said, trying to casually walk on his way.

The fellow would have none of it. "You ain't got laundry in there, so I says you've got food. Or something else worth hiding." He cocked the gun. "How dumb do you think I am?"

"I got no opinion." Quinn held up one hand congenially while the other slipped to the knife tucked in an outside pocket he'd rigged into the sack. "I just want to get on my way."

The man gestured toward the sack with the point of his gun. "And what if I says no?"

Quinn drawled out his speech to match the southern twang of his opponent. "I ain't got no argument with you. I'll just be going."

"And I says *no,*" the man growled, even as he stumbled a bit. Quinn considered that even a skilled swordsman couldn't best a drunk with a loaded gun. A fight was definitely not in his interest. Even if the scuffle didn't draw blood—which was a big if—it'd most definitely draw attention.

When the man clicked the hammer back on his gun, Quinn ran out of options. Drawing the knife, he flashed it towards the man's face, hoping to startle him just long enough to knock the gun out of his grasp. The man was big and quick, however, despite the drenching of alcohol, and things dissolved quickly into a dangerous tussle of arms, elbows, punches, and grunts. Quinn, weighted down by the pack, was seriously handicapped. After what seemed like hours but was probably only half a minute, Quinn managed to bring the heel of his boot down on the man's shin. In the handful of seconds the brute doubled over, Quinn ducked out of his grasp and set off running.

He'd gotten perhaps twenty paces when the heart-stopping sound of gunfire exploded through the alley. Quinn tripped as a hot sting tore in his left side, accompanied by a desperate whizzing sound. I'm shot, he thought with a clarity too sharp for panic. *Lord Jesus, save me, I'm shot.* He forced in a deep breath, discovered his lungs still worked, and set off at a stumbling run toward the darker part of the alley away from the shouts gathering behind him. He'd always imagined getting shot would hurt worse, always pictured it as an instant blackness stealing his life. Yet, he could still run, still breathe. Grasping his side as he willed himself to put one foot in front of the other, he reached toward the source of the stinging pain. Quinn's fingers discovered a gaping, singed rip in his shirt but surprising little wetness. Still running, still surprised that each breath came and kept coming, he pulled his hand up in front of his face, bracing himself for a bloody sight. A small amount of blood stained his fingers, even though his side stung worse than a gallon of iodine. Had he been only grazed? Had he indeed been graced by that providence Reverend Bauers never called "luck"?

After a minute or two of more running, Quinn ducked into a dark doorway and waited for his pulse to stop slamming through his chest. You are breathing, you are alive, he found he had to tell himself over and over. He'd heard of men who never felt their mortal wounds—whose bodies numbed themselves as the blood drained out. He looked back down the alley, scanning the bricks for a trail of blood. There was nothing. Quinn looked back down at his shirt and felt his side—which still bled a small amount—but nothing indicated the fatal shot he feared. He had, in fact, been grazed. Another handful of inches to the right, and he'd be lying in a heap in some corner of the city. It seemed bizarre to him to live through yet another close call. Perhaps it wasn't so far-fetched an idea that God was saving him for a special purpose. If I were a cat, Quinn thought dryly, I'd only have seven lives left. Maybe six.

The sobering thought of his survival just made Quinn's resolve that much stronger. It felt just like when he was dueling Major Simon. He could take the fear or the anger and force it into focus, channel it into an energy that strengthened his skills rather than detracted from them. If I'm supposed to live, he reasoned, then I'd better do something good with that life.

In all the chaos, he'd managed to keep hold of the sack of goods that had been headed for camp. A quick peek inside showed that while surely jostled, the contents hadn't been harmed. If he could calm himself enough to stay smart, there was no reason not to continue his mission. In fact, Quinn had new incentives to get these goods to the folks who needed them.

With quick steps, a long prayer and several deep breaths, Quinn set out toward Dolores Park.

Mama and Aunt Julia were simply delighted to be playing the role of hostesses. Although no match for their previous dinner parties, it still felt extravagant and celebratory. Nora was pleased to see Reverend Bauers again, even though she'd long since suspected her father's agenda for the evening. Papa and Mama had both made it abundantly clear that they much preferred Nora restrict her charity to the much safer confines of Grace House. Papa hadn't gone so far as to stop Nora's mail cart visits, but he was close. Of course, if Mama or Papa ever knew the full details of her scrape with Ollie, things would be much worse. Which made Nora wonder: how much worse would things get if they knew the way her heart jumped when Quinn took her hand? When she discovered Major Simon—proper, eligible and appropriate Major Simon—had been invited, Nora began to wonder if she hadn't hid her feelings as well as she thought.

"Oh, you look lovely." Mama smoothed a wayward lock of hair as Nora came down the stairs. "How good it feels to have guests on the way. It's such a simple dinner, one I'd be embarrassed to serve back…before… but still it is a pleasure just to set a decent table again."

"Major Simon is accustomed to army rations," Papa reasoned, "I'm sure he'll appreciate whatever you set before him. And Reverend Bauers's ample middle tells me the man simply likes to eat, so you've no worries about your meal. I admit," he sighed, letting Mama straighten his tie, "it is refreshing to do something simply for the pleasure of it again."

When the approach of the visitors was announced, Nora went to the front window to find a most amusing scene—Major Simon in full uniform, next to a humbly dressed Reverend Bauers on the bench of a dilapidated sort

"Good evening and good welcome!" Uncle Lawrence greeted. "It feels wonderful to open our doors to guests."

Nora asked as many questions as she could devise about the ministries at Grace House. Not only did it provide for an entertaining conversation—for the reverend was always quick with an amusing or poignant story—but it pleased Mama and Papa. Still, for every story Bauers told about God meeting needs at Grace House, Nora recalled four similar notes up on the post. She admired Reverend Bauers, but to her his work didn't convey the affirming connection that she felt to the struggling residents of Dolores Park.

That she felt while with Quinn.

"I hear you are as brave as the good reverend in many respects," came the major's voice, pulling her from her thoughts as Reverend Bauers finished up yet another story of derring-do in the name of Christian charity. It came as no surprise that Nora found herself seated next to the major. "Tell me," he inquired, "do you think the Good Lord sends such adventures to Bauers, or does he simply go looking for them? I find I can't decide."

Nora had to chuckle, for in truth, she'd wondered the same herself. "God does seem to indulge his appetite for the unusual. He's only begun to tell me of his missionary adventures, and already he's described so many exotic places."

"The way I hear it, one does not have to travel far with Reverend Bauers to find adventure. Did you know he claims to have been an accomplice of the famous Black Bandit?"

"I had not heard that, for I've only just met him, but I must say it doesn't come as much of a surprise. He is very resourceful and not at all…shall we say…conventional?"

Now it was Simon's turn to laugh. "Not at all conventional. I like that. Mind if I borrow your astute description?"

"After calling me both brave and astute, how could I refuse?"

He looked at Nora for a long moment. "You shouldn't." Up until tonight, Nora had seen the major's interest in her family as being purely the product of her father's position. They were, after all, partners in the logistical quagmire that getting goods in and out of San Francisco had become. And she had assumed that tonight's invitation had been at her father's instigation. Now, aware of the major's gaze, Nora began to suspect Simon had done a little instigation of his own. He was considerably older than her, but he possessed many of the qualities Mama would find "appropriate" if not downright "desirable" in a suitor. He was very formal—almost stiff—but managed an agreeable smile now and then. He was a steady, stable fellow, not dashing or charming, but friendly enough. He was fit but stocky, a barrel-chested, solid build that spoke of more strength than grace. Had the events of the last months not happened, Nora would probably have been open to the major's attentions.

The trouble was, the events of the last months *had* happened, and none of the ways in which Nora measured life—and men—survived the upheaval. Nothing in the major's interest ignited that deep, highly charged captivation every thought of Quinn produced.

*Quinn.* She used his first name with startling ease. Her mind played back to the power in the way he walked. The effortless grace of the way he moved, the corded muscles of his arms that showed when he rolled his sleeves up to work. He was an exceedingly handsome man, Quinn. She did not even know Major Simon's first name.

"What do you know of this post set up in Dolores Park?" Simon asked her, pulling her yet again from her distraction. Did he think her flighty, that he had to keep fetching back her attention? If he did, it didn't show in his eyes.

"It is the most amazing thing, Major. Brilliant, when you think of it. At first it was only to serve as a message board of sorts…"

"Like the fountain downtown," he said.

"Yes, but then someone posted a need—something small, I think, like nails, and someone saw that need and filled it. When all you see is need all around you, it's such a powerful thing to see a need being met."

"Hope is a very powerful weapon, Miss Longstreet. Even the army has nothing to match it."

He actually seemed to understand what she saw in the post. "I think hope may be the very best weapon we have."

"I'm sure Bauers would agree with you there. Even the army could take a few lessons in the hope-wielding department from him. We're good with logistics, and the whole business of keeping order, but we need some help in the morale department now and then."

Everyone simply expected the army to sweep in and take charge. Yet, it had to be frustrating and difficult for them as well—no one thought about that. They were, after all, men far from home living amid such destruction for months on end. "Has it been overwhelming?"

she asked, turning toward him. "All the wreckage and supervision and sheer enormity of it all?"

His brow furrowed. "My men are exhausted. Some days I am astounded at what we are able to do. Other days, I find myself having trouble believing it will ever be enough. I've served several places, and this is by far the most devastation I've ever encountered. Were it not for the kindness of San Francisco's good people, I would surely lose heart." His smile hinted that perhaps he meant it in a more particular way than the mass support of the city's people.

"*Everyone* is grateful for what you do." It was better to keep such conversations out of particulars.

"Actually, some are decidedly ungrateful. But that is not a story for a young lady's ears. Tonight should be about hope and other pleasant things." With that, the major stood and offered a most eloquent toast to Nora's father, to Reverend Bauers, and the "many hopes for a pleasant future."

Mama looked pleased indeed.

# *Chapter Twelve*

Quinn showed up early for the mail cart, taking his place across the street long before anyone else gathered. He told himself that it was to discreetly take down requests from today's messages at the post, to see if word of last night's deliveries had traveled around camp, but it wasn't that. Those things were necessary reasons to be there ahead of time, but Quinn's eagerness had far more to do with Nora's recent dining companion than any missions of mercy.

It irked him to think of Major Simon enjoying all the pleasantries of dinner with the Longstreets. Not that fine dining was ever a part of his life, but just to think of her chatting and laughing with Simon over dinner made him lose his own appetite. His imagination toyed mercilessly with him all evening. No doubt Mr. Longstreet offered Simon encouraging smiles instead of the stern glares he reserved for Quinn. How instantly, violently jealous Quinn was of the major's ability to waltz through the Longstreets' front door invited; his own appearance at that door would hardly meet with such a welcome. Simon had access to a world Quinn had never cared much about before. Now, Quinn felt his exclusion from it all too keenly.

Still, he knew that's not how Nora saw it. She saw *him,* his worth, his abilities. Not his status or his education or what he knew folks of that sort would call "prospects." In a perfect world, that'd be all the connection they'd need. Pity that these days, San Francisco was about as far from a perfect world as a soul could get.

And then again, were it not for the quake and all the destruction, would they have met at all? Could he be thankful for that course of events despite all everyone had lost? Reverend Bauers would probably have some wise remark about God turning evil to good, or as he put it, "turning the world upside down." He must be right, for Quinn could find no other explanation for his recent ability to feel on top of the world and at the bottom of it at the same time. "Upside down" surely was a good description of how he felt.

He felt a whole host of other things as the cart rolled into view, even though he caught a heavy exchange of glances between Nora and her father as they arrived. He hadn't seen her since the incident with that louse Ollie, and he worried that Mr. Longstreet would banish her from the mail run once he knew. Admittedly, things looked strained between Nora and her father, and it was clear her presence wasn't sitting well with Mr. Longstreet, but she'd either hidden the worst of what happened or managed to convince her father not to let it stop her from helping. Either way, Quinn found himself breathing out a relieved prayer of thanksgiving when the cart pulled to a stop and she caught his eye.

He squeezed his hand more tightly around the small object in his pocket. He was glad he had it to give to her today, even if it served his own selfish motives. Too wound up from the events of last night's close call, he'd spent the time he should have been sleeping managing the promised repairs to the tiny locket. And, in an act even his own mother would have called hopelessly romantic, he'd found a pair of tiny blue flowers and pressed them to fit where the photos had been. The locket looked so sad emptied of its images that he had to do *something.* At least it felt less foolish to think of it that way.

"You look worn-out today," Nora said when he finally crossed the street. "Was the weather awful last night?"

He slept in a shack. She slept in a house. Everything felt like a reminder of their different worlds. "I'll be fine." He changed the subject. "Edwina was running around the camp showing off her doll yesterday. You'd think the thing came from the finest store in the city to hear her tell it. I haven't seen a face that happy since... well, quite a spell."

"She liked it then?" Nora fairly beamed despite her efforts to keep her speech casual.

"She loved it. And why is it, by the way, that she came straight to me?" He scratched his head, mocking deep thought. "I can't recall making any dolls."

Nora reached to accept a sack-wrapped package from a family waiting beside them. "Ah," she said after the family had left, "but *you* made the message post. And no request for a doll could have been made without a certain post." She nodded at him. "So the credit belongs to you."

Quinn shook his head. "That note could have stayed there a hundred days and never gotten an answer if it weren't for a pretty lady with a very big heart. *You* made her happy."

"That's nice to hear. It makes it easier to forget about what happened…afterward."

It was as if a cloud passed right over her face—the glow left that quickly and that completely. It made Quinn want to go after Ollie again this very minute. "I can do better than that," he said, reaching into his pocket. For a moment he was ashamed of the coarse piece of string that held the locket instead of the fine chain that had broken, but the look on her face wiped that away. "It's not perfect, but it'll close now like before."

She took it with delight. Without his prompting, she somehow knew to open it, and he could tell when she caught sight of the two tiny flowers. If he'd been afraid that she'd find the arrangement crude—the flattened blooms were held in place with a tiny crisscross of wires because there was no way to replace the glass—he was wrong. The wonder in her eyes sunk deep into his heart.

Again, neither one of them seemed to have words big enough to fit the moment. A whole host of things passed between them in a silent exchange. She knew how he felt. He knew he had no reason to be jealous of Major Simon's access. He'd just gained an access of his own that no one could ever take away from him. While it made no sense and it offered no prospects and only a fool's chance of going any further, Quinn felt as if he'd gained the world in the space of seconds. God had given him the chance to give her some happiness, to restore the tiniest sliver of her world to rights, and it felt better inside his chest than the dozens of shiny medals Major Simon boasted on his.

"Mr. Freeman," she managed, and he wondered if anyone else could hear the tears lingering on the edge of her voice, "how is it you are always managing the most astounding things with lockets?"

"I'm clever that way." It delighted him to twist her words back on themselves.

"You are, indeed. And most kind." She looked as if she would have said a dozen other things if they were alone, and that hummed in his chest. "Whatever should I do without you?"

He managed a wink, sure he would overstep his bounds if he stayed a moment longer. He was dead tired, and she looked so breathtakingly beautiful. "Don't find out."

Tipping his hat, Quinn whistled as he walked back across the street, pretty sure his world had turned upside down yet again and not minding one bit.

"A gun?"

Quinn held up the shirt with the singed stripe just to the left of where his heart ought to be. It was only the grace of God, Quinn thought, that his heart was still around to keep beating. "I'm thankful to be alive this afternoon." He briefly recounted the details of his scrape the other night.

"Most of San Francisco could say they are grateful to be alive, Freeman."

"I'm telling you, that was too close a call. You said it yourself, I'm of no help to anyone if I'm dead." He pointed to the swords. "If these are all I've got to work with, it won't take long."

The major looked at him with an expression Quinn

couldn't quite read. "The Bandit didn't carry a gun that I know of."

"I'm not the Bandit." It was as if the concept, which had been vaguely bumping around in his head for days, had finally crystalized into clear thought. Quinn knew, somehow, that he wasn't going to be a second Bandit. A sort of bone-deep instinct that the Bandit wasn't what God had in mind. What God did have in mind, Quinn couldn't say. He'd be something else, he just didn't know what quite yet. In truth, he didn't like not knowing. Having only an insistent discomfort with the idea of stepping into the Bandit's boots wasn't nearly enough to go on. Certainly not enough to get killed over. He would rather God send a thunderbolt of clear suggestion down on him— and soon.

"I can't say I'm that surprised you want to be armed." He motioned to the swords. "These are fine weapons, but you're right—they won't be enough to accomplish your, shall we say, *unique* objective."

"So you agree?" Quinn suspected the major would object to arming him. Before last night, he'd have done his best to steer clear of adding a pistol to his weapons. But last night had been a harsh awakening. If armed assailants could take his cache, then he needed to be the right kind of man to stop them. To defend himself. "I want to stay alive, not to blast around the city taking down anyone in my way. I want to be able to shoot someone in the foot or leg. To wound him but not kill him. I want you to train me."

"I will. But as far as I'm concerned, you had to ask the right way first. I wasn't about to hand you a gun so you could…how'd you put it? 'Blast around the city taking down everyone in your way'? I make it a policy never to arm an impulsive man." Major Simon went to a shelf and flipped open the lid of a box to reveal a silver-colored Colt .45 pistol. "Here, take a look."

It wasn't that Quinn had never seen a gun before. It was just that it was a very sobering sensation to be looking at *his* gun. He glanced up at Simon, hoping he didn't look as taken aback as he felt.

"That's good," Simon remarked in low tones. "Honestly, I'd have worried if you snatched it up."

Slowly, Quinn lifted the firearm from its place in the box. He expected it to feel foreign and foreboding in his hand. Quinn flexed his fingers in a half dozen different configurations until they settled themselves around the handle.

"You know, it is easier to be careful with a gun than with something so dramatic as a sword. But a man has to come to that conclusion on his own."

Quinn eyed Simon, not quite sure what to make of such a remark.

"Can you shoot? Have you ever shot a gun?"

For a moment, Quinn second-guessed his impulse to tell the truth. He'd never needed one. He'd managed just fine by out-thinking anyone looking to harm him. "I know how."

"It's not that hard a concept. But knowing and doing are a mile apart. "Let's go outside to the firing range and find out just how clever a messenger you can be."

"I can't explain it," Quinn admitted as he put his shirt back on that evening after Reverend Bauers had mended both shirt and side. He'd come to Grace House not only because he couldn't safely explain the singe burn in his side or hole in his shirt to Ma, but because his thoughts were in tangles. "It was like the pistol was just there, waiting for me. But it's a gun. I own a gun."

"There's a difference between a gunslinging outlaw and a deliberate marksman." The reverend put away his bandages and mending supplies, shelving them in his study-now-pantry between a large book and a tin of beans. "After all, no one would compare the sword-play of the Black Bandit with that of a pirate. You're using it as a deliberate defense, not an impulsive act of aggression. You'll need to defend yourself if you're going to do…what you're going to do." The old man heaved himself down on to a crate. "Glory, but I think I'm getting too old for all this. Such drama is best left to younger hearts. Speaking of which…"

Quinn shot the old man a look. He'd seen this coming a mile off. Expected it yesterday, as a matter of fact. "Don't start."

"And here I was thinking I'd jumped to conclusions."

"You have."

"I don't think so." He held Quinn's eyes for a long moment, his expression so neutral Quinn couldn't say if he was about to be chastised or encouraged. Or both. "Miss Longstreet is an admirable woman, Quinn. Any man in the county would look at her twice. And you two seem to have much in common." There was an unspoken "but" in his tone. Bauers raised one eyebrow in silent invitation of a reply but didn't expound on what he was thinking.

Quinn was glad for that. Maybe. He fiddled with the box of noodles at his feet. "I can't stop thinking about her. No one else seems to see the things about her that I do. People dismiss her. Why doesn't anyone understand what's important to her?"

"And by that you mean her father?" It should have sounded judgmental, but it didn't.

"I know he's a friend of yours." On one level, Quinn knew Mr. Longstreet wasn't acting any different than most fathers. But he didn't seem to understand that Nora wasn't most daughters. She was so different…so amazingly, wonderfully different…that Mr. Longstreet's ordinary, protective behavior didn't sit well with Quinn.

"And he's a good man. He is a good father, too, even if that might be hard for you to see at the moment. After all, if something precious to you survived the earthquake, wouldn't you feel all the more protective of it? Isn't her locket—the one you found—even more valuable for surviving the fire?"

Bauers wasn't being helpful. Quinn needed no reminding of the mile-high wall between him and Nora. He thumped a tin of beans down on a nearby shelf with more force than necessary.

Reverend Bauers shook his head. "Your problem, Quinn, is as old as time. I find it rather encouraging to know some things will go on as they did despite all this. You and Nora come from different worlds. And while they may have come crashing down side by side, the distinction between those worlds hasn't altogether disappeared. You'd best remember that. But you'd also do well to remember," the reverend continued, turning away from Quinn and busying himself with a small stack of books, "that the truly extraordinary matches often make no sense whatsoever. If you're asking me, I'd take a reckless heart over a sensible one any day."

There was a long moment of stunned silence before Quinn replied, "Simon tells me reckless is bad."

"Of course he would. He's got the army teaching him

how to live. You, you've got your heart and life and God guiding you. No sir, reckless has its uses. Messengers who go wandering around past midnight need to be a bit reckless."

*Messengers. Midnight.* The words clicked together in Quinn's brain to solve the one detail in all of this that still eluded him.

Quinn stared right at delightful, frustrating Reverend Bauers, who had no idea what he'd just done. "I know who I am now." No, Bauers had not solved the larger question of what to do about Nora, nor fixed the challenges of delivering goods, but he had just answered a small but frustrating question. "Thanks."

Bauers looked stumped. "For what?"

"The name. I'm not the Bandit. I never wanted to be another Bandit anyways. I'm the Midnight Messenger."

"The Midnight Messenger?" The reverend squinted up his eyes, as if trying the thought out for size. "It fits. It works. Yes, I believe you are the Midnight Messenger. Good gracious, what have I done?"

"Become an accomplice. Again." Quinn pointed at the old man. "I *knew* God wasn't done with you yet."

# Chapter Thirteen

It was an unlikely crowd that gathered in the street between Dolores Park and the official camp later that week. Nora and her father stood with Major Simon, Reverend Bauers and Quinn Freeman, staring at the deluge of messages that now covered the post. While Nora was surprised that her father agreed to a further inspection of the notes when Reverend Bauers had asked, she was thankful he didn't seem to view the gulf between the two camps as wide as he had in earlier weeks. As it was, Nora sent up a prayer of praise that these five people could stand here together. She found herself thanking God daily for the wealth of experiences she'd had since that fateful Tuesday morning.

There was almost always a knot of people gathered around the column these days. Word of goods and foodstuffs arriving mysteriously in the middle of the night had spread quickly. Nora knew she had granted Edwina's wish for a doll, but that didn't explain how one family received the blanket they'd requested. Nora heard another story of a woman who tacked up a request for sewing needles, only to find them stuck in her door the next morning.

Suspicious, Nora had asked Quinn what he knew, but he denied any part in the thing. He had no reason to keep it from her, but then again she had no real claim to his confidences, did she? No matter who was behind it, the good news shot a sense of hope through the camp like a burst of sunshine after so much pain and suffering. Not every need was filled—from the looks of the column, perhaps only one request in twenty met with success—but even those odds seemed enough to fuel a surge of optimism.

Bauers folded his hands over his round torso. "From the looks of it, we'll need a second post by the end of the week."

"I had the same thought," Quinn agreed. "But a length of wood that big will be hard to come by. Folks are already saving every scrap they can find in hopes of rebuilding."

That gave Nora an idea. "Papa, what about the column you kept from our old house? We could use that, couldn't we?" It was charred and had a large chunk out of the top, making her wonder if her father had hauled it out of the rubble for purely sentimental reasons. It didn't look to her as if it could serve much use holding anything up anymore, so why not use it here where it could do a world of good?

"It was one of the few things we could save, burnt as it is." Her father pondered the idea for a moment, his reluctance obvious, and Nora thought of her locket, so precious to her even though it was battered almost to uselessness. Sometimes people just needed to hang on to something no matter how little sense it made. She was just about to take back her suggestion when Papa shrugged his shoulders and said, "I don't know why I saved it, to be honest. I suppose this is as good a use as any."

"You know, Longstreet, there's no reason to think it can't be returned to you later," Major Simon offered. "It might even be quite a conversation piece when you rebuild."

"I'm sure it would do good," Nora added. "We should do it."

"I could come over this afternoon and fetch it back," Quinn offered.

"Yes, then, why don't you?" Mr. Longstreet finally agreed.

Nora smiled. "Oh, Papa, I'm so delighted it's coming from our house."

Papa cleared this throat. "The question remains," he looked from Reverend Bauers to Major Simon, "*who* is it we are aiding? Reverend, do you know how the first requests were met?"

"Well, some of them have been met through Grace House and its benefactors, that's to be sure, but there is definitely another party at work. And no, I don't know who they are."

"I do worry that this 'generosity' is really the result of theft," Papa said, stroking his chin. "I'm not for helping out some misguided Robin Hood."

"I suppose it's always a possibility, but I'm inclined to think otherwise," Reverend Bauers said. "Until we have evidence that wrongdoing is involved, I choose to encourage this charity. Think of it as merely another version of postage—you are delivering communication, just by a means other than mail."

Major Simon cast his gaze up and down the first pole. It had so many notes upon it now, wood could no longer be seen. "Still, the postmaster has a point. Another column means twice as many notes. How many notes will be too many? Unmet expectations can be a dangerous tinderbox."

"We've already survived the firestorm," Quinn said. "What's a little more tinder if it might do some good?"

Papa sighed. "Mr. Freeman, I'll expect you this afternoon, if Reverend Bauers or the major can supply you with a wagon."

"Consider it done," Quinn said.

Nora tried to dismiss her twinge of excitement as simply the satisfaction of helping more people. That was a lie. It was far more about the prospect of Quinn Freeman coming to her house this afternoon. She just hoped her father couldn't tell the difference.

When Mr. Longstreet had mentioned he had a usable pillar stowed away in his backyard, he hadn't mentioned that it was hidden under a pile of other rubble and broken furniture. Hadn't Quinn stood on that far corner just days ago, bemoaning his lack of access to Nora's world? *I never learn, do I, Lord?* Quinn grunted and pushed a heap of old bricks out of the way.

Out of the corner of his eye, he saw Nora's face dart away from a window to his left. How long had she been watching him work? He pulled his shirt back on, suddenly feeling the effect of knowing her eyes were on him. *Does it have to be so hard, Lord? Do You set up a man's heart for this foolishness on purpose, or do we do this to ourselves? Surely You didn't bring me through a disaster only to watch my heart break, did You?*

"You look like you could use a drink." Nora appeared on the porch a few minutes later with a large tin cup in her hand. "We've not had ice for weeks, but the water's still cool."

Quinn thought he would have gladly drunk hot water just for an excuse to walk up onto the porch and catch a whiff of her hair. "I sure could use any kind of water. That post's heavier than it looks, I'll tell you."

He drained the cup quickly, glad to have the cool water slide down his parched throat. "Hard to imagine how a house full of sturdy wood came down so quick, isn't it?" He handed the cup back to her after spilling the last bit of the water on his hands and splashing it on to his face.

"The house across the street took three days to fall over. It felt like ours came down in half a minute." Quinn could practically see the memory darken her eyes as she leaned against one of the back porch's columns.

"I'm sorry," Quinn said, meaning it. So sweet a face should never bear that pained expression. "Some awful things happened in our neighborhood, too. A chimney fell on a man right in front of my mother. She has nightmares about it now and then, but it's getting better."

Nora eased herself down the length of the post to settle on the edge of the porch. She was quiet for a moment, fingering the hem of her skirts. "I used to dream about the ground swallowing up Annette every night. I'd wake up feeling like it all just happened, like it would never go away but just keep swallowing the both of us over and over. It was awful." She looked up at Quinn, who stood on the ground with one foot on the steps below her. "I haven't had that dream since you gave the locket back to me. Not even after I lost her photograph, although I cried when I got home." The tenderest of smiles fluttered across her face. "Thank you for fixing it."

It was a little thing, and then again not so little. He wanted to do so much more for her. "It's not the same. I'm sorry about that."

"I am, too." Her hand went up to the locket, and a surge of satisfaction came as her fingers traced his handiwork. She let out a sigh he felt as much as heard. "But nothing's the same, I suppose. We simply have to find the good where we can, make do."

Quinn couldn't help himself when her voice got that wistful quality. "There is good, you know," he said softly, daring a long look into those violet eyes. "More than I ever thought, actually."

She smiled. Not the frail smile of a moment before, but a warm, radiant one that seeped into him stronger than the sunshine. "There is, isn't there? Some wonderful things have happened. Things I can't help thinking wouldn't have happened if everything went on the way it was before. I had that thought just this morning as we were all standing around looking at your wonderful post. And now there will be two." She widened her eyes. "Did you hear the talk as we were standing around? People were saying the loveliest things. They were excited to be receiving gifts and to know that people cared about their needs. Reverend Bauers said that he thought maybe God was giving San Francisco a chance to show the world a good side no one thought was there. Do you think that's true?"

Quinn crossed his arms and leaned against the post opposite Nora on the porch's back stairs. "I don't try to think what God's motives are. He knows what He's got planned, and I expect we wouldn't understand it much if He did tell us the whole scheme. I've got enough on my plate just working out my little part in it, much less the bigger picture."

"Oh," she said, "I think you have an enormous role in it."

Had Bauers told her something? Did she know his role in those deliveries? He didn't like that idea—the Midnight Messenger could be a very dangerous business, and he didn't want her mixed up in it, even if she did want to fill a few of the requests on the pillars. "How so?" he asked carefully.

"The posts, of course. I think God set you right there with that clever idea just like He set you in the camp with the teeter-totter. Like He set you to save me from Ollie. Or to find my locket." She looked right into his eyes, and Quinn felt his stomach drop out through what was left of the soles of his shoes. "You'll probably think it's silly, but you've been such an encouragement to me. Here I was thinking God had left me alone, and you do all those things—those little but very big things— that let me know He's still minding my path. You're an answer to my prayers, Quinn Freeman. How does that make you feel?"

He knew the exact moment his heart left his body. The exact instant it disobeyed all the good and solid reasons he had for not pining over Nora Longstreet and left to follow her of its own accord. He stared at her, knowing his affections had just overstepped all kinds of bounds and not caring. He no longer had any choice in the matter. "I'm thinking it might not be wise to answer that, Miss Longstreet."

She held his stare with an expression almost too bold

for her delicate features. "Nora," she corrected quietly. "And what if I told you I think I might already know?"

"Nora," he said unsteadily, feeling the sound of her name play all kinds of havoc with his composure, "you do already know. I'm just not sure it will change anything." He waited a long moment before he added. "And that's a shame."

"I wish the world were different," she said. "Do you think the world can be different now? That the earthquake can change more than just...the buildings?"

Was she asking him if he was willing to defy all that stood between them? Did she realize how dangerous a question that was? "I know how I'd have things if it were up to me." He tried to tell her, without saying the words, how much that was true. He hoped his eyes showed her what her eyes were showing him. And at that moment, sore and sweaty with the sun beating down on his head, Quinn thought if the only reason God spared him was so that he could feel what he felt from her gaze, then he'd consider it a fair trade. He could do the work of twelve if he could see that look every day. "If God left it up to me... I'd..."

Somehow, some remaining shred of reason stopped him from finishing that sentence. As if it'd lose all its wonder if he tried to put it into words. But she knew. He could tell.

She, however, was willing to go further. "You're one of the very best things about all that's happened, Quinn." There was a power in her eyes that made him want to swoop down and carry her off to whatever future they could discover together. But he didn't want to steal her off her aunt's porch like some kind of marauder. If God ever gave him the chance to claim her for himself, he'd walk through the front door with the admiration of everyone who cared about her.

"You are a wonder, Nora Longstreet," was all he could manage, inadequate as it was. He covered the incredible longing in his chest with a teasing tone. "As big a wonder as they come."

"What will happen now?"

Quinn pushed off the porch steps and willed his feet to take steps in the direction of the cart. It'd take hours of hammering to squelch the humming in his gut right now. Tired as he was from all this work, he was glad to know more work—not to mention another attempt at a delivery—awaited him. He was lost, good and lost. "I've got to work that out," he said, snatching one last look at those memorable eyes, "but you'll be the first to know."

## Chapter Fourteen

Nora sat gazing out her bedroom window that night, trying to make sense of her feelings. The warmth that surged through her when Quinn Freeman looked at her had yet to subside. His shoulders were so broad and his skin so tanned, she found her breath catching as she watched him work. Quinn was much more than just physically handsome—he had an energy about him, a presence that pulled feelings from her she'd never known before. Feelings so strong, in fact, that Nora was continually surprised that Mama or Papa hadn't noticed. She felt so changed that it must surely show.

Annette had talked about such feelings. She had been quite taken with a young man named Eric just before her death. Nora and Annette had stayed up many nights talking about him and, unfortunately, how Aunt Julia and Uncle Lawrence would react if they knew. Annette was a beautiful girl—the violet eyes they shared looked stunning against Annette's dark hair—and Aunt Julia had considerable plans to strike her an advantageous match. It was only Annette's fiery nature that had delayed such a match—her cousin had managed to sidestep many of her mother's attempts by proving herself "a bit too spirited." While Nora loved that about her, Aunt Julia considered it an unfortunate trait best stamped out at every turn.

Nora desperately longed to talk with Annette, to share with her the deep care growing in her heart for Quinn. A care she was sure would meet the same scorn as Annette's feelings for Eric. She'd lost so much when she lost Annette. Aunt Julia had moved her out of the pallet in the living room and into the room that had been Annette's—a touching and costly gesture for Aunt Julia, who had spent so many hours in Annette's room just after her death. Mama would find Aunt Julia wandering silently around the room, touching things, straightening the mess left by the earthquake, folding and refolding clothing. It was both comforting and harsh to be sur-rounded by Annette's things. As if she were all the more here and all the more gone at the same time. Without really meaning to, Nora found herself wandering the room just as Aunt Julia did, sorting through her pos-sessions with aimless fingers.

She wasn't sure what made her look under the bed. Maybe it was the many times they'd played under there as girls. It was just no fun to explore alone.

As she poked her head under the dust ruffle, Nora noticed a whole host of articles that had been dislodged and scattered by the earthquake. Even the houses that suffered very little structural damage had been shaken like a snow globe with often disastrous interior results even if the exterior looked fine.

There was a small brocade sack. Nora recognized it instantly as the place where Annette kept her private treasures. She hadn't even remembered about the cache until seeing it just now. It would make Aunt Julia so happy to know she'd found it.

Until she remembered that it was where Annette kept her diary. And Annette's diary would surely be filled with entries about Eric. Nora didn't have the heart to open that Pandora's box up for Aunt Julia. What Annette had planned for her and Eric would only make Aunt Julia sadder, and what would be the use of that? She'd only just barely stopped moping around the room, only just begun to rejoin the world and resemble herself again.

Pulling out the sack, Nora peered in to find Annette's brown leather journal. Perhaps she had been sent Annette's companionship—even if only in her words and thoughts. Reading Annette's thoughts and feelings for Eric would be so great a comfort. Nora clutched the book to her heart, thinking it a gift from God. There were no issues of violating Annette's privacy. On the slim chance the diary contained no mention of Eric (which was possible if Annette truly feared her mother discovering the book) perhaps by reading it she would know she could turn it over to Aunt Julia with confidence. If not, Nora said silently, closing her eyes and hoping Annette could somehow hear, I'll keep you safe to myself. It's the least I can do.

Nora stayed up for hours that night, poring over the nearly year's worth of diary entries. Several times Nora found herself laughing at Annette's atrocious grammar or spelling. She had never been one to tend to her lessons, no matter how many times Aunt Julia scolded her for it. Her penmanship, however, was artistic and lovely, with lines as long and flowing as her onyx hair.

Annette had been in love. Dramatically—as one

would expect from such a spirited soul—and danger-
ously in love. She and Eric had been more serious than
even Nora knew. According to her entries, the couple
would have eloped by now. It struck Nora that earthquake or no, she'd have lost Annette—for the young
couple would surely have run far away after their secret marriage. But I would have been able to say goodbye. To know you were happy. Aunt Julia, however,
wouldn't share her good wishes. With a small smirk,
Nora couldn't help thinking her aunt would see the
elopement scandal as worse than a dozen earthquakes.
Only you, Annette, could make me thankful for an
earthquake in some ways. Yawning, Nora finally tucked
the diary back into its brocade case and slid it to the
bottom of the small drawer than held her nightgowns.
God had sent her a bit of Annette after all. While it still
stung to have known Annette kept such secrets from
her, and her heart ached for the tiny photographs lost
from her locket forever, her heart burned in a new, unfamiliar way for the man whose flowers were tucked
in their place.

Now, it seemed, Nora had a secret of her own.

Ma stood in the doorway, staring holes in Quinn's
back as he finished shaving outside and splashed the
last of the morning's water on his numb face. "Did you
think I wouldn't notice?" she barked finally.

Every muscle in Quinn's body ached beyond reason.
He'd spent the afternoon sinking the second post into
the ground, made a pretense at a few hours' sleep after
dinner, then slipped off to make a few deliveries. He'd
managed only three of the five requests before time
and fatigue had caught up with him, forcing him back

to bed if he stood any chance at making it through the day's paid labor ahead of him.

*Heroes need better wages, Lord.* Quinn prayed as he willed strength and reason to seep into his brain from the coffee cup he currently held. He needed to be three separate people in order to keep all this up.

"Notice what?" He didn't look at her, but he didn't even need the mirror's reflection to tell him his evasion wouldn't succeed.

Ma spun on her heels and turned back into the shack. "*Notice what? he says,*" she addressed the empty shelter loudly enough for him to hear. "As if fooling his ma comes easy to him now. It's come to that, has it?" Quinn wasn't quite sure who she was conversing with, but it was clear that he shouldn't answer that question at the moment. He followed her inside, only to have her turn on him with angry eyes. "Who is it you're keeping all kinds of hours with, Quinn? Out half the night, carousing with the likes of Heaven knows who? There's nothing but drinking and gambling happens that time of night. I'm no fool." The look of disappointment in her eyes fell to the pit of his stomach like a dozen rocks. "You had such sense before, son. Where's it gone?"

She thought he spent his nights drinking. While it had never occurred to him she'd come to such a conclusion, once he thought about it there wasn't a single good reason she shouldn't suspect the worst of his midnight disappearances. Many a good man had let the stress and grief of the disaster lead him straight to the bottle. His own da had tripped along that path—to his own eventual end—years before with nowhere near the desperation that gripped the city lately. "No, Ma," he said, not having another excuse but not being able to bear the look in her eye.

She looked as if the loss of another of her men to the bottle would be her undoing. "Don't make it worse by lying," she said quietly. Her knuckles were white around the spoon she held.

Quinn took an enormous, burning gulp of coffee and looked her squarely in the eye. "I'm not drinking, Ma. I promise. I couldn't. Not with Da…"

One hand flew up to stop his words, as if even his name caused her pain. She turned away, shaking her head. Her disbelief stung him worse than the bullet graze he still nursed on his left side. In all his eagerness for secretive heroics, he'd never considered it would cost him Ma's trust to be the Midnight Messenger. Still, it had to be that way. Telling her where he really was would only place her in danger if things ever went wrong. But he couldn't bear her thinking he was slipping down to his father's ugly end at the bottom of a bottle. He had to tell her something, and quick. Blurting out the first thing that came to his mind—mostly because it never left his mind—he offered a sheepish grin and said, "You'd like her, Ma."

Ma went still, staring at him. "A woman?" she said suspiciously.

Well now, he hadn't thought through the details. What woman of decent character would keep the hours he'd been keeping? No woman of decent character. He could practically see his ma come to the base conclusion that his "woman" was no "lady." "No, Ma, not that, either."

Ma's hand went to her heart. "You're not giving me much hope to go on." She got a straight-to-business look on her face and sat down on her chair, placing her teacup carefully on one knee. "How about we try this again, and with the truth."

There wasn't another way. At least not one that he could see at the moment. "The truth is, Ma, that I can't say. That's the whole of it and the best I can give you. But I can tell you that it's not drink. But you can't know more than that, and I've my reasons."

"What kind of reasons would make a son lie to his mother?"

"I've not lied to you, Ma. And I'll make a promise to do my best never to lie to you. But that means you'll not get answers to some questions. At least not now." If he made enemies as the Messenger—which he most surely would—anything she knew would put her at risk.

She narrowed her eyes at him. "What in Heaven's name are you up to, lad?"

"You can't know, Ma, and it's as simple as that." He felt ancient this morning, and it had nothing to do with lack of sleep. "But you can know that I doubt I can do it well on an empty stomach."

Ma addressed the empty room again. "All secrets, but I'm to feed him breakfast. What's happening to the world, I ask you?"

"It's getting a little bit better day by day, Ma. And that's the truth of it." He reached out and gave her a hug, noticing how small she felt in his embrace. It felt odd to think of her as old, nearly impossible to think of her as frail, but the months had taken their toll on her much more than they had on him.

She opened the little tomato box that had become their pantry, pulling out a hunk of cheese he'd managed to procure the previous afternoon. "Is there really someone," she asked with careful words, "or were you throwing up smoke to your own ma?"

Quinn polished off the last of his coffee. "There is, and there isn't."

His mother cut the last of their bread into two thick slices. "What kind of answer is that to a simple question?"

"I suppose Reverend Bauers would say some simple questions don't have simple answers."

She only heaved an enormous, burdened sigh as she handed him the bread and cheese. "I suppose I can only pray for you. God Himself only knows what to make of the likes of this."

With a sad smile of his own, Quinn thought his mother was absolutely right.

Quinn slowly squeezed his finger and felt the gun's kick as it released its bullet.

Square into the straw target Simon had set up a good distance away. Quinn turned out to be an excellent shot. Within a week of training, Quinn already bested most of the regular infantry and half of the officers. While it surprised him that such a dark skill came to him so readily, he couldn't ignore the admiration and respect fellow infantrymen gave him when he shot as well as he did. He understood how the Wild West got so wild now—and why Ma had been so against him owning one. Guns gave very attractive power on very short notice.

Major Simon took off his hat and squinted down the line at the hit target. "I ought to enlist you," he said with a dark look. "This minute."

Quinn shook off the tired ache in his neck, aimed

and fired. A hole burst dead center on the second target. It rarely took him a second shot.

Simon shook his head. "You're wasted on the swords, Freeman. The pistol is your weapon by far."

It was the first compliment Simon had paid him in days. Things had been tense between them since the major's oh-so-well-received dinner with the Longstreets—but the tension had mostly been on Quinn's part. From what he could see, Simon was oblivious. Part of him knew the circumstances held immovable obstacles between him and Nora.

Another part of him refused to accept it. It was as if he and Nora were cut from the same cloth, but neither one seemed suited for their present circumstances. She was bolder than society cared to allow young women, and he craved more than what society cared to allow men lacking a formal education. It seemed unjust that neither of them be able to reach toward the middle ground they somehow seemed to share. He was not at all bothered by her boldness—something men like Simon probably considered unfortunate. He'd heard Simon speak of young, bold recruits as "loose cannons" or "liabilities." Quinn, on the other hand, was fond of Nora's boldness almost as much as he was fond of her eyes. No one should tamp down Nora's boldness any more than they should change her eye color. It was how God had made her.

"I'm not sure how you did it, but word is out," the major said once they returned inside, handing Quinn a cloth to clean the pistol. "People are talking about a mysterious 'Midnight Messenger.' Very dramatic name, by the way."

Quinn had "signed" one or two of the deliveries as

the "Midnight Messenger." It was important that folks in Dolores Park knew someone was out there on their side. He'd done it as an act of reassurance more than any ploy for fame. "I wasn't shooting for drama. Just something people could remember."

"Oh, they're aware of you, all right." The major looked as if he didn't think that was such a good idea. "Now that you've got an identity, I'd venture people will be out looking for you. And not everyone will want to shake your hand, if you catch my meaning. I suppose the mask isn't such a bad idea after all." Simon nodded toward the ordinary-looking rucksack Quinn used. Inside were the costume and weapons of—now—the Midnight Messenger. Major Simon kept the bag inside a locked chest in a closet near his office, setting them alongside the supplies on delivery nights.

With Reverend Bauers's help, Quinn had fashioned a fabric version of the Bandit's mask—a sort of dark bandanna skullcap with a two-holed flap that folded down over the eyes to tie behind his head. It covered Quinn's visibly blond hair, hid his ears and brow, and worked just as well under a hat as without. Quinn could almost feel himself transforming when he put it on. Still, these people needed so much more than what he'd been able to give them. "These provisions aren't enough," he informed the major. "I'm going to need more."

"Don't overextend yourself, Freeman."

Quinn didn't care for his I-know-better tone. "I think I know how much I can do. I don't need you setting limits on me. If you can provide it, I'll find a way to deliver it."

"And your cocky attitude will fast find a way to get

you killed. You're exhausted, Quinn. You won't be any good to me dead."

Any good to "me"? When had this become about Simon? "I'll admit I'm tired, but I'm not one of your liabilities. If I need rest, I'll get it. If you're so intent on my backing things down a bit, give me some extra provisions to take to Grace House. I'll let the reverend be the hero for the evening, feeding folks who need to be fed. A good meal's hard to come by, with cooking fires being outlawed and all."

Quinn pushed out an exasperated breath. Even he had to admit the last remark was an underhanded blow. Everyone hated the army's banning of open flame— necessary as it was to ensure public safety. It wasn't Simon's fault people couldn't cook for themselves. Maybe he really was too tired if he let the major's superior attitude get under his skin like that.

Simon looked annoyed, but didn't rise to Quinn's challenge. "I just took a delivery of some bacon, beans and even a little sugar. And because its kitchen is intact, Grace House can have flour for baking. I'll throw in three extra sacks. Bauers can feed extra mouths and keep everyone occupied for a day or so. Will that convince you to slow down?"

Quinn was smart enough not to let his temper get in the way of a good solution. He'd never admit it to Simon's face, but the prospect of a night off was sorely tempting. And although his cot called to him, Quinn knew exactly where—and with whom—he wanted to spend his newfound free time.

# *Chapter Fifteen*

Nora stood in the living room later that afternoon watching glances bounce back and forth between her parents and Reverend Bauers. The reverend had just come to the house—under "major's orders"—to ask Nora to help with a last-minute army distribution of foodstuffs and supplies.

"I know Nora wants to help, but I need to be cautious about when and where she lends a hand, even at the request of Major Simon." Nora hoped her father wouldn't force her to decline such a perfectly good reason to visit Dolores Park.

"It is a testament to you that your daughter is so willing to be of assistance. She'll be back for supper, madam." Reverend Bauers folded his hands seriously across his chest. "You have my word. She'll only go to the very edge of the park, and she'll be escorted by Major Simon himself at all times."

Mama acquiesced first. "Please tell the major he is most welcome to stay for dinner when he brings Nora back."

They pulled up to the park edge to find Major Simon

smiling on the back of a large wagon mounded with a variety of clothing, blankets, building supplies and tins of various food. "How delightful to have your help, Miss Longstreet. It is a great pleasure to see you again. If you would be so kind as to sit behind this table and make a list of each family as they receive their goods? Just names please, as Sergeant Miller here will take note of the particular items over at the cart." He handed her a ledger and pencil.

She settled herself behind the table, and as the major attended to the other officer, Nora discreetly swept her eye around the gathering crowd. No Quinn. Not even after an hour's worth of listing names. It was foolish to expect him to find her every time she set foot near the park. She was chastising herself for giving in to such disappointment when Reverend Bauers came up to the table.

"Miss Longstreet," he said, "you'll be pleased to know I've persuaded the major to accept your mother's kind offer of dinner. I wonder if I could persuade you to offer me a moment of your time to help with the posts?"

"Please, Reverend, tell me whatever it is you need." Nora stood up and the reverend tucked her hand into the crook of his elbow. They had walked the half a block to the post when Bauers stopped and whispered into her ear. "What I need, my dear, is to get him what he needs."

Nora pulled back. "What who needs?"

Suddenly, Nora heard a voice from behind her other shoulder. "I need to see you." It was Quinn's voice, right behind her.

She moved to spin around and face him, but the reverend held tight to her arm. "Quinn, can we at least *attempt* to be careful?"

Nora's eyes flew wide and her spine stiffened as she realized that Quinn had actually put the Reverend Bauers up to this meeting. "Quinn?" Nora fairly gasped.

"Mr. Freeman," corrected the elder minister.

"Quinn is just fine." Nora could hear the smile in Quinn's voice even if she couldn't turn to see it. "I had to see you." She heard him shift his weight and groan. "Reverend, give me a minute?"

The minister tightened his grip on Nora's arm. "Within eyeshot of the major? Certainly not." His voice was stern but Nora could clearly see the twinkle in his eye. "Nora, would you be so kind as to write down a dozen or so of these requests as I point them out to you? It should only take…" he inclined his head in Quinn's direction "…two minutes at the most."

"Five."

Nora was so flustered by the "conspiracy" and Quinn's nearby voice that it took her a moment to grasp the chalk and slate Reverend Bauers produced from his coat pocket. "Certainly. I had…very much…wanted to come back here and see…the posts." It was like trying to have six conversations at once. "Papa is so very cautious now."

"As well he should be," the reverend chimed in, at which Quinn produced an exasperated groan from somewhere just off her left shoulder.

"I need to see you."

Nora looked at the minister. How could she possibly answer such a question with a reverend inches away? As if hearing her thoughts, Reverend Bauers found something fascinating in the sky to look at and began to whistle softly.

"I... I don't know. I don't know how."

"I'll just talk to your father. Explain what's..."

"No," Nora countered. "He'd never listen. Not yet."

She heard him blow out an exasperated breath behind her. "I'd make him understand."

His determination made her heart pound. "Perhaps you could, in time. But not yet." The memory of Papa's scowl darkened her words.

"Your window is on the south side, right?"

Nora startled. "On my house? Aunt Julia's house?"

"Does it have a balcony?"

"Have you been reading *Romeo and Juliet?*" the clergyman asked in an exasperated tone.

Nora swallowed a laugh. The vision of Quinn Freeman scaling Aunt Julia's rose trellis made her want to giggle and sigh at the same time. "That's not wise."

"To say the least," Reverend Bauers said. He pointed out a message from the post asking for a hymnal and socks. "A meeting at Grace House is wisest. I told you that, Quinn. See here, Nora, there are three requests for dolls like the one you gave Edwina. I don't think the Ladies Aid society would see fit to provide those, but perhaps if Grace House supplied the materials you could make more."

"I told him," Quinn said. "Edwina was so happy."

"Her grandfather came to services at Grace House the following weekend. I gather he's not darkened the door of a church in ten years."

Quinn's voice was low and close. "You did that, Nora."

Nora's satisfaction ran so deep she could almost

soak in God's smile coming down on her from Heaven. "That's wonderful," she whispered, having to work hard to concentrate as she wrote down the three other names. "Of course I'll make more."

"If you bring them to Grace House, I can meet you there." The urgency in Quinn's voice made the back of Nora's neck tingle.

"I could be there Tuesday," Nora replied. Tuesday seemed like a million years from now.

"Tuesday." Quinn's single word seemed to echo her own frustration. Nora closed her eyes, feeling his gaze burn into her, sense his presence in the air just behind her, hear his breath. Her hand moved to grasp the locket around her neck.

"Tuesday it is. Take care, you two, we walk a knife's edge with this."

Nora felt Quinn's exit as much as she heard his footsteps. After a moment, the minister pointed out another two or three requests tacked to the post, and somehow she managed to write them down.

"Why are you helping us?" Nora had never used the word "us" before. It seemed terribly important that she had now.

Reverend Bauers turned to her with a smile that wiped years—perhaps even decades—off his face. For a moment she saw the dashing young adventurer he claimed to have been in his youth. God's provision over the years had made the reverend a very brave and daring man—Nora felt a stab of guilt at thinking of him as just a gentle old preacher. He was gentle, and old, but he was so much more than that. Nora wanted, at that moment, to know that at eighty *she* would look back on her life as full of God's adventures.

"Why? Is it not obvious?" He chuckled. "The man is absolutely relentless."

She smiled. "I believe I am coming to feel the same way."

They returned to the table and Nora did her best to wrestle her attention back to the task at hand. There was a moment, a frozen moment in time, where she looked up and caught Quinn's eyes as he stood at a distance. Even from far away, the gold of his eyes glowed like topaz, the intensity of his stare stole her breath and flushed her cheeks. She glanced around, sure the whole world saw the power of their locked eyes, but everyone bustled by unawares. Life pulsed by all around them, noisy and busy and ignorant of the air that hummed between Quinn and her. She could live to be a hundred and still be able to recall the amber glow of his eyes in that moment.

Suddenly, Romeo facing death to scale Juliet's balcony didn't seem so melodramatic. She had thought herself too old for such childish romance, but with her heart beating as wildly as it did, Nora felt perhaps the heart's distinction between brave and foolish was a very fine line, indeed.

A thud and a yelp dragged Nora from her thoughts. Something had fallen off the piles of goods that filled the cart. When white powder pooled out of the burlap sack, she could hear the reaction by those who saw. Flour ranked as one of the most coveted and least available supplies anywhere—everyone wanted some and it was nearly impossible to get any. As a matter of fact, the army was saying there wasn't enough to distribute outside of the official relief stations that were cooking for hundreds of refugees daily and supplying the endless bread lines.

"Flour!" one woman called out, pointing to the snowy mounds. "You've got flour in there! I want some of that."

Major Simon stiffened. Clearly this wasn't a good thing. "Sergeant?" he said in a cautionary but commanding tone.

"I don't know, sir, it must have been in there by mistake."

The woman who'd first cried out pushed her way to the front of the crowd. "They told us there isn't any flour to give out. Only there is, isn't there?"

Simon moved between the woman and the flour. "There isn't a way for you to use this. Baking requires fire, and fire is too dangerous right now."

"For who?" a man jeered. "You got enough to lose track of, then I say you got enough to let decent people do their own cooking."

"Who knows what else they been keepin' from us?" a second woman said, peering into the back of the cart. "I heard you been sellin' the flour rather than give it to us. Making profit off our need, are you?" This started a chorus of accusations against the army. Major Simon frowned and held up his hand to quiet the crowd, barely succeeding.

"We sell flour you can't use and buy things you *can use* with the money. One carelessly tended stove could start another fire. You know we can't have that. I know this is difficult, but…"

"Don't you get all fancy-worded on me. Ain't right to go profiteering off of folks in need. You think you know better than me, that's what I think. Well, you don't. You're just another one of them, you are. Don't really care a fig for what happens to us so's long as you can keep us fooled."

"No one's trying to mislead you," the major said in a forced calm. "We're trying to give you what you need as fast as we can, but you've got to understand the dangers. The few common fire pits are the best we can do for now. We simply can't have you people using ovens. I'm sorry."

"Yeah? Well, I'm hungry. Which of us is better off?" some man called out from the back of the crowd.

"The Messenger could get us flour," the first woman declared.

"I'd hope the Messenger would care about the safety of your family as much as you do, ma'am, and he'd tell you what I'm telling you now." The major was trying to stay calm, but the crowd had turned on him.

"Hang your 'care,' captain. I'd rather have your flour. Wouldn't we all?" the man called out again.

"Let's try to see the bigger picture here," Reverend Bauers interjected, coming to stand next to the major. "Safety is absolutely vital. Times are challenging for everyone."

"Some more than others," a thin woman grumbled as she tossed the pair of shirts she'd just collected back on to the cart. Several others followed suit, and Nora could see the major's jaw clenching.

Nora felt the tension gather in the air like a storm. Suddenly, it felt as if all of Reverend Bauers's promises of a safe visit were going up in smoke. She looked up, needing to find Quinn's eyes, wanting to know he would step in and save her, yet again, if things got out of hand. But Quinn had vanished. Her pulse began to rise. Forcing calm into her voice, Nora turned to Reverend Bauers. "Perhaps it might be best if we left now and saved the rest of our efforts for another day."

"Indeed. And perhaps it would be best not to ask the major to make good on his promise of escorting you home."

As voices rose, Nora craned her neck around against Reverend Bauers's pull on her arm, striving for one last glimpse of Quinn, who surely must be somewhere in that crowd. Tuesday felt years from now.

"That was a disaster." Major Simon let out a few choice words as he threw his gloves and hat down on the table in his office. He hadn't called for Quinn to come and see him, but it didn't take a genius to know that thanks to this afternoon's fiasco, the Midnight Messenger wasn't going to get the night off he'd planned. He and Simon stood in the major's office, staring at each other. It was the first time he'd seen Simon lose the edges of his slick control.

It was also the first time since he'd started that Quinn felt a pang of regret. Fear, even. It had been adventurous, a satisfying chance to make hope-sparking deliveries for people in Dolores Park. Now, Quinn felt the demands coming down on him like an avalanche. He was only one man—and yet the cries of that crowd seemed to expect him to do what even the U.S. Army seemed hard-pressed to do. "We set out to make a solution," the major continued, "and we've made a monster."

"The people want flour. Donated flour's coming in by the tons. How can we deny them things as if they're children?"

Simon sat down behind his desk. "And have them

burn the city down all over again? They've no real ovens. They've no safe storage. One careless spark, Freeman, that's all it would take. We've got to be vigilant. We've got to make decisions based on what's best for the entire city, not just one family's stomach. You heard me explain it—we've sold most of the excess flour to buy things they really can use."

"I heard you," Quinn replied, letting his tone show what he thought of that particular strategy. "You sold our relief supplies." It sounded wrong, no matter how the major put a shine on it.

"It's best." Simon's tone held a challenge of its own.

"And *you* know what's best?" Quinn felt as if that black shirt and mask were now made of iron, clamping down on him with heavy solidity. People expected the Messenger to give them what they wanted.

"Tight authority means life and death these days. We can't afford another rebellious mob scene like that."

Quinn forced civility into his words. "So what will we do?" He had a hunch he wouldn't like the answer.

"My grandfather taught me an old saying." Simon began writing something out on a slip of paper. "When you don't have what you want, make do with what you've got." He stood and called, "Private!" out his office door, handing the paper to the tense-looking young man who appeared seconds later. Quinn wondered, by the major's behavior, if he'd even remembered he was in the room.

"This is a requisition for two dozen blankets from the barracks warehouse. Tell them to make sure the blankets are in good shape and have the army markings on them. I want them in my office within ten minutes. Understood?"

"Directly, sir." The young man barely paused to salute before bolting from the room. Simon pulled the office door shut after his private.

"They want flour, so you're going to give them blankets?" Quinn had serious doubts it would be seen as a fair trade. You could hardly eat a blanket, after all.

"No, *you're* going to give them blankets. Army blankets. It's high time we let everyone know the Messenger's on *our* side. You've lost your night off. I'm sorry for that, but I'm sure you see the urgency of the thing."

Quinn wasn't liking this at all. "Wouldn't it be better to get the people to understand why they can't have baking fires? I don't see how tossing army blankets at them helps."

The major frowned. "You cannot reason with a mob. Only distract it. You watch—that post will be filled with requests for flour tomorrow morning. Flour they think the Messenger can find for them because they think we've hid it from them. Nothing personal, Freeman, but you've become a temporary liability, and we need to recast you from rebel to partner. We can't have people thinking the Messenger is out there outsmarting the army. You saw how fast things escalated out there—the Messenger has to be seen as working *with* us."

Quinn had the disturbing feeling that he'd been enlisted without his consent. That he'd just been sucked up into the army machine, forced—albeit kindly—to do their bidding and serve their purposes. Major Simon had done so much for him, and yet it was hard not to feel as though it had all been for some convenient purpose. Like the small pawns in the chess game Reverend Bauers was forever trying to teach him. Scooted about to serve some larger aim without much regard for his own health and safety.

Yet, Simon had a valid point—one careless spark could start the firestorm all over again. And Simon had given him weapons, training and was by far his best source for goods. Quinn couldn't be the Messenger without Simon's help—at least not yet. "And what are *you* going to do?"

"Oddly enough, the most important thing I can do right now is to do nothing. To behave as if all were well, as if there were no cause for concern whatsoever." He raised an eyebrow at Quinn, who tried to swallow the knot currently balling up in his throat. "Which means, thankfully, that it is in the city's best interest that I dine at the Longstreets' tonight as if there were not a single demand upon my time this evening."

Quinn hoped his mouth wasn't gaping open. It should have been.

"Word of my calm dismissal of any problem will travel through the city as fast as word of your deliveries will fly through camp. We're both making vital deliveries tonight. Just different kinds."

Quinn let his frustration grind a sharp edge on to his words. "So you solve this by eating a fine meal while I help you by spending another night hiding in shadows?"

Shrugging his shoulders, Simon said, "Would it help if I bought you a steak tomorrow night?"

"Only just." Quinn was glad no one required him to salute as he left. The Messenger was suddenly feeling less like a calling and more like a punishment.

# Chapter Sixteen

Quinn stalked through the kitchen at Grace House. "I've had about enough of this. He's the one with the problem, so why am I the one staying up tonight to fix things? He's the one denying people what they want." He turned and glared at Reverend Bauers, not bothering to hide his frustration. "Yet he's with her, and I'm here."

Reverend Bauers gave out a lumbering sigh and put down the box of silverware he was shelving. "Except that he's right, and you know it. People can't have the flour, even if they think they need it. Simon is right, Quinn, but it's not really why you're rankled, in any case."

Quinn ignored that last remark. "We should be equals in this, but I've got the short end of the stick by far. I can't remember the last time I slept an entire night. Tonight I was…" He stopped himself. He was going to try and find a way to see Nora, that's what he was going to do with this evening. And now, not only had that opportunity been plucked from his hands, it seemed to have been handed—on a silver platter—to Major Simon. Really, if Simon had asked him to distribute army blankets on any other night, he would have donned the Messenger's black bag and gladly made the deliveries.

"You were going to what?" Bauers knew the answer. The knowledge in his eyes was disarming even if it was softened with understanding. "I was standing right next to you, you know. Balconies. You really do have a flair for drama, Quinn." He walked entirely too calmly over to Quinn, reaching up to tap Quinn's throbbing temples. "Use your eyes, man. You stare enough at her, surely you see it. You've no rival in Major Simon. She's as much drawn to you as you are to her. It's her parents who are your rivals. Their views and their expectations for Nora's future." He clasped Quinn's shoulder and returned to shelving the supplies that were finally leaving his study for their former places in the mission kitchen. "Why do you think God called you to be His messenger?"

His messenger? Quinn thought that made him sound a bit too much like the angel Gabriel. And Quinn wasn't feeling very angelic at the moment. "I don't know, actually."

"I do. Nora would too, if she knew. You're clever and quick and brave…and willing. Most times, all God really needs is a willing soul—he can always make up for the rest if a man is willing to step out in faith."

Quinn picked up a stack of plates and put them on a high shelf. "You make it sound noble. I doubt it will feel very noble at three in the morning when I'd much rather be home in bed."

"It *is* noble. And very few noble things in this world come without great cost. It cost you to help those people. It will keep costing you—probably more as this goes on. The question is, are you going to let that stop you? Or are you going to keep on in the faith that God will keep on providing?"

"Simon's begun treating me like I'm some sort of secret army weapon. He's using me for his own end."

Reverend Bauers sat down on one of the kitchen's large wooden benches. How many times had the food Quinn had gobbled down in this kitchen been the only decent meal of the day in his childhood? The wood creaked under the reverend's weight—most of the Grace House furnishings were old and worn, leaving Quinn to wonder how much longer many of them would last. "You can always just quit," Bauers offered, resting his elbows on the table. "Stop. No one would be the wiser."

"And just let people think everyone's given up on them? Just vanish, even after people have come to have a bit of hope? What would that solve?"

"Exactly," Bauers replied. "What would that solve?" He motioned for Quinn to sit. "It wouldn't solve anything to your liking, Quinn. You care. Perhaps too much. But don't let some useless worry about Major Simon muddle your thinking here. You've a mission, and Simon's part of that mission. You need to trust God with the details, even if they don't seem to your liking. God knows what you feel for Miss Longstreet, and He knows what Miss Longstreet feels for you."

And that was the question, wasn't it? What did Nora feel for him? He thought of her eyes as she held his gaze on the porch the other day. He could dive inside those eyes and live a happy man forever. They seemed to pour courage and purpose into him—as if he caught the world by the tail just by catching her eye. She felt for him what he felt for her. He'd seen it, felt it. He knew she cared for him; he'd just let Simon's arrogant remarks fester a groundless doubt about it. "What is God up to here, Reverend?"

The question made the old man laugh heartily. "I ask myself that nearly every day lately. I've got an inkling, but if I knew for certain, well then there'd be no use for faith now, would there? Do I believe God sent an earthquake? Can't say that I do. I don't believe God sends evil upon us. But I do believe evil happens and then God works wonders to pull all the goodness he can out of those circumstances."

"Tell Him to pull harder. I'm running out of steam."

Bauers laid a gnarled hand on Quinn's forearm and bent his head. *"Holy Father, bless this man, your servant. Grant him strength and endurance. Keep him safe, honor his efforts to serve Your children. Tend to his heart as You tend to his soul. He is near and dear to me, Lord, and I would grant him the world were it up to my wisdom. But it is Your wisdom, Lord, that is always best."*

The reverend kept Quinn's arm in his grasp, and Quinn's breath caught at the surge of emotion that welled up in him. There was a time, when he was a young and angry teenager, when he'd tried to bolt from the house after an argument with his father. Ma caught him as he attempted to burst out the door, grabbing on to him with a fierce grip that seemed impossible for her size. She pulled him firmly to her, hugging him even though he struggled against it. He'd ended up clutching her to his shoulder—even then, he was taller than she—fighting the sobs that wanted to come tumbling out of his chest at how unfair the whole world seemed.

It was as if she knew of the coming storm and made herself his anchor.

She'd settled something in him that day. Passed some kind of strength through from her heart to his, something that enabled him to stand firm when things got worse and worse with Pa. He felt the same way again, now, only deeper. As if Reverend Bauers had passed a strength of soul between them, lent him the steadfast faith it would take to see this thing through. Not a certainty, not a plan, not even a calm, but the steadfast faith that didn't need calm to stand firm.

Matthew Covington had once told him he was sure God ordained him to be the Bandit. Quinn thought it high-minded talk at the time. From out of the mist of his memory, a verse came to him. A blessing, as it were, from within. *"Be confident of this very thing, that he which hath begun a good work in you will perform it until the day of Jesus Christ."*

Major Simon was staring at her. Not in the open, unabashed way that Quinn had, but in glances and gazes over the conversation he held easily with her father. Ease. It was the single strongest word Nora could use to describe Major Simon. He was at ease with himself, at ease with his position, at ease with the chaos he'd been chosen to supervise and at ease with the obvious eagerness at which the Longstreet family welcomed him into their home.

That same eagerness made Nora uneasy. Despite her "advanced" years—most of her friends had been married off by now—she had never felt pressure of any kind to wed. Her parents had always patiently expected the right man to simply present himself in a matter of time.

Now, the earthquake's brush with death had made them anxious. Not in the "imminent disaster" kind of way, but more of a "life must be accomplished as soon as possible" outlook. As if Nora had managed to beat the odds by surviving, but had best grab the elements of life—husband, children and such—quickly, before the odds caught up with her. In fact, record numbers of couples had married since the earthquake. Albert Simon, with his charm and credentials, seemed to Nora's parents to be the perfect solution to all life's problems. The way Mama fussed over him, one would think they'd been betrothed since childhood.

"Nora," Mama said as if she'd been impatiently waiting for Nora to come up with the idea on her own, "why don't you show Major Simon the garden?"

"The garden" was a stretch of the term. In truth, it was a scratched-out patch of the backyard where Mama and Aunt Julia had managed to coax a few flowers into sprouts. Aunt Julia only had a kitchen garden before the earthquake, whereas Mama had tended a variety of overflowing flower beds. Nora wasn't sure if the new flower garden was for Mama's comfort, or just the only way Mama could think to engage Aunt Julia's increasingly withdrawn disposition. Either way, it struck Nora as the same intent as Quinn's teeter-totter—a "luxury" that was, in fact, very much a survival necessity. It was a pathetic display by Mama's former standards, but then everyone had had to redefine their standards lately, hadn't they?

"You've a garden?" Nora wondered if the major's impressed tone would survive the tour of the tiny seedling patch. She thought of Quinn's frequent reply of "only just," but swallowed the urge to use it.

"We've done what we could, given the circumstances," Mama said, smiling at Aunt Julia. Behind Mama's forced smile, Nora could see the hints of longing for her own garden, for her own home. Papa had begun the process of rebuilding just last week, but it would be weeks if not months before they were back in a home of their own, and Papa had decided to move them farther away from the bay. They'd be farther from Dolores Park and farther from Grace House once they left Aunt Julia's. Nora couldn't help but worry how Aunt Julia and Uncle Lawrence would fare, wandering around in their own freshly empty home once her family left.

Major Simon gave that grandly easy smile of his. "I'd like very much to see it." He looked right at Nora when he said it. The directness of his gaze ought to have disturbed Papa, but instead Papa looked supremely satisfied with the major's obvious interest. For the first time in her life, Nora felt the social expectations of a young woman's future tighten around her. As if she were standing with her feet in a fast-moving river, facing the very real threat of being pulled out into the rapids.

# Chapter Seventeen

"I find them rather eager, don't you?" Simon surprised her when they'd closed the door behind them on the back porch. "Is there some sort of horrid fact about you they've yet to disclose? I can't possibly be the first caller you've had." He'd identified himself as a "caller"—knowing all that the term implied—with an unnerving confidence. As if they'd spoken of it for years instead of days, if not hours. As if there was no question how things would proceed from here. "They do seem in a hurry all of a sudden." It seemed the most neutral thing to say.

He tucked his hands in his pockets and walked out on to the lawn toward the rows of green shoots surrounded by a makeshift fence. "Many are, you know. It's a natural reaction to a shock such as the disaster."

Yes, he had several years on her, but even aside from that, Major Simon looked as if nothing ever shocked him. She had a sudden vision of him standing amid the roiling army barracks, legs braced wide on the shuddering ground, timing the earthquake on his pocket watch. "Were you frightened?" she asked. "When the earthquake struck?"

He raised a dark eyebrow, stumped by her sudden change of subject. He left his inspection of the fence to look at her for a moment. "I'd not be much of an officer if I panicked in a tight spot, now would I? I must be ever the stoic and fearless Major Simon."

Nora leaned back against one of the fat pillars that held up the porch. "I'm not at all sure I'd trust a fearless man. There are many real things in life to be afraid of. And after all, 'fear of the Lord is the beginning of Wisdom.'"

"I leave those ponderings up to the reverend."

"You're not a man of faith, sir?"

"All men pray in battle, Miss Longstreet."

Nora crossed her arms over her chest. "And that is not an answer, Major Simon."

He looked at her for a long moment. She could see him think, see him weigh her question and analyze its intent. "That is an important question for you, isn't it?"

"Yes, it is."

Simon clasped his hands behind his back. "Faith, to soldiers, is a luxury. Obedience and survival are our anchors." He returned his gaze to her. "I suppose the best answer I can give you is that I *could* be. Perhaps that is one of the things I might learn from you. If we were to…pursue things."

"I could never give you faith, Major. That is something only God can do."

"Perhaps," he said, his smile broadening. "But there is something I know you could do."

"And what is that?"

"You could call me Albert." He looked around. "At least, in less formal circumstances."

How had her parents, who never seemed to view her "spinster" circumstance with any anxiety before, suddenly become so focused on marriage? She supposed the great, awful lesson on life's fragility they'd all had was at the root of it. It wasn't hard to grab at happiness with both hands when even the slightest prospect of it rose. The number of marriage licenses issued since the earthquake proved there was an overwhelming, unspoken fear that destruction could happen again at any moment. That the whole world could shake and tumble off into the ocean tomorrow morning. It made some people desperate to do "what's right." It made other people desperate to do whatever it was they most wanted.

Calling him "Albert" should have come easily. Still, Nora found the only reply to his request she could manage was to say, "Perhaps someday." When his face fell at her response, she added, "Soon."

He crossed his arms over his chest, narrowing his eyes as if she had just become an objective. She could literally see him setting, as Mama would say, his cap for her. "You'll find I'm a persistent fellow."

Nora lay awake for hours, pondering her life's current complexities. She'd stayed up at first to merely read more of Annette's journal, her guilt at opening the private book overcome by the joy of just hearing her cousin's thoughts again. Annette was gone forever this side of Heaven, but reading the diary, Nora could imagine her sitting on the edge of the bed, recounting the dramatic details of her secretive meetings. Annette's life was such a tumult, it made her own life seem settled by

comparison—even with the sudden social acceleration
going on. Why were Mama and Papa suddenly eager to
marry her out to a man she'd just met and a dozen years
older than she? Stability? Protection? To simplify the
rebuilding of their own home and lives? Suddenly, everyone had layers that weren't there before—Annette,
Mama, Papa, Major Simon, even Reverend Bauers and
Quinn—and clarity eluded her as surely as sleep did.

*Quinn.* She welcomed the use of his first name, clung
to it, even though she'd resisted with… Albert. She tried
his given name out in her thoughts, inspecting how it
felt. It failed to hum in her head the way Quinn's name
had. As if the word itself had colder, sharper edges instead of the curled warmth of Quinn's. The two men
couldn't be more different. From a sheerly practical
standpoint, she had no business even considering Quinn
Freeman at all. Then again, Annette had been beyond
impractical in her association with Eric. And yet, it had
made her desperately happy. Ready to risk all she knew
and loved to make a future with such an unknown, inappropriate man. It was romantic. It churned up a vibrant
sense of adventure Nora had almost lost in all the day-
to-day survival of the post-earthquake city. Everything
had been so very serious for so very long.

*What am I to do, Lord?* Nora sat back, clutching Annette's diary tightly to her chest. *Surely, You've spared
me for some reason. Let me find Annette's journal for
some purpose. Is it fair to ask for more guidance? For
some sign as to where I go from here?* It was larger,
even, than the two men. She was powerfully drawn to
Dolores Park and its courageous occupants. The desire
to help them was like a pulse in her head, making her
look at every scrap of food or clothing with keen new

eyes. Could this be used here? Could that be put to use there? The world, which had tucked itself neatly inside the confines of her house and social engagements, had suddenly expanded outward with connections and relationships feathering out in all directions to a variety of fascinating people. *You want me to do something, Lord. I feel it. I think I've grasped on to it a time or two, like with Edwina or Sam, but I can't see the whole of it.*

She thought of the woman, Sister Charlotte, that Reverend Bauers had told her of the other day. The frail nun, now older than Reverend Bauers, had once been an outrageous diva of the stage. A societal maven, one of those people whose parties ended up in society pages from a grand time when Nora was young, according to the reverend. When her husband had died, Charlotte had opened up her huge estate as almost a public haven, helping just about anyone who came knocking.

Evidently, Sister Charlotte still raised eyebrows, for Mama's nearly shot into her hair when Nora asked if she could go with Reverend Bauers to meet her. God had certainly charted a wild course for the woman— even after decades in the church, people still tittered about how any woman like that could take vows. Had Charlotte heard God crystal clear to make such risky choices? Or was she just groping her way through the fog as Nora seemed forced to do? *There must be something I'm supposed to do. Some difference I'm destined to make.*

Nora went to her window, wanting to see the expanse of stars. They weren't always visible in San Francisco's fickle climate, but the vastness of them was a comfort to Nora when she could look up and see them. Great swaths of them were visible in between patches of clouds tonight. It was as if God was reminding her they were always there, even when the clouds hid her view. It was not much as signs from Heaven went, but it would have to do. Sighing, Nora peered down into the little, optimistic garden Mama and Aunt Julia had made. It would have to do, too.

She noticed it, just before she turned to go to bed.

A small bouquet of blue flowers, tied to the post that held up one side of the makeshift fence. Larger versions, Nora realized, of the tiny buds Quinn had fastened into her repaired locket.

He'd been there.

Yes, of course some other explanation was possible, but somehow Nora's heart was sure Quinn had left those flowers. The thought of him staring up into her window in the moonlight was so potent it stole her breath. They'd talked about how her window looked out on to that garden. She was even sure he'd caught her watching him as he removed the house column that had become the tent city's second message post. Quinn had been here. Tonight.

She yearned to dash downstairs, throw the back door open and peer around to find him waiting on the edge of the lawn in the way he waited across the street. To find those golden eyes amidst all the blue cream of the moonlight. Surely he must be awake, waiting, imagining. It was as if she could feel him out there in the night.

Quinn slumped on to his cot with such force he was sure Ma would wake from the sound. There must be some psalm filled with ache and misery to describe his current state, but he hadn't enough energy to recall a single verse. *It's too much, Lord,* he lamented in silent prayer. *There's just me and so much need. I've never been so tired.* So tired he'd almost been caught. The fog of his fatigue had made him sloppy, and he'd almost walked headlong into two men with guns. In that hollow gap between his mistake and his safety, he mind went straight to Nora.

I don't want to die without kissing her. That had been his thought. There, in the dark, his longing galvanized into something almost reckless. She would know, however he could manage it, what she meant to him. He would never take a kiss that hadn't been freely given, but if she gave him her affections he would grab at that treasure with both hands. *If you grant me her heart, Lord, I could take on anything.*

He walked out of that close call steeled to one purpose: letting her know.

How, exactly, does one man let a woman he can't see know what she can only guess, in the middle of the night? Quinn looked up, as if to dare Heaven to solve this whopping riddle, and saw his answer: in the flower box above his head was a collection of blue flowers. Nora's flowers, as he'd come to think of them.

It probably took more time, but it felt like mere seconds before he'd cut half a dozen from the flower box, pulled a handful of threads from the woven edge of the blanket, and ran all the way to Nora's home. A smile swept across his face when he saw what Nora must have thought of as the "rose trellis"—it was merely a fence post around the tiniest of gardens. Even if it held his weight, it would have provided four feet of altitude at best—hardly enough to reach the corner window he knew opened into Nora's room. He stood staring at the window for a while, willing her to come to it despite the lateness of the hour. Imagining what he would say, what he would do if she appeared.

It was probably God's grace that she didn't, for he was sure all his restraint would be lost if he saw her. Just before he left, Quinn ran his finger along one of the blooms, wishing it was Nora's cheek he touched. *She'll know.*

He repeated that thought—the half declaration, half desperate prayer that she would know his heart—as he lay on his cot. *I can't bear it if she never knows, Lord. Even if she doesn't feel the same, I need her to know.*

But she did feel the same, he was almost sure of it.

He fell asleep praying for God's mercy to find some way through the multitude of hurdles that kept them apart.

## Chapter Eighteen

By Tuesday, Nora felt time had crawled to a halt. She was grateful to have the task of doll-making, for the days seemed to lumber by, mocking her impatience. A struggle raged inside her: she needed time to assemble the dolls well, but she couldn't get to Grace House fast enough. Nora knew the flowers were a gift from Quinn, even if her mother persisted in her belief that Major Simon left them as a token of his coveted esteem. It seemed an act of God's kindness that Albert's schedule kept him from a visit—Nora wasn't at all sure what she would do when she faced him again. She had no idea how to handle his advances when she felt such an impossible and unlikely longing for Quinn Freeman.

And she did long for him. By the time she finally sat beside Reverend Bauers on his cart as it wound through the city, it had grown close to the desperate craving that Annette described in her diary—a nonstop fixation. But then again, it seemed entirely different. Annette talked of Eric's physical characteristics, things he did that made her feel special. Nora did find Quinn exceedingly handsome, but her attraction to him ran far deeper than that. It was his character, more than his eyes, that stole her breath. His thoughts, how he saw the world, how tenderly he treated Sam or Edwina. Certainly his eyes were capable of taking her breath away—even from a distance, as they often did—but it was the soul she glimpsed behind the eyes that captured her heart.

He *had* captured her heart. No matter how appropriate her parents found Major Simon, Nora's heart was no longer hers to give. Marriages for love did happen, but rarely. Did every woman let go of her heart in order to marry a suitable husband? It just seemed so wrong— so far from what God surely meant for His Holy Sacrament of Marriage.

"I need your help with a most peculiar problem," Reverend Bauers remarked jovially as they turned the corner toward Grace House. "What should I do about the persistent man pacing in my study? He's been hounding me daily regarding a certain woman. Miserable that Tuesday has taken so long in coming. I'm besieged."

"How unfortunate," she teased in return, delighted to know Quinn found the gap between this meeting and their last as unbearable as she had. "Tell me, Reverend, do you believe them well-suited for each other?"

"Oh, aye, I do indeed. It's true, they are worlds apart in life, but a perfect pair in spirit. Were they any other pair, I would count the obstacles between them as insurmountable."

Insurmountable. It was the perfect word for the sadness that overtook Nora at times when she thought of Quinn. It did seem as if the social chasm between them loomed insurmountable. *Were they any other pair...* She loved how Reverend Bauers had phrased it. "So, you do hold out hope for their prospects, then?"

"Oh, my dear, there is always cause for hope. Hope can accomplish the most amazing things." The reverend turned to look at her for the first time in their journey, and the knowledge in his eyes sparkled deep in her chest. "Yes," he said, at what must have been her desperate expression. "I am on your side, Nora. And his."

She wanted to wrap her arms around his shoulders and plant an affectionate kiss on his round cheek. "Reverend," she said, gazing into his amused eyes, "what are we to do?"

"Beyond prayer?"

"Yes, Reverend. Beyond prayer. I have prayed until my soul hurts and still feel like a storm surrounds me at every turn. It feels as if everything is against us. So if you have encouragement for me, I'd very much like to hear it."

"You have great reason to be encouraged, my dear. You have the heart of a relentless man of astounding character. Quinn will find a way. He found a way for you to meet today and will continue to vault over every hurdle between you, if I know him." A twinkle lit the old man's eye. "He simply can't bear to be separated from you, and as you know, your Quinn is not the most patient of men." He leaned in. "But you must take care, too. You will not be able to hide this for long, and I fear your own challenges once your family finds out. Society has some walls even an earthquake can't tear down."

*Your Quinn.* No, she wouldn't be able to hide this for long. His name hummed in her chest, and her hands tightened around the bouquet she seemed unable to put down since this morning. "He did arrange this, didn't he?"

"Of course he did." The old man laughed as if it were obvious. "And he tried mightily to convince me to fetch you yesterday—and the day before that. I was hard-pressed to get him to see reason and be patient. Even so, he has been at Grace House since sunrise, and I fear he won't last the day if we tarry much longer." His face grew more serious. "I'll be honest, my dear. I fear the strength of his affections may drive him to act unwisely. The two of you face so many challenges." He directed the cart around a corner, clucking his tongue as if he'd been negotiating rubble-filled street all his life. She wondered if it was age or faith that enabled him to face all that chaos with such calm. "Major Simon, among other things."

"Major Simon," Nora repeated, trying not to let her heart sink. "You know about him?"

"Albert Simon is an ambitious man. When he knows what he wants, he gathers every ally he can find to get it. Yes, he has asked me to speak to your father on his behalf. He is most taken with you. And I don't have to tell you Quinn is most disturbed by the rival." He leveled his dark brown eyes at Nora. "Should he be?"

She supposed a more sensible woman would have considered the situation carefully. As it was, "Not at all," came gushing out of her as if she were a schoolgirl. She felt her cheeks redden and cast her gaze down into the now-wilting flowers. She should have pressed them, but she couldn't bear not to have them near.

"Tell him so. You have much to say to each other." He winked. "But I believe he needs to hear that most of all."

Nora leaned over and gave Reverend Bauers a kiss on his cheek. "You are a dear, dear man, Reverend."

"Nonsense," he said, his smile warm and broad. "I

am an idiot who doesn't know when to stop tilting at windmills. It is a good thing God suffers fools gladly, don't you think?"

"You are no fool," she said, wanting to get out of the cart and run the last few blocks while at the same time needing a host of hours to calm her nerves. "You are a very wise man."

"Remember that when we are all knee-deep in trouble."

Quinn looked at his reflection in the small, round mirror above the fireplace in Reverend Bauers's study. He wished mightily for a better shirt, for an unmended pair of pants. He looked at his bruised fingers, the ones that flexed so easily around the Bandit's sword, and willed himself to have Matthew Covington's elegance. That man was dashing and well-spoken. He? He felt like a joke of God's purpose, a fluke born of disaster and circumstance. More than anything at this moment, he wanted to feel worthy of Nora Longstreet.

It was, as Reverend Bauers was fond of saying, a God-sized wish. He heard the cart coming up the alley, and shut his eyes for a moment, drawing in a deep breath to slow down the cannon fire going off in his chest. He could have been sixteen instead of twenty-six the way his pulse was thundering. He was going to see Nora, alone. Not glancing over his shoulder or hers, but saying freely the things that had hung in the air unsaid between them. How he felt.

Hearing her say—and, mercy, he didn't know what he would do if he didn't hear her say—that she felt the same way about him.

The creak of the back kitchen door sounded her arrival, and Quinn dashed to the kitchen. She was looking down as she stepped through the door, her hat hiding her face, but when she met his eyes, a glow flooded his chest and banished every hint of worry. He understood now why men conquered the world for love. He remembered thinking Matthew Covington had gone mad when he watched that heroic man go completely foolish around Georgia Waterhouse. Back then, at his tender years, he'd thought Covington a fool. He didn't think so now. Had she asked him, in that moment, to lasso the moon, he would have said yes without thought or doubt.

"And hello to you, too, Quinn," the reverend said, having a grand time with Quinn's current speechless state. "Glory, it is worse than I thought. Why don't we all sit a moment and have a cup of tea. I'm sure cook has made some, and if not, I do remember how myself."

"I'm not thirsty," Quinn said, not taking his eyes off Nora.

"Perhaps Miss Longstreet…"

"Not at all, Reverend." After a dumbstruck second, she blinked and added, "Thank you."

Her eyes said everything he needed to know. He longed to sweep her into his arms that very second and defy the world to ever part them again.

Reverend Bauers stepped into his sight, mock sternness on his amused face. "I was thinking about how very nice it would be for Miss Longstreet to see the volume of Shakespeare sonnets Mr. Covington sent over earlier this year. The binding is exquisite." Quinn stared for a blank second. Reverend Bauers's foot gently tapped Quinn's boot. "Get out of the kitchen before you make a fool of yourself, man," he said in low tones. Raising a conspiratorial eyebrow, he returned his voice to a more public volume. "I simply haven't the time to show it to her properly. Do you think you could manage?"

"I'm sure I could, Reverend." With a grin he had no hopes of hiding, Quinn extended an elbow to Nora. "Reverend Bauers's study is just down the hall." As he turned to leave the kitchen, feeling the rush of having Nora's arm on his elbow, he caught sight of Reverend Bauers holding up ten fingers and mouthing the words "ten minutes."

Not likely. There'd be no rushing this moment, not for all the danger in California. Quinn forced his feet to move through the hallway at a casual pace, as if he were about to show Nora Longstreet the most mundane object in all the world.

Instead of showing her his heart.

Nora had thousands of thoughts tumbling through her head, feeling half her age and almost weightless as they walked down the hall. "You're hurt," she remarked, noticing new bandages on his left hand, just as the right hand's wounds were healing. "How hard you must work to always be nursing wounds."

Quinn opened the study door. "Many are hurt worse."

After a quick glance up and down the hallway, Quinn closed the study door behind them. It wasn't as if Nora hadn't been unchaperoned with a man before—she'd been ostensibly alone with Major Simon just days before—but Nora's heart was pounding so hard she fought against the urge to put her hand to her chest.

Her chest, where her locket lay. The locket housing the tiny buds Quinn had given her. Her hand found its way to the locket anyway, and she felt Quinn's eyes on her hand. On his gift. "Where is this book?" she managed to choke out.

Quinn's eyes glowed. "There is no book."

"So, I've been tricked?"

"I hope not." He looked at her, a long, unguarded gaze that sent her pulse skipping. "Have I?"

"I don't think so." Surely, the air had been cooler in the kitchen. "Those flowers, they were…"

"…From me," he finished for her, taking one step toward her. She'd known it all along, of course, but it felt so different to hear him claim them out loud. "I knew you'd recognize them." He took another step toward her. "I'm done hiding it, Nora. I don't want to talk around it or pretend it's not there or pretend I don't think about you all the time or want to show you every pretty thing I come across. There's so much awfulness around right now not to…" He flushed, as if he hadn't meant to be so forward.

Nora felt for the chair back behind her, suddenly needing something solid to hold on to. "Not to what?" She wasn't even sure she'd managed to say it out loud. His straw-colored hair refused to stay the way he'd combed it. He was standing close enough to her that she could smell the soap he'd used.

"Not to grab at the one thing, the one amazing thing that's come out of it." His face broke into that deep-down confident smile of his, a "count on it" quality that made her believe they could do anything if they were together. "It is amazing, isn't it?"

For a second, propriety made her consider denying it, but it would be useless. Even if she told him there was nothing between them, Nora was sure her eyes and her very breathlessness would give her away. "Surprising."

"Don't you think there's something planned here? I found your locket, I found you, all the ways you've helped?" He paused slightly before adding, "All the ways you've cared?"

He was right. It was as if forces had been pulling them together since that horrible morning. As if God had handed her some glimpse of dawn after so much darkness. Now, looking at the blaze in his eyes, it seemed completely useless to fight against it for a moment longer. And she didn't want to fight it. She wanted to be with him, to spend time with him, to share in the things he did and the thoughts he had. A determination—a defiance, even—sprung up where all the denial had been. "Yes," she said, a surprising strength in her voice. "Yes, Quinn, I'm sure I…"

She was going to finish that thought. Just as soon as she remembered what it was. At the moment, the look in Quinn's eyes sent every shred of logic packing. His smile broadened. He closed the distance between them and put his hand to her cheek. His hand was warm and rough and exquisitely gentle. Nora thought the room would dissolve away to nothing around her, felt as if the floor would give way and the walls would fall over. She closed her eyes for a moment, hoping to memorize every detail of his touch, sure this stolen moment would be the only one they had. Life was too sensible to allow something like this to endure. This was fantasy and folly and…and she'd fight to keep it with everything in her power. "I'm sure," she said again, whispering it this time as she opened her eyes to see him gazing at her. She brought her hand up to rest atop his, desperate to hold on to him as he touched her face.

One thumb traced a slow arc across her cheek. "I

don't know *how,* yet." His voice held the same determination that drummed in her heart.

"There has to be a way."

"I'll find it. After all, I found you, didn't I?" He looked at her with wonder, as if the thought just struck him anew. "In all the city, I found you. After all this, I found you."

Nora let her head fall against his strong hand. "Find us a way, Quinn."

It was as if the topaz in his eyes ignited, as if she'd unleashed something fierce and powerful in him. He took both her hands in his and kissed them gallantly. "There's not a thing can stop me now."

She had to laugh at his exuberance. "What about Reverend Bauers and his ten minutes?" She held up her fingers the way the reverend had.

He laughed as well. "Never you mind that." He pulled her a bit closer. "Say my name one more time. Say it." He looked like he would spin them around the room any moment.

"Quinn, be careful."

"Not at all. I'm done being careful. Can't you see that?"

His defiance lit fire to hers. She brought both his hands to her lips and kissed them tenderly. He began to pull her closer. Neither one of them heard the knock on the door until it opened and Reverend Bauers cleared his throat with mock alarm.

"Good Heavens, I see I've come just in time."

Quinn scowled. "Go away."

"I think not."

Quinn's eyes closed. "Go *away,* Reverend, sir."

Nora felt flustered. "Reverend," she interjected,

squeezing Quinn's hands, "You've been so kind to us. How can I thank you?"

"By taking this fine thing God has given you and being wise. Keep our friend here from crossing the line from brave to foolish. I'm afraid I haven't had much success in that department."

Surrendering to the interruption, Quinn reached out and clasped the old man's shoulders. "You've got too much of the fool in you yourself, old man. And I'm glad of it, I am." His gaze wandered back to Nora, as if he couldn't take his eyes off her for more than a second or two. "And grateful."

"And one or two other things I won't go into, I'm sure," Bauers said. "But time's not on our side. Part ways, you two, before anyone's the wiser or I'll live to regret this more than I do."

Quinn's eyes conveyed a million things, even if he only returned his hat to his head and said, "Soon." She found his smile the most remarkable sight; the glow of it seemed to settle beneath her ribs and warm her from the inside.

"Soon," she almost whispered. Even a second earthquake wouldn't prevent them from being together again.

Reverend Bauers folded his hands together across his stomach after Quinn left. "He's a most remarkable young man, but I gather I've no need to convince you of that."

"No, Reverend." She sighed. "I'm quite convinced."

The clergyman's voice fell to an oddly serious tone. "He faces more challenges than you know. And I fear things will only get more difficult for him in the coming days. He'll need to draw strength from you." He walked toward her, clasping her hands in his. "But I see great strength in you, too, so I think that perhaps God does indeed know what He's up to."

Hadn't she wondered the same thing?

# *Chapter Nineteen*

Quinn lay the list on Major Simon's desk. "I don't know whether to be flattered or worried." People's faith in the Messenger's abilities had expanded to some rather challenging requests. Pins and basic medicines were one thing. Some of the items on the posts this week made for tall orders. One man had actually asked for lumber—the largest request yet.

"Lumber is gold at the moment," Simon responded. "I can't get enough to fill my own needs much less extra. Besides, I don't much like the idea of people building on to their shacks. We can't have people thinking of Dolores Park as anything but temporary."

"Temporary? After three months?"

Simon gave Quinn a hard look. "You think I don't know most of these people don't even have two timbers left of their old homes to nail together? I know I'm not dealing in reality, Freeman. But I've got to work as hard as I can to give the right impression." He looked down for a moment and swore for the first time since Quinn had met him. "The general got a wire from the president yesterday. The whole world is watching." Major

Simon was normally such a cool-headed character; it was more than a bit unnerving to watch him fray around the edges. If the pressure was getting even to him, it must be huge.

"All right then, no lumber. I don't know how I'd carry it anyway." Quinn scooped the bits of paper back up.

Simon let his head fall into his hands and heaved out a sigh. "Their wants aren't your fault." He looked up, attempting a weak smile. "Now look who's gone off and shot the messenger, hmm? You've done an amazing job."

Again, Quinn was glad for the praise, but just a bit leery of Major Simon, who seemed to think the Midnight Messenger was an army recruit. He'd made a point to call them "partners" earlier in the discussion, but the relationship was feeling more lopsided day by day. Quinn had already decided it was time to seek out a few sources other than the army. *Lord,* Quinn prayed as he tucked the batch of papers into his pocket and said goodbye to Major Simon, *if You can bring water from a stone, and manna from Heaven, a dozen tins of peas should be easy, right?*

Actually, it was. For all the talk of scarcity, Quinn had secured half of what he needed from sources outside the major in the space of two hours. Things could be found with a little clever trading here and there. It took time, connections and creativity. The last two Quinn had always had in abundance. Time, however, was growing as scarce as sleep. By dinner, Quinn only had left the last four items on his list: two Bibles and two revolvers. He'd already decided not to even attempt the revolvers, and he had a pretty good idea where he could manage the pair of Bibles. He needed a safe place—other than Major Simon's cache or his own shack at the camp—to stash his Messenger "booty" anyway, and the Grace House basement was ideal.

"Glory!" Reverend Bauers remarked when Quinn came up the basement steps in the full Messenger gear he'd pulled from its hiding place at the army base, suddenly uncomfortable with it staying there. "You look dark and dangerous. I venture even the Bandit would be wary of you with that pistol at your side."

"I haven't used it yet," Quinn remarked, adjusting the large duffel that was beginning to wear permanent bruises in his shoulder.

"I pray you never do," Reverend Bauers said, "but that's optimistic, I fear." He handed Quinn the two Bibles he'd requested. "I feel much better knowing you've gotten even two requests for God's word. I know it's my weapon of choice against all we face these days." He stopped for a moment, considering Quinn with a wistful look. "'Blessed are the feet of him who brings good news,'" he quoted.

"Maybe, but sore are the feet of him who brings canned peas." He shifted the sack again, straining under the weight, cringing when the tins inside the sack clanged against each other despite the careful packing he'd done. "I'm delivering those first. No one had better ask for potatoes this week. Or anvils." Quinn turned his back to the reverend so he could untie the top of the duffel and tuck the pair of Bibles inside.

"You've still your humor about you," Bauers said as he retied the bag. "I'm glad of that." He gave Quinn's shoulder a quick clasp. "And you have much to be glad of, especially today."

"I'm glad of *you*." Quinn was pleased to have an ally in the old man, especially in terms of Nora. "Thanks."

"The glint in your eyes is thanks enough." Bauers moved aside the scraps of cloth that had been hung in the mission kitchen as make-do curtains. "It's good and dark out now. Off with you, and take care. Come back when you need anything else."

Quinn settled his hat down over the mask. "That won't be long, you know."

The night was thick with mist, hiding the slip of a moon that had appeared earlier in the evening. It made travel easier in some respects, with more shadows for hiding and bad visibility. The lack of vision, however, seemed to amplify sounds so that Quinn stilled and flinched every time the tins clanked against each other.

Inside Dolores Park, deliveries were always challenging. Close quarters granted all kinds of nooks in which to hide, but it meant eyes were everywhere. The camp never really went to sleep—someone was always up somewhere—but the lack of lanterns, fires, or streetlamps made concealment easier. Quinn had become so acquainted with Dolores Park's cracks and corners he could probably find his way blindfolded.

Saying a prayer of thanks for his gift at memorizing things, Quinn ticked down the list of who got what in his head as he peered down the next aisle. Two tins of peas to the third shelter on the left, one of the Bibles to the last shack on the right. Just before setting the tins down outside the structure, Quinn wet the nub of charcoal he'd found yesterday and used it like a pencil to add his new flourish—a large "MM" on the top of the tins. Not quite the Black Bandit's calling card of a

white ribbon—frankly, he found that a bit overdone—
but a mark of his own. Something to let folks know it
wasn't just the United States Army looking out for their
welfare. He did the same in the dedication page of the
Bibles, and on every other item he'd procured himself
rather than from the army stocks.

It was near three o'clock when Quinn finally folded
the dark duffel and the other Messenger items into their
new hiding place at Grace House, yawned, and headed
for home. Just before turning in, Quinn removed a small
square of lavender soap from his pocket, marked its
muslin wrapping with the double M sign and hung it
with a set of pins to their door for Ma to find.

Nora came downstairs later that week, still smiling from a bouquet of blue flowers that had once again
found their way to the backyard garden fencepost. Even
better, attached to the flowers this time was a large
lump of sugar—something nearly impossible to get
lately, and she had no idea how Quinn had acquired
it. How clever he was—it was an ideal token to offer
to her parents.

The packet fell from her hands on to the hall table,
however, as she turned into the front room. Mama and
Aunt Julia had the most dreadful looks on their faces.
She hurried into the room, worried as to what could
have made them so upset.

Until she saw what Aunt Julia clutched to her breast
with brittle, shaking hands. She remembered now. She
had heard a rustle in the garden last night, and had stolen out of bed to find the flowers and sugar tied to the
fencepost as the bouquet had been the last time. It had

been nearly impossible to fall back asleep, and instead she had stayed up until nearly dawn, reading.

Reading Annette's journal, which had become a treasured companion to all the emotions roiling around inside her. And she had fallen asleep, journal in hand, sleeping late into the morning. She had not realized, until just this horrid moment, that while the flowers and sugar were still on her coverlet, the diary was gone when she awoke.

Of course it was gone. It was now in Aunt Julia's hands. They must have found it when her mother came in to wake her. Nora squeezed her eyes shut against the wall of remorse that stole every drop of the joy she'd felt only seconds before.

"Yes," came Aunt Julia's tight, sharp voice, "I found it. Or rather, your mother did."

"Nora." Her mother's voice was laced with disappointment. "Why did you not bring this to us earlier? How could you have kept all this from us when we might have prevented…" Nora was glad Mama thought it too cruel to finish the sentence.

"I only just found it," Nora admitted, "I didn't know…before. I had no idea."

"You two shared everything." Aunt Julia jabbed the words at her. It was a fair accusation.

"I thought we did."

"You thought." Aunt Julia seemed to be a coarser, angrier version of the gray ghost she had become on the day of the earthquake when Annette's body could not be found. Annette had been sleeping at Nora's house the night of the earthquake. No one could ever understand why she had wandered off in the melee. It had been assumed, for comfort's sake Nora supposed, that she'd made her way home more quickly than the others in a desire to see her mother and father safe. As she stood there, watching her aunt's spirit seemingly die right in front of her, Nora realized that it was more likely Annette went looking for Eric. Which, according to the hints in the diary, was right into the heart of the destruction. It seemed so terribly, inexcusably cruel for Aunt Julia to know this now, when it did no good at all.

"Heedless child!" Aunt Julia hissed, her fingers nearly scraping at the bindings. "My own flesh and blood, capable of such…such *wanton* behavior." It was as if the very words left a foul taste in her mouth. Her face pinched tighter as tears reddened her eyes. Mama reached for her hand but Aunt Julia knocked it away. "And they've paid for their sins, her and that…shiftless cad. What snake of a man lures a young woman like that into plans to abandon us? It's this city, I tell you. This vile, sinful place…"

"Now, Julia." Mama reached out again, to no avail.

"Reverend Mansfield is right. We shouldn't be surprised. How much longer did we expect God to endure such blatant, sinful ways?" The pastor from the church Aunt Julia and all of Nora's family attended had been vocal in his condemnation of the city's sin. He was one of those people who saw the earthquake as God's judgment sent down upon an evil city. Nora could never see his viewpoint, especially now.

"God struck down the city," Aunt Julia continued. "And now I have to live with the fact that he struck down *my own daughter* with it."

Reverend Mansfield would surely see it that way, too. Nora's heart burned with regret for letting the secret slip when only pain would come of it. There was too much pain already.

"You've had a terrible shock, Julia," Papa said, coming into the room behind Nora. Land sakes, did everyone in the house know it all by now? "We all have."

"I want to leave. I want to leave this horrible place and never look back. There isn't a thing left here to want."

"That's not true," Nora said before she thought better of it.

"What do you know, you silly thing!" Aunt Julia snapped, making even Mama and Papa flinch. "You didn't even know enough to stop your cousin from walking into her own doom. We've taught you nothing about what's right, *nothing!*" With that, she threw the book on the divan next to her and left the room, her sobs wafting through the house until they all heard her door slam shut upstairs.

Nora went to pick up the journal. Awful as it was, she couldn't bear to think what Aunt Julia might do to it, and it was her last piece of Annette. On her knees in front of the divan, Nora slid the book to her lap and looked up at her mother. "I didn't know, honest. And once I found it, I only thought it would hurt Aunt Julia worse to know."

Papa came up and sat on the other side of the divan, so that Nora kneeled between her parents. "You really had no idea what this man was planning? You knew nothing of Annette's…" She could tell Papa was trying to think of a delicate term, "indiscretions?"

"I suppose I suspected something. She told me she fancied some man Aunt Julia and Uncle Lawrence wouldn't like. But running off with him? I never dreamed she'd keep something like this from me."

Mama laid her hand on Nora's arm as it stretched across the divan's thick brocade cushions. A color Annette had helped to choose, Nora suddenly remembered. She was so fond of burgundy. They'd planned to have a portrait of her painted this summer, sitting on this very spot. With a sad twinge, Nora realized it would never have been painted either way. For either way, Annette would have been gone.

But gone was not the same as dead, even if Aunt Julia would disagree right now.

"It is one of life's great tragedies, the things that have been done to innocent young ladies who do not guard their way. You see, now, why your father and I have been so very careful with you. So much can be lost."

Nora's heart shuddered.

"It is a horrible thing to think, but I can't help wondering if God has been kind in taking Annette when He did."

"Papa!" Nora said, pulling back.

"I know it seems harsh," Papa said, "but do you have any idea what kind of life awaited your cousin if she'd have gone through with this mad plan? A man from the docks? It's a terrible squalor of a life, Nora. Why do you think I'm so worried about you at Dolores Park? These are coarse, desperate people. Full of violence, drink and disease."

She'd never heard her father talk so. "But they aren't all bad. You help them. Papa, you spend *every day* helping in the official camps."

"It's my duty to serve those camps." He said it as if his mercies were an unpleasant but necessary task, like swallowing castor oil. "It's the duty of every good Christian to help those in need." The words didn't seem to include those in need in Dolores Park.

Nora ran her hand along the book. "Annette loved him." It was an odd thing to say, but she felt that someone ought to at least make it clear that Annette was not duped or kidnapped or stolen in the night. "He loved her—or she believed he loved her."

Mama reached out and smoothed Nora's hair, much as she had done when she was a small child. On the floor, at their feet, it did feel as if she'd become small again. "It isn't a fairy story, Nora. This would never have ended well. Only pain and heartache and much worse would have come to Annette. She must have known how dreadful it was to keep it even from you." Mama's eyes looked from the book to Nora. "You can't keep it, you know. And you must never speak of it." The warning in Mama's eyes made Nora clutch at the diary involuntarily. "I suppose it's up to Julia and Lawrence, but I wouldn't fault her if she chose to burn it."

"Burn it?"

"It's far better if no one else knows." Papa seemed to actually agree with Mama on this terrible suggestion. He looked at Nora. "Reverend Mansfield might make an example of Annette if he learned of it, and how could you put your aunt and uncle through something like that? Haven't they been through enough without adding such disgrace to their pain?"

A startling panic grabbed at Nora. "No one will know. I'll hide it. I can't bear to lose another piece of her."

Mama looked at her as if she were a petulant child. "I think you meant to hide it now, and we all see what has happened. Surely you won't put your needs before Annette's own mother and father's?"

Papa reached down and took the book gently from Nora. It took an enormous amount of willpower not to snatch it back out of his hands and run from the room. Everything seemed to be crumbling around her, and just at the time when things seemed to be springing to life. Any chance of Mama and Papa's ever approving of Quinn slipped through her fingers as she knelt on the parlor floor. "Perhaps," Papa said in a quiet, managerial tone, "this is best decided in a while. Everyone has a lot to think about."

Nora leaned back against the divan, feeling drained. *If only you knew how much there is to think about, Papa.*

"What was that you were holding when you came down this morning?" Mama's voice held a forced brightness, as if she were packing up all this unpleasantness to stuff away in a closet and wanted something nice to take its place.

"Sugar," Nora said, still too stunned to evade the truth.

"Oh, my. Received a trinket from our dashing major, have you?"

Of course Mama would think the flowers and sugar came from Major Simon. He'd made a spectacle of himself bringing sugar when he came to dinner—Mama was beside herself at having a "true cup of tea" after dinner. Nora didn't answer. She had no idea what to say, especially in light of all that happened.

"Now, don't make Nora blush," Papa said, smiling. It was clear from the look that passed between him and Mama how pleased they were at the major's attentions.

And yet how was she acting any different than Annette, sneaking around, whispering affections behind closed doors? "Perhaps you should come on the mail run with me this afternoon after all. I'm sure I could send word to Major Simon to meet us, and I'm equally sure he'd prefer to hear your gratitude in person."

Any chance at seeing Quinn—however small—was a treasure. She needed his help to figure out what to do next.

Or did she? Was she simply letting some insipid passion pull her off the sensible course? She had never been one to second-guess things, had always thought of her decisiveness as a quality, not a fault. She'd loved it when Annette called her bold.

And where had Annette's even greater boldness—which Nora had always admired—gotten her? The urge to see Quinn now vied with an equally strong mistrust of her instincts. The result was a frustrating paralysis.

Papa laid his hand on her shoulder. "Come now, you mustn't let Annette's misfortune weigh down your own future." It was the oddest thing to feel his offer of comfort, knowing he had no idea of the true reason for her upset. Like having two conversations at once. Now Papa was encouraging her to visit the camp?

Not the camp. The major.

# *Chapter Twenty*

Dolores Park buzzed with talk of the latest Midnight Messenger visit. One sack of goods—well, actually two, for Quinn had to make a second run with all those cumbersome tins of vegetables—had launched a fast and ever-exaggerating chain of gossip. As he stood in a bread line for unofficial camp residents after several hours' work cleaning bricks this morning (gratefully, a seated task; his feet throbbed), Quinn heard the pair of men behind him boast that the Midnight Messenger had brought an entire ham to a shack in Dolores Park. The truth had been slightly less heroic—a can of some sort of luncheon meat—but it made Quinn smile just the same. He smiled for a good half an hour, until it came to him that perhaps he ought to worry about what kinds of requests would turn up today. Someone had even come from another unofficial camp several blocks away, pinning a handful of requests to the Dolores Park message posts.

Major Simon had advised Quinn to only pull a handful of requests on an irregular schedule, but he'd long since begun augmenting his army-supplied runs with

Messenger deliveries of his own procurement. There was just so much need.

"Beware expectations," the major had warned. "When unmet, they can be dangerous things."

"Kind of odd when you think of it," the man behind Quinn said. "We got us a whole army what's supposed to be lookin' out for our needs, and turns out one fella in a dark suit bests 'em all."

That made Quinn raise an eyebrow and listen harder.

"How do you know the Midnight Messenger wears a dark suit?" the other asked suspiciously. Evidently, he suspected his partner knew more than he was letting on.

"I hear tell. Besides, what do you expect someone called the Midnight Messenger to wear? Pink?" He lowered his voice. "I heard he's a big fella. Over six feet."

Quinn hunched.

"With long, flowing dark hair, like one of those pirate types."

Quinn straightened up again, laughing at his own prideful caution.

"I reckon he works for the army," the second man suggested. "So's they can cut corners and all."

"Or spy on us," the other countered. "He's got to be a sneaky one if no one's caught up with him yet." Quinn bent down, pretending to have something wrong with his shoe, so that he could angle his face just enough to catch a glimpse of the pair. He thought he recognized the voices, but the faces were unfamiliar. Never mind, he knew which aisle they lived in by the can of meat he'd delivered there.

"Of course, if he works for the army, no one's *gonna* catch up with him, are they?"

"I hope they don't. My wife needs a tin of powder

for her stomach troubles, and I don't hardly think an army that won't give us flour will give us medicine for my Laura." The man grunted. "I'm fixing to put a message up on the post. I figure it's the postmaster who's got something to do with it. He don't ever cross to our side of the street, but his pretty daughter does. I seen her write things down once."

"I heard someone tell that Major Simon fella to expect the postmaster and his daughter at today's mail run. Could be you're right, Mack."

Only sheer strength of will squelched Quinn's urge to turn and look at the pair. Who was sending word to Simon that Nora was coming? And why? Had her father suddenly decided to encourage Nora's visits to Dolores Park? Or had Major Simon stepped up his efforts regarding Nora?

Nothing, not the longest bread line in history, not even the throbbing of his tired feet, would keep Quinn from today's mail run. He forced patience into his fidgety body as the line inched along by reciting, "Mack and Laura, stomach powder, same row as the ham."

Nora looked upset. She smiled pleasantly, casting her eyes out over the crowd with every piece of mail, but Quinn held back, suddenly unsure if her quick, searching glances sought him or Major Simon. He'd thought she'd be beaming after the flowers and sugar. After their declarations in Bauers's study. He'd felt like nothing would come between them after they'd spent that time together. Himself, he'd been walking on air for the hours since she kissed his hands. Now, he felt sore, exhausted, and naggingly uncertain. What he wanted, what he *needed,* was to speak with her. He thought of

the pirates, the buccaneers the men in the bread line had
likened to the Midnight Messenger. If I were a pirate, I
would steal her away, he thought. Take her to some foreign shore where no one cared what cut of coat a man
wore or who his parents were. Or weren't.

When Simon came to the mail cart, it only got worse.
Mr. Longstreet beamed over the major, offering jovial
smiles and knowing glances that lodged in Quinn's gut
and simmered there. The only thing that made the whole
scene bearable was the sure sense that Nora wasn't really happy to see Major Simon. Oh, she feigned it well,
all smiles and downward glances, but the way she held
her head and the way she flailed her hands gave it all
away. When Nora was happy, her hands were calm and
graceful. When she was upset, they traveled about like
bees, flitting from her neck to her waist to her skirts.
And he, he knew that about her like he knew a thousand other little details his heart had memorized. Because he knew *her*—the true Nora, the Nora inside what
other people saw.

He lingered on his side of the street until she'd finished her pleasantries with the major. Then, as Simon
and the postmaster exchanged confident looks—he dis-
liked the sense of negotiation their glances gave him, as
if Nora were a spoil of war—Nora went back to taking
in the mail. Watching how she served those in line, his
resolve grew stronger. She was in his life for a reason,
and he in hers. All the conventions in the world couldn't
alter that truth.

She looked his way, finally, catching his eye. For a
moment, there was the unchecked affection he'd seen
in Bauers's study. Her eyes glowed, her lips parted just
the slightest bit and he could almost hear her suck in

a breath. For the tiniest moment the world fell away around them.

Then, as if a drape came down, he watched caution come over her. While she still held his gaze, it was with doubt rather than joy. Her eyes told him a sort of war was going on inside her—the possible fighting the probable. Affection and longing and fear and sadness all stuffed themselves into those few seconds.

Something had happened. He didn't know what, but he did know he couldn't let her alone. He pleaded to her with his eyes, hoping he could tell her to hang on, to give him just a moment to work something out. He held up a finger, arching his eyebrows and mouthing "wait," then ducked around the corner to find Sam.

It took all of ten minutes to contrive a reason for Sam to bring Nora to the teeter-totter, but Quinn was pacing madly by the end of it. His imagination had come up with a dozen scenarios—each more catastrophic than the last—as to what had happened to make Nora look at him with such worry.

"What's wrong?" His effort at a conversational tone failed miserably.

"Nothing."

Already she was lying to him. "That's not true. Something's wrong. I can see it."

She looked up at him. "This can't work. Quinn, surely you know that. We're foolish to think it can."

"You didn't feel that way earlier. You've never felt that way. What's happened?"

She glanced around nervously. "Annette. She kept a journal, and I found it. She was…involved…with someone and they were going to run away together just as the earthquake…" Her hand went to the locket again.

"Everyone is so upset. Her parents are furious, they're saying she's better off dead."

"We're not them, Nora. I'll go to your parents." The conviction roared up inside him. "I'll make them see. And if they don't…well, I won't be without you. We belong together and they'll just have to see that."

"They won't," she nearly wailed. "You should have heard them, Quinn. They said the most horrible, judgmental things."

"Do you believe that? What they said?" Suddenly, he needed to know that more than anything. Needed to know if she could defy them and their thinking.

Nora looked at him with stormy, sad eyes. "It's not just them. What kind of future could we possibly expect?"

"The same future anyone's got a right to expect. To be happy. To be with someone you care about. Nora, we'll never be running off in the night, I'll tell you that right now." He wanted to grab her hand and shake her, knock this new layer of fear off her spirit and bring her back to the courage he'd seen before. Instead, he gripped his hat and tried to hold her with his eyes. "I'm sorry about your cousin. But your parents are wrong. And we're right. I don't know how I'll convince them— how *we'll* convince them, but we will."

"I can't see how. Not now."

He reined in his frustration. "Not yet. Maybe you're right, and now's not the time, but soon enough *we will*. Do you trust me to work it out? Do you trust us to work it out?"

"I don't know."

"I do." He held her eyes, wanting desperately to hold her to his chest but knowing this wasn't the time for it.

"I do know. Sure as anything. We'll find a way, Nora, you hang on to that." He locked her in his gaze until she straightened and nodded.

*Hold her in Your palm, Father,* Quinn prayed as he motioned for Sam to come walk her back. *She's my whole world now.*

Nora walked back across the street clutching Sam's hand. It was the mirror image of the first time they'd walked together. That first trip, Sam had grasped her hand tightly, all his fear clenching his fingertips as he led her to his father's shack. Now, she felt as if Sam led her through her fear back to her father's cart. She was grateful for the tiny escort—her mind was in such a tumble she didn't know how she'd have found her way alone.

She had fooled herself that it would sort itself out. That she would see Quinn and suddenly know her course. Instead, her heart tottered like the toy Quinn had built—one second thinking the safety of Major Simon and her parents' approval was so wise, the other second falling into a rush of emotion when she looked into Quinn's eyes. When he looked at her so fiercely, with such a command to trust him, she felt what surely must be passion. An overwhelming, powerful sense of need and "rightness" that let her believe they had a future. That the two of them had been uniquely paired in all the world, uniquely completing each life to the betterment of the other.

And a life with Major Simon? The most she could say was that it felt stiflingly arranged.

Why did life suddenly have such urgency anyway? Why, if she had gone on unpaired for this many years, did her heart and her parents suddenly demand up-heaval?

*The ground has shaken things up enough, Lord,* she prayed as she gave Sam a hug goodbye and walked up to the mail cart. *Must You shake up my whole soul in the process?*

"Major Simon left something for you while you were gone," Papa said, as he offered his hand to let his daughter up onto the mail cart. He smiled with undiluted pleasure as he pointed to a small package on the bench of the cart. It opened to reveal a stack of cloth in various bright colors, small samples of yarn, a few bits of lace and a handful of buttons. Along with a small package of lemon drops. She read the accompanying note:

*Reverend Bauers told me you needed more supplies to make dolls. I hope these will help. The lemon drops are for the dollmaker, from her admiring major.—A*

"Why are we meeting here?" Quinn looked at the desolate corner of the scrapyard where Major Simon had asked him to meet. Even for their unusually discreet relationship, this seemed a bit much.

Simon picked up a tangled piece of steel and spun it to catch the orange sunset. "Because I have an important question to ask you. A sort of unofficial question on a rather unconventional matter. Not exactly army protocol."

Quinn didn't think anything he and Major Simon did fit within army protocol. "And what's that?"

"Are you ready for things to get complicated?"

Sitting down on a barrel, Quinn had to laugh. "They already are."

"True." The major stuck the shaft of steel upright in

the dusty ground and sat down on a second barrel. "I suppose I mean, are you ready for things to get *quite* complicated?"

"Why?" Quinn replied. "What is going on?"

"I don't have to tell you," Simon began, "that a whole lot of people are watching how relief efforts get handled around here. If things go well, it could not only mean help for many people, but things could go well for me, personally. And," he added, looking straight at Quinn, "you as well. If we go about it in the right way."

"Our way isn't perfect, but it works."

"It could work better, I think. But like most good things in life, it's going to be a bit risky and I daresay unconventional." He shifted his weight on the barrel and gazed at the sun as it began to dip into the water. "Do you know how the great fire was eventually put out? Why we used all that dynamite?"

Quinn knew the basic concepts. "To burn things ahead of the fire so it didn't have enough fuel to move on. Starved it rather than drown it, I heard one man say."

"Exactly. We fought fire with fire. I'm proposing, Freeman, that we do the same here. Only the fire I'm fighting now is grift. Corruption. People abusing the relief system for their own good. It's making my job harder and your job more necessary. I wouldn't need the Messenger if things got *where* they were supposed to *when* they were supposed to. I'd like for the army to be out of the relief business, but not if it means the marketeers are all that's left. Despite my best efforts, relief is ending up in greedy hands."

Quinn thought Simon didn't need the Messenger as much as the people in the tent cities needed the Messenger, but he got the major's idea. "I don't want the marketeers to win either, Major. It's not right. All the generosity we've seen shouldn't be ending up in the places it is."

"I'm glad you agree. And I think your unique talents put us in a place to do something about it. A real something that gets results. But we're going to have to bend the rules a bit to get what we need."

Quinn smiled. "I'm no stranger to that."

The major laughed. "That much I knew. But for what I'm about to ask, you need to come out on top of this as much as I."

"Go on."

"I don't think I can stop the thieves in any conventional way. But they'll stop each other in the name of greed. That's what I mean by fighting fire with fire. I've got a pool of money—gold, to be exact—at my disposal. We're going to offer gold for information on how supplies are slipping out of army hands. Pay these grifters to turn each other in. Or, rather, turn their information in to the Midnight Messenger. Then you use the information, get the goods and deliver them to the people who needed them in the first place. You know parts of this city I don't. You can go places I can't, can do things that...well, let's just say fall well outside of army protocol. I supply you the gold to pay the informants, with any extra means you need to get and deliver the relief supplies and everybody wins."

Quinn took off his hat. "Except me, when I get shot for playing both ends against each other."

"There is that. It'd be far riskier than what you're doing now. But eventually, you'll make it unprofitable to steal from the army while still getting help to the unofficial camps I'm not really allowed to service. Think of it, Freeman. You could be the single most beneficial man in San Francisco."

"Only no one will know. They'll just know the Midnight Messenger did it."

"I've considered that," Major Simon said with a wry grin, "and I've a plan for that, too. I think that once the tension has died down and we've gained the upper hand, that we should reveal you as the Midnight Messenger. With, of course, a whole lot of army gratitude, a public commendation and a commission in the Corps of Engineers for you to get a draftsman's education and apprenticeship. It's never been done, but then again I don't think a lot of what I have in mind for you has any kind of precedent at all. You'll be a hero."

Quinn pulled in a surprised breath. The Army Corps of Engineers would have a huge hand in rebuilding San Francisco. He'd be building, fulfilling that dream of studying architecture if what Simon said was true. He'd never considered signing up, fearing they'd never grant a real education to a man of his status. Why haul bricks for the army when a civilian firm paid just as well and no one shot at you? He could never reveal his role as the Messenger on his own—it'd be far too dangerous— but with the army at his back, he could take real credit without risking harm. If he lived through double-crossing half of San Francisco's underbelly. "It's a big risk."

"It's a big reward. I'm offering you an entire new standard of living, Freeman. For you and your mother. You'd be able to provide—very nicely—for all the people you care about. Isn't that what all this is about, anyway? Providing for them?"

Most of the people in Quinn's life who had power had gotten it by dark means. Influence that was more about fear than respect. The docks were a system of predators, a jungle that had finally consumed his pa and lots of other people he knew. Wasn't it worth any risk to escape that? To count for something in the world, be educated and have a real hand in rebuilding this city? It called to the deepest part of him, answered a need so basic he hadn't even named it until now.

And then there was Nora. What price wouldn't he pay to be able to be seen as "a man of prospects" by her family? To lay aside all the secrecy?

It was the opportunity he'd survived for. The reason God had spared him, had given him the talents he had and the past that now made him so useful.

"I'm in," Quinn said, without a shred of doubt.

## Chapter Twenty-One

"Were these with the other supplies?" Quinn watched carefully to ensure his conversation went unobserved, and made his voice husky so that Leo, a man who most people knew as the butcher but was known to Quinn to have many other well-connected occupations, wouldn't guess his identity.

"No. Finding those'll take some asking around," Leo replied. His current target was a shipment of hospital supplies that had gone missing from Fort Mason yesterday. Personally, Quinn was in search of crutches for a young woman from the northern part of Dolores Park. The army hospital had a storehouse of crutches, but Quinn wanted to see if he could secure a pair on his own, outside of army influence, as long as he was casting about for information on the missing supplies. He'd been successful. The young lady would find the pair of crutches, with a MM carved into one side, lying outside her shack when she woke tomorrow morning.

"I've heard of a man with tents for sale," Leo said. "Army tents. Along with some ether. I think he might be who you're looking for. An awful lot of things seem to wander off the official camps when he's around, seems to me."

That's exactly the information Quinn was after. "Like I said, I can pay well for information like that," Quinn said quietly. "And do something about it besides."

Leo was the first man who dared take the Midnight Messenger up on his offer. The offer had been out on the dock's unofficial grapevine of gossip for a handful of days with no results. Folks were right to hesitate. Men who hoarded supplies for the black market weren't the kind of people to take kindly to exposure. Quinn had been forced to offer a whole lot more gold than he'd originally planned before Leo finally came forth. "Ain't cooperation a profitable thing?" Leo said, keeping his back to the Midnight Messenger as instructed. "Tomorrow, two o'clock. You bring the money, I'll bring a little map showing you where you can find 'im. But I'll need twice what you offered."

Quinn winced. Until folks realized they could deal with the Midnight Messenger and not get shot themselves, it was going to take a whole lot of convincing— the shiny metal kind—to gain conspirators. Success was getting very expensive. "Done." Quinn tossed a single gold coin at the butcher's feet. "For your time."

"Pleasure doing business with you, Mr. Messenger." Leo picked up the gold and tucked it in his pocket. He walked slowly away, whistling into the night.

It's started, Quinn thought to himself. Let's hope I'm alive to see it finished.

It had been an insufferable week. The unspoken tension in the house choked the sunlight out of the air. Nora did not see how Annette's unfortunate romance altered the sorrow of her death. In fact, Nora took some solace in knowing Annette had been so happy before her life was cut short. No one—most especially Aunt Julia—shared her point of view. Everyone clipped all mentions of Annette or romance or secrecy from their words, lest Aunt Julia fall into another of her crying spells upstairs in her room.

Her own parents took all the regret as fuel to watch *her* with excruciating caution. One more not-very-well hidden sermon on the values of propriety and familial respect, and Nora thought she'd burst. It was odd to have one's life boxed up like a curated museum piece when one had just survived one of the most devastating disasters in history. She couldn't persuade her mother or father that she was not a fragile lily on the verge of being crushed by the slightest misstep. Did Mama and Papa think that all her sense and intelligence had fled at Annette's words?

She knew better. Her chafing came from the inescapable fact that her parents had good reason to worry. She would close her eyes and try to imagine Major Simon kissing her hand in the tender way Quinn had. But she could not recall the color of Major Simon's eyes. And she saw the particular gold of Quinn's eyes in all sorts of things: sunsets, leaves, this color silk or that painting.

Albert Simon was a respected man, and a foundation for a solid marital future. Quinn, for all his impossibility, was a storm she could not escape or contain. He had character but few prospects, passion but earned little respect—at least from those who did not know him, for she knew him to be highly respected and loved throughout Dolores Park. At best, Simon had a space he held open for faith, whereas Quinn had a faith that seeped into every part of his life.

It could not be denied. She was, quite irresponsibly, in love with Quinn.

Nora had somehow become a different woman. The combination of disaster, Annette's death and secrets, and the laid-bare world she now saw had added a new layer to the old Nora Longstreet. Life wove complexities and consequences into threads she hadn't seen before. Her world had expanded, deepened, and her emotions had undergone the same transformation. She needed time, space and interactions with people to help her work through it all.

All she had were relatives, prayer, confines and the poor distraction of making a dozen or so rag dolls.

It was nowhere near enough.

Her prayers for a chance to get out from under the stifling supervision of her parents were answered, oddly enough, by Major Simon. Word had reached him, evidently through her father, that the supplies he'd given her had been made into dolls that were now ready. As such, he'd sent a young officer to oversee a trip to Grace House so that she could meet with Reverend Bauers to see about their distribution. She would much rather have been escorted to Dolores Park itself, but she knew that to be unlikely. Still, she hoped Reverend Bauers might know more about someone called the Midnight Messenger. For several weeks now, Papa had brought home tall tales of blankets, medicines, foods and such that had been snatched from the hands of marketeers and delivered to those in need. How this dark hero managed to slip in and out performing such deeds of bravery and compassion without anyone discovering his identity amazed her. She imagined he worked somehow with Quinn's posts, and that pleased her immensely. This hero sounded amazing enough, even if Papa's talent for exaggeration did leave some room for doubt.

"I think Simon's behind it," Papa had told her last night after seeing her eyes go wide with the latest re-counting. "Finding a way to expand the relief efforts outside of the boundaries the army has set for him. He's denying it at every turn, but there's something behind the man's eyes. It's a pity you won't see him today. I suspect you'd be able to charm the truth out of him."

Whether or not Albert Simon was involved, Nora was grateful for the major's latest heroic act: getting her out of the house. She was utterly delighted to climb into the army cart with her basket of dolls.

"Marvelous!" Reverend Bauers exclaimed upon her arrival at Grace House. "I have missed you greatly, Miss Longstreet." He gave Nora a hearty kiss on the cheek as if she were his granddaughter. It was a pity the man had no family of his own. Then again, perhaps God had granted him a whole neighborhood as his family precisely because his heart was large enough for the task. "There has been so much commotion about lately. Politics and accusation and midnight deliveries. It is a sorry thing that no one here has any appetite for discussing adventures. I've been starved for good conversation."

He took one look at the very dutiful-looking private who stood by the cart as if his career hung in the balance. "The good major's not told you to stay the entire visit, has he?"

"Yes, sir."

Bauers waved him off as if he were an insect. "Glory, how wasteful that man can be. Surely there are more important things to be doing these days than guarding a young woman in a house of worship. Go find yourself something to eat in the kitchen and tell Major Simon I wouldn't hear of your staying and shall return Miss Longstreet safe and sound myself. Tell him I insisted." He gave the private a wink. "My boss has more authority than even his."

When the private hesitated, Bauers nearly bellowed, "Off with you, then!" and chuckled when the young man fairly scrambled in the direction of the kitchen.

"I've no mind to be supervised," Bauers said, tucking Nora's basket into one arm and her hand into his other elbow. "Nor, I gather, do you. Captured our good major's attentions, have you?"

"I fear it's more the work of Mama and Papa than anything I've done. I hardly need to add two words to their efforts. I've not had much opportunity to do anything. Mama and Papa have kept me under lock and key since…" She stopped herself, realizing she'd said too much already.

"Since what?"

She shook her head. How could she heap more shame on to Aunt Julia and Uncle Lawrence by telling a man of God what Annette had done? Then again, this man of God was not the sanctimonious Reverend Mansfield. She couldn't help thinking Reverend Bauers probably would have helped Annette and Eric if they'd come to him. Here, out of Aunt Julia's parlor, with all Bauers knew, she could at least speak freely and sort out her thoughts. Hadn't she just prayed for some help in dealing with the storm swirling around inside her?

"It is a long and private story, Reverend. But perhaps it is best that I talk to you about it."

"Let me attend to a quick matter, and then we'll have tea sent into the study," Bauers said. "We can talk for as long as you'd like."

Quinn was asleep when he felt his mother push at his shoulder. As he pulled his aching body upright on the bed, she handed him a note. "Come to Grace House?" he yawned aloud, looking up at her.

"Don't you be lookin' at me, boy," Ma said sharply. "No one tells me anything." She wasn't at all pleased, and she had good reason. Notes and messages and generally suspicious behavior had been the norm for Quinn for weeks now, and when she'd see him—which wasn't often—she'd look at him with disappointment and anger. Quinn knew she thought he was up to twelve kinds of no good, and it pained him to let her think the worst of him.

*Hurry up the day, Lord,* Quinn prayed as he avoided Ma's glare. *I'm tired of waiting for everyone to know what I'm up to.* After a particularly close call the other night, Quinn had begun to say prayers for his safety nightly and had asked Reverend Bauers to do the same. Bauers knew he was the Messenger and was storing additional supplies at Grace House for him, but even Bauers didn't know how far things had gone.

"It'll be all right, Ma." It was a poor excuse for a response, but Quinn had no other. "Just a little while longer."

She narrowed her eyes. "Isn't it funny how those same words come out of every mouth these days. If I go to my grave never hearing again about how everythin's coming soon or on its way or in just a while, I'll die a happy woman."

Quinn pulled on his boots and kissed his mother on the cheek. "Just mind it's not that grave that's coming soon. I need you."

Her gaze softened. "Aye, that you do. There'll be no rest for me until I see you off and settled with a family of your own. And high time it is for that, too. Not that anyone can make plans for any kind of future while we're here." She waved her arm around the shack while she pushed out a disgusted breath. "Oh, for a real roof over my head again."

Quinn grabbed his hat and two of the biscuits that sat on a tin plate by the door. "I'd say soon, but you might cuff me."

"If you were goin' anywhere else but Grace House, I just might, but for the size of ye."

These days Quinn actually had enough money to occasionally ride the streetcars, so he arrived at Grace House in one-third the time it would have taken to walk the trip. Bauers met him at the door with an assessing stare. "It's as bad as I thought," he remarked, crossing his arms over his chest. "How much have you slept this week?"

"Just enough."

"You can't keep this up for much longer. You know that, don't you? Exhausted men make foolish mistakes." They walked into the hallway toward Bauers's study. "Simon pushes too hard, I think."

"He's enough of his own worries. I'll be fine, Reverend. I doubt it'll be much longer."

"Until what?" The reverend regarded him with a narrowed eye. Bauers was clever enough to sense he hadn't been told the whole story. He might have worried less if he knew the entirety of the Messenger plan, but that wasn't safe. Quinn had already decided only he and Major Simon would know all the elements of how the goods found their way to refugees. Everyone else got only pieces.

"Now, you know better than to ask me that." The constant evasion was wearing on Quinn, tired as he was.

Bauers's worried look mirrored Ma's. "I'll just have to content myself with a safer question, such as, can you stay an hour or so?"

"I can." Bauers must have had some request of him to send the note. "What did you need?"

"It's not I that's needing. It's you. When was the last time you've spent more than two minutes in prayer, man?"

"You'd be surprised. They might be short prayers, but there's heaps of 'em every day."

"The chapel is a healing place to be, Quinn. I want you to spend some time there. I want you to know you're right with God while you walk this perilously thin line. And don't think I don't suspect just how thin it is."

Quinn had seen Reverend Bauers force folks into the chapel before. Bauers had actually barred the door behind him once when he went on the one and only drinking binge of his youth, and he didn't doubt the good reverend would do it again if he felt it necessary. Truth was, he did need to pray. He needed to pour out his hopes and fears to his Father in Heaven. Right now the thought of an hour in the chapel's cool, peaceful darkness seemed like the only thing that would keep him going. Quinn smiled at the wise old man. "How is it you always know what I need?"

Reverend Bauers smiled. "I listen to the One who really does know what you need."

"You won't have to bar me in this time. I know where I need to be."

"You know—" the reverend's smile broadened into a look of fatherly pride "—I believe you do. What a man of faith you've become, Quinn. I couldn't be more proud of you." He punctuated his smile with a wink. "But I'll still come check on you in half an hour. The spirit may be willing, but I suspect the flesh may fall asleep, at the rate you've been running."

Quinn could only return the smile as he walked off toward the chapel, knowing he was indeed headed in the right direction. Twenty minutes later, with a world of weight lifted off his shoulders, Quinn turned at the opening of the chapel door behind him to find the most beautiful reassurance God had ever sent.

## Chapter Twenty-Two

How he'd gotten Quinn inside Grace House without her knowing, Nora couldn't guess. But when Reverend Bauers pushed open the door to the chapel and the wedge of soft light revealed that head of sandy hair bent over the front pew, Nora's heart tumbled. When he turned and looked at her, his gold eyes shining their surprise, the connection was as powerful—and unsettling—as it had been that first day at the ceremony.

She somehow managed a quick glance back at Reverend Bauers, who merely offered the most knowing of grins and pulled the door shut behind her.

Quinn stood. The chapel was so small that even though they were on opposite sides of the room, she could hear him clearly when he whispered, "You're here." The grateful amazement in his voice unraveled something in her chest. Something she'd been clutching tightly but now couldn't hope to contain.

"I've been here for most of the afternoon," she said, wondering how long he'd been here and exactly how much planning Bauers had done.

Quinn laughed softly and shook his head. "I wonder if God realizes how devious our good reverend can be."

She laughed herself. "I believe He does, and makes good use of it besides."

He looked as if he were a thirsty man drinking in the sight of her. She felt the same sensation—the very sight of him soothed her. Her heart was at once both pounding and wonderfully settled.

"Glory, but I've missed you," he said, crossing the distance between them. "I haven't slept a whole night in forever, but every time I close my eyes, I see you."

She knew now what drove Annette, for if he told her to take his hand and run away at this moment, Nora would have done it. "I… Quinn, I'm frightened." And she was. This thing between them seemed so much stronger than she could control. And so much of her didn't want to control it.

He took another step toward her. "We'll be together. I know it, now more than ever."

He closed the distance and reached up one hand to brush a thumb across her cheek. "If I tell you that in a little while, if you just keep your fight alive, there will be a way, will you believe me?" He feathered his fingers along the side of her hair, and she reached up to hold that hand against her face, treasuring his touch. She could believe there was a way. That tiny spark of determination leapt from his fingers and lit the fire waiting inside her.

"Yes." And she did want to. With a power she didn't know her heart possessed. Without another thought, Nora threw herself into his embrace. His arms were warm and strong and she knew they could hold the world at bay.

She felt him shudder at the contact and knew it sealed for him what it had sealed for her: their fate. Only it felt more like stepping into a wonderful, adventurous future God had yet to reveal.

She kissed him. The gentle kiss went through him like cannon fire, shaking him so deeply he could never hope to describe it. All the doubt, the envy, the worry fell away in the heady bliss of knowing she was his. He sighed and wrapped his arms more tightly around her. Nora Longstreet was in his arms. It was beyond imag ination, and then again, it seemed as if it could never have been otherwise. She was so perfect within his embrace, so absolutely, wonderfully near him, that all his efforts to return the kiss gently were lost. It was not a gentle kiss. Fierce was the wrong word for it—although it seemed to wield the power of the universe. Passionate was too coarse a term. His meager education failed him any vocabulary save the thought that pounded throughout his body like a heartbeat: I love her.

The vitality she'd lost roared back into her eyes. When she threw her arms around his neck, he picked her up and spun her for the sheer happiness of it all. He kissed her again, just because he could. He could fuel a hundred Midnight Messenger missions on the surge it gave him.

"I've been so worried about you," she said when they finally pulled away to sit breathlessly in the pew, his fingers threaded between hers. He couldn't stop his thumb from tracing the back of her hand. "There seems to be so much going on. Papa has been bringing home the most incredible stories."

"Really?" Quinn worked hard to hide his amusement, pretty sure where this was heading.

"This Messenger fellow, he's filling requests from your posts, isn't he? You must know who he is. That might become very dangerous for you. He's made some people very angry, Papa says."

You've no idea how dangerous or how angry, Quinn thought. He hung on to the decision not to tell her, even though the spark in her eyes was making him work hard to do so. She would be so astounded once she knew. And then there was the very tempting prospect that revealing his role as the Messenger might raise his standing in her parents' eyes. Pleasing as that was, it came at too high a cost. If he revealed himself, even to only Nora and her family, it ran the risk of the secret getting out. He'd lose every advantage anonymity gave him, not to mention placing them at risk.

As Nora recounted a few of the stories she'd heard, Quinn grew shocked at the amazing deliveries folks credited to the Midnight Messenger. Exaggeration had stretched the truth far and wide in camp gossip. His heart was so full at the moment, however, that he felt capable of the astounding feats she listed. "He is a very clever man with some powerful helpers—or so I'm told," he offered. "I don't know that much."

"He uses your posts." She looked up at him with admiring eyes and he thought himself the most blessed man on earth. "Doesn't that make you feel wonderful, to know your idea is doing so much good?"

"You use my posts, too, for your dolls. And so do other people who send help. I only make sure folks know what people need. People are mostly good if you give them the chance. I just give them that chance."

She frowned. "People are worse and worse from what Papa says. You'd think I was in braids again from the way he and Mama watch me. I know it's just everything that has happened making them so cautious, but I can't bear it sometimes. There are as many wonderful things out here as there are bad. How is it I can feel so much life when they seem to be surrounded by fear?" She tightened her hand against his. "Honestly, I don't know how I shall ever manage to see you again soon enough."

He touched her cheek. "I am very clever, you know. And God's given me a very resourceful partner in our good reverend." The mission bells rung four, and he knew their time was close to over. "I suspect we'll find a way," he said, pulling her up to standing. They walked hand in hand to the back of the chapel.

"Reverend Bauers would say this is a time for God to be mighty."

He smiled. "He'd be right."

When they'd reached the small cross hung in a nook by the chapel's rear door, Nora took both his hands and held them fast. When she bowed her head, the moment felt rich and deep. One of the few times in Quinn's life he felt the word "holy" truly applied.

*"Father God, protect this man."* Quinn closed his eyes, feeling the closeness of her prayer as if God's hand had indeed rested on his shoulders. *"Be gracious and mighty to us as we try and work our way through these times. Grant us wisdom and courage. Thank You so very much for how You've brought us together, for saving us from dangers. I'm glad You know my heart, Lord, for it's too full to find words. Be with us, go before us, keep us in Your mighty protection until we're together again. Amen."*

A knock came on the chapel door, and Reverend Bauers leaned into the room. "It's time to fetch you back, my dear. I do hope you've given him the encouragement he needs."

Quinn nodded, sure he must look beyond smitten. No doubt it'd be a week before he could wipe the grin from his face.

"If there are two happier people on God's green earth at the moment, I'm sure I couldn't find them."

Nora rushed up to the reverend and grabbed his arm. "You are the dearest man in the world, Reverend."

"Only just," Quinn added, who was at that moment counting Bauers as the finest friend a man could have. "You see her home safe, now."

"You've only enough time to make your appointment, Quinn. Off with you now before you're late."

Nora grasped his arm and kissed him on the cheek. "Be safe, Quinn."

"Always," he said. It felt like yanking his heart out of his chest to leave the room. "Watch for me, I'll find a way."

If there was ground under his feet as Quinn walked to his next training session with the major, he hardly knew it. Today, the Midnight Messenger walked on air.

Just as dawn was slipping strands of pink into the sky, Quinn leaned against the wall and sighed. "You're sure? You're absolutely sure?" Quinn had been dealing mostly with small-time grifters who'd started hinting that there were much bigger forces at work. When he'd relayed his suspicions, Simon promised to look into any large shipments that would be particularly attractive to the marketeers, and he'd identified one later that week.

"Gospel truth," Leo said. "He's only the front man. It's Sergeant Miller that's got the other half."

"Theft from the inside? Why would the army steal from the army?"

"When some things fetch so high a price, ain't too many men can resist. This kind of thing's been happening all along. It's just worse now. I know of three others besides."

"Three other army men?"

"Well." Leo cocked his head to one side. "One of 'em's navy."

Quinn let his head fall back against the wall. "Outstanding."

"What's the matter?" Leo flipped one of the coins and caught it midair. "Army own you or something?"

"No one owns me."

"So, take them down with the rest of the lot. It'd be nice to see some of the high-ups fall."

Quinn reconfirmed the address of the stockpile again with Leo. How this simple butcher got the information he had, he didn't know. And didn't want to know. Leo had friends in places Quinn hoped he'd never have to go. Even more than before the earthquake, there was a whole other city lurking under the one people saw. "You're sure?" he said once more.

"Dead certain."

"Let's hope I'm not dead if you're not certain."

Leo made a derisive sound deep in his throat. "No one'd shoot you. You're a legend."

"Read some history," Quinn said as he ducked back around the corner. "Too many times it's the legends that go down first."

Quinn managed to get half the shipment redelivered

to the official camp the following night. It took four trips—one of which entailed an entirely too close call with a nasty fellow bearing a nastier knife. The other half found its way to both Dolores Park and one of the other unofficial camps nearby. A few things were just too large for one man to carry, and Quinn decided it was worth letting those go. Truth be told, he wasn't quite sure how to tell Major Simon that it was one of his own army officers doing the stealing. On one hand, Quinn supposed Simon expected the ever-present corruption to work its way into army ranks eventually. On the other hand, Simon looked so pressed at their last meeting, Quinn feared the major might explode at such news. Is wasn't as if things weren't working. People in both the official and unofficial camps got help now. Quinn decided to bide his time, to look for another way than the Midnight Messenger to expose the grand-scale thieves. A way that didn't entail him meeting the business end of an army pistol.

## Chapter Twenty-Three

Papa came to sit beside Nora in the bay window as she stared out into the street after breakfast. If you didn't peer too closely, things were beginning to look something close to normal. Streetcars went by, even if not nearly as often as they used to. Had it really been months since the earthquake? So much had changed, so many wounds were still fresh. Sam's foot had completely healed, banks and shops had reopened, but Aunt Julia still cried, people still lived in shacks and stood in line and Nora could still not look at the photograph of Annette on the piano without getting a lump in her throat.

"So quiet," Papa said, fingering one of Nora's curls. "Yet, you still think louder than anyone I know." Papa always said that he could hear her brain turning over a problem from across the room.

"The world is different," she said, thinking it a vague and cumbersome response. Still, how could she even begin to talk to her father about all that was swirling around in her thoughts?

"I'm glad you see that," he said, leaning back against

his side of the bay window seat. "It is a far more dangerous place out there these days. These are troublesome times. I worry for you and your mother."

Funny, Nora had meant the *better* sort of different. She had lived, she realized, in a glossed-over world. A delicate, cultivated world where faith was more of an intellectual, spiritual pursuit rather than a daily act of trust. God as "daily bread," had become so much more real to her. God was somehow nearer. Clearer. She saw His hand in places she'd never even thought to look before.

Nora turned to her father. "Do you believe Reverend Mansfield when he says God sent the earthquake as punishment?"

"Do I think God smote San Francisco for her sins?" Papa sighed. "Most days, it's easy to say no. But I've seen things that make me wonder. This seems to have brought out the best and the worst of our city. People have stolen from charity. But then people like Major Simon have done so much good."

Nora decided to ask. "Do you think Major Simon is the Midnight Messenger?"

Papa stroked his beard, smiling. "Well, now, I have to say I haven't given the idea consideration. I've always guessed he had something to do with all of it, but is he the actual man? I couldn't say. He strikes me as a bit…" Papa hesitated "…too mature for such exploits himself. It'd be quite a story if he were, wouldn't it?"

Messenger or not, it was certainly hard to improve on Papa's opinion of Simon.

"I do know," Papa continued, leaning in, "that he greatly admires *you*. You should be very flattered, my dear."

Nora didn't know what to say. Papa mistook her downturned eyes as modesty instead of bafflement, and perhaps that was for the best. How on earth could she ever tell her parents what she felt for Quinn? They'd never understand, nor would they ever approve. She did not yet know if she could be brave enough to defy her whole family. When Quinn looked at her, she felt strong enough to challenge the world. But here, alone, she faltered.

Papa tipped up her chin, much as he had done when she was a little girl. "What are your feelings on the matter of our renowned major, Nora? I'm of the mind he is seeking a match, and I'd like to know where you stand."

Nora had hoped it would not come to this. There seemed no way through this conversation without an outright lie to her father, and she didn't want that. "Where I stand? In regards to Major Simon?"

"Exactly. Should he come seeking a match, what would your answer be?"

"He is very well regarded."

She was stalling and Papa knew it. "That's true enough, but I am not asking what others think of him. I want to know what *you* think of the man."

"I think him well-bred, distinguished and very clever. He is certain to do great things." She didn't lie. Major Simon was those things. But he had not captured her heart. She could no more make herself love him than she could make herself stop loving Quinn.

She loved Quinn.

"Do you care for the man?" Papa asked it so tenderly, she couldn't lie to him. Most especially about this.

"No," she said softly. "He is an admirable man in

many respects, but he has not captured my affections, if that's what you're asking."

"That is exactly what I am asking. And yet, seeing you talk, I would not say that you find the man repulsive. I am wondering, Nora, if you read too many novels to see what constitutes a marriage in the real world. I did not sweep your mother off her feet when we first met. In fact, we mostly were afraid of each other. But I love her dearly now. We were a fine match then, and it grew into a fine marriage. I want the same for you. And so I ask you, if you do not care for the man yet, could you see coming to care for him as time went on?"

Perhaps before. But now her heart was no longer hers to give to someone else. She knew that if she married Major Simon, it would be turning from love forever. She knew so many women who took a sensible, lukewarm marriage on themselves without a moment's hesitation. A lifetime of mutual regard, of domestic partnership. Before the earthquake, before all that had happened to her, she suspected she could have done the same.

She could not now.

"I can't say." It was the closest she could come to the truth without rejecting Papa outright. Even the concerned disappointment in his eyes just now was painful to bear.

"You are old enough to know your own mind, Nora." Papa sat back. "But you have also been through a terrible ordeal. Let us simply say that more time is needed. It would be too soon and too cruel to move in such a direction in light of your Aunt Julia, anyway. But we will talk of this again soon, hmm?"

Nora could only nod. Nod and trust that Quinn had

indeed found a way. *Be very, very mighty, God,* she prayed for what seemed like the hundredth time since leaving the Grace House chapel.

Nora was out in the tiny garden, tending to a forlorn patch of flowers she was trying to coax into bloom when a pebble fell at her feet. She thought nothing of it until a second fell a foot or two away toward the backyard fence. And then a third, closer to the edge of the fence. Someone was trying to get her attention from the other side of the fence. It didn't take much imagination to wonder who it was luring her to the secluded corner of the alley. Peering into the kitchen window to ensure no one watched, Nora nevertheless gathered up the weeds she'd just pulled and made it look as if she was meaning to toss them beyond the fence.

Quinn's face beamed as she turned the corner, and his smile melted her heart. She did love him. The world felt disjointed when they were apart and centered when they were together, no matter what the circumstances. She realized, as she slid her hand into his, that any efforts to build a future without him would never work. His future had been intertwined with hers. Her heart had moved from "if" to "how."

Quinn pulled her into his arms and kissed her forehead. "I can't seem to breathe without you." She felt his deep breath and knew what he meant. She'd become so acutely aware of his absence, so needful of his presence that it did feel as if she choked without him. He pulled her back to look at her. "Ma suspects."

"How?"

"Well, it might be closer to say she suspects something. She told me this morning I looked…oh, what was the word…besotted. And she had the oddest look when she said it. Something halfway between a scowl and a smile, or both together, maybe." He curled a lock of her hair around his finger. "I feel distracted all the time. You make it hard for a man to concentrate, did you know that?"

Nora melted against his chest. "How much longer? We don't have much time."

"We've time enough." When she shook her head, he pulled back to look at her again. "What's the matter?"

"Papa asked me to consider Major Simon. Wanted to know what would be my reply if the major…declared his intentions."

She felt Quinn stiffen. "Has he?"

"Not directly. But believe me, he's getting plenty of encouragement from Mama and Papa. I suppose I should be glad my father asked my opinion at all, from the way he talks."

"He'd better ask your opinion. You've the right to your own mind on this, surely."

Nora pulled out of his embrace to pace the alley. "He feels I'm too troubled by all that's happened to see clearly. I hesitated all I could, but he saw that hesitation only as confusion, not reluctance. I couldn't lie to him. I couldn't say yes just to please him, but I couldn't say no yet, either."

"You'll have to tell him outright, sooner or later."

"You know it's not that simple. My parents' anger aside, Major Simon isn't the kind of man to take such a rejection easily. I fear he would make things very difficult for my family, if not just you and I."

Quinn's features darkened. "If he knows your heart is elsewhere, why would he pursue you?"

Nora leaned back against the fence. "Papa says matches of quality can't always be about love. He's going to ask me to trust him for what's best for me, I know it."

He looked at her, intensity sharpening his gaze. Quality had been exactly the wrong word to use. "And will you?"

"No," Nora said, turning to face him. "Even as I was talking to him I could see how impossible it was." She took a breath, realizing now was indeed the time to say it. "I love you. My life lies with you. I can't turn my back on that even if it made all the sense in the world." She put her hands on his chest. "You've got to find a way because I've got to be with you."

Quinn took her face in his hands, staring so deeply into her eyes she felt the ground drop out from underneath her feet. "I love you, Nora." His voice was deep and warm, yet very serious. "I'll not let another man take what I know God's given to me. We belong together. The how and the when, they're just details. You hang on to that. I love you." He kissed her—a declarative, powerful kiss that seemed to stake his claim to her heart and dare the world to do anything about it. They were so much stronger together than they were apart.

It seemed far too short a time before he sighed and said, "You'd best get back. I've loads to do and your ma will worry if she looks out the window and sees you gone." He kissed her hand, grinning as he had that first time back in Reverend Bauers's study; a cocky, dashing smile that melted her heart all over again. "I'll come again soon. Count on it. You hold fast and leave the rest to me."

Quinn pulled on his boots with a troubled heart. Simon was stepping up his pursuit of Nora. He was also stepping up things all over the camp and the regiment—the man was on the move. Toward what, he couldn't say. He had the most foreboding sense of collision, however. Of the impending crash of so many intentions—his, Nora's, Simon's—that worked against each other. If Simon succeeded, if he brought the relief efforts out from under the corruption, it'd be partly through Quinn's own hand as the Messenger. And Quinn would come out as a man of position because of it. Her parents might hold him in higher regard once they knew he was the Messenger. Yet, there was the stark truth that even with an army commission and the shot at a draftsman's training, he still couldn't compete with Simon's pedigree and standing. Would it even matter if Nora expressed her own mind on the subject? Simon's success meant his own, but it still might not prevent his defeat where Nora was concerned.

And then there was the small matter of army corruption. Could the Midnight Messenger really be selective in exposing the grifters? Make trouble for the small-time marketeers on the outside but leave those inside the army alone? Or did he have to bite the hand that fed him and trust God with the consequences? *I'll need so much wisdom tonight, Lord, You'd better be watching my every move.* Tonight he was tackling one of the larger shipments rumored to have been diverted by Sergeant Miller, right under Simon's nose. How it would all end, Quinn had no idea.

The shipment that night involved a variety of things—foodstuffs, building materials, medical supplies, dry goods. The selection wasn't that unusual, but the quality was the sort that would bring a particularly high price to the right set of deep pockets. He'd managed one trip to fetch the wayward goods without incident and was doubling back for a second when he spotted the sergeant himself standing guard. Someone had evidently realized things were going missing. By the time he'd managed to fill his duffel a second time, he'd been spotted. Shouts turned to drawn pistols, and Quinn found himself dodging bullets as he made his escape. It was far too close a call to chance a third trip—the rest of the goods would have to fall into the wrong hands. Not only that, but the shouts he heard as he fled made one thing crystal clear: the army grifters knew the Midnight Messenger had discovered them. How Simon would handle it from here, Quinn could only guess. There was no hope of keeping it quiet any longer.

Simon was curt with Quinn the next morning, but said nothing at all about the night's developments. It seemed odd—foolish, even—not to deal with the problem at hand, but the major's tension was all too obvious. Perhaps he had some reason for not discussing it. He was, after all, a very clever man who knew the army's intricacies far better than Quinn did. When he handed Quinn a relatively minor list of supplies for the Messenger this evening—hidden at a location off Fort Mason property this time—Quinn assumed Simon was backing off until a strategy could be developed. Minor was good. The location was also appealingly close to Nora's house. If he were quick about it, he might find a way to see her or at least leave some kind of gift. That proved too enticing an opportunity to miss. Quinn hadn't had a night he would classify as "minor" in two weeks.

The evening proved far from minor. Rather than an easy delivery, Quinn found himself escaping down the

alleyway at full speed. The small stockpile of fabric
and beans in no way merited the four men with very
large pistols who were guarding it. Quinn ducked left
as shots whizzed by him to the right, hearing a tin in
his duffel hiss as it took an entirely too-close bullet.
Where had all these armed thugs come from in this
neighborhood? Why now, when tonight should have
been easy pickings? Panting, Quinn tucked and rolled
behind a barrel as another handful of bullets peppered
the wall to his left.

Like a bolt of lightning, it hit him; this was no ordinary defense. These men were after him, and they
weren't treading softly. After a quick glance at his sur-
roundings—which offered painfully few options—
Quinn shed his duffel and ducked into a cellar doorway.
If there was any chance at all the pursuers were only
out to retrieve their goods, the abandoned duffel should
take care of that.

Peering around whatever cellar he'd entered, he saw
only rubble at first, and then a small window on the far
side of the building. Small enough, he hoped, to allow
his exit while being too tight for the band of husky thugs
at his back. As he made his way across the pitch black,
he prayed the duffel had been prize enough for them.
A storm of yelling and footsteps behind him told him
otherwise. Quinn began leaping over boxes and beams,
heading for the window with all the speed in him. If he
had to dive through the glass to make his escape, a few
cuts and bruises would certainly be better than whatever waited for him in that crowd.

Quinn pulled his mask off his face, wrapped the
cloth around his hand and punched through the window
at a run. Already earthquake-damaged, it gave way eas-

ily, and Quinn felt a flurry of scrapes on his knees and arms as he began scrambling out the broken window.

"Don't kill him, ya fools!" A voice came from behind him as Quinn worked to get the rest of his body out the window and on to the glass-strewn street. "The army only pays if he's alive."

"Nah, kill 'im. I heard a couple of fellers on the police force will pay more for him dead!"

In the split second Quinn paused to realize the army had put a bounty on his head, the bullet hit him. It was as if a cannon had gone off in his thigh, a burning, explosive sensation that shook the breath from his body. *Lord, save me, I'm shot.* It shocked him that his leg still worked, although every movement sent shards of pain throughout his leg. He grabbed at it, not daring to look down, and rolled away from the window as a second shot rang out. He fell more than ran around the corner, out of sight of the heads now surely poking out the window. He didn't stop to find out if they fit through the opening to follow him. Quinn ran until the edges of his sight began to swim, stopping only to take the bandanna and tie it around his throbbing thigh.

He was nowhere near Grace House, nowhere near Dolores Park, nowhere near help of any kind. *Father God, I'm done for. Help me!* He couldn't go home— this crew would think nothing of shooting mindlessly in the camp aisles, and too many people could get hurt in those close quarters. He couldn't go to Grace House— he didn't think he could make it that far. He certainly couldn't go to Simon at Fort Mason. He was injured, losing blood fast, and in very real danger of passing out.

He had to get help, and he had to get it without revealing who he was. Which meant he had to get his

mask, shirt and guns out of sight. With another prayer
and a deep breath, Quinn looked around. There was a
postbox at the end of the street. Ironic, but useful. It
was the slimmest of chances that the Midnight Messenger's costume, if discovered in a postbox, would
wind up in Mr. Longstreet's possession. And it was as
good a place as any to shed his "identity." Wincing as
he pulled the mask cloth from his leg, he shed the dark
shirt, hat and boots, dumping them into the postbox
with a sour thought: I'm going to die half-naked and
alone. It was the furthest thing from the new future he'd
thought to grasp.

Assessing where he was, there was only one place
close enough. While it pained him to even think about
bringing this to her doorstep, his only real hope of survival was the Longstreets. At least I'll see her again
before I die, he thought, as he limped off toward her
street, praying he stayed conscious long enough to die
in her arms.

Nora was startled awake by the commotion. She panicked instantly, her body going back to the horrible
earthquake morning before she was completely awake.
There were voices, shouting, but nothing shook or rumbled. She heard her father call for something, heard
Aunt Julia yelp as if something had frightened her. She
found her wrap as quickly as she could, tucked her feet
into slippers, and headed out the bedroom door without
even bothering with a light.

Mama, Papa, Uncle Lawrence and the cook were
huddled around the front door. Papa was calling for
water, the cook was grabbing bandages from the basket

that was supposed to go to Grace House this morning and unrolling them. Had someone been hurt?

She'd just made it down the stairs when Aunt Julia grabbed her arm, pulling her into the front room. "Stay away, Nora!" Julia said, her eyes wide with alarm. "Who knows what that ruffian's brought into my house!"

"Nora." A voice moaned from the center of the commotion.

The room went still. Mama turned to look at her, her face a silent shocked question as to why the person on the floor knew Nora's name.

Papa moved his arm, and Nora realized why her heart filled with fear.

It was Quinn.

## Chapter Twenty-Four

Quinn Freeman lay bleeding on the foyer floor, his naked chest covered in bloody smudges and smears of dirt. His leg was soaked in blood, and every spark she'd seen in his eyes was gone when he turned to look at her. "Quinn?" she said before she had the chance to think better of using his given name.

Papa stared. Mama's hand went to her chest in shock. "You know this man?" Papa said, his voice dark with alarm.

"Papa," Nora said, pulling out of Aunt Julia's arm to kneel down. "This is Quinn Freeman. The man who brought me Annette's locket." For a minute she was astounded Papa didn't recognize him, then she realized Quinn didn't look at all like himself in his condition.

"Good Heavens!" Aunt Julia gasped from behind them, as if the thought of this bloodied thug touching her daughter's belongings made her ill.

"He's been shot," Papa said. "He's lost a lot of blood, from the looks of it. Call the police."

"No!" Quinn gasped.

"Why ever not?" Nora asked, brushing back the hair

from his eyes. He just stared at her, hard, then squeezed his eyes shut as cook tied off the bandage tight over his wound. The bleeding seemed to have been stemmed, but it still looked ghastly.

"He needs a doctor," Papa said, more calmly this time. "Call Major Simon—Fort Mason has the closest."

"No!" Quinn said through clenched teeth, pulling himself to sit upright against the wall this time. "Not Simon. I need Bauers."

"But Simon knows you, that makes no sense. We really should call the major," Nora said, looking at her father.

"No," Quinn insisted. "Get Bauers."

"Reverend Bauers?" Papa furrowed his eyebrows. "You're talking nonsense, man, you need a doctor, not the reverend."

"Bauers only, please," Quinn pleaded. He shifted his gaze to Papa. "There's a reason."

"There had better be a very good reason you're skirting the authorities, Mr. Freeman, and you'd better have out with it right now. I'll not have you bringing any danger to this household." As if the improbability of him falling on to their doorstep in the middle of the night had just hit him, Papa suddenly leaned in. "Why *are* you at our door, Mr. Freeman?"

For a moment Nora thought Quinn was rattled enough by his wound to simply state the truth. She caught his gaze and tried to hold it, fearing there was no way she could discreetly tell him now was not the time to declare affections.

"I was close by. I recognized the house. From when I came to get the pillar."

"Does it hurt?" Nora asked, before she realized what a foolish question that was.

Quinn actually managed a wink. "Only just." Nora noticed a sickeningly red spot now blooming on the white bandage cook had just tied. Something had to be done, and quickly. There wasn't time to stand here and argue whom to call.

"Papa, he's been nothing but kind to our family. He must have some reason, and Reverend Bauers is surely more used to these kinds of emergencies than we are. I think he even has basic medical skills. Please, Papa, can we send word to Grace House?"

Mama looked as though that were a thoroughly dreadful idea. Actually, she looked ready to thrust Quinn back out into the street to fend for himself. Aunt Julia looked like she could barely stand one more minute of this ruffian staining her front foyer carpet. Papa, however, seemed to actually consider her request. "Lawrence," Papa said to Nora's uncle, "help me get him onto the back porch." As Uncle Lawrence and Papa helped a swaying Quinn to his feet, Papa gave orders for cook to send her son off with the mail cart to Grace House, returning with the reverend at all possible speed. Much to Nora's dismay, he also told the boy that once he brought back the reverend, he was to turn right around and deliver a second message to Major Simon.

At least Bauers would get here first. At least Quinn wasn't tossed back into the alley. At least Quinn was still alive, although she had no idea what had happened. Whatever it was, it was more than some stray bullet or scuffle, for Quinn looked as if whoever shot him might burst through the door at any minute.

Heaping trouble upon trouble, Mama had seen too

much. She'd stared at Nora with suspicious eyes, cataloging every look she gave Quinn or instance where she touched him. Papa hadn't guessed it yet, but Mama knew. In truth, her face looked as pained and wounded as Quinn's. It was difficult to guess which set of wounds to tend first.

Mama made the decision for her, snatching her elbow as she went to follow Papa and Uncle Lawrence. "What have you done, Nora?" Her voice was low, her words clipped.

"Nothing, Mama." It was such a useless reply. Nothing but fall in love, actually, but she couldn't put words to that just yet. Not with the look in Mama's eyes. "I know him."

"How well do you know this man?" It was an accusation, not a question.

"Well." It said everything and nothing at all. Nora cast about for a better answer but found none.

Aunt Julia called Quinn a slurry of names Nora was glad he could not hear. "He's hurt, Mama," she said, pulling herself up with a strength she hadn't realized was in her. "He needs help. Now." Before Mama could reach out and stop her, Nora turned and walked down the hallway toward the back porch.

Quinn blacked out twice before Reverend Bauers came rushing out the door on to Nora's back porch. He went to work immediately, motioning for Papa and Uncle Lawrence to put Quinn up on a nearby table. "We'll need a candle if not a lamp." Suddenly, the gentle pastor she'd known was replaced by a fiercely calm commander, moving with military precision. She'd heard Quinn say once that Bauers hadn't been in the clergy all his life, and for an odd moment she wondered what kind of adventures he'd had before joining the church. Papa acquiesced and lit a lamp, bringing it over to where the reverend began peeling back the bloody bandage. Nora felt the room sway and backed up a bit to cling to the porch pillar. "I'd feared something like this would happen," Bauers said, fishing into a bag of medical supplies he'd put on the table. "No good deed goes unrewarded these days." He poked around in the wound, which snapped Quinn out of his faint to hiss through his teeth. "You're blessed. The bullet went clean through from the looks of it. That means you'll heal fine if you don't bleed to death first."

Quinn only moaned. And then did a bit more than that when Bauers began poking around some more. Nora wanted to rush up and hold Quinn's hand, to put a cloth to his forehead and let him know she was here, but Bauers managed to catch her eye and give her a barely perceptible "no" shake to his head. The point seemed moot when Quinn blacked out again once the reverend poured a generous dose of iodine into his wound.

"It's not ready to stitch yet. We'll have to pack it to stem the bleeding, then stitch it later. Until then, he can't be moved."

Papa did not look pleased. Nora was secretly glad to know Quinn wasn't going anywhere. At least she had a chance to find out what on earth had happened, and why Reverend Bauers didn't seem terribly surprised to find his friend shot.

The reverend looked at Uncle Lawrence. "I wonder if you wouldn't mind sitting with the man while I have a conversation with Miss Longstreet and her father. I doubt he'll come to anytime soon, but I wouldn't be surprised if he tried something reckless if he did."

That didn't do wonders for Uncle Lawrence's confidence, but he agreed to stay out on the porch with Quinn while Reverend Bauers asked if Nora and Papa wouldn't sit down with him and hear what he had to say. Nora had no idea what to expect and settled herself into a chair in the front room with the two men. *Lord, what is happening here? Stay close to Quinn. Stay close to me. I have no idea what's unfolding.*

Reverend Bauers eased himself into a chair and chose his words carefully. "There's more to this man than appears, especially tonight. I've no doubt he came here only out of desperation, for he's been taking pains for quite some time now to keep this from you." Nora could only guess what dark secret Bauers seemed to be alluding to, and it grew even worse when the reverend looked right at her. "He's sought only to protect you from any harm, Miss Longstreet."

Papa looked as though he was bracing for the worst. Nora wasn't far behind, as a long list of horrible secrets ran through Nora's imagination, chopping her breaths into short, anxious gulps.

"The man on your back porch is the Midnight Messenger." Bauers folded his hands and waited for the fact to sink in.

"Quinn?" she nearly gasped.

"Him?" Papa pointed in the general direction of the back porch. "That man is the Midnight Messenger? You can't be serious."

"It's precisely Quinn's…shall we say…'colorful' background that gave him knowledge and access to a certain side of the city the Midnight Messenger needed.

In a city as large as this, one clever man can make himself rather invisible."

Nora thought she ought to shake her head to clear it. On the one hand, it seemed utterly impossible. On the other hand, it made all the sense in the world. He had access to all the requests from the posts. He always looked tired. Her gifts in the garden always arrived at night. And he was infinitely clever as well as caring to a fault. He was as strong as he was impulsive. Why couldn't he be the Midnight Messenger?

"All those times he said he knew someone who could help, all my questions he dismissed, they were all..."

"To keep you from any danger your knowing might bring," Bauers cut in. "As you can see, the Midnight Messenger has made enemies. He's taken many great risks to help the refugees in the unofficial camps, exposed a great many evils, but he'd never bring that risk to your doorstep."

"Which is *exactly* what he's done." Papa was trying not to shout for Mama's sake.

"And I'm guessing there must be a very good reason for that, but we might not get the chance to learn it tonight."

There was a scuffle in the back hallway. Nora heard Uncle Lawrence shout something and was just rising from her chair when Quinn stumbled into the room.

Quinn's gaze flashed from her to Papa to the reverend. "You told them," he growled at Bauers. Quinn's eyes held the same barely checked temper she'd seen when he confronted Ollie.

Nora rushed up to steady him as he leaned against the wall. "Nora!" Papa said, his disapproval radiating out of the single word.

She ignored her father, locking her gaze on Quinn instead. "Is it true? Are you the Messenger?" He only nodded, and she didn't even need to see that. It was clear in his eyes.

"Impossible," Papa argued, although Nora could hardly guess why. He'd just as much admitted it and Bauers had little reason to lie about such a thing.

"I shouldn't have come here." Quinn pulled away, but only succeeded in making it one or two steps down the hall before he fell against the wall again.

Bauers had found a wooden chair from the hallway and essentially shoved it under Quinn. "If you won't lie down, at least *sit* down. You're too big for me to haul off the floor alone."

Papa stood up to pace the floor, and Nora could see his thoughts churning. Her thoughts should be in a tumble, too, but somehow she saw how the puzzle pieces fit together almost instantly. It seemed impossible that she hadn't put the facts together before, now that she knew them.

She put her hand on Quinn's shoulder, ignoring the dark look it produced from Papa. "Seems to me this business is best sorted out by Simon or the police," her father said wearily. "He'll settle it soon enough when he arrives."

That made Quinn nearly bolt out of his chair, almost sending Nora tumbling. "Simon's coming?"

"He's on his way now."

"Simon's the reason I'm shot!" Quinn exploded, and Reverend Bauers's hand thrust on to Quinn's chest with a power and speed she'd never have attributed to a clergyman in his eighties. "The army's put a price on the

Messenger's head, and the police seem to have upped the offer. I'm as good as dead now."

"Why?" Nora nearly shouted, planting herself in the middle of this trio of angry men. "What's Major Simon to do with this?"

"He's been getting me the supplies," Quinn said. "He's been part of it from the beginning. Only things went a bit deeper than that, and he began giving me gold to buy information on where stolen goods were being kept."

"So Major Simon *has* been in on this?" Papa asked, wiping his hands down his face.

"He trained Quinn and served as a supply source," Reverend Bauers explained. "It served the army's purposes to see that goods got where they ought to have gone. Major Simon is clever enough to see that one renegade could spur a thousand stories of good deeds, and do any number of things an army couldn't. Or shouldn't."

"Oh," said Quinn with a dark laugh. "You'd be amazed what the army can do. I proved too smart for my own good when I figured out half the trouble was coming from within the army itself." He glared at Bauers, who looked as if that was news to him. "Don't you see? Marketeers weren't just finding their way to the army, it was a couple of rats on the inside selling freely to the marketeers. And I knew. I've become an embarrassment because I can expose the corruption *inside* the army. Under Simon's own nose. And only he knows I'm the Messenger. If he didn't *start* the manhunt, he did nothing to *stop* it, and I'm sure there were dozens of volunteers. I haven't exactly made friends with this."

No one knew quite what to say. It seemed so impossible.

Quinn sunk into the chair and looked up at Nora. "He said he was going to tell the whole city what I'd done when it was time. Give me a commission in the Army Corps of Engineers. An apprenticeship as a draftsman. I'd be someone you could…" His words fell off. Nora held his eyes, perhaps more in love with him at that moment than she had ever been.

"He told you this?" Bauers obviously knew nothing of this new bargain.

"And I believed him," Quinn replied bitterly. "I took all those risks on his word, fool that I am."

"Major Simon is an honorable man who's given me no reason to think he'd do something so outrageous," Papa said.

A knock came on the door, bringing everyone in the room to a standstill. Papa looked at Bauers, then at Quinn.

"That has to be Major Simon," Nora said, coming over to her father. "Papa, don't let him in."

"Of course I'm going to let him in. It's the only way we can get to the bottom of this."

"He'll deny it. It'll be his word against mine." Quinn called after Papa to no effect. Despite his injuries, Quinn looked as if he might bolt for the back door at any minute. In his condition, he'd get all of two blocks before Simon or who knows how many other members of the army would be at his heels. Panic burrowed under Nora's ribs, stealing her breath and making her heart gallop.

Simon strode into the room as if he ruled the world. "Quinn, are you all right?"

How he managed to appear so concerned was beyond Quinn's reckoning. "Only just," Quinn ground out through clenched teeth. He found himself using every ounce of the major's lessons on focusing anger— all trained on not thrusting a knife into the man's ribs this very minute.

"He's been shot," Nora said curtly. "As I assume you know."

"Nora!" Mr. Longstreet didn't much care for his daughter's tone. That was fine with Quinn; he didn't much care for his so-called ally's betrayal, either.

The major only raised an eyebrow. "So your man told me. I'd actually heard from one of my regiments that there was talk of the Messenger being shot." Simon looked straight at him. "I was out looking for you…"

"Or sending thugs out after me?" Quinn cut in.

"…when one of my lieutenants came to find me, saying someone had come to the fort pleading for me to come here. Here, Quinn? However did you end up here?"

"A man can only go so far with a bullet in his leg," Quinn replied darkly, "But then again you knew that. I suppose I should be thankful not all your trainees are as good a shot as I am, Major?"

"Gentlemen!" Reverend Bauers stood between them. "Can we please remember where we are?"

"So you admit, Major, that Freeman is the Midnight Messenger?"

"He was working for me as that, yes."

"I do not work for *you!*" Quinn shot back. He'd always known Simon thought of him merely as another gun in his arsenal.

"It was actually me who put these two together, Mr. Longstreet." Bauers put his hands up between Quinn and the major. "I knew of Quinn's desire to help in this…unusual fashion, and I felt the major's skills and resources would make for an excellent partnership."

Some partnership. Quinn could barely keep from voicing the thought.

Bauers looked at Simon with narrowed eyes. "Did I misjudge, Albert?"

"It was a brilliant idea, Reverend." Simon leveled his glare at Quinn. "At the time. I fear it's gone too far for all concerned."

"Do you, now?" Quinn's knuckles itched to knock a dent into that dignified jaw. The searing pain in his thigh was making it harder and harder to keep a lid on his temper. He felt Nora's hand settle on his arm, cool and steady, and he willed those qualities into his thundering nerves. Major Simon saw her gesture, and raised an eyebrow again. Quinn didn't care one bit for the look of disdain that settled in his eyes.

"I wasn't aware," Major Simon said as he took very particular notice of Nora's gesture. "How unfortunate a complication. Quinn, you exceed my expectations at every turn."

"I expect I do," Quinn said. He felt his body begin to break out in a sweat and wondered how much longer he'd be able to stand.

"Mr. Freeman claims he was fired upon by your orders." Mr. Longstreet sounded entirely too much like he'd already made up his mind on the subject. Quinn wondered why he was surprised. What good was the word of someone like him against the upstanding Major Simon?

Simon looked from Nora's father to Quinn. Could no one else see the supreme annoyance, the carefully veiled anger in Simon's eyes? Quinn realized with a sinking sensation that the major could lie through his teeth this very moment and everyone in the room would believe it. His future was lost; any chance at the education or commission—if he lived long enough to even consider it—was long gone now.

"I believe," Simon said smoothly, "that the Messenger has made enemies. Enemies that might go to great lengths to make him suspect his own had betrayed him. As such, I have no doubt that Mr. Freemen believes I sent those thugs after his life."

"I never *said* anything about a group." Quinn pointed a finger at Simon.

Simon didn't skip a beat. "It's always a group. Cowards travel in packs." Simon turned to Nora's father. "I'm so sorry this business has ended up on your doorstep. Why don't you let me see to Freeman's wounds at the fort infirmary. We can protect him there, too, from whomever it is that's done this. And I insist we post a guard outside this house for the next twenty-four hours. I've no intention of your kindness bringing you further trouble."

"Papa, don't you dare let him take Quinn!" Nora burst out. Quinn's heart both swelled at the thought of her championing him and broke knowing that her efforts would come to no use. Defying her father only made it worse. The strongest-standing wall in San Francisco—the mile-high societal wall—had defeated him in the end. The only thing he could do now was save Nora from her own sweet loyalty to him. He tried to slide her hand from his shoulder, but she only clasped him harder, puzzlement in her eyes.

"Nora, I think you should go upstairs and join your mother and aunt." Mr. Longstreet was dismissing his daughter with the same patronizing tone Simon used with Quinn.

"Absolutely not. I will not stand here and allow you to send Quinn off with someone who means to do him harm. Not after all he's done for this family. For me."

Simon looked at Nora. "Do you really believe me capable of such evil, Miss Longstreet? I'm disappointed. I'd rather thought I'd made quite an impression on you." He actually smiled, and Quinn realized he'd underestimated Simon's cleverness. "Let's have this business over with, Longstreet. I'll protect the man until we can get to the bottom of this."

Quinn shot a panicked look to Bauers, knowing all too well what fate awaited him if he went to Fort Mason tonight.

"Perhaps it would be best for all concerned if I took Quinn with me," Bauers offered. "Grace House is as safe a place for him as any, and I'm sure I can tend to his wounds. There's no need to trouble the major further."

"Oh, I hardly think that's wise," countered Major Simon.

"No, I think that's by far the best choice," Nora declared, coming round to stand in front of her father. "Until we can sort this out."

Quinn had had just about enough of people thinking for him. "It's clear I'm not dying," he said, looking at the reverend, "so I'll make my own choice, thanks. Reverend, if you'll drop me off, I'll tend to *myself. At home.*" He didn't care one whit that no one in the room seemed to think this a good idea. With a wave for Bauers to follow him, Quinn pushed himself down the hallway toward the front door.

And watched it fade into a yawning cave of blackness.

## Chapter Twenty-Five

Nora thought she would never survive the night. It was getting on toward dawn, and she hadn't slept one wink. It was bad enough that she'd barely convinced them to let Reverend Bauers take Quinn back to Dolores Park on the shared but unspoken idea that Quinn would probably only make it as far as Grace House. Bauers pushed hard for this, despite Major Simon's objections. When Quinn slumped to the ground a second time as they argued, Nora burst out crying. Papa was so shocked—and Simon so disgusted—that the whole lot of them left in such a commotion that Nora realized she never did learn where Quinn would spend the night.

She was angry enough with herself for that bit of foolishness, but the scolding Mama gave her after everyone left was worse. She looked so disappointed in her, so incapable of understanding why Nora would ever do something so irrational as take up with "his kind." As if Nora had betrayed her entire family and everyone's hope for happiness. The only reason Mama stopped short of likening her to Annette and her terrible fate was that Aunt Julia had come downstairs.

No one seemed to care that her own happiness was in more ruins than the city. Perhaps that was what made it so easy to throw all caution to the wind, get dressed and go find Quinn. The soldier Major Simon had posted in front of their house evidently didn't take his charge too seriously, for she found him fast asleep on the house's front stoop. The sun was just coming up as, with a calm that certainly didn't fit her reckless circumstances, Nora set out.

The only reasonable place to start seemed to be Grace House. Still, it wasn't as if she could simply waltz out her front door and amble down the dark street before dawn alone.

Or could she?

The clang of a streetcar bell confirmed that the cars did run this early…after all, the docks never really shut down and people had to get to work. It struck her that she'd never thought about anyone having to get to work at such a terrible hour, but certainly it happened to people every day. There was so much she never saw before this. So much she never considered.

It was colder than she expected, and by all rights she ought to be tired, but the exhilaration of her mission made the blocks fly by. It seemed only a matter of minutes before she was reaching into the pocket of her coat and handing coins to a very surprised man aboard the streetcar. She was glad that while his expression said "Out and about at this hour?" he never actually voiced it.

She'd never seen Grace House—or any of this part of the city, for that matter—at dawn. Despite the signs of destruction that still lingered everywhere, the neighborhood had a delicate calm, tinted rose and gold by the sunrise and peppered with tiny clusters of people coming and going. There was something poetic and uncluttered in the simplicity of the people going about their daily business. Quinn had once used the word fussy to describe things in Lafayette Park. He'd meant it as a jest, a good-natured teasing when she'd turned her nose up at something, but looking around, the word fit. She realized, as she turned the corner into the back kitchen door of the friendly, tattered mission building, that perhaps its unfussiness is exactly what attracted her to Grace House. Why the simple chapel felt more holy to her than the starched formal sanctuary of their church up the hill in the "better" part of town.

Quinn *had* to be here. She couldn't fathom that Reverend Bauers would agree to let him be carted off to some horrible fate at Fort Mason. And he couldn't go home, not in that state, although she didn't think Quinn had many other choices. The cook looked surprised—and rather annoyed—at being roused hours before breakfast.

"What are the likes of you doing here? At this hour?" He yawned.

"I'm looking for Reverend Bauers…and Quinn Freeman." When the hefty man stared blankly at her, she added, "It's terribly important."

"I imagine it is," he said, motioning her into the cold kitchen. The fires hadn't even been lit for the day's meals yet. "You sit here and I'll go fetch him."

"Thank you." It suddenly struck her, as she sat down on one of the benches that lined the worktable, how cold and tired she really was. Everything seemed so out of joint and jumbled. What must Quinn be feeling? Thinking? Was he in much pain? He was so very dark and angry—a side of him she'd only seen even a glimpse of the time he'd rescued her. *Oh, Lord, watch over him. I don't know what to say to him, what to do.*

"Odd," the cook remarked, yawning again as he came back into the kitchen. "He ain't here. Looks like he left in a hurry, though. One of the boys says he ain't been back for hours now."

So he *hadn't* been successful in keeping Quinn from the major. The thought turned Nora's blood to ice. *No.* She wouldn't consider that possibility. The reverend must have found some way to get him all the way to Dolores Park. Or elsewhere. Maybe the resourceful Reverend Bauers had many secret hiding places. There really was only one place to go next: Quinn's mother in Dolores Park.

Twenty minutes later with her pulse pounding in her ears, Nora took a deep breath and knocked on the entrance to Quinn's shelter in Dolores Park. "Quinn?" she called, even as she knew the folly of thinking he'd actually made it here, "Mrs. Freeman?"

After a moment of rustling from inside, Mrs. Freeman poked a half-asleep face out of the doorway. "Miss Longstreet?"

"Is…is Quinn here?"

She frowned even as her eyes widened. "What's happened to Quinn?" she asked, alarm cutting sharp edges on her words.

There was nothing for it. Nora lost her battle with her composure and began to cry. "Something's happened, Mrs. Freeman, something terrible."

Mrs. Freeman pulled Nora into the shelter and sat her down. A quick version of the entire story was nearly impossible, but Nora did the best she could as Mrs. Freeman sat astounded. "Quinn? The Midnight Messenger? Of course—how could I not see it? All that time gone, those nights, the things that arrived. God save him, he's been the Messenger from the beginning."

"But now it's all come crashing down," Nora said, clutching Mrs. Freeman's hand as she relayed the story of the shooting, the confrontation in her parlor and how certain she was that if Quinn was not here, then he was surely in the clutches of Major Simon, and no good could come of that, even if Reverend Bauers was still up and about and trying to save him. "They fought terribly. Quinn is sure Simon put the price on his head, but I don't think my father believed him. Major Simon will do something to him, I know it."

Mrs. Freeman, who now fought back tears of her own, stared at Nora for a long moment. Sighing, she reached out and touched Nora's cheek. "You care deeply for him, don't you?"

"I love your son," Nora said, feeling the declaration of it settle her, drawing a surprising strength from the ability to say it out loud. "And I believe he loves me."

Mrs. Freeman's eyes fell shut for a brief moment, then opened with such a tender expression in them. "I know he does, child. I'd suspected he'd finally lost his heart to someone, he just wouldn't tell me who. Now, perhaps I know why. Oh, darlin', I wouldn't wish such trouble on any lass."

"It's Quinn who's in such trouble. I've got to help him. There *has* to be a way." Quinn was so clever. What would he have done? Could she be as clever as he, now that his life might depend upon it? She tried to look for connections in all the various pieces of this mess. People. People loved the Messenger; they might rise up to save him if they knew he was endangered. Or at least keep Simon from doing anything that might be poorly misconstrued. Simon was on the lookout for his good prospects—maybe there was a way to leverage that. A plan—one might even say a scheme—began to form in her head. There wasn't time to think it all the way through—she'd just have to make it up as they went along. "Mrs. Freeman, how many people know Quinn?"

"Nearly everyone. Quinn's always had many friends—at home and here. And I'd guess the Midnight Messenger has even more."

"What if… Mrs. Freeman, can you pull together an army of your own? Major Simon would never do anything to the Midnight Messenger in public, so I think we'll simply have to bring the public to the Messenger."

"Fill the fort with people? Wouldn't the army shoot at a mob like that?"

"Not if reporters were there. And if it was clear the people were looking for the Messenger, the army couldn't do anything that might get in the papers. Simon will have to bring Quinn out. He's got to be in there, Mrs. Freeman, I can't see where else he'd be. It's the only thing I can think of to do."

"Well now, I don't see how I've got much choice. Got my son, does he?" Mrs. Freeman stood up. "I'd say it's high time Major Simon had more visitors that he'll know what to do with."

Nora felt her strength mount as she walked back to Grace House. The sun was up, she'd fashioned a plan even Quinn would admire and her determination to see it through was galvanizing with each step. She prayed as she walked, beseeching God to bless her efforts and to keep Quinn safe—even though the panicked thought occurred that it might already be too late if Major Simon was as dark as she suspected. *"No,"* she prayed aloud, *"Lord, You can't have brought him through the earthquake only to meet that end. I won't believe it."* I can't, she added in a tight, frightened corner of her heart.

Grace House held good and bad news. Reverend Bauers was there—looking exhausted and worried. Still, he confirmed that Quinn was still alive although in bad shape. He was being kept at Fort Mason for his own protection, the reverend reported with an expression that told Nora he shared the same doubts as to Quinn's prospects under the major's watch. The challenge came when Papa stormed through the front door in search of his daughter.

"Come back home," he ordered. Nora thought being in a house of God was the only thing currently keeping a lid on Papa's temper. She'd never seen him like this, and it should have frightened her into submission. It didn't. Instead, it steeled her determination to do what she knew was right. Papa could not see that now, and that couldn't be helped. She'd spend all her efforts to convince him later, but for now defiance was the only route open to her.

"I'm sorry, Papa," she said in a voice so steady it surprised even her. "I must do this."

"Do what?" Papa said, exasperated. Reverend Bauers stood between them, cautious but willing to let her have her say.

"Try to save Quinn."

Nora expected Papa to ask "from what?" thinking his high regard for Major Simon wouldn't allow for the possibility of Quinn's current danger. Instead, Papa asked the most dangerous question of all: "Why?"

It should have been difficult. Frightening, even, to declare it to Papa after all his lectures. Instead, it came out with the ease of truth, necessary as breath. "Because I love him."

Papa stared. For all Mama's suspicions, evidently Papa was genuinely stunned by her admission.

Reverend Bauers chose that moment to step in. "There's a good deal to sort out, no doubt, but I do agree with Nora that desperate measures are in order. Let me accompany her to Fort Mason and you have my word she will talk with you further about this. For the moment, time is very much of the essence."

Before Papa could even gather his wits to respond, Reverend Bauers had Nora by the arm and they were heading out the back door to climb aboard the minister's rickety cart and head to Fort Mason. Nora prayed for Mama and Papa the whole way, for in some very real sense they'd lost the daughter they once had. She hoped the new, transformed daughter they now gained would still be welcomed when today's dust settled.

Annette would have been proud. For all her adventures, Nora's bold cousin had never spent a day such as this. As she stared out the window of Major Simon's office at Fort Mason, Nora could scarcely believe the size of the crowd Mrs. Freeman had gathered outside. Or that her plan had worked. Then again, perhaps Major Simon never stood a chance; once Mrs. Freeman discovered someone had placed her son in harm's way for his own gain, Nora was sure God's ears burned with the justice she called down upon the major's head.

He'd never looked so unnerved. "Are you quite sure, Miss Longstreet, that your father's only the postmaster?" His words were smooth, but his knuckles were white as he put down his pen. "It seems to me you've a politician's blood running through your veins."

"I'd think twice about that phrase 'only the postmaster,' Major," Reverend Bauers advised. "This entire plan was Nora's doing. I fear she could easily devise another one nowhere near as favorable to you. And I am quite astounded at how enamored with her those two reporters are at present."

When Major Simon had refused an earlier meeting, Nora wasn't surprised. She hadn't ever expected the major to cooperate. Instead, Nora asked Reverend Bauers to take her to the offices of the city newspaper. It had been far easier than she imagined to get the reporter to follow her back to Fort Mason. The exclusive revelation of the Midnight Messenger's true identity was far too good a story to miss. And evidently, when one reporter rushes out of his office, others hear about it soon enough; now no less than four photographers were currently waiting outside with the crowd of refugees from Dolores Park.

Bauers had been busy as well. As Nora met with the reporter, he'd used the newspaper wire service to arrange for a hefty reward for the names of the army officers who'd been given the instructions to let word out about the price on the Messenger's head. The size of the reward wired from one Sir Matthew Covington—a friend of Quinn's from England, who, thanks be to God, happened to be in New York on business—ensured quick success. In addition to that, Nora could now ensure that the men's corroboration of Quinn's story reached her parents' ears.

"You have the papers?" Nora extended her hand to receive what she had just watched Simon write: Quinn's commission into the Corps of Engineers, his subsequent draftsmanship education and even a decoration for outstanding citizenship. "I'll find it difficult to be cooperative outside without this in my pocket."

"He'll come to no harm. I had no intentions of having him shot," Simon asserted.

"I cannot believe you," Nora said calmly. And she couldn't. She slipped the folded paper carefully into the pocket of her skirt, feeling jaded.

Major Simon eyed her. "If I'd have wanted him dead, Miss Longstreet, he'd have been shot hours ago. I have enough authority to control someone like Freeman without having to shoot him, you know."

"No, I don't know that." And she'd done her best to make sure he couldn't shoot Quinn now. Not with the crowd outside his window. She was glad for that, seeing the unnerving darkness in the major's eyes.

The strength of the midday sun was broiling the crowd into impatience. They could either learn enough to cheer Simon for his accomplishments, or learn more and jeer him for what he would have done to the Midnight Messenger. Nora would be lying if she said the thought of publicly humiliating Simon didn't appeal to her at the moment. The simple truth was that Simon was currently the lesser of all available evils, and he was still very good at what he did. To remove him from the relief efforts entirely would do little more than heap chaos upon chaos.

She didn't need revenge or glory; she needed Quinn.

Unharmed and with the commissions Simon had originally promised him. All she was really doing, Reverend Bauers reminded her, was using the leverage they had—namely the press and the mayor's keen need of good news to tell the world on behalf of their damaged city—to ensure the major kept his original word.

A knock came on the door, and the reporter poked his nervous head inside. "It's a powder keg out there. If you're going to make an announcement, you'd best get to it." As if on cue, a wave of cries for the Messenger could be heard outside. They'd been told they'd find out who he was today, and they didn't seem much in the mood to be patient about it.

"Remember, my good major," Bauers said as he walked over to stand beside Simon. "I'll be listening to every word. I'm anticipating a lovely speech. It'll be a grand day for San Francisco. And you get the rarest of all opportunities—a second chance to do the right thing."

Someone splashed water on his face. Quinn moaned, knocking the hand away without even opening his eyes. He knew he'd ended up in some kind of cell, but not much more. During several waking moments over the course of the night, he'd managed to surmise that his attempts to go home had failed. The last thing he remembered was making for Nora's front door, then it all went black until he woke up here.

He had a pretty good idea where "here" was. And who held the keys.

"Freeman, up with you," a gruff voice said.

Quinn's head pounded, his ribs ached, he still had cuts on his hands and arms from climbing out the broken window, and his leg felt as if it would burn right off any second. He definitely was in no mood to stand up and be neighborly. Why they hadn't simply shot him yet, he didn't know. Actually, he didn't want to be shot again, ever. Last night had put him off guns for life, even if life only lasted a few more hours.

It had all come unraveled. All the help he'd been was of no use. In his arrogance, his craving to be a man of importance, he'd misread God's calls to him in ways that hurt everyone he loved.

Nora worst of all. The one detail he did remember last night was the scorching look in her mother's eyes when Nora'd touched him. As if she'd committed some unforgivable sin by loving him. He'd tainted her future by trying to graft it on to his own. She deserved far more than he could give her now. The physical pain couldn't hold a candle to the gnawing ache in his chest. It felt like his very soul had been yanked out of his body.

"Wash up, you've got company and an appointment to keep."

An appointment with the business end of an army rifle, no doubt. Why on earth did they think it a good idea to wake him up to shoot him? Or dress him? Somebody threw a damp towel and some clothes at him. An army uniform. Quinn was really starting to hate Simon's sense of humor.

"I don't care what he looks like," someone said outside his cell door. "I insist you let me in right now!"

He must be delirious—the voice sounded like Nora's. Well, God had answered his prayer—he'd at least gotten to kiss her. He rolled his body away from the light, sinking back into the pain that pulsed with every heartbeat. "I hope Heaven hurts a whole lot less," he muttered.

"I hope you don't see it for a very long time," the

tender voice said, and he felt a cool, smooth hand on his brow.

He rolled back over and forced his eyes open. Nora's sweet face stared down at him like God's gift from Heaven. "Am I alive?" he whispered, reaching out, expecting his hand to slide through the mirage.

The mirage smiled. "Only just." She grabbed his outstretched hand and kissed it.

It was her. He pulled her hand toward his face, pressing it to his cheek. Glory, it really *was* her, here with him. His pain-fogged brain couldn't make sense of it.

"You've got to get up and put these on, Quinn. I haven't time to explain more."

Something had happened. People were rushing about, there were shouts and yells outside. He pushed himself upright, hurting everywhere. Nora took the towel beside him and began wiping his hands. "What's going on?" he asked, shaking his head in an attempt to clear it.

"You're going to need to stand in a few minutes. Can you do it?"

He took the towel from her and wiped his own face. The cool cloth brought him a shred of clarity, and he looked at the vision of beauty in front of him. Without a moment's thought, he took that face in his hands and kissed it. Soundly. Bliss. She tasted like sheer, sweet bliss.

"Time's a wastin', Romeo," the gruff voice said from behind him. "There'll be time enough for that later."

Later? There'd be a later?

"You're to be announced as the heroic Midnight Messenger in a few minutes," Nora said, blushing. "We need to get you cleaned up and dressed."

"I don't understand…"

"I've found a way. Don't worry about that right now, just trust me and put these on."

"They're army clothes!"

"Indeed they are."

"Am I going to be shot?"

"No, Quinn, I think they said you're going to be a corporal."

The sunlight stung his eyes. Reverend Bauers had a hand on his shoulder, helping him stay upright. The bandage on his leg was too tight, a throbbing distraction, and sweat was pouring down his back. He didn't care.

He did care that Nora was yards away from him, standing next to a fellow with a camera and notebook instead of by his side. She had yet to explain why Major Simon was making a speech about the Midnight Messenger, saying all kinds of wonderful things about the "hero who slipped through the night to help those in need." Reverend Bauers had only barely stopped him from lunging at Simon when they finally met up just inside the doorway. *"Touché,"* was all Simon had said, tipping his hat in what could only be called a simmering resignation. He held Quinn's gaze with a nasty glare that evaporated instantaneously the moment the major stepped on to the podium placed on Fort Mason's front steps.

And then he heard his name.

Bauers led him forward as the crowd cheered so loud Quinn thought his head would split open.

People cried out his name and the mayor came to shake his hand. He'd been revealed as the man behind the Midnight Messenger, as a hero. He saw Ma, standing down off to his left, her face a mixture of joy aimed at him and an anger he guessed was aimed at Major Simon. She knew. Still, Quinn couldn't figure out how they'd gone from last night's chaos to this morning's glory.

And glory it was. Simon continued his speech, describing the commission he'd originally promised, eliciting more cheers from the crowd. Quinn would begin serving as a draftsman's apprentice the moment he was well enough to do so. He'd been made a corporal in the United States Army Corps of Engineers. An officer. More men shook his hand. Amazing as it all was, the edges of Quinn's vision begin to blur and turn colors. "I can't stand up any longer," he whispered to Bauers. "Get me out of here." How funny that a moment he'd been dreaming of for weeks was not nearly as pleasant as he'd imagined. He was grateful—deeply grateful— but all he wanted right now was Nora and sleep, in that order. Glory, it turns out, hurt a lot.

Ma came rushing through the door a few moments later, bouncing back and forth between fussy praises for his deeds and teary-eyed scoldings for keeping such secrets from your own Ma.

"Where is she?" he asked Bauers and his mother, hoping at least one of them would fill in the host of missing details.

"Your Nora?" Ma said, smiling. "She'll be along. Don't you worry about that."

"I worry about that," he said trying to peer around Ma and Bauers to the door that still opened on the activities outside. "Where *is* she?"

Bauers's hand came down on his shoulder. "I imagine she's with her mother and father by now. I asked them to come. I doubt it will be a short conversation, so you'd best find some patience."

At that moment, Major Simon came in through the door, surrounded by a quartet of very official-looking men. Quinn stood up, wobbling a little when he did. He held Simon's eyes until the major said, "Excuse me for a moment," to his companions and walked over. Bauers and Ma both tensed.

"They were only supposed to bring you in. I'd no plans to do you harm," Simon said, nearly under his breath.

"I don't believe you," Quinn returned, equally quietly.

"I suppose you wouldn't." The major extended his hand. Shake his hand? Now? After all he suspected happened?

Quinn took that hand and gripped hard enough to hurt Simon. It may have looked like a handshake, but it wasn't. It was a warning. "I ought to run you through right here, in front of all these people," he murmured loud enough for the major to hear. "But someone once taught me to do the unexpected to my opponents."

Simon pulled his hand away.

"I don't know what all happened," Quinn continued, "but I will. I won't stop watching you, Simon."

"You got caught in the cross fire, Freeman, nothing more."

"I don't see it that way."

"And now is not the time to have this conversation," Reverend Bauers cut in between them. "Let the matter rest for the moment, gentlemen, too many eyes are watching."

"You're *blessed* I'm in no shape to do anything more," Quinn growled.

Major Simon paused for a second before replying, "Perhaps I am."

# Chapter Twenty-Six

Quinn was tired of sitting. Funny, he could remember the days he'd give anything to sit for hours on end, but now the inactivity was driving him crazy. "Where is she, Ma?"

Ma looked at him as if he were no older than Sam. "It's not yet two o'clock, Quinn. The sun doesn't hurry across the sky just because you're in love." She looked at the pile of goods filling their shack. "Someone brought more sugar. Why people think the Midnight Messenger needs sweets is beyond me. Where do they think we can bake out here?" She pointed at him. "Bring me a real oven and a real kitchen to put it in, then I'll sing and dance."

"I'll dance with you now, Ma."

"Ye will not at that." She scowled at him playfully. "You're supposed to be off that leg for another three days."

"Three days… I'll go mad," Quinn moaned.

"Keep looking at those books the army sent over. I can't imagine how much you've got to learn."

"Sam!" Quinn yelled. "Sam, come here!" Ma gave out an exasperated sigh. Sam poked his head into the shack a moment later. "Go see if Miss Nora's come yet, would you please?"

Sam was no fool. He looked straight at Ma, who pulled a watch out of her apron pocket and shook her head. "It ain't two," Sam said with an annoying amount of authority for someone who came up to Quinn's waist.

"I'm outnumbered." Quinn let his head fall back against the cot where he was propped up.

"Even heroes have to do as they're told," Ma said teasingly. "On occasion."

Quinn sighed, picked up one of the dry texts he was trying to make his way through before he started studies next month and thought patience was highly overrated for heroes. Even ex-heroes.

He'd lasted no more than ten minutes, when he heard Nora's voice call out from beyond the shack door. "Hello, Mrs. Freeman, hello Quinn!"

He went for the door, but Ma thrust a hand to his shoulder. "Back down with you. She can take the six steps it takes to get inside, son, there's no worries there."

Quinn sat up and ran his hands through his hair just as Nora ducked inside. Followed by a sight he never expected to see: Mr. and Mrs. Longstreet. "I've brought someone with me," Nora said, smiling.

It was an awkward moment, to be sure. Mr. Longstreet looked uncomfortable, Mrs. Longstreet looked downright panicked. Nora wore a cautiously hopeful expression, and Ma looked flustered. A bristling silence filled the crowded shelter until Ma flung up her hands and said, "I think I'll make tea. We've got real sugar, we might as well enjoy it."

Nora reached out her hand to Ma, smiling. "That'd be lovely, I think. Mama, why don't you sit here?" She motioned to the shack's only chair and motioned for her father to take a seat on the large trunk nearby. When her parents were seated, Nora perched on the edge of the cot by Quinn. He wanted to reach out and touch her, but the moment seemed too delicate.

"Thank you for coming," he managed, sure his face was flushed. He knew what it cost them to make this trip, the grace they'd somehow found a way to extend to him, And their daughter.

"How are you healing?" Mr. Longstreet said stiffly.

"I expect I'll limp for a while, but good as new eventually." He looked at Nora. "Maybe better."

"Oh," said Nora, giving Quinn a package he hadn't even noticed she was holding. "Reverend Bauers sent this over for you. It came all the way from New York."

"Who'd be sending me something from New York?" Quinn asked, looking at the package. He grinned when the return address read "Sir Matthew Covington," care of some fancy-sounding hotel with a New York address. He pulled open the package to reveal a handsome set of drafting tools. A thick card with elegant handwriting read,

> *I hear you've put my last gift to good use. I pray you'll do as well with these.*
> *Best,*
> *Matthew Covington.*

"Glory," said Quinn, running his hands over the unfamiliar tools. "They're something, aren't they?"

"Lord Covington seems to think rather highly of you," Mr. Longstreet offered.

"He's been a good friend." Quinn looked up into

the older man's face and offered a smile. "We got off to a very bad start, he and I, but things managed to improve after a bit."

"You have many good friends," Nora said. "And much to look forward to."

"Perhaps," Mr. Longstreet said, planting his hands on his knees and looking at his wife, "this is one of those times where it was darkest before dawn. Perhaps a better day is coming for all of us, hmm?"

It wasn't much of a speech, but it said everything Quinn had been hoping to hear. "I hope you're right, sir. I sure hope you're right."

Mrs. Longstreet actually managed a nod. He nodded back, knowing how big a step that was for her. Over the course of the many hours he had to sit and think it over, he'd come to feel compassion for Mr. and Mrs. Longstreet. How wrong was it for them to want the best for their daughter, to cling to their familiar standards when everything else was collapsing around them? They loved Nora as much as he did. Surely there had to be a way to find some common ground in all that. God was a mighty God, after all, and He'd shown Himself in ways mightier than even Quinn could have dreamed.

He'd decided long ago that there'd be no stealing Nora away in the middle of the night. He'd wait until they came around. By the looks of today, just maybe they'd begun.

Mr. Longstreet checked his watch and stood up. "Well, it's nearly two o'clock, there's mail to tend to across the street. Nora dear, why don't you stay here for a bit. I think I can manage a little while without you."

He reached for his wife's hand, and while she hesitated, she took it and they ducked out of the shack together.

Quinn managed to count to five before he grabbed Nora's hand and pulled her to him. She was a wonder. The finest thing God had ever sent to him. Her kiss could convince a man the world was a wondrous, hopeful place. "You're mine, love, and I'm yours." He kissed her, feeling its warmth fill up the room and spread all the way to Heaven. "It's only a matter of time now. And you know how impatient I am."

"I do, indeed." Nora nestled her head on to his shoulder.

He kissed the top of her head and closed his eyes, oblivious to the world—until Ma's voice pulled him from bliss.

"Well, I see you've run off our guests already, before anyone's had tea. Do you think you two lovebirds could manage to tear yourselves away long enough to suffer a cup with your own mother?"

"Only just," they said at the same time, catching each other's eyes.

# *Epilogue*

Surely my heart will explode, Nora thought as she stood trying to breathe in Reverend Bauers's study. I won't survive the day, much less the ceremony.

Papa caught her hand, the tenderest of looks in his eyes. "My brave Nora? Trembling? Surely it can't be the prospect of marrying Quinn to put such fear into you." He was teasing her, dispersing the tension, but the edge in his voice gave away his own frail composure. "My baby girl, no longer a baby girl." He sighed. "And hasn't been for some time."

"Oh, Papa…" Nora couldn't hope to finish the sentence. A featherlight kiss on her cheek was his only reply, and Nora thought the combined lumps in their throats might render them speechless for the rest of the year.

The mission bell chimed the hour, signaling it was time for the ceremony to begin. Papa swallowed hard as he opened the study door and offered his elbow. "Best not to keep Corporal Freeman waiting. I imagine Quinn's current state would rival yours, impatient as he is."

Nora's steps down the hallway felt heavy and ill-placed. She feared her grip on Papa's elbow was so tight he'd cry out any second. Not one part of her considered this wedding a mistake, and every fiber of her being yearned to be Mrs. Quinn Freeman, but the sheer enormity of the moment seemed to pound down upon her. In a split second's musing, she wondered if Reverend Bauers was having any luck keeping Quinn from pacing the altar.

A cascade of lovely notes wafted down the hallway. Mama's friend was certainly working wonders with Grace House's old, cranky organ. Despite all the—what was the word Mama had used?—"rustic" charm of Grace House's chapel, to marry Quinn anywhere else would simply seem wrong. Grace House, and all it stood for, was too much a part of her life and Quinn's to join them elsewhere.

Turning the corner to start down the aisle, Nora thought she'd simply cease breathing and fall on the spot. Until her eyes met Quinn's. His gaze erased the distance between them in a heartbeat, calming her with the warmth she saw there. She watched him go still, saw his shoulders settle from their panicked breaths, felt them find their home in each other's eyes as they would for the rest of their lives. She would always draw her strength from this man God had sent her. Just as she would always pull from within him the man God intended Quinn to be. They were, truly, God's gift to each other. The phrase seemed timeless now, instead of trite.

The ceremony unfolded around them and still she spent it transfixed in Quinn's eyes. Both mothers cried and kissed their children, vows were spoken, blessings asked, rings exchanged. All of these things made them "married." But it was the time-stopping kiss, the tender-sweet seal of their union surrounded by raised army swords and the enthusiastic pealing of the church bell, that made it real.

She was his and he hers. Today was full of joy and celebration. When tomorrow dawned, Corporal and Mrs. Quinn Freeman would deliver a new message to the world: all the hope their hearts could hold.

\* \* \* \* \*

*Historical Note*

There really was a heroic postmaster during the San Francisco 1906 disaster. I chose not to use Arthur Fisk's real name or his personal details, but to base my story around his generous declaration to deliver mail regardless of postage. He says it best himself: "The Postal Service as a means of communication among hundreds of thousands of distressed people was, I believe, an untold blessing." His awareness of how the littlest of things can hold back despair became the seed from which this novel grew. It is, of course, fiction. There was no Black Bandit (save a cheeky stagecoach robber in the 1880s), nor a Midnight Messenger. The U.S. Army, presented with the gigantic task of holding the city together in its darkest hours, did an outstanding job. While there was plenty of corruption to go around, the army marketeering in the novel is more my invention than any real historical suspicion. Careful researchers will note I've played a bit with the geography, and I trust they will forgive my liberties in service of the story. One important and amusing fact to relate is that, in fact, a record number of marriages and romances are attributed to the disaster. A good reminder that love does, indeed, conquer all.

# WE HOPE YOU
# ENJOYED THIS BOOK!

SPECIAL EXCERPT FROM

*Love Inspired*®

*Carolyn Wiebe will do anything to protect her late sister's children from their abusive father—even give up her Amish roots and pretend to be Mennonite. But when she starts falling for Amish bachelor Michael Miller, can they conquer their pasts—and her secrets—by Christmas to build a forever family?*

*Read on for a sneak preview of*
An Amish Christmas Promise *by Jo Ann Brown, available December 2019 from Love Inspired!*

"Are the *kinder* okay?"

"Yes, they'll be fine." Uncomfortable with his small intrusion into her family, she said, "Kevin had a bad dream and woke us up."

"Because of the rain?"

She wanted to say that was silly but, glad she could be honest with Michael, she said, "It's possible."

"Rebuilding a structure is easy. Rebuilding one's sense of security isn't."

"That sounds like the voice of experience."

"My parents died when I was young, and both my twin brother and I had to learn not to expect something horrible was going to happen without warning."

"I'm sorry. I should have asked more about you and the other volunteers. I've been wrapped up in my own tragedy."

"At times like this, nobody expects you to be thinking of anything but getting a roof over your *kinder*'s heads."

He didn't reach out to touch her, but she was aware of every inch of him so close to her. His quiet strength had awed her from the beginning. As she'd come to know him better, his fundamental decency had impressed her more. He was a man she believed she could trust.

She shoved that thought aside. Trusting any man would be the worst thing she could do after seeing what Mamm had endured during her marriage and then struggling to help her sister escape her abusive husband.

"I'm glad you understand why I must focus on rebuilding a life for the children." The simple statement left no room for misinterpretation. "The flood will always be a part of us, but I want to help them learn how to live with their memories."

"I can't imagine what it was like."

"I can't forget what it was like."

Normally she would have been bothered by someone having sympathy for her, but if pitying her kept Michael from looking at her with his brown puppy-dog eyes that urged her to trust him, she'd accept it. She couldn't trust any man, because she wouldn't let the children spend their lives witnessing what she had.

*Don't miss*
An Amish Christmas Promise *by Jo Ann Brown,*
*available December 2019 wherever*
*Love Inspired® books and ebooks are sold.*

LoveInspired.com

LIEXP1119

Looking for inspiration in tales
of hope, faith and heartfelt romance?

Check out **Love Inspired®** and
**Love Inspired® Suspense** books!

## New books available every month!

---

## CONNECT WITH US AT:

Facebook.com/groups/HarlequinConnection

Facebook.com/HarlequinBooks

Twitter.com/HarlequinBooks

Instagram.com/HarlequinBooks

Pinterest.com/HarlequinBooks

ReaderService.com

# SPECIAL EXCERPT FROM

*Can a mysterious Amish child bring two wounded souls together in Cedar Grove, Kansas?*

**Read on for a sneak preview of**
**The Hope** *by Patricia Davids*
*available December 2019 from HQN Books!*

"You won't have to stay on our account, and we can look after Ernest's place, too. I can hire a man to help me. Someone I know I can…" Ruth's words trailed away.

Trust? Depend on? Was that what Ruth was going to say? She didn't want him around. She couldn't have made it any clearer. Maybe it had been a mistake to think he could patch things up between them, but he wasn't willing to give up after only one day. Ruth was nothing if not stubborn, but he could be stubborn, too.

Owen leaned back and chuckled.

"What's so funny?"

"I'm here until Ernest returns, Ruth. You can't get rid of me with a few well-placed insults."

She huffed and turned her back to him. "I didn't insult you."

"Ah, but you wanted to. I'd like to talk about my plans in the morning."

Ruth nodded. "You know my feelings, but I agree we both need to sleep on it."

Owen picked up his coat and hat, and left for his uncle's farm. The wind was blowing harder and the snow was piling up in growing drifts. It wasn't a fit night out for man nor beast. As if to prove his point, he found Meeka, Ernest's big guard dog, lying across the corner of the porch out of the wind. Instead of coming out to greet him, she whined repeatedly.

He opened the door of the house. "Come in for a bit." She didn't get up. Something was wrong. Was she hurt? He walked toward her. She sat up and growled low in her throat. She had never done that to him before. "Are you sick, girl?"

She looked back at something in the corner and whined softly. Over the wind he heard what sounded like a sobbing child. "What have you got there, Meeka? Let me see."

He came closer. There was a child in an Amish bonnet and bulky winter coat trying to bury herself beneath Meeka's thick fur. Where had she come from? Why was she here? He looked around. Where were her parents?

*Don't miss*
The Hope *by Patricia Davids,*
*available now wherever*
HQN™ books and ebooks are sold.

HQNBooks.com

Looking for more satisfying love stories
with community and family at their core?

Check out **Harlequin® Special Edition**
and **Love Inspired®** books!

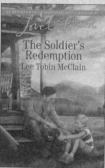

**New books available every month!**

---

**CONNECT WITH US AT:**

Facebook.com/groups/HarlequinConnection

 Facebook.com/HarlequinBooks

Twitter.com/HarlequinBooks

Instagram.com/HarlequinBooks

Pinterest.com/HarlequinBooks

ReaderService.com

⬦**HARLEQUIN®**

**ROMANCE WHEN
YOU NEED IT**

## Inspirational Romance to Warm Your Heart and Soul

Join our social communities to connect with other readers who share your love!

Sign up for the Love Inspired newsletter at **www.LoveInspired.com** to be the first to find out about upcoming titles, special promotions and exclusive content.

### CONNECT WITH US AT:

Facebook.com/groups/HarlequinConnection

 Facebook.com/LoveInspiredBooks

 Twitter.com/LoveInspiredBks

LISOCIAL2018